Jessica Ruston was born in Warwickshire. Her career began in the worlds of theatre, film and publishing, and she has written screenplays and two non-fiction books. Her previous two novels were highly acclaimed. Jessica lives in Brighton with her husband. For everything you need to know about Jessica, visit her website www.jessicaruston.com.

JESSICA RUSTON

The Darker Side of Love

headline
review

First published in 2012 by HEADLINE REVIEW
An imprint of HEADLINE PUBLISHING GROUP

1

Cataloguing in Publication Data is available from the British Library

ISBN 978 0 7553 8360 3

Typeset in Sabon by Avon DataSet Ltd,
Bidford-on-Avon, Warwickshire

Printed and bound in Great Britain by
Clays Ltd, St Ives plc

Headline's policy is to use papers that are natural, renewable and
recyclable products and made from wood grown in sustainable forests.
The logging and manufacturing processes are expected to conform to
the environmental regulations of the country of origin.

HEADLINE PUBLISHING GROUP
An Hachette UK Company
338 Euston Road
London NW1 3BH

www.headline.co.uk
www.hachette.co.uk

For my girlfriends.

Acknowledgements

Thanks to Mr Simon, Ariella Feiner, George Lewis and everyone at United Agents; to the whole team at Headline, in particular Sherise Hobbs, Leah Woodburn, Helena Towers and Lucy Foley. Thanks to those friends who helped me understand a little of the City and the recession, either knowingly or unknowingly. Some of the characters in this novel started life (mostly with different names) in a serial called 'Come for Dinner', written for *The Lady* during 2010; thanks to Rachel Johnson for that original commission. Thanks to my parents and sister for their constant cheerleading and love, and to Judy and Joe Ruston for the same, and for providing me with a place to write this book. Most especially, thanks, as always, to Jack, for far more than I can list here, but particularly for ensuring that I see the lighter side of love.

Prologue

The Lodge
April 2010

From his position on the floor, in the corner of the room, he could see a sliver of sky. It was the shape of a scalene triangle – one with no equal sides – like a shard of broken glass. Scalene, isosceles, equilateral. Funny the things you remembered from school. Mr Humphreys had been his maths teacher back then, a thin, stooped man whose brow furrowed above the bridge of his glasses as he endeavoured to explain equations and trigonometry to his young charges. He wore a rotation of woven ties and he would put his hand to them as he leant over your desk so that they didn't flop on to your exercise book, a gesture of respect for your personal space that was notable because it was so unusual. No other master at his school would ever have considered whether it might be annoying to have someone else's tie slither about on your desk as they explained the finer points of how to solve an equation. Mr Humphreys had been his favourite teacher. He and the master who had taught English lit and drama – what had he been called? Wright, that was it. He had been another kind man. He remembered Mr Wright's soft, lisping voice urging him to 'feel Romeo's desperation' as he had stood, feeling ridiculous in his school uniform, trying to pretend

1

that he was in a dimly lit churchyard facing his enemy, sword in hand, rather than in a chilly assembly hall waving a hockey stick at his best friend, Mr Wright looking helpless.

He still remembered the words, though, so Mr Wright couldn't have been as ineffectual as his manner might have indicated.

'Good gentle youth, tempt not a desperate man; Fly hence, and leave me. I beseech thee, youth, put not another sin upon my head, by urging me to fury: O, be gone! By heaven, I love thee better than myself; for I come hither arm'd against myself: stay not, be gone, live, and hereafter say, a madman's mercy bade thee run away.'

His eyes filled with tears. He had had no understanding then of what it might be like to feel that desperate, that driven to dreadful acts. No wonder he had giggled and hammed as Mr Wright became more and more frustrated. How could he have understood? He'd been fourteen, with no clue about how life itself could squeeze the air out of you until you gasped for oxygen and your arms scrambled and grasped on to the nearest thing for bolster, and your legs kicked, kicked to find purchase. Now, though, things were different; the words were all too appropriate, the meaning behind them intimately familiar.

Now he knew what lengths a man could be driven to by a chain of events that weren't even really a chain; a chain made them sound logical, consecutive, as though there had been a plan. The things that had led him here had no logic to them, as far as he could see, and, God knew, he had spent enough time thinking about it. Hours and hours, turning over the events of the last few years. He could see all too clearly the mistakes he had made that he could not reverse, could pinpoint the moments when he might have changed things but hadn't. Because he had been too weak, or scared, or felt too trapped, because his sense of pride had stopped him or because he had been trying so hard to impress. To be the big man. He could see all of those things, laid out before him like a battlefield.

But there was still one question – the big one, really – that he could not answer, no matter how he turned it around in his head and looked at it from different angles like a Rubik's Cube. How had he become the sort of person who picked up a gun?

He was not that man. He was no action hero, no bank robber, no street-smart kid with a bad attitude and a worse upbringing. He was – or he had been – normal. Or so he told himself. Because when it came down to it – who was?

Chapter One

10 December 2007

Caroline breathed in as her bridesmaids began to do up the back of her dress – not that she needed to, for if anything the dress was a little loose. She had lost more weight since the final fitting, despite strict instructions from her dressmaker that she shouldn't. It wasn't intentional, but she hadn't been sleeping well, and there always seemed to be something else to do, some errand to run. She had ended up living off snatched half-sandwiches and unfinished lattes. She wasn't sorry, though; her cheekbones were sharp and she had a pleasing dip below her collarbone that had never been there before. Bart liked her new, more gym-honed self as well, admiring it daily, and she had vowed to keep up her twice-weekly sessions with her personal trainer after the honeymoon and not let herself slip back into the dangerous habit of serving herself man-sized portions at dinner every night and become the clichéd slightly dumpy newly-wed. She had never really been slim before – never fat, either, but her legs had always been chunky and her face rounded out with what people called puppy fat, even when she was in her late twenties and no longer any kind of pup. She was enjoying being the sort of girl who could walk into a shop and be able to pick up even the slimmest-fitting pair of trousers and know that they would slide on easily.

She liked being able to undress in front of Bart and feel him looking at her bottom and know that it was not going to let her down, that he was focusing on its pertness and the perfect crease below it, rather than the gentle ripple of cellulite that she had worried about before.

Before. Before Bart. BB, as her friends sometimes joked. Harriet had coined the phrase, she thought, and Izzy and Stella had quickly taken it up. It had become part of their language, the lexicon that bound the four of them together, a tightly woven alphabet of old memories and in-jokes, oblique references to previous boyfriends and even more oblique references to current ones. She and Harriet had the oldest stories, of course – they'd known one another since they were thirteen, after all. The best part of twenty years. A lifetime's worth of evenings out and late-night chats; long afternoons drinking coffee and eating carrot cake in the café round the corner from her parents' house; sleepovers and glasses of wine in the kitchen at parties.

Izzy she had known the next longest, her brother James's wife whom Caroline had made it her business to befriend when they had first got together, so enamoured had she been with both the idea of having a sister, even a sister-in-law, and with Izzy herself, who was glamorous and ambitious and tough, who wore sequinned minidresses that showed off her long legs and who kept an unruly crew of cooks under tight control in the restaurant kitchen that she used to run. She had been from a different world. But far from being haughty or stand-offish, she had pulled James and, with him, Caroline, into that world with her, taking them to restaurant openings and giving them the chef's table in her kitchen one Saturday night, taking Caroline shopping away from her comfort zone of Liberty and John Lewis, into markets and funky little boutiques in the depths of the East End that Caroline would never have had the courage to enter if she hadn't been with Izzy.

And then had come Stella, with her wide grin painted scarlet and her fingers dripping with vintage jewellery, her easy laugh and her ability to turn any gathering into a party. A friend of Harriet's to start with, she had slotted into place in their little group as though the space had been waiting for her, and the four of them had become a unit. Well, more than the four of them, of course, because there were the boys as well – James, Caroline's brother and Izzy's husband; Will, Harriet's boyfriend and James's oldest friend from school; and then with Stella came Johnny, wild, uncontrollable Johnny, who was a musician and who they were all fascinated by, because he seemed to live utterly outside the realms of normal life. It had always been the seven of them, and there was an awkward space where Caroline's man ought to be, although the rest of them pretended it wasn't awkward at all and ignored the fact that when they got together for dinner in a restaurant the waiter would hover expectantly, waiting to see whether they were going to be joined by someone else, or that when the girls got together for lunch, all of the others would get to moan about something their other half had done and Caroline would just have to smile and giggle and roll her eyes along with them and act as though she knew just what it was like to live with someone. To have their dirty socks on the floor and their boots by the front door, to have someone coming in asking what was for dinner or making sure the back door was locked before they went up to bed.

BB. It felt like a long time ago now, those days. It had been as though she were living her life inside a slightly murky vase, one whose flowers had been left in too long, leaving the glass all smeared, and he had come along and smashed it and suddenly the world had been brighter. Sharper, full of possibilities and light and – fun. Caroline had never been a fun sort of a person; she had always found it worrying and a bit intimidating when, at university dinner parties, someone had inevitably suggested a game, with a glint in their eye. 'Truth or dare,' someone would cry, or the one where you had to guess the name stuck on a Post-it note on your forehead, or drink while you think, and she would get panicky and hide in the loo for as long as she could get away with. But Bart had stopped her hiding, and made her realise she didn't have to pretend to be someone she wasn't. 'I can't bear those sort of stupid, inane games, and I'm glad you don't like them,' he said. 'Just don't bloody play them. If your friends can't cope with you just being with them and not joining in, then they're not very good friends.' And with him she felt brave enough to say that, or at least some approximation of it. 'Sorry, I'm really terrible at these things and I never enjoy them,' was as bold as she got, but that was enough, it seemed, and he was right, people didn't mind, and she could go back to sitting at the table, sipping her wine and happily watching as the evening descended into a mess of bits of paper with names of famous people scrawled on them and half-drunk shot glasses of sambuca that would leave sticky rings on the table.

They, she and Bart, had a different sort of fun, a more grown-up sort. They went to private views of exhibitions, and openings of smart new shops, and talks given by eminent people with question-and-answer sessions afterwards and canapés. They weren't always the events Caroline would have chosen to go to, but they were important for Bart to be seen at, and they did usually end up meeting one or two interesting people, even if Caroline did often have the feeling that they were slightly more on the edge of things than Bart would have liked, and it meant that she always knew about the latest restaurants and things in town, which made her feel – more useful, she supposed. Her friends phoned her up when they were looking for some-where to take their parents for dinner, or a date for the afternoon, and she could flick back through her diary and see what they had especially enjoyed recently (she put a gold star by particularly successful outings, in part for this very purpose) and make thoughtful recommendations.

Bart would have booked their honeymoon, which he had insisted on keeping a surprise, through the same concierge service, she was sure. He used the company, Henry Butler's, which was owned by Will, to run his life, or that was what it sometimes felt like, and when they were first living together, Caroline had once worried aloud whether it was because she wasn't organised enough. 'I'd like to help you, darling,' she had said. 'I'm happy to do things like – I don't know, arrange for your shirts to be collected by the laundry service, look into theatre tickets. I have time.' He had smiled that wide, white-toothed smile at her that made her feel as though she were at the centre of the world, and kissed her fingers. 'I know you're happy to do it, darling, but I'm not. I don't want you becoming my drudge, your diary full of errands you have to run for me. I want you to be my girlfriend, not my PA. And before long you won't have time for it anyway.' He had grinned again then, and waggled an eyebrow at her, and she had known he was talking about marriage, a wedding, and then babies, but she had refused to be drawn into asking him what he meant and so had just kissed him lightly and said, 'You're right, I am getting busier at work these days,' and gone back to flicking through her diary looking for a suitable date to take her niece and nephew to the zoo. 'And it's Will's company, it's good to keep it in the family, so to speak, surely? I'm happy to be able to give him the business. James seemed pleased when I signed up.' He was a bit petulant now, the emphasis on the word 'James'; the slight implication that Caroline hadn't been as pleased and jovial as her brother hovered behind the words, and that was the last thing she wanted Bart to think, so she abandoned her diary and slid her arms around his waist. 'Of course, darling,' she had murmured into his neck, as she dropped the little light, nibbling kisses on to it that never failed to make him groan. 'It's brilliant that you're supporting Will, he's been working so hard to make the business happen and he's practically family, like you say.' 'And me?' he had asked, pushing his hand down into the front of her trousers, his voice low. 'How about me?' She had gasped, as the fingers of his left hand began to work at her and he pulled her top up with his right, his breath hot on her skin, and the words had escaped her mouth like a sigh. 'You're everything,' she had gasped. 'You're everything.'

'Caroline? What are you thinking about? You've gone all pink. I know you're the blushing bride and everything, but you don't want to look like you're having a hot flush. Shall I get the powder?'

Caroline looked in the mirror, and pulled herself back to the room. Harriet was right, she was all pink-cheeked. The blushing bride indeed.

She turned to Harriet, and shook her head. 'Sorry, just – just felt a bit hot for a minute. I'm fine. No, don't open the window, honestly. I'm fine. Just a bit emotional, I suppose.'

Harriet handed Caroline her glass of champagne, and perched on the edge of the bed. The four women – Caroline, Harriet, Izzy and Stella – and Izzy's daughter Pearl were all crammed into Caroline's childhood bedroom, which was full of make-up and tulle and high heels. In the corner of the room, the photographer had all their bouquets lined up in a row, Caroline's in the centre, pink and white roses, and her three bridesmaids' beside, smaller bunches of pink roses, and was taking close-ups of them.

'I'm not surprised. Big day. Biggest day of your life, or so they say. Does it feel like it?'

Caroline smiled. 'I don't know, really.' She turned back to Harriet. 'Is it all going to change, do you think?'

Harriet raised an eyebrow. 'You're asking the wrong brides-maid, darling, aren't you?' She turned to Izzy, who was in the corner of the room trying to persuade a stubborn Pearl to wear the floral circlet that had been provided for her hair. Pearl's bottom lip was jutting forward like a ledge.

'Iz – Caroline wants to know the secrets of married life.'

Izzy looked over her shoulder, her expression taut. 'God, don't ask me, I can't even get my own child dressed.' She gestured to Harriet to top up her champagne glass. 'Who'd have thought I once ran a kitchen full of alpha males with a rod of iron, eh? Why did no one tell me they were so much easier than children?'

'No one tells you things like that, you silly cow,' came a voice from the windowsill, where Stella was sitting, legs drawn up in front of her, holding a cigarette out of the window. 'It's part of the covenant. Just like no one tells you how *fucking* much labour actually hurts, and how completely disgusting the whole thing is. It's like a gentlemen's club or something. A cult. You don't know what it's really like until it's too late.'

'Oh for God's sake, Stella.' Izzy rolled her eyes. 'Having children is not like being in a cult.' But she didn't sound a hundred per cent sure.

'It bloody is. They exhaust you until you're weak-willed, and then before you know it you're spouting crap that a few months before you would have scoffed at. You give up all the fun things in life so you can follow a small creature around who shows no interest in anything other than screaming and sleeping. You develop an unnatural and many would say unhealthy interest in its poo. And even when it's cross-eyed and covered in cradle cap, you tell anyone who listens to you for more than thirty seconds how incredibly beautiful the little bugger is. How else can you explain that, if it's not like being in a cult?'

Caroline laughed, a little nervously. 'I'm sure it's all really exciting, though.'

Stella looked at her and smiled. 'Oh, Caroline. So innocent. So young.' She gave a fake sob and covered her eyes with the back of her hand.

Harriet stood up and smoothed her dress down. 'Stop it, you two. You'll have her running for the hills before we've got her in the car.'

Caroline shook her head. 'No. I can't wait to get there. I'm so excited.'

Harriet rolled her eyes behind her friend's back, and Stella saw her and winked. Caroline's devotion to her fiancé was touching but occasionally impossible not to mock.

'Of course.' Harriet nodded, reached for Caroline's veil. 'And who wouldn't be. Ignore these two old crones. Marriage has made them bitter and sour. Like raisins. Or something.'

'Sorry, Caroline,' Izzy said. Pearl was now wearing the floral headdress at an angle that could only be described as rakish. Izzy had given up fighting with her. 'I'm not trying to put you off. Some bridesmaids we are, eh? You're going to be very happy. I know you are. Getting married is . . .' She paused. 'Getting married is going to change your life.'

'She's right, Caro,' added Stella. 'You're going to be the perfect wife. Look at you. An hour before I got married I was – I think I was having sex, actually.'

'Please tell me with Johnny,' Harriet sighed.

'Of course with Johnny! Anyhow, the point is – I was hungover, and I wore a red minidress and leopardskin shoes and – well, I guess we started as we meant to go on. Everyone does. Izzy, what were you doing an hour before you got married? Something incredibly efficient, I bet. Organising everyone. Opening a restaurant in the morning, getting married in the afternoon?'

Izzy laughed. 'Not too far off, actually. Our caterer was ill, so I was in the kitchen, preparing canapés for a hundred and fifty people, because I didn't trust anyone else to take over at such short notice.' She coloured a little at the admission and held her hands up. 'Control freak, much?'

'Ha!' Stella whooped. 'See? Start as you mean to go on. Me, irresponsible, Izzy, control freak, you – perfectly calm and sleek, like a princess.'

'Oh for God's sake,' huffed Harriet, as she affixed the veil onto Caroline's head and began to do it up at the back. 'Stop talking utter crap and let's get this princess bride dressed and ready to become Mrs Beauman.'

But despite her protests, Harriet had to admit that Caroline did look absolutely perfect. And as she pulled the dress together and did up the row of tiny lace-covered buttons that ran down the back of it, she wondered what she might be doing an hour before her own wedding, and how Stella would analyse that as being typical of her. If she ever got there, that was. If she ever got there. Will was showing no signs whatsoever of wanting to be the next in line to walk up the aisle, and they had been together for longer than any of the group. She bit her lip. No, she told herself, not today. This day is not about you and Will.

She straightened, and the three women stood behind Caroline, facing the mirror, in silence.

'Oh darling,' Izzy said softly, 'you look absolutely beautiful.'

Caroline held her breath. She had never in her life felt beautiful before. Pretty, sometimes, yes. Attractive, reasonably often. Well-groomed, most of the time. But beautiful? Never until now. She smiled, and looked to her friends. They were right. She was starting as she meant to go on. Surrounded by the ones she loved, about to marry her soulmate, and happier than she had ever been. Her life was about to change, and she was going to savour every last moment of it.

'Look! Oh Caroline, didn't you look beautiful.' Izzy Rathbone craned her neck over her sister-in-law's shoulder, bottle of champagne in one hand and tray laden with cutlery tucked in the crook of the other, and kissed Caroline's cheek as she went past. The long oak table in James and Izzy's kitchen was full, all the cutlery and plates and napkins for the party laid out in neat rows and piles, the rest of the surface covered with photos from the wedding.

Izzy counted out the pieces of cutlery in her head as she admired the photo of Caroline and Bart taking their first steps as husband and wife. She always seemed to be doing one thing and thinking about another. She was used to splitting her brain like this. It was one of the first things you learned when you became a mother. Her eyes ran over the forks, all on their sides, all facing the same direction, curved tines fitting together.

She had covered the table with a white tablecloth, and moved it against the wall of the big, light kitchen diner. They had done the side return of their three-storey terraced house last year, pushing the room out to the full width of the building and adding a glass roof over the new space, which caught the afternoon light and sent shards of sunshine over to the big range oven. They'd redone the kitchen at the same time, new Shaker-style wooden units hand-painted in a soft greeny grey, and a big granite-topped island with a sink in the centre that had a special tap for boiling water and one of those swooshy chef's taps that James had wanted, and which she had wished she had never agreed to, because it sent jets of water shooting around the kitchen if you angled it slightly the wrong way, or if a small child managed to climb up on a stool and get their hands on it, which they did almost daily once they had realised the mess-making potential of the thing.

Izzy glanced down to the far end of the table. The knives were annoying her. Lining them up took up too much room, putting them in a glass when the rest of the cutlery was on the table looked messy; she had not yet found a satisfying solution. She sighed, and returned her gaze to the wedding photos, passing the bottle of champagne to James as he walked into the room and giving him a *topping up the drinks is practically your only bloody job, why am I doing it?* look. He gave her a wink as she did so, and she softened, and smiled. It was one of the things she liked about having been with someone for so long – the ability to read one another's minds, finish their sentences, signal a whole conversation with a glance.

Caroline gazed at the photos in front of her, knowing that she should gather them together and put them away before everyone else started to arrive or something got spilled on them, but not wanting to. The fizz of the day was still floating around her shoulders like a cloud: she was still the bride, still glowing with her honeymoon tan and her wedding manicure still intact. And the photos were not only a reminder; they gave her a glimpse of all the bits she had missed, the expressions she hadn't noticed, the way things looked from the outside that she had only seen from the in.

There was one of her small bridesmaids – Pearl, her niece, and Betty, her god-daughter – with circlets of roses on their heads, faces solemn with the magnitude of the task ahead of them. Here was one of her favourites – her grown-up brides-maids outside the church. She mentally marked this photo as one that she would get framed – they were walking up the path towards the doors, she in the centre, her brow furrowed a little. They were early, but she was worried that they were going to be late, so she was making them all walk quicker, except her progress was impeded by her dress and her high heels, so that she was doing a strange duck-like waddle, her hips uneven and her elbows sharp. Stella's head was thrown back, her hair messy, a rose jammed in behind her ear, unashamedly laughing at Caroline's ill-concealed panic, a final cigarette between her fingers, her other hand reaching into her bag for perfume that she would shortly spray over them all so that they walked into the church smelling of the same, unmistakably Stella scent; sexier and more adult than anything Caroline would have worn and distinctly un-bridal. Izzy was reaching for her sister-in-law, a reassuring hand to her elbow. 'Slow down,' she was about to say. 'Caroline, we aren't late, honestly, people are still sitting down. Stop panicking or you'll get there all out of puff like you've run the sack race.' Harriet was a step behind her, holding her veil and train away from the ground, trying to keep up as Caroline powered ahead. Her girls. She would get four copies of it made and have them framed, she thought now, give them to them as thank-you presents. The picture summed the four of them up so completely.

She turned it over and moved on to the next photo, and this one made her heart leap. It was of Bart, so handsome in his morning suit, standing outside the church flanked by his ushers, his face calm, his demeanour unruffled. The one sign of anxiety something only she would have noticed – the fact that he was rubbing the ends of his fingers together as he waited. The guests, hands holding their hats in place against the bluster as they walked down the path towards the church entrance, lit with flares in the fading winter light. Izzy straightening Caroline's train as she waited in the porch of the church, Julian Rathbone, her father, standing bolt upright like the ex-military man he was, pride visible in his very spine.

'Ready for the off?' he had whispered to her as she took his elbow. She remembered that her bouquet had been shaking slightly, an extension of the tremor that ran through her arm.

She'd taken a deep breath, and given a small nod. 'I can't wait to see him. To stand next to him. It's just – well, the thought of getting there's suddenly a bit daunting, Daddy.'

He had patted her hand, cool and reassuring as always. 'Chin up, girl. Eyes straight ahead, and don't whatever you do look at your mother. She's cried twice already, I don't want her setting you off before you've even got up the aisle.'

Caroline laughed. 'OK. Let's do it.' And once she had reached the altar, she had been right. All of her nerves had melted away, and it had been just her and Bart, and the vicar marrying them, and no one and nothing else had mattered.

Bart squeezed her hand now, and she smiled at him. Three weeks married, and it was New Year's Eve. Life was good.

'Come on,' he said. 'We'd better put these away. You don't want them to get messed up. Can't have you all upset because someone's upended a glass of champagne over them.'

'I know.' Caroline began gathering the pictures into a pile.

'Oh my God! Do you think they . . . ? I bet they did. Look.' Stella Albright's voice rang out in a scandalised and thrilled stage whisper as she picked up the photo of one of the ushers, an old school friend of Bart's, dancing with a single friend of Caroline's, his hand sliding down the satin back of her dress towards her bottom, drawing her towards him on the dance floor. 'The little hussy. I'd never have thought that one had it in her. Good on her. I must give her a ring.'

Stella leaned over and kissed Caroline with her ever-red-lipsticked lips. 'Hello, darling. Welcome home. Bart.' She pecked Bart on both cheeks. As usual, she smelt of scent and sex and cigarettes.

'Careful of the photos,' Bart muttered as she picked up one of Caroline's mother, Ginny, between navy-blue-painted fingernails. Underneath it was a photo of Harriet, looking over at her boyfriend Will as Caroline and Bart stood at the front, hands interwined. In the picture, Harriet's eyes sought him out at the back of the church, where he had been handing out orders of service and where he now stared fixedly at one of those same pieces of stiff white card, pretending to read the words of the hymn as he sang loudly, calling for his bow of burning gold, vowing not to cease from mental fight, when all the time Harriet, and anyone else who cared to think about it, knew that he had been singing it regularly since childhood.

'I am being careful. Look at this. Shame.'

'What do you mean?' Caroline leaned in closer. 'It's lovely of Hats.'

Stella raised an eyebrow. 'Lovely? Look at her. She practically combusting with envy.'

'Do you think?'

Stella snorted. 'Darling. It's written all over her face. Now, where's the champagne? You're all miles ahead of me, I'd better play catch-up.'

Caroline nodded as Stella left, continuing to stare at the photo. She hadn't seen it before. But now, thanks to Stella's writers' eyes, she could. Stella always saw the story behind things. Suddenly it was clear. Harriet's gaze resting on Will, him feeling it and pretending not to. Now she could see the yearning in Harriet's eyes, the unasked question palpating like the wings of a butterfly across the space between them. Harriet's mental fight. Marry me, she seemed to be silently saying, like a prayer. Marry me. It's been seven years and people have given up glancing at my ring finger after Christmas and New Year, or Valentine's Day, or my birthday. It's been seven years and I'm the last one and I know it shouldn't matter, it should all be about us, but it does matter. It does.

Caroline shivered, and put the photo to the bottom of the pile so that Harriet would be less likely to see it when she and

Will arrived. Then she slid the pictures back into their protective plastic sheath, and went to tuck them away somewhere safe, thinking as she did so how lucky she was to have found Bart.

7.12 p.m.

Harriet Bailey sat in the front seat of Will's clapped-out old Land Rover, and wished, not for the first time in their relationship, that she had worn something warmer. A pair of tights wouldn't have gone amiss, or even a pair of Spanx that would hold in a bit of extra warmth along with the lumps and bumps, rather than the stupid underwear that Will had given her for Christmas. She rubbed her hands together and fiddled with the heating dial, though she knew from long experience that it was futile, it wouldn't pump out anything other than icy-cold air. 'Damn.' She got a blast of it now, and put her hand back down, before turning to rummage in the back seat for a scarf or something. There was only Will's old Barbour, which was covered in dog hair and the stain of something unspeakable down the front – pheasant blood or worse, probably. She spent a second weighing it up, then pulled it over the seat and put it on. It was filthy, but comforting; it smelled of Will, of the woody aftershave his father gave him every year and had been doing since he was fourteen, of cigarettes and Fisherman's Friends, and of Labrador. Not exactly how she wanted to smell on her arrival at James and Izzy's, but her fingers were turning blue at the ends, and she liked huddling down in its too-big shape. She leant over and pressed down on the horn.

'Come ON, Will, for fuck's sake! What are you *doing* in there?' she muttered. She knew exactly what he'd be doing, though. Sitting on the loo. What was it about his bowels that meant that he had to wait until the second before they were due to leave, which was already half an hour later than they should have left, because he was incapable of knowing how long it

19

took him to get ready, always proclaiming he'd be there in 'two minutes, darling, I've just got to have a quick wash', before blithely getting into the bath where he would promptly fall asleep, waking up only when either the water started to cool down or she banged on the door, and then he would have to shave, and all the while she would be waiting, keys in her hand, by the front door, until she gave up and shouted, 'I'll be in the car,' in the hope that it would chivvy him along.

It never did. So she always ended up sitting here in the cold, her breath crystallising in front of her, fuming with irritation yet too proud to go back inside and sit at the table and wait for him there.

7.34 p.m.
'I'm not driving back, you know,' she snapped at him as soon as he got into the driving seat and put the keys in the ignition. 'It's not my fault you left it too late to book a cab.'

Will shrugged good-naturedly. 'We'll call one later, pick the car up tomorrow. Or we can just walk back.'

He put the car into reverse, waited for it to pop out of gear as it always did, shoved it back in, and began to back out of the parking space.

'I'm not sodding walking, Will. It's freezing, and I'm wearing stockings and stupid shoes. I'll freeze to actual death. If I don't break an ankle first. I don't know why you didn't organise it through Butler's. What's the point of running your own concierge company if you can't use it to actually sort some of your own life out?'

Will smiled. 'They're all booked up, weeks ago. With bookings from paying customers. Which is what we need, not me using it as a penis extension to show off with. We've got a perfectly good car' – as he said that, the Land Rover sputtered, as if even it didn't believe in its own reliability – 'and if the

20

worst comes to the worst we can crash at Boner's.' Will and James had been at boarding school together, and still sometimes called one another by the nicknames they had been given in their first few weeks there, based on their surnames: 'Boner' for James, and 'Skinny' for Will. Harriet flung her head back against the seat in annoyance. She couldn't bear the stupid public-school monikers, or the daft voices her boyfriend and his best friend used to greet each other with them, like they were on the rugby pitch, booming and drawing the last syllable out. Inane.

'Anyway, sod the car. Much more interestingly, what was that you said about stockings?' And Will took his left hand off the wheel and reached over and ran his hand up under Harriet's dress, squeezing her thigh and then bending his fingers around higher, working them inside the silk band of her knickers, and she was glad she had decided against the Spanx.

8.40 p.m.
'What are we going to tell them?' Harriet shivered as she walked up the path towards James and Izzy's front door. This year's wreath was a silvery-blue pine, studded with cones sprayed silver and glowing white sprigs of mistletoe.

'What do you mean? We don't have to tell them anything.'

'Will! We're an hour late. It's so rude.'

'You're so rude.' Will growled, and bit Harriet's neck, pinching her bottom at the same time and sending a jolt of memory through her of how he had jerked the hand brake on and left the car running in the street outside their house, leaning over and unclicking her seat belt despite her protest-ations and pulling her back inside the house, where he had lifted her up on to the big wooden chest in the hall and fucked her as she perched on the edge of it, holding her steady with both hands on her bottom as he did so. She could never stay cross with him for long.

'They won't care.'

'They'll be able to tell.'

'So? It is allowed, you know, darling. We're practically—' He broke off. 'We're grown-ups.'

They both looked ahead. Ignored the unspoken word. Practically married.

'Hello! Happy New Year, come in, come in, everyone's here . . .' Izzy's voice held a slight question, and Harriet rolled her eyes at her as they walked into the warm hallway, mouthing 'sorry' as she did so, correctly hoping that Izzy would assume their lateness was down to Will. And it was.

9.53 p.m.

Izzy cleared a tray of half-eaten canapés from the table and replaced it with one of mini eclairs and tiny tartes Tatin, all neatly lined up in rows. For a second, as she put the tray down, she couldn't decide whether she felt proud or embarrassed by the fact that she had spent three hours piping choux pastry into little lines that afternoon. It was absurd, really, to have done so. Everyone was drunk, no one would notice, or care, that she had made them herself rather than ordering in from the local patisserie.

Oh stop it, Izzy, she told herself, stop feeling sorry for yourself. You have a perfect life, a life thousands of women would kill for. She knew it was true. She knew how lucky she was. And that made the fact that she felt so trapped in this perfect life, so bored by it, all the worse. There was no one she could tell, no one she could confide in. It would be horribly ungrateful, cruel even, to go to Harriet or Caroline or Stella and moan about the fact that she was bored to tears, so bored that she sometimes felt as though she could not last another day of her life, and that she had, on at least three occasions in the last month, looked up flights on expedia.co.uk, playing travel roulette, clicking the buttons and seeing just how far away she could get for five hundred pounds, or some other arbitrary sum of money. Because they wouldn't understand. They would think she had gone mad. Anyone would. She had a good husband, two healthy children, enough money to stay at home with her family. Who could ask for more? And yet. Every day when she woke up, she yearned for the excitement she used to feel when she was going in to the restaurant, gearing up for a long shift. For the ache in her muscles after it was all over. For the burns and cuts that had marked her hands and arms – hands and arms that where now soft and smooth, bearing only faint memories of their previous life. Like her. A faint memory of the woman she had once been. She knew it. She was sure James felt it as well. Her absence, her lack of – Izzyness. But she had no idea how to fix it.

She passed Will a plate of home-made champagne truffles, and gestured to him to pass them around. He was mid conversation with Julian, her father-in-law, and neither man looked up.

'. . . and the beauty of it is that we vet all the parties involved, so it's just an extension of Henry Butler's. You're not going to arrive at your chalet in Val d'Isère to find that you've been lumped in with a group of people you've got nothing to say to. You'll be with people like you.'

'What's this?' James asked, taking a swig from his beer.

'Will's new wheeze,' Julian said. 'He's trying to convince me it's going to be the next big thing.'

'It could be huge, Julian. You mark my words. But I won't be offended if you're not interested in coming on board. I think Bart is, though.'

Will clapped his arm around James's shoulders. 'Posh timeshares and group holidays, basically, mate. We buy a load of chalets, big swanky villas, that kind of thing. Clients can either buy a chunk – x thousand pounds for however many weeks a year, but in a fuck-off villa in Barbados or Tuscany, or even on a yacht – or they can go as part of a group. Singles, couples with no kids, few friends, that kind of thing. We organise it all, make sure the right people go together, provide all the staff. Holiday matchmaking, if you like.'

'Sounds good,' James said. 'Big outlay at the beginning, though.'

Will rubbed his chin. 'Yep. But no one's done anything quite like it before. We'll get loads of press. And the demand's there.'

'Is it?' Julian asked. 'Times are tough, Will. A project like this . . . Well, I can see how it could have worked a couple of years ago. But people are nervous right now. Is it the right time to be expanding?'

Will grinned. 'It's always the right time to be expanding. Onwards and upwards, you know that's my motto.'

Will was still holding the plate Izzy had passed him, unaware of her waving her arms at him and mouthing 'pass them around' from the other side of the group. Eventually she gave up and went back to the cluster of men to retrieve them.

'Thanks, darling,' James said absent-mindedly as she took them away.

'Caroline's Bart?' Julian's eyebrows caterpillared towards each other.

'Mm, he sounded keen, anyhow. You sound surprised.'

'Oh no. Not really. Just thought he was focusing on – I don't know. New media or something.'

Will shrugged. 'I think he likes to have his fingers in plenty of pies,' he said.

'Well, sign us up for a fortnight somewhere without the kids, eh?' James smiled. 'Could do with a bit of a break from the ankle-biters.'

Izzy suppressed a frustrated sigh. Classic, the way James made it sound as though he was beset by children all day long.

Last weekend he had spent the sum total of an hour with them, when she had been at the supermarket, and she had returned to find him playing some game on the computer and them with half a pot of jam in their hair.

'You could? You're always complaining that you don't get enough time with them. Make your mind up, darling. And try and keep an eye on people's glasses, will you?'

James raised one hand to his forehead in mock salute, and she flicked him with a tea towel and left them to it.

11.32 p.m.
Stella stood in the small downstairs cloakroom, reapplying her lipstick and listening to the chatter of the party going on outside the door. She opened her squashy leather bag and pulled out her perfume, spraying a thick cloud into the air around her head. She looked up at her face in the mirror, leaning forward to touch up the thick flicks of eyeliner rising up from the corners of her dark blue eyes. A quick poof of her teased and backcombed bleached hair and she would be done.

As she got her comb out, there was a light tap on the door. 'S'busy,' she called. 'Won't be long.'

'It's me.' Izzy's voice came through the door. 'Open up.'

Stella reached out and unlocked the door with one hand, her other holding the twist of hair she was working on above her head. 'Hey. Good party. Amazing food, again.'

'Thanks.' Izzy closed the door behind her, a flute in one hand and bottle of champagne in the other, leant her head against it and closed her eyes. 'God. I'm knackered.'

She opened her eyes and her gaze met Stella's in the mirror. 'I look about a hundred,' she said, lifting her fingertips to her forehead and stretching the skin a little. 'What do you think? Five years younger?'

Stella shook her head. 'Don't be stupid. You don't need any

of that crap. You look amazing.' She put her comb away and began applying another layer of mascara.

'What, for thirty-five and two kids?'

'No. Just amazing. Full stop. You're gorgeous, you know you are. The perfect yummy mummy.'

Izzy groaned. 'Great.'

'I know, it's a vile phrase. Sorry. But, you know, if the cap fits . . . Here, do you want?' Stella held out a small fold of paper, and looked at Izzy questioningly.

'I shouldn't. I haven't since the kids.'

'Up to you. You don't mind if I . . . ?'

Izzy shook her head, and Stella unfolded the wrap and shook a little pile of white powder out on to the glass basin surround. She took a credit card from her purse and crushed the small lumps down into a fine dust.

'Fuck it. Do me one. Not too big.'

Stella held out a rolled-up twenty-pound note, and Izzy took it and snorted the line of coke. 'Fuck. Gosh.' She held her nose, wincing slightly as the powder rushed through her sinuses.

'OK?' Stella asked.

'Yup. Just . . . wow. It's been a while.' Izzy opened her eyes.

'When was the last time you did that?'

Izzy thought back. Before the children. 'Five years? More? I forgot how – zingy it is.'

'Zingy. Oh Iz. Only you.'

'What?'

'Nothing. You just manage to make a line of coke sound like a particularly refreshing shower gel. Zingy!'

The two women laughed.

'When did I become so tragic?'

Stella laid her hand on Izzy's shoulder. 'Darling. You didn't.' She paused. 'You've *always* been tragic.'

She laughed, and ducked as Izzy took a swipe at her.

'Sorry, sorry . . . Bart and Caroline seem happy, don't they?'

'Blissfully. I'm so happy for her.'

'Yes. Was beginning to wonder whether she'd be single for ever.'

'I think she was too.'

'I'm sure. What are we going to do about Will and Harriet, then?'

Izzy rolled her eyes. 'Don't. Poor thing, she's desperate for him to propose.'

'Do you think he will?'

'He should do. He doesn't know how lucky he is to have her.'

'Oh, I think he probably does.'

'Well she doesn't think so. If he's not careful, he'll lose her.'

Izzy straightened her top in the mirror. 'God, I should stop gossiping and go and make sure everyone's got full glasses for midnight, and then fetch the kids – we promised we'd wake them up. They'll be hell tomorrow.' She groaned. 'God. Bloody children. I love them, God knows I love them. But why do they have to be there ALL the time.' She laughed. 'I'm so bored, Stell. You're so lucky to be able to work, to do something that fits around Viking.'

'Ha.' Stella zipped her make-up bag shut and turned to face Izzy. Stella and Johnny's son was a little over a year old, and Stella, a freelance journalist, had been back at work part time after a couple of months. 'It's not luck, darlin', it's necessity. You try being married to a musician. They're terribly pretty and they woo you with amazing songs, but when it comes to paying the mortgage, Johnny's about as much use as Viking, bless him.'

'But at least you're both doing what you want to do. You have that freedom. I can't do what I want to, because working six till midnight in a kitchen is hardly conducive to bringing up kids, James is sick of his job, but he can't really do much else now, and he has to keep the ship afloat. He hardly ever sees the kids, I see altogether too much of them . . . We're stuck.' Izzy sighed.

Stella raised an eyebrow. 'There are always choices, Iz,' she said, a little sharply.

Izzy refilled their glasses and took a gulp of champagne. 'I know. Sorry. We're lucky. We're all lucky.'

Midnight

'Ten . . . nine . . . eight . . . seven . . . six . . . five . . . four . . . three . . . two . . . one . . . Happy New Year!' The large flat-screen TV in the corner of the living room burst into life with the fireworks over the Thames, and the bongs of Big Ben echoed throughout the room as the group of friends and family kissed and cheered and shook hands, and party poppers flew into the air covering the room with multicoloured streamers. Johnny picked up one of James's rarely used electric guitars that he had plugged into an amp in readiness, and strummed the opening chords of 'Auld Lang Syne'. The notes reverberated around the room, and Will cheered and pushed everyone into an impromptu circle, Ginny on one side of him, looking flushed and a little overwhelmed, Stella on the other, and they linked arms across their bodies as Johnny played, and sang, up to the bit that no one ever knew the words of, where they just sort of la-ed along. James held the small, sleepy Alfie, who was eighteen months, as he rubbed his eyes and gazed at the spectacle in his living room, and Pearl skipped around in the middle of the circle of grown-ups, gazing up at them, a balloon in one hand, delighted to have all of the people she loved most in the world in one place.

'We'll take a cup of kindness yet, for auld lang syne . . .' The room broke into cheers again and Pearl clapped happily along with them as the circle broke up and people returned to their little groups. Julian and Ginny began to gather their coats and everyone protested for a minute and then let them go out into the night, a flurry of goodbyes and thank-yous and Happy New Years following them into the cold street, and then it was just the eight of them, and Pearl and Alfie had fallen asleep on James's lap, and he took them back to bed, slipping their warm bodies under the covers and kissing their foreheads, before going back downstairs for port, a plate of cheese and a game of liar dice with the boys, while the girls kicked their shoes off and curled their legs up under them on the sofa, gossiping about the evening and eating leftovers. And it was the eight of them, James and Izzy, Caroline and her beloved newly minted husband Bart, Harriet and Will, Stella and Johnny. They were an eight, they were two fours, they were four twos. They were not perfect, but they were together, and that was what mattered, and they were lucky. They were lucky.

Later, after everyone had left, Izzy reminded herself of that as she shut the door after Harriet and Will, listening to them stumbling noisily down the path, slipping on icy stones, giggling and whispering to each other. You are lucky, she told herself, as she turned off the lights and climbed the stairs to bed, following in James's footsteps, treading softly so as not to wake up her sleeping children. You are lucky, she told herself, as she paused outside their bedroom doors for a moment, listening to their snuffling, regular breaths. You are lucky, she told herself, as she went into the room she shared with her husband and began to undress. And with every silent reminder, she wished, secretly, for something – anything – to happen.

Chapter Two

January 2008

Keys, phone, wallet, changing bag, snacks; keys, phone, wallet, changing bag, snacks; keys, phone, wallet, changing bag, snacks . . . Izzy ran through her mental checklist over and over again as she picked up the items she needed to take with her to the gym and crèche. She pulled open 'the drawer', which was the kitchen repository for stuff that had no obvious home – rubber bands, highlighter pens, takeaway menus and lumps of Blu-Tack – and reached to the back of it, her fingers feeling for the rectangular travel-sweet tin she kept there. She opened it, and took a single cigarette out of the pack of Marlboro Lights. Her one sliver of self-indulgence in the day. She would smoke it after her session with her personal trainer, as she walked to pick up Alfie through the leafy gardens of the Bovingdon, the private club that she and James had joined when they bought their house.

'Mumm-eeeeee! Alfie's done a poo and now it's on the floo-oooor.' Oh Jesus. Great. Poo on the floor and it's not even – Izzy checked her watch – not even half past nine. She raced up the stairs two at a time, fumbling with the catch on the stair gate at the top and heading into Alfie's room to find him sitting quite happily in his cot, small nuggets of poo dotting the floor surrounding it.

'Shit. Shit, shit, shit.' Izzy swore under her breath. She couldn't be angry with Alfie, not really, it was her own fault for leaving him in his cot without a nappy on while she sorted their things out. A flash of guilt that he had been doing this while she was worrying about getting her daily cigarette out of its hiding place and sliding it into her pocket. Bad mother, the little voice in the back of her head whispered, the voice that had appeared recently and would not quieten. Neglectful, selfish, bored. Bored by your own children. She pushed the voice down, and lifted a chuckling Alfie out of his cot, scooping the remaining poo from underneath him with a nappy as she did so and carrying him at arm's length into the bathroom.

By the time she had cleaned up Alfie, and taken the dirty sheet from his cot and put it into the machine, and sorted out the carpet in his room as best she could with a can of Vanish – she would have to get it steam-cleaned – she was late for her appointment. On a whim, and in a moment of small rebellion, she decided not to run in order to try and make it, doing only half a session, but to cancel it completely and take the kids for cake at the café round the corner instead. The café did home-made iced buns with pink icing that Pearl adored, and Ailsa, the Syrian woman who owned it, always gave her an extra big one and made a fuss of her. It was a bit cramped, and a bit shabby, but Ailsa made good coffee and none of the local mums tended to go in there, and while Izzy usually liked the company that she found at the Bovingdon, today she felt like being left to her own thoughts.

James had been coming in later and later from work. She tried to pinpoint when it had started, but, like her own feelings of frustration, she could not find the end of it to thread the needle. She thought it might have been since he went back to work after the New Year. But then maybe it was before

31

then. The days and weeks melted together like candle wax. He said it was because work was busy, that they were over-stretched after one of the team had left and not yet been replaced, but Izzy wasn't sure. He'd always had to travel a lot with his job, making frequent, sometimes twice- or thrice-monthly trips to the States, days in Germany, France, Belgium. She wasn't a suspicious person, had always prided herself on not being one of those awful jealous, clingy women who needed to know where their men were every second of the day, quizzing them every time they walked through the door about where they had been and who with, as though they were trying, hoping, even, to catch them out. But something was – not quite right. She didn't think James would have an affair. Dispassionately, disregarding the natural self-protection (ego, maybe?) that instinctively leapt up inside her to deny that he could betray her in that way, she just didn't think he was the type. He wasn't naturally duplicitous, he was loyal and honest, and they still had sex regularly. She didn't feel it likely that he would risk their family life for – for what? A fling carried out in hotel rooms and quickies in the office after hours with a secretary? No, it just wasn't him.

But still, there was something unspoken forming a membrane-like barrier between them, and she couldn't catch hold of it for long enough to work out what it was.

The café was full of a warm, nutmeggy fug, and Izzy felt herself relax as soon as she pushed the buggy through the door. Ailsa bustled over to help her, a tiny ball of energy and thick black curls. She hovered as Izzy got the children out of their straps and settled into the small wooden chairs.

'Horrible day, wet and cold, English January, so I've made baklava, you want some, or you want lunch?'

Izzy looked over at the pile of little pastries dripping in honey under their glass dome, and nodded. 'Baklava, please, and buns for the littles. And a . . .'

'Double-shot latte with soy?'

Izzy nodded.

'Coming right up. Babyccinos for them?' Ailsa made small cups of frothed milk sprinkled with chocolate powder for the children who came to the café and wanted the same drink as Mummy.

'Thanks, Ailsa. How was your Christmas?'

Ailsa began to work the huge red coffee machine, twisting the handle of the dispenser round and packing it full of fresh ground grains. She shrugged. 'Not so good,' she said over her shoulder. 'My mother's sick. She's dying, they think. So, I have to go back home to look after her.'

'Oh no, Ailsa, I'm so sorry.' Izzy felt a little uncomfortable. The women had exchanged pleasantries for months, chatted about Izzy's children and the local area, complained about the council's slackness with rubbish collections and extortionate taxes, but had never talked about anything really personal. 'Has she been ill for a long time?' she ventured.

Ailsa shook her head as she carried a plate of sticky sweets to Izzy's table, being careful to put them down out of Alfie's reach, and touching his hair as she did so. 'No, just a couple of months. But at Christmas she got a lot worse. I'm an only child, she's my only parent left. So, we're selling up.'

'You're selling the café?'

'I can't leave it to be looked after by someone else, I'd always be fretting about it. I can't allow my mother to be looked after by strangers. And maybe me and John will stay in Syria once – well, for good. We've talked about it before. Maybe . . .' Ailsa shook her head and wiped the sadness from her face. 'Maybe this is a good thing, you know? Sometimes change finds you.'

Izzy nodded, slowly. Her mind was filling with images,

despite herself, as her eyes flicked around the small space. She felt sorry that Ailsa was leaving, sorry that she was having to go in this way. But she couldn't help it. An image of a new space was appearing, fully formed in her mind's eye. A deli counter stocked with delicious things, more adventurous meals than Ailsa's moussakas and pyramids of falafel. Lunchtime dishes aimed at the carb-shunning women she knew from the club, who could probably be tempted to take a change of scenery every so often with good food that fitted in with their diets. Home-made cordials and flavoured syrups for coffees; big sandwiches for the blokes, really good ones, her meatball subs and proper sausage and bacon sandwiches at weekends. Some shelves along the left-hand wall selling the things you really needed in a local shop – not the pretty but fairly useless packs of squid-ink spaghetti and amaretti biscuits that Ailsa stocked, but the things you suddenly ran out of and couldn't get in Tesco Metro. She made a mental list – Maldon salt, good olive oil, balsamic, free-range eggs, unsalted butter, Parmesan . . . Could she get an alcohol licence? she wondered. A small list of wines by the glass would go down well with the local wives on Friday lunchtimes and days when the nanny was there. She could do a special deal: carb-free pasta and sauce (she had perfected the art of making a bowl of spaghetti-like strands from courgettes and carrots) or a big salad and a glass of wine for a set amount. Healthier versions of takeaway favourites like she made for her family – spicy fried chicken, posh kebabs in flatbreads with hummous, slices of home-made pizza . . . Her mind was buzzing.

She put a baklava into her mouth and chewed over both it and the idea that had begun to form in her mind. There was a chunk of money, savings, rainy-day money, in a couple of ISAs and a savings account. Most of James's salary went on the mortgage and household bills and car payments, club fees, holidays, the usual set of expenses, but there was a bit of capital floating around that she could lay her hands on. Stella might be up for a nanny share; she was working much more now that Viking was that bit older. She could maybe juggle that and the crèche at the Bovingdon while she did the refit, and look for someone full time for when she opened. Ailsa's words echoed in her brain. *Sometimes change finds you.*

'Ailsa?' she called across the room, and the woman nodded and came over to her table. 'Have you found a buyer yet?'

Pearl was giggling gleefully as James came in through the front door, pulling his carry-on case behind him and leaving it propped up by the coat hooks in the hall. Two pairs of wellington boots with eyes like frogs sat next to it, alongside Izzy's leather boots and a pair of his deck shoes.

'No, put the blueberry in your mouth, Pearl, that's right, and another one, or I'll take them away. No, not UP YOUR NOSE!'

'What are you putting up your nose, you little monkey?' James called out to Pearl, who squeaked with excitement. 'Daddy! Present!'

He walked into the kitchen, picking up Pearl as she swivelled in her chair and held her arms out to him, and leaning down to kiss Izzy, then Alfie, who was sitting, solidly, being fed oatmeal. He ignored the kiss and opened his mouth wide for another spoonful.

'Hi, darling. They been OK?'

Izzy nodded. 'You know, fine. Alfie's had a bit of teething tummy. He's better now.'

She looked at her husband. She wanted to blurt it out immediately, her plans, her vision, how excited she felt, how she could see a future stretching ahead of her for the first time in months. It was only since talking to Ailsa that she had realised how small her world had become. Until today, she hadn't been able to look beyond the next weekend, because all of her days were the same. Now, all of a sudden, her mind was racing. She had to keep putting Alfie down to make a note of something she had remembered she wanted to stock, or a menu idea. It was like her brain was waking up and stretching.

Not now, though. James was distracted, his mind still on work and travel and getting home; he would not respond well to being bombarded with this straight away. She would wait. She *must* wait. She felt as though her chest would explode.

'Thank God you weren't too delayed. I have to leave soon and Janey can't get here till ten. I was going to have to take them with me.'

'Where are you off to?' James looked grumpy – his hoped-for post-plane nap would have to wait until later.

'Oh . . . a meeting.' Izzy bit her lip. Tried to keep her voice light, casual. As if it were no big deal that she were going out to a meeting on a Saturday morning when her husband had just got home.

'A meeting?' James raised his eyebrows. Stay-at-home mothers didn't have meetings.

'Mm.' She picked up her keys. Waited.

'What meeting?' There it was.

'I'll tell you later.' She couldn't help but smile. She was so excited. The meeting was with the solicitor she had found to deal with the lease. That was another reason for delaying the conversation – she wanted to make sure everything was in place before she told James what she was up to. He was much better at dealing with things when he knew there was a plan. She was making her plans.

Izzy grinned and put Alfie's spoon down, pulling on a long cardigan over her weekend uniform of T-shirt, skinny jeans and boots. 'I'd better go,' she said, kissing James on the cheek as she hooked her bag over her shoulder and picked up her large diary-cum-notebook. 'Try and take them to feed the ducks or something if you get a chance,' she said. 'It chucked it down all day yesterday, so we went to soft play with Stella and Viking.' Izzy rolled her eyes and James winced, sympathetically. 'I know, I don't know what I was thinking. Viking bashed Alfie on the head in the ball pond and they all came out smelling faintly of pee. Remind me if I ever suggest going back there, will you, that it's the seventh circle of hell?'

James gave her a little salute, and a wink. 'Roger that. I'll take them to the Bovingdon to go on the swings.'

'And for chips,' Pearl interjected, firmly. 'Chips and ketchup.'

'Chips and ketchup, eh? Well, maybe. ONLY if you go and watch *Pingu* for half an hour while Daddy has a shower, like a good girl.' Pearl's eyes lit up and she raced off to the living room and the DVD player. *Pingu*'s plinky-plonky music started up, and James scooped Alfie out of his high chair and held him slightly at arm's length. The boy's face was covered with oatmeal, which had gone hard, giving him the look of a neglected pot of wallpaper paste, and Alfie was poking his tongue out of one corner of his mouth, trying to reach a final morsel. James and Izzy both looked at him and laughed. 'Think I'll just take him in with me,' James said. 'Come on, you.'

'See you later,' Izzy called from the front door as James carried his son upstairs. 'Oh, and I booked us a table at Corton's for tonight.'

James paused. Corton's was his favourite local restaurant, a little bistro around the corner. She waited for him to protest that he'd be too tired, that he'd rather stay in. Held her breath. He loved Corton's. It would put him in a good mood.

He smiled. 'Great. It's a date.'

*

'Is it about the money?' Izzy asked, after the waitress had cleared away their main-course plates, quickly and quietly, picking up on the tension that hovered over the table between them. She tapped her wedding ring on the side of her wine glass.

'Of course not,' he said. 'Well, not really. I mean, it is a lot of cash, Izzy.'

'I know it is. But it's worth it.'

'Easy for you to say.'

Izzy bit her bottom lip. She mustn't cry. She must. Not. Cry. 'That's not really fair, is it? I'm so bored. I'm bored to sodding tears, James. You have no idea what my life is like day to day.'

· 'I'm sorry. I never realised your life was so awful.'

She exhaled in frustration. She hated this. She couldn't express herself, couldn't find the words to get him to understand her. She felt like an angry child full of tantrumming rage with nowhere to put it. 'It's not. Of course it's not.'

James's face was stony. Izzy reached across the table and took his hands in hers.

'I'm sorry. I know I've been really lucky to be able to spend the time at home with the children. I do know that.'

James paused before replying. 'Well. We've both been doing our bit.'

She bristled. 'Yes. We have.'

There was a pause. Neither of them looked the other in the eye. 'So, what are you saying? That because I'm not the one who's been out earning, I don't have any claim on the money?'

James looked uncomfortable, and shook his head. 'That's not what I said.'

'Why not? You might as well. Admit it. It's how you feel. Isn't it?' Her torso was stiff in her seat. She fell quiet as the waitress returned and swept the crumbs from their table. Smiled a quick, terse smile as they were handed pudding menus. They both put them down without looking at them.

'I just think it should have been a joint decision. It affects all of us, after all. It's not just about whether we can afford it.'

He was avoiding the question, and they both knew it.

'Fine. So let's make it a joint decision. Let's discuss it.'

'What's the point? You've already made your mind up. I can't stop you. What sort of git would I be if I said you couldn't do it?'

Izzy shrugged. 'If you're dead against it, then I don't want to do it.'

James smiled. 'Don't be petulant.' But his voice was joking now, and she sighed.

'I need you behind me. Starting a business is *hard*.'

'Especially at the moment.'

'Exactly. I don't want to do it – I can't do it – if we're not together. If you don't believe in it. I need this, darling. I really need it.'

He rubbed his thumb over her hand and nodded.

'Looking after the children full time – it's not them. It's not that I don't want to be with them. It's just – it's the relentlessness of it. It's like a treadmill. The same thing over and over again, the same questions, the same meals, the same snotty, bored women at the playground. I'm going out of my mind and I have to get off the treadmill, I have to feel like an actual person again or I don't know what I'll do. I know you hate your job . . .'

'I don't hate it. Not really. It doesn't set me on fire, true, but . . .'

'You do. And I'm sorry. I know you've got a bit trapped, and a bit stuck, and you pay for everything. But imagine if this works. If it does really well. It might, you know. I used to be kind of good at what I did.'

'You were incredible. You still are. It's what made me fall in love with you. That truffle risotto . . .' James groaned at the memory.

'And there I was thinking it was my ravishing good looks and enchanting sense of humour.'

He pretended to think. 'Nope. Still the truffle risotto.'

She paused. 'I need to do this, James,' she said quietly, after a while. 'I'm sorry for going about it stupidly and not talking to you first. But I really need to do it. And I really need you to help me.'

He lifted her hand to his lips and kissed her fingers. 'Of course. Of course I will.'

Izzy grinned at him. She felt as though the world had opened up in front of her. 'Thank you. Darling. Thank you.'

Harriet stood in front of the pasta counter in the brightly lit food hall in Selfridges basement. It was her default destination when they had people coming round for dinner; the little office that she and her business partner ran their small PR firm from was just around the corner, and she often popped in after work to pick up something for supper. Sometimes at lunchtime as well, which was a bad habit; it was far too expensive to really be able to justify buying her sandwiches here.

She smoothed down the front of her dress while she waited. It wasn't just her wallet that was suffering from her lunchtime sandwich habit, it was her belly as well. Harriet had never been overweight; she had slim, muscular legs that remained taut from her years of playing hockey and tennis at school, and a narrow waist, but these days it was topped with a small pot belly. There was a pocket of fat that had positioned itself there soon after she had turned thirty and that she couldn't seem to shift (not that she had tried all that hard, admittedly). It was too late for New Year's resolutions. Maybe she should go on a diet and think of it as a spring-clean.

'Some of the wild boar tortelloni, please,' she requested, pointing to the little yellow pillows when her turn came. 'Enough for four. Four greedy people. So if you think six.' She had salad and pecorino in her basket already, and a loaf of squidgy white bread to mop up the sauce; she just needed something for pudding. She took the paper package from the server and put it in her basket.

'Harriet? Hattie?' Harriet turned, automatically reaching her hand up and smoothing down her straight brown hair, tucking it behind her ears. 'Oh my GOD!'

Harriet's face froze into a mask of wide smiles as inside she cursed herself for not leaving the office five minutes earlier, arsing around on Facebook instead.

Tasha James. Just her bloody luck. The pointy face of the single most annoying and competitive girl that she and Caroline had been at school with swooped towards her like an eagle seeking its prey. Tasha now lived around the corner from Izzy, in a large, flamboyantly expensive house.

'Tasha! Wow, how nice to see you.' Harriet put her basket down on the floor and the two women kissed on both cheeks. Harriet felt Tasha grab her hands as she pulled away.

'How ARE you?' Tasha gushed, still grasping her hands, lifting them up slightly now as though in great affection. Harriet knew better, though.

'Oh, fine, fine, really good actually. The business is going from strength to strength, just booming,' she babbled, hating herself as she did so for trying to get in a defensive strike before Tasha hit her with the ace she knew was coming.

'You and Will still together?' Tasha asked with a sweet smile that Harriet knew from experience covered a rabidly pushy soul. Tasha James had been the girl who had tripped up her best friend in the third-year relay race on sports day and blamed it on slippery ground and badly fitting trainers. But everyone knew.

'Yes, still together.' Harriet tried to stop her smile from turning into a grimace. Here it came. Brace position.

'Not married yet?' Tasha's voice was macaroon light. Harriet knew it, had known that was what was behind Tasha's faux-affectionate grasping of her hands: she'd been checking by touch for the presence of a ring on the right finger. Busted, you spiteful cow, she thought. But simply said, 'God, we just don't seem to have got around to it, we're both so busy with work. You know what it's like, when you run your own business you're never off duty.' Point to Harriet – Tasha had no idea what it was like; she had worked for the same marketing company since leaving university. And her words could imply that Will had asked her, that he was keen, couldn't they? Just haven't got around to it could mean that they were both desperate to tie the knot, just too frantically busy to have time for anything as trivial and girlish as organising a wedding. *Gah, why are you even thinking about this? She's a witch, she always was and she always will be. Just say you have to go and leave. Stop playing her pathetic game.*

But Tasha was nodding now. 'I *so* understand,' she was saying, lifting her left hand to her mouth and turning it slightly towards Harriet so that she caught the full glare of the stack of diamonds on her ring finger: a wedding band studded with them, then a trilogy engagement ring, its stones fat like little eggs, and then an eternity ring, more diamonds glinting smugly. 'Hubby's company has just gone public,' *oh of course it has, you hateful, hateful woman,* 'and the weight of it is a real burden on him sometimes. So it's my job to keep the home fires burning and give him all the support I can.'

Unlike you, running your own business as a pathetic attempt to fill your day and cover up the fact that Will doesn't love you or value you enough to actually ask you to marry him. Harriet heard the real meaning underneath Tasha's empathy.

'And of course it's not going to get any easier in a few months; we'll both be on duty around the clock,' she added, pushing her chocolate shearling aside and revealing a tiny cashmere-covered bump above her Seven maternity jeans.

'Number four!' she said, smugly. The bump wasn't much bigger than Harriet's newly acquired pot belly, she thought sadly. For a brief, slightly insane moment she was tempted to claim that she too was 'in the club', like those moments where you drive along the motorway and imagine, for a fraction of a second, what it would feel like to just spin the wheel.

'Oh, Tasha, congratulations, how lovely for you both,' she said instead. Of course. She played the game, and eventually managed to refuse Tasha's suggestion of a 'quick drink at the champagne bar, well, fizzy water for me, of course!' that both of them knew wouldn't happen – 'Sorry, I'd so love to, but I have to dash home and get dinner on. I've got friends coming and I'm making something special. This? Oh no, this pasta's just for the freezer' (*liar, stop lying, you fucking idiot, just tell her you're serving your friends bought pasta and you don't give a fuck because you have better things to do than slave over some River Café recipe that requires a certain type of flour only available from a special deli in Rome and butter that's been clarified three separate times*) – and escape into Oxford Street, where she almost tripped over a *Big Issue* seller in her rush to get outside and light a cigarette, her fingers clicking the lighter catch in irritation until it finally caught, then leaning against the wall of the department store, her shopping on the ground between her feet, unsure whether she hated Tasha more or herself. Or Will.

Chapter Three

April 2008

James was tapping at his laptop, his fingers moving fast over the keys, faltering only occasionally, when he paused to think, his lips moving as he tried to word the email in the right way.

I appreciate your predicament . . . – no, that wasn't right, too stiff, he sounded like an old git. *I appreciate that this must be difficult for you* . . . – something of an understatement, but it was an improvement. *But I am unable to* . . .

The words trailed off. He turned his head and looked out of the small window next to him. Clouds puffed up underneath the plane and beyond, as though they were forming a bridge to their destination. It was the fourth time in five weeks that he'd crossed the Atlantic, and he was tired.

Maybe he'd be able to sleep for a few hours before they landed. After he'd finished this blasted email.

He turned back to it.

I am unable to be the person you are looking for me to be. You must understand . . . Must she? She had never been an especially understanding sort of person. She was unlikely to understand this.

I hope that, in time, you will come to understand . . . Better.

And true. He did hope, very much, unlikely as he felt it to be . . . *why I must refuse your very reasonable request.* Should he say very reasonable? If it was so reasonable, why was he refusing it? *Why I must, with regret, refuse your request.* Christ, not a sentence anyone with a lisp should attempt out loud, but it would do.

His fingers hovered. He should say something else, something to stop him sounding, and, more to the point, feeling, like such a complete heel. He wriggled his toes. The cashmere socks that Izzy had given him in his stocking, which had seemed like a girlish indulgence at the time, had come into their own during his frequent flights (Izzy had smiled smugly when he had told her, and he had realised that was exactly why she had given them to him, and felt a bit mean for his initial ungratefulness, even though he hadn't said anything, had thanked her effusively before putting them to one side). They were much warmer than the nylon sheaths you got in the amenity packs, and they didn't have that horrid nylon feeling that made his teeth itch. He was a lucky man.

The thought spurred him on. *Please respect my decision. I trust that you will find the money I have transferred to your account of some assistance with bills and so forth, both past and present. Sincerely, James.*

He let the mouse hover over the send button.

'Another glass, sir?' The air hostess, all hairspray and sensibly heeled shoes, was next to him, a bottle in her hand, and he nodded and pushed his glass over towards her, then clicked send before he could start fretting about the sign-off, or changing his mind, and shut the laptop firmly. There. It was done. The money would leave his account in a few days, he estimated, and he could put the whole thing behind him and move forward. He had done the right thing – the only thing – for the sake of his family, he told himself. It had been the only choice. He would rather have sent the money – a reasonably large sum, a number that he had come to after much deliberation and mental toing and froing – in cash, and have had it done with, but Izzy had cleared out their savings account and then some buying the café that she was refitting, and anyhow, he wouldn't have been able to hide the disappearance of such a large amount. The loan he had taken out in his sole name was much safer.

For now, he could simply sit back and enjoy the last couple of hours free of children and responsibility and domesticity. He loved his family, but they were so – noisy. He smiled as he sipped the wine, and accepted the plate of cheese and biscuits that the flight attendant put in front of him. Bliss.

Caroline and Bart and Will and Harriet were due to arrive at Ginny and Julian's for supper in under an hour. Ginny had been looking forward to it all week; she loved having a houseful of her children and her children's friends. Missed it. Tonight, though, she couldn't disappear into her cooking as she normally did. She was distracted. A wicked feeling, the knowledge that she had done something she should not have – and got away with it – flickered inside her. She stirred the risotto and tried to suppress the guilty smile that threatened to creep up towards her cheeks.

She had loaded the shopping into the back of her car and gone to wheel the trolley back to park it. She was having a morning of errand-running – Waitrose first, so she could get it all back home in time for Paulina to help her unload it and put it away before she left at eleven to pick her little boy up from his minder (Paulina came three mornings a week for a couple of hours each time, and Ginny often thought that she would give up the use of her legs rather than the Polish girl). Then she had to go to the optician, to pick up the new prescription sunglasses she had ordered, smart ones with Chanel frames that she was vainly proud of; the post office to collect a parcel she had missed delivery of; and the dry cleaner for this week's batch of Julian's shirts (she had refused, early on in their marriage, in an uncharacteristic fit of feminist wrath, to spend hours every day starching pink-striped collars and cuffs, and so he had always sent them out. She did make the concession of dropping them off for him and collecting them, and worried at the beginning whether this was a betrayal of the sisterhood, but then decided that she was overthinking things. Not everyone could be Andrea Dworkin, after all – nor should they aspire to be, in Ginny's opinion; she had never been able to understand why feminists had to look so – hirsute).

She got back in the car, pulling her padded body-warmer firmly down so that it fitted snugly under the seat belt; she couldn't bear it when it got rucked up when she was driving, it made her feel all fidgety. *Woman's Hour* was on, with some woman talking about emigrating to the south of France and how it hadn't been as easy as she had been expecting, to plug her book about life on a lavender farm. *Stupid cow, you didn't even speak French and you thought you'd be able to slot right in. What on earth were you thinking? I'm surprised they didn't bury you under your precious lavender bushes*, Ginny thought, and then felt mean-spirited and a little shocked at herself. She turned off the radio as well as the heater, as a sort of punishment.

The post-office queue was long, and Ginny let her weight rest on one leg, then the other, as she stared at the back of the neck of the man in front of her. It was slightly greasy-looking, and the collar of his jacket was dusted with dandruff. Ginny felt uncomfortable, and looked away. It felt too intimate, too much like an intrusion.

She felt around in her pockets for some distraction, but came up with nothing. Not even an old Locket. The magazine rack on her left had a strict sign on it forbidding customers from leafing through them, written in thick blue marker pen. She turned to her right. A shelf of stationery was at elbow level, neatly stacked green ring-bound notebooks and packs of envelopes, and she fingered them absent-mindedly. The queue moved forward a step. Now the stationery shelf got a little more interesting, plastic wallets full of felt-tip pens arranged in a rainbow, and tiny notebooks with bright plastic covers on key rings. Pearl would love one of those, Ginny thought, they were just the right sort of fiddly little thing that she liked to collect, squirrelling them away in her box of treasures. She picked one up. Pink, everything had to be pink. They had miniature pens attached to them as well, that clipped on to the side with a tiny popper. Yes, she'd love one of those.

The till where you paid for purchases from the shop part of the post office was at the front, by the door. They wouldn't let you buy chocolate bars, or even envelopes or anything like that at the post-office counter. Ginny had been caught out by that before; you had to queue separately. There was a line of people waiting at the front till. Ginny picked up the notebook, and, as the queue shuffled forwards once more, put it into her pocket.

'Mrs Rathbone?' The shop-owner's daughter called out her name as she walked past the front till carrying her parcel (a new dog bed for Mr Butterworth, of the kind that he especially liked with a furry lining, which, predictably enough, were only available via mail order from Germany. Mr Butterworth had turned out to be an extremely high-maintenance dog, despite the breeder's assertions that he came from a long line of hardy, easy-going ancestors. If that was true, Mr Butterworth was a throwback – he had got to the point where he would only eat poached chicken and a particular type of expensive dry dog food, which also had to be ordered specially and collected from the vet).

Ginny wanted to freeze and squeeze her eyes shut like a child, in the hope that it would make her invisible, but instead she just carried on, pretending she hadn't heard the girl, the weight of her deception heavier than the bulky parcel she was carrying. Her heart thudded and she focused on the bright street outside. On the pavement, a child was whizzing past on one of those scooters, and Ginny kept her eyes straight ahead.

'Mrs Rathbone!' The girl's voice was louder, and Ginny could feel a couple of people looking around. Oh damnation. She was right in front of the wretched girl now, she couldn't pretend she hadn't heard her that time.

She turned, smiling politely, trying to look a little confused, a little vague. As though she had no idea why the girl was calling her back. What would she say, what on earth would she tell them? 'Yes? How are you?'

I didn't have a spare hand, she would say. *I just slipped it in there while I was waiting and then clean forgot about it*. Would it be enough? *If you didn't have this ridiculous system of two tills for the different queues*, she could always add, if the girl looked liable to make a fuss about it, *then it would never have happened*. Righteous indignation she could resort to, if necessary. She steeled herself.

The girl was holding an envelope out to her. 'Your newspaper bill, Mrs Rathbone. Could you possibly take it while you're here?'

Ginny paused. 'Yes. Yes, of course.' She tucked the dog basket under one arm and held out her hand for it.

'Thanks so much. Don't worry about it now, no hurry. I can see all your hands are full! Just drop a cheque in next time you're here.' The girl grinned at her, her plump face friendly and warm, her fine filigree gold earrings jangling gently, and Ginny swallowed the nugget of guilt that rose up in her gullet. She didn't even know the girl's name. And she was being so kind. Suddenly she felt like crying, and handing back the silly toy that was burning in her pocket. But she didn't. She thanked the girl again, and promised herself that she would find out her name and use it next time, then walked out of the shop. And as she got into the street, the feeling of guilt and remorse left her, soaring out of her like a bluebird from its nest, and was replaced with a little fizz of excitement. She had got away with it.

'This is one of the first properties we're buying,' Will was saying, his finger hovering over a photo of a large, dazzlingly white villa. He leafed through the sheaf of papers in his hand. 'And this one, as well.' The second was a chalet, French by the look of it, surrounded by snowy peaks that sparkled just as brightly as the painted walls of the first building. Bright blue and bright white was what people seemed to want from their holidays these days, Ginny thought. Blue skies, blue sea, white sand, white snow. None of the sludgy greens and heathers of the holidays they had always taken the children on when they were small, in Cornwall and Scotland and France. She pulled her thoughts back into the room. Will was chatting easily, his shirt open at the neck, his arms moving in big arcs as he enthusiastically talked the table through his plans. Harriet looked as though she were miles away, distractedly turning her coffee spoon over and over in the pot of sugar.

'How's your work, Harriet?' Ginny asked her, as she sat back down next to her, refilling her coffee cup from the cafetière.

Harriet looked up and smiled. She was a good-looking girl, Ginny thought, handsome, maybe, rather than pretty, but always so well dressed and neatly groomed. Quite a contrast to Will, who might have found the contents of his wardrobe in a charity shop or his grandfather's closet – quite probably had done.

'Oh, it's fine. Very busy. We won some big new clients

recently, so I'm spending a lot of time on projects for them.'

Ginny got the feeling that Harriet wasn't keen to go into more detail about her job, so she changed the subject. 'How wonderful. You are clever. And your parents? How are they?'

Harriet's smile became a little wan. 'In the final throes of wedding mania. Em's wedding's in six weeks. Mum's doing WeightWatchers and is seriously tetchy, as is Dad because she's making him eat all sorts of vile calorie-counted meals. And Mum keeps ringing me when I'm at work to ask who she should put people next to. I don't know why she thinks it's my job, it's not my sodding wedding to worry about.'

'Because you're the eldest, and she trusts you,' Ginny suggested gently. Oh dear. The change of subject didn't appear to have been a successful one.

'Yes. Well. That's all well and good, but I don't have time to worry about the finer points of my sister's reception, when the sister in question is only worried about how she's going to look.'

'Oh dear. I'm sure she's just nervous. It is quite a stressful time.'

'I know. So everyone keeps telling me.' Harriet bit her lip and then turned her head to Ginny, an apologetic look on her face. She glanced over at Will. He and Julian were deep in work chat, but she lowered her voice anyhow. 'Sorry. Tempers a bit frayed around the subject just now.'

Ginny patted her hand. 'It's all right, dear. It can't be easy for you.'

Harriet took a deep breath. 'You know the worst of it? The bridesmaid's dress she's making me wear. Actually, no, I'm a "maid of honour", apparently. Em reckons you can't have a bridesmaid older than yourself.'

Ginny winced.

'Yes, she's deeply tactful, my sister. Anyhow, here it is, this'll make you laugh.' Harriet reached down under the table and took her iPhone from her bag. She slid her thumb across the screen to unlock it and tapped in her pass code, before scrolling through her photos until she reached the one she was looking for. 'Here.' She handed Ginny the phone.

In the photo, Harriet stood grim-faced and stiff-backed in a brightly lit changing room. She wore a tight-fitting strapless dress made from taffeta of a colour so unflattering Ginny was quite sure no one had even bothered to name it yet. It was a sort of peachy coral, combined with a green-tinged pale gold; the two colours mingling and shimmering together in the shiny fabric. It made Harriet's pale skin look sallow and her eyes sunken. The dress was topped with a bolero made from the same fabric, which had short sleeves that ended just at the wrong point of the upper arm, making Harriet's slim limbs look chunky and ham-like. Her face was grim, and Ginny didn't blame her. *Good heavens*, she thought to herself, *I'm not surprised Will hasn't got around to proposing to her if he's seen her in this. Is the poor girl's sister deliberately trying to make her look like an unripe pumpkin covered in grease?*

There was a choked gasp from next to her as Harriet spluttered on her coffee, and Ginny spun to face her, putting the phone down as she did so.

'Goodness, are you all right, darling, did it go down the wrong way? Here . . .' Ginny grabbed her napkin and handed it to Harriet, mopping at the spilled coffee with Harriet's own. She noticed, as she patted at Harriet's top, that the girl was staring at her with something that looked a little like horror. 'It's all right, Hats, don't worry, no harm done,' she said kindly. 'There, see?' She gestured to the tablecloth; she had covered the coffee stain up with her white napkin. 'It'll come out in the wash.'

Harriet shook her head angrily and stood up, pushing her chair back from the table with a scrape. 'Thanks for that, Gin,' she said. 'Thanks very much.'

Ginny blinked. 'I . . .' She looked to Julian, realising as she did that the men had all gone rather quiet, and that Caroline had broken off from her adoring of Bart to stare at her, furiously. She had a quiet temper, Caroline, always had done; it was slow to rise up, but when it did, it burned stubbornly.

'Mum,' she said now, 'how could you? When we were all having such a lovely evening? Why would you even think something like that, let alone say it? I don't understand you.'

Harriet had left the room and was pulling on her coat in the hall, crossly getting tangled up in it in her haste to leave, eventually giving up and simply throwing it over her arm. 'Thanks for supper,' she said automatically. 'Julian, lovely to see you. Sorry, I have to – early start.' She opened the front door. 'Will?'

Will gathered up his papers and threw his tweed jacket on. 'Blimey, Gin,' he said under his breath as he leaned over and kissed her cheek, 'you've dropped me right in it with that. Still,' he winked at her as he shook Julian's hand and clapped him on the shoulder, 'you're not wrong. Unripe pumpkin covered in grease! Good one. Poor old Hats.'

As they made their way down the steps, through the formal front garden and to the car, Ginny could hear fragments of Harriet's icily furious voice carrying through the night air and the slightly open kitchen window.

'Bloody woman, I don't fucking believe it ... worse than your witch of a mother . . . everyone judging me . . . *so* embarrassing . . . don't understand . . . different for men . . . oh just FUCK OFF, Will!'

As she listened, she knew that it was all her fault, knew by the faces of her family that she was to blame, that she had somehow said out loud the shamefully unkind thing she had been thinking. But she had no idea how it had happened.

*

Caroline and Bart didn't stay for long after Harriet and Will left; they helped Ginny clear up, despite Caroline feeling furious with her mother, and then made their excuses and got in the car. Caroline was driving, as she usually did these days, giving the excuse of having to get up early for work the next day, or feeling a bit under the weather. No one commented, as they would have done a few years ago, no one tried to persuade her to leave the car, just have one more drink, 'sod it, get Scootercab out'. They just smiled tactfully and nodded and assumed.

She wished their assumptions were right. She wished that the sparkling water that she sipped with a wedge of lime, hoping that it might look like she was holding a G&T, was a sacrifice she was making for the sake of the baby they all thought she was already carrying. Instead, it was no consolation at all, just a bland, tasteless reminder of her desperation to conceive and her inability to do so.

It was so unfair. She was doing everything she could. Not drinking, apart from the odd glass of red wine when she got her period, as consolation and salve. Exercising enough, but not too much, eating at least seven portions of fruit and veg a day, including plenty of leafy greens, avoiding processed food and transfats and making sure all her meat was organic. She had banned Bart from sitting with his laptop on his lap, had tried to get him to cut down on his drinking as well and had swapped the coffee in the machine at home for decaff (she knew he was still mainlining espressos at work, but also that that was a battle she would never win). They had sex regularly, more often when her Persona indicated that it was her fertile time (not that she needed it – she had become expert at recognising the revoltingly but accurately named egg-white cervical mucus that signalled the same), and vigorously, though Bart was beginning to seem less enthusiastic about the somewhat military-style programme of shagging she had him on.

She should make an effort to seduce him when it wasn't time, she thought, as she started the car, so that he didn't feel as though she only wanted him for his sperm. She did want his sperm, very much, but she wanted him as well. She caught his eye in the rear-view mirror and gave him a grateful look. 'I can't believe Mum tonight,' she said.

'Strange, wasn't it? I thought she liked Harriet.'

'She does. Loves her. Always has done.'

'What do you think it was all about, then?' he asked.

Caroline shook her head. 'No idea. She's been behaving a bit weirdly recently. I wonder if things are OK with her and Dad.'

'They seem fine. Always think your parents are a pretty good advert for marriage, for people who've been together for as long as they have. They seem relatively happy.'

'Mm.' Caroline reversed out of the drive. 'It's not as simple as that, though, is it?'

'What do you mean?'

'You know what I mean. I told you what happened.'

'What, the other woman?'

Caroline nodded.

'Come on. It was years ago, you said. Anyhow, it's hardly that big a deal, is it? Can't have been.'

Caroline bristled. 'Why? Of course it was a big deal – *is* a big deal.'

'If it was that bad, she'd have kicked him out. Surely?' Bart squeezed Caroline's knee as she drove. She shifted it away from him slightly.

'Come on, Caro. Don't be silly.'

'I'm not being silly. You obviously don't think fidelity in a marriage is "a big deal". That's new information. So at least I know what to expect.'

Bart shrugged. 'She just said what she was thinking. Hardly

a great crime. She'd had a couple of glasses of wine; we all had.'

'She wasn't drunk. And I hadn't had anything.'

'No. I know. You're very virtuous.'

'What's that supposed to mean?' Caroline jerked her head towards her husband.

'Just that you're making quite a point of your clean-living lifestyle at the moment. It's difficult for the rest of us to come up to scratch.'

'The rest of who, exactly? It's no one else's bloody business if I'm trying to look after myself better and it's not my problem if other people can't cope with it.'

'Not your problem.'

'No.'

Caroline's chin jutted out stubbornly, and they moved forward through the light traffic in silence.

'Doing it all by yourself then, are you? Trying for a baby by yourself? Going to raise it by yourself as well?'

Caroline shook her head. 'That's not what I meant.' She tried to keep the tears that were stinging her eyes from falling. 'I'm just doing everything I can. That's all. I don't want to fight with you, Bart.'

'I'm not fighting.'

'I know.' She took her hand off the wheel for a moment and laid it on top of his. She had learnt early on in their relationship that Bart's stubbornness was immovable, especially when he had been drinking. His words had felt cruel and they had hurt her, but he didn't mean it. He didn't mean it. 'I know.'

And then she lifted her hand back up to rub away the tear that had fallen on to her cheek.

The art gallery where Caroline worked was in a small side street near St James's, next to a cigar shop, and sold mainly water-colours and drawings, both old and contemporary. It was a quiet, calm space, with limestone floors that made a soft tapping noise when you walked on them. Caroline loved the peaceful bubble that the owner had created in the middle of the city, she loved sitting at her small writing desk in the corner and talking to clients about what they had in mind and where they were going to put it, she loved the fizzy excitement of a new collection and organising the private view with careful, precise attention to detail. It was her little domain, and she ran it calmly, efficiently and with grace.

She was not an ambitious woman in career terms, had never had the urge to work her way up some metaphorical ladder to achieve – what? She wasn't sure. Achievement for her wasn't something that was measured in promotions or salary raises. She didn't feel the need to be the best, to win. She'd never been competitive, was too kind. She had got in trouble at school for slowing down when she was about to win the relay race so that her nearest competition, who was one of her friends and who had hurt her knee, might cross the line at the same time, and had then been confused and hurt when the other girl had sped up and left her behind. She just didn't have that aggressive instinct. She had enough money, especially as she did not have particularly expensive tastes or extravagant habits. She wasn't a dedicated shopper like Harriet, who whipped through Selfridges with the speed of a scorpion's sting; nor did she have two children and the sort of domestic and social life that ate through cash like Izzy; she didn't have the party lifestyle and haphazard way with money of Stella. Out of the four of them, she was by far the most sensible. And that was fine with her. When she had been single she had been content to spend her Friday nights in front of a box set with a bowl of pasta, only venturing out when one of the girls dragged her to the pub or round for dinner, and now that she was married she was not just content but happy to do the same with Bart, and occasionally to entertain their friends at home. They went out more than she would have chosen to, because he felt it important for his work, and that was fine – it was part of her job now. Because that was how Caroline measured achievement. Her career was her marriage, it was the best thing she had ever done and it was the most important. Her parents' marriage had taught her that two people could overcome anything if they tried hard enough, if they both wanted to. Caroline really believed that most people who got divorced just hadn't *tried*. She was not, however, foolish enough to voice this opinion in public.

She looked up to smile at the potential customer who had just entered, and her smile widened when she saw that it was not a stranger, but her husband.

'Darling!'

She got up from her desk and came over to him, putting her arms around his neck and kissing him.

'Hello. How lovely. There isn't something wrong, is there?' Her brow crinkled, and he kissed it.

'No, nothing at all, don't worry. I've just come to whisk you away, that's all.'

'Where? What do you mean? I don't finish until five.'

Bart grinned, and pulled an envelope out of his jacket pocket, waving it at her. 'You do today. I've already spoken to Charles. Come along.'

He strode into the back office and picked up her coat, flinging it over one arm, and her handbag. 'But, what is that . . . what are you doing . . . ? Bart, I can't just leave, I've got . . .'

'Anything else, or is this it?' He held up the bag.

'Yes, that's it. But – Bart, where are we going?'

He handed her the envelope and watched with pleasure as she opened it and delight spread across her face. 'Oh my God. New York. Oh Bart, I've always wanted to go. For how long?'

'Just the weekend. I know, I know. It's seriously indulgent.

And we've only been back from honeymoon for a few weeks. But here's the thing.'

He took her hand and led her outside. A black cab was idling by the kerb.

'It's exactly a year since we met. Right there, in that room.' He pointed to the gallery.

'Oh Bart. I had no idea.'

He took her hands in his. 'I just thought we should do something special. Treat ourselves. A year and a day ago we hadn't even met, and now you're my wife. If that doesn't deserve to be celebrated in style, then I don't know what does.'

He kissed her, and held the door open for her as she got into the cab, and as he did so, he slipped a small box into her handbag, making sure it went into the side pocket where she kept her phone, so that when she pulled it out, as she inevitably would before long, she would find it there. It contained a platinum eternity ring, with a line of diamonds channel-set into the metal, one for every month they had known one another.

He sat back as the cab pulled away and out into the traffic, feeling pretty pleased with himself. He thought he was probably due the best blow-job of his life when they landed in New York.

The city was as exciting as she had always imagined it would be. The first night, Caroline sat in the window seat of their small but luxurious hotel room in the Mandarin Oriental, her knees drawn up to her chin, and gazed out of the huge window overlooking Columbus Circle and the corner of Central Park. Orange tail lights glowed and sirens blared, and she could feel the buzz and thrum of life pulsing through her veins. It made her fingertips tingle.

She had wanted to come here since she was eighteen and got hooked on *Friends*, watching it every weekend in the TV room of her parents' house, eating ice cream and dreaming of having a group of friends like that, a life like that. Of feeling like she really fitted in to a group of girls, the way Monica and Rachel and Phoebe all did, of being at ease with boys and dating. Dating. She had never been on a date, not a proper one. TGI Friday with her brother's friends didn't count. To them, she was just James's little sister, and always would be. Even to Will.

She had known Will for five years by the time she fell in love with him. Properly, smack-in-the face, bite-your-own-fist-off-so-you-don't-say-anything-stupid-in-front-of-him in love with him. She'd had a crush on him for as long as she could remember, but that had been silly schoolgirl stuff. Now she was eighteen, and this was grown-up love, not to be sniffed at. It had been when they were watching *Withnail and I* together, the four of them, she and Harriet, Will and James, that she had first realised it. They'd been lounging in the garage that her parents had converted into a sort of den for the kids, with a ping-pong table, and an old sofa and a pile of beanbags arranged in front of a TV and VCR.

'I must have some booze. I demand to have some booze!' Withnail was commanding, and Will was reciting the lines along with Richard E. Grant, standing in by the television, one arm raised in the air in a fist. James leapt up, and, joining in the act, grabbed an empty wine bottle from the bin where his parents stored them before taking them to the tip. Will raised it to his lips and pretended to glug it down, wiping his mouth flamboyantly on his sleeve as he finished. 'This is a far superior drink to meths,' he continued to quote. 'The wankers don't drink it because they can't afford it.'

He held the bottle up in the air triumphantly. 'Every line,' he said, proudly, 'I can do every line.'

'Sad,' James said, chucking a ping-pong ball at him. 'Get a life.'

But Caroline had just gazed at him, standing there, bottle in his hand, in his threadbare grey V-neck with holes around the cuffs that he stuck his thumbs through, his faded blue jeans and his Converses, and thought he was perfect.

Then she had looked over at Harriet, lovely Harriet, who was her best friend at school, and who was funny and clever and sharp, and saw the look in her eye, and then Will's as he looked at her, and knew that it was never going to happen. Her first big love was over before it had begun.

It hadn't stopped her secretly pining for him, though. Caroline sighed quietly now as she watched a bagel seller pack up his stand far below her, and thought how many hours she had wasted dreaming about Will, about him suddenly seeing her as if for the first time, turning to her and telling her she was beautiful, telling her he had always yearned for her (yearning always seemed to be a significantly grown-up sort of a word, with its undertones of a sexuality that Caroline did not yet quite comprehend), had wanted to ask her out for ages, but had been held back by some kind of mysterious male valour and loyalty to his friend. In her fantasies, Caroline would blink, and tell him he had been foolish, but would secretly be impressed by his sense of honour and would love him all the more for it. And then he would kiss her, a proper, full-on snog that she had imagined so many times that sometimes now when he kissed her on the cheek when they saw one another, which was often, she would be reminded of it and blush and have to hide it while the memory of her teenage passion faded away once more.

Bart turned over in the bed and reached his arm out, sitting up blearily when he did not find her there. 'What are you doing?' His voice was full of sleep.

'Jet-lagged. Just enjoying the view.'

'It's pitch black, you lunatic. Turn the light on if you want.'

'No. I'm fine. Go back to sleep.'

He grunted and rolled over, pushing the sheet from him. He got hot when he slept, giving off waves of heat like a radiator. She loved knowing that about him. It was one of the things that told her: now you have a place. Now you fit in.

Chapter Four

July 2008

Johnny's head lay lightly on the pillow, the muscles in his neck taut, a curved gap between the top of his back and the cotton sheets. The girl slid her hand into it, pulling his face closer to hers. He could feel the warmth of her breath on his cheek as she exhaled.

'Stay,' she whispered, sliding her body over to him in the bed and laying a leg on top of him. 'Stay.'

He smiled, and kissed her, letting his hands drop to her waist and down over her hips, naked below the T-shirt she wore, with the logo of a heavy-metal band on it. His fingers reached the tiny silver ring that pierced her clitoris, and he flicked it gently, enjoying the tremor that it sent through her body.

'I mean it,' she said, her eyes closed, 'I want you to stay, Johnny.'

'I'll be here when you go to sleep.' He kissed her shoulder. She pulled it back, away from his lips.

'But not when I wake up.' She wriggled her hips backwards, away from his hands. He sighed, and turned away to sit on the edge of the bed. His shirt was on the floor, a plaid shirt in soft grey and charcoal check that Stella had got for him last Christmas, and he pulled it on, clicking the little mother-of-pearl-covered press studs shut.

'You know the answer, Lila.' She flopped on to her back, letting her arms fall back above her head. The street outside the window was dark, and an orange light glowed.

'No, I can't. No, I have to go home. No, no, no.'

She propped herself up on one elbow and reached for her pack of cigarettes. Her black hair shimmered over her shoulders as she pulled one out and lit it, sitting back against the wall and watching as Johnny pulled his jeans on.

He forced himself to dress, looking at the rain that trickled down the windowpane, glistening against the glass. It would be east to stay. Easy to take his jeans off again, slide back under the covers with Delilah's warm body alongside him, slip back into sleep and the soft powdery smell of her skin. Not go out into the cold, the wet, not get the night bus back home, not tiptoe in through the hall and be faced by the empty kitchen with the lights off, Stella's laptop on the kitchen table, a single empty glass beside it, a silent recrimination that would remind him of the fact that she had been sitting there, writing, alone, while he had been out. Not sit, a whisky in his hand, watching the moon as his wife and child slept upstairs and trying to figure out what the fuck he was doing. Just – not.

But he couldn't do that. Whatever happened, however hard he partied, he always went home. It was just the deal.

'You know I have to, Lila. De-li-li-li-lilah,' he said, leaning over and stealing a puff of her cigarette. She watched him with kohl-rimmed eyes, her make-up still heavy from her show, a ghost of the evening painted on her face. Delilah Kitten was a burlesque dancer, performing fifties-inspired numbers with big marabou fans and champagne coupes in bars and clubs around London.

She shrugged. 'You don't have to do anything,' she said, one eyebrow tilting at him.

He laughed. 'Yeah, I really do,' he said quietly.

'I don't like it, Johnny.'

'Me neither. But I don't like the alternative either.'

Delilah pouted. Johnny's was a strangely honest form of cheating. He never pretended that he wasn't in love with his wife, that they no longer had sex, that they had 'grown apart'. She'd respected that about him at first, when it had just been talk and banter and chat. Had liked the fact that he made no attempt to hide his love for the blonde, red-lipsticked girl whose wedding photo he still carried in his wallet, and the fat baby they had made together. But that was before they had started sleeping together, and before the tendrils of jealousy had begun to grow inside her, winding their way around her heart. Now his honesty simply frustrated her, and despite it having been one of the things she had first fallen in love with, she wished he could be a little more like some of the other married men she had been with in the past. She wished for more duplicity, more pretence.

'Go on then. Fuck off.'

He stood and smiled at her. 'OK.' He didn't move.

'I mean it. Go, if you're going.'

'I'll see you soon.'

She shrugged a shoulder.

'Don't play games,' he said, still smiling.

'Why not? You are.'

He shook his head. 'Delilah Kitten. Impossible girl.' He bent down and kissed her, and then picked his keys up from her bedside table, and left.

The street outside was colder than it looked, and Johnny pulled up the collar of his leather jacket against the chill as he walked to the bus stop, trying to keep a little of the warmth from Delilah's body and bed around him before it faded away. He was stuck in a sort of limbo, he always felt at times like this, when he was on his way to or from seeing her. Either trying to shake off the memory of one of them, or trying to keep it huddled around him, as though the women's presence were like a scent.

Maybe it was, he wondered; maybe Delilah could smell Stella on his skin, and his wife his mistress. Stella certainly sensed that something was up, he knew it. She had become – awkward around him. Not angry, or suspicious, in the usual way, but almost embarrassed. More conscious of her body when she dressed in the morning as he lay in bed watching her, more aware of her movements around him. Like they were strangers suddenly forced to share a living space, unsure of what the rules were, of what was polite or not.

It was because he had changed the rules, he knew, as he stood at the bus stop and lit a cigarette; he had changed the rules and she could sense it. Never before had he seen the same girl more than a handful of times; never before had he made the fatal mistake of getting to know one before sleeping with her. Never before had he cared. He shouldn't have done it, he knew that. Should never have let himself slide from flirting to friendship, and then into bed. But he had been bored of one-night stands, if he was honest, and instead of doing what he knew – he *knew* – he should have done, and going back to his wife, like he always had done, letting her remind him exactly why it was her that he always returned to and could never be without, he had been seduced by the unavailability of the girl whose body was on show for all to see, but whose heart was locked firmly away.

The bus came, and he got on it, passing his Oyster card over the sensor and slipping into one of the seats by the window. A drunk snuffled in the back row, and they trundled past shut kebab shops and newsagents as they worked their way south.

Eventually the bus juddered to a halt by the church around the corner from Johnny and Stella's house, and he hopped off the step, shoving his hands into his pockets and heading home. He wanted to smoke a cigarette, but didn't want to take his hands out of the fleece lining to do so, so instead he walked faster. He would have one at home, with a whisky, before sleep.

Johnny had never had to make plans; he just did stuff, and it either worked or it didn't. Meeting and marrying Stella and then having Viking had worked, from the start; his career, if you could call it that, had worked in that he was busy enough, he kept himself more or less afloat, though he was aware that with a bit more of what some might call 'application' and thought, he could be doing much better. But he didn't really want to plan and get a manager and make proper decisions about it, so instead he hid it under a head-shaking, helpless 'state of the music industry these days' attitude, and just carried on as he always had done. It infuriated Stella, who, despite her boho, party-girl exterior, was an astute and ambitious woman with big plans for her future, but there it was. She had known it when she married him, known that if she wanted a careerist she should look elsewhere, and she had not done so.

There was no easy answer to his dilemma, and he knew it. He had no intention of leaving his wife, breaking up his family, and never had done. But then nor did he have any real intention of changing, of giving up Delilah, who he had come to see as an important part of his life, or, if he was really honest, the other girls, the ones who floated through in a steady trickle of blow-jobs in back alleys and heavy, heated encounters after gigs. He didn't see why he should have to, as long as everyone was happy. Though as things stood, he wasn't at all sure that that was the case.

Just a couple of hours later, he woke. Stella was standing in the doorway, damp from her shower and wrapped in a towel, her hair twisted up in a turban. Johnny tilted his head to look at her, and winked.

'Morning. Nice to see you readying yourself for my return.'

Stella rolled her eyes. 'I wish. I've got a meeting with Benjy today.' She wandered over to her clothes rail and started flicking through the hangers.

'Where?'

'Shoreditch House.'

'Oh. A lunch meeting, then.'

Stella looked over her shoulder at Johnny, who was now holding Viking upside down by his feet. Was that a note of jealousy in his voice? Probably not. Benjy, her agent, was forty-five but thought and acted like he was twenty-five, and they were meeting to talk about a ghost-writing project she'd been offered, the 'autobiography' of a reality-TV star who was hot at the moment and who wouldn't be next year but whose publishers thought had just enough mileage for a book if they got it out quickly. She hadn't told him about the novel she was writing yet, but she thought she might, over lunch today. She'd written thirty thousand words now, and figured it might be time for someone to tell her whether it was worth continuing to lose sleep over.

'Mm. I'm hoping he's got some good news for me. I need some work. We're running out of money. Again. How about you?'

She didn't know why she was bothering to point this out to Johnny. He was worse than useless with money. If she left things to him, bills would pile up in big sheaves of red paper by the front door until they blocked it.

She took a black jersey dress off its hanger, and looked for a cardigan to go with it. Something light; it was going to be warm, but if they ended up sitting outside on the roof then she'd be glad of it. You felt the wind up there. She found a fuchsia-pink one with a round neck and fitted shape, and pulled it on.

'Session for Mac later, doing some backing vocals for him.'

'Can you take Viking round to Julie's? I need to file a piece before I go.'

Johnny looked at her. 'OK. Sort his bag out and I'll do the rest.'

The rest was walking Viking and his stuff around the corner to the childminder; it was getting his bag ready with snacks and the right toys and a change of clothes that took the time and the thought. But if she told Johnny he had to do it, she'd only have to cope with the inevitable stream of questions about what Viking had to eat and what clothes he fitted into now, and then there'd more than likely be a phone call from Julie later asking where his spare nappy was, and it was just easier all round to do it herself.

'Sure,' she said, squirting serum on to her fingers and rubbing it into her skin. 'I look about a hundred years old,' she muttered, loading her make-up brush with foundation.

'You're beautiful,' Johnny said. Automatically? She looked at him in the mirror and he blew her a kiss. 'Mummy's beautiful, isn't she?' he said to Viking. 'Pretty Mummy. Like a princess.'

Viking stared at her, his thumb in his mouth. 'Daddy,' he said, turning away from Stella and burying his head in Johnny's shoulder. 'Daddy.'

Stella rolled her eyes. Typical.

'. . . She threw a complete tantrum when her publishers told her she'd just missed the longlist, demanding to know why and who hadn't pushed it hard enough and which other books had been put forward and not made it and, you know, all the usual.' Benjy grinned at Stella, his whitened teeth bared and slightly moist.

'Blimey,' said Stella. 'Was she really expecting to be on the list then? I didn't think the book was all that.'

'On the list? She'd already picked out her frock and written her acceptance speech. I think she might fire me.' Benjy sounded singularly unbothered about this possibility, folding up a slice of pizza into a parcel and shovelling it into his mouth. Stella sipped her glass of rosé.

'Silly cow,' she said.

Benjy lifted one shoulder in a shrug. 'Her sales have dropped anyway, and she hasn't brought me any new projects in a while. I don't need to carry the dead weight, to be honest, Stell. Not these days.'

Stella nodded. 'Speaking of which . . .'

Benjy looked up at her over his plate. 'Oh, fucking hell, you're not buggering off, are you? If you leave me and go to Gerald Harris I'll never forgive you. I saw him chatting you up at Jackie's launch.' Gerald Harris was another powerful agent, and Benjy's biggest rival. The two men were constantly taking potshots at one another.

'Don't be silly,' Stella said. 'You represented me when I was a struggling writer with hardly a credit to my name. Well, I'm still a struggling writer, with a few more credits to my name now, but you know what I mean. I'll never leave you, dahlink.' She spoke the last sentence as though she were the heroine of a war film, clipped and full of mock restrained passion, and Benjy laughed.

'No, I mean about new projects. I've been working on something.' She could see Benjy's antennae prick up. The man was an agent through and through.

'Go on.'

'It's a novel.' She spoke the words quickly and then bit her lip. Just saying it felt dangerous. Exposing. But Benjy just nodded.

'Good,' he said. 'Give me something to sell. How much have you got?'

'Almost thirty thousand. I think it'll be about a hundred when I'm done. Maybe a bit more. It might be rubbish.'

'Might be. Let's see, shall we? Send it over this afternoon. I'll read it at the weekend.'

He leaned forward and refilled her glass. 'Now. Are you going to take this ghosting gig, or what?'

Stella nodded. 'Course I am. Thanks, Benjy. I appreciate it.'

And the conversation moved on to contracts and interview schedules and deadlines. And in the back of her mind she felt a little bubble of excitement that could not yet be burst. She had taken the first step. The novel might suck, Benjy might hate it and dump her, but none of that had happened yet. For now, it was still a clear pocket of possibility, and she held on to it, tightly.

It was almost six by the time she got home, lunch having turned into coffee, and coffee into a cocktail with a couple of journo friends she had bumped into, and then more coffee and a couple of lines to try and cancel out all the rest before going home and picking Viking up and making his tea.

She was fine, though. Fine. The key stuck in the door and she gave it a shove, before pushing Viking's buggy in through the doorway and parking him at the bottom of the stairs, still strapped in, while she ran upstairs to pee. Viking yelled angrily as he tried to follow her and realised he was imprisoned.

'Coming, poppet, coming in a second.' Stella finished peeing and washed her hands, checking her reflection in the mirror as she did so. She ran a finger underneath her eyes in an attempt to wipe away the smudged liner.

Downstairs, she freed Viking, who immediately toddled down the hallway towards the kitchen. 'Sausages,' he shouted – at least Stella knew that was what he was trying to say. To the untrained ear it would have sounded rather more like 'shoj'. The child was obsessed with cocktail sausages. She got a pack out of the fridge and turned the gas on, putting a dozen links in the pan with a bit of oil. She'd have whatever he didn't eat. Lunch felt like a long time ago now. She put the pack of sausages back in the fridge and pondered the half-open bottle of white wine in the door.

'Shoj!' Viking cried again.

'I'm doing them, darling, you have to be patient.' She closed the door, leaving the wine where it was. It had been full this morning, she was sure. Still, who was she to be judgey about lunchtime drinking, especially today? She didn't at home, though. Not when they didn't have people round.

She sighed and put a pan of water on to boil for the peas that she knew Viking would reject. When had she started sighing? She sounded like her mother. God, what a depressing thought. Stella's mother had spent her life sighing, and resenting, and silently begrudging with pursed lips, and Stella had vowed never to become like that. Never to turn into the woman who had made her childhood so heavy with guilt and the sense that she was a burden, never to tut at her husband when he came in through the door, never to stand by the stove muttering to herself about how no one appreciated her. She'd thought she had been doing pretty well. But now, the sighing had started. She felt herself almost do it again at the thought, and shook her head. *Sighing at the thought of yourself sighing, you idiot.* Maybe she would have a glass of that wine after all.

Johnny's laptop was open on the kitchen table, and instead of getting her own out, she ran her finger over the touchpad to wake it up and check her emails. There was one in there that she should reply to from one of her editors about a feature she was working on. She must check her eBay account as well and see if any of the stuff she was watching needed attention. She was bidding on an old steamer chest to use as a coffee table, and keeping an eye on a Perspex Louis Ghost chair that looked as though it might go cheaply. Over the years she'd got rather good at spotting the items with poor photographs or little in the way of description that meant other people were likely to overlook them and she could pick up a bargain during the last few minutes of the auction.

The screen came to life and she saw that Johnny's Twitter account was open, the background to his profile a black-and-white photo that she remembered taking. It had been a couple of years ago, when Johnny's old band had been playing at the Isle of Wight festival. He was standing on stage in the photo, guitar in one hand, other arm raised in the air, his hair thick with sweat and his eyes shut as the song and the set came to a close. It had been a triumphant day, full of applause and whoops from the crowd, and they had been convinced it was the start of great things for them. It hadn't been – at least not for the band. They'd broken up not long afterwards. But for Johnny and Stella, who was, without knowing it, carrying Viking, it had been.

Stella went to shut the window down, but before she did, and without even really thinking, she clicked on the 'messages' tab. Later, she would wonder what had made her do it, what had made her change the habits of a marriage, the promise she had made herself that she would not snoop, would not drive herself mad with suspicion and wondering. Would not be that woman and would not become her. And she would wish beyond wish that she hadn't, had not seen the long list of private messages between Johnny and a girl called Delilah Kitten, messages that she sat down and read, obsessively, unable to stop, as she fed Viking chunks of cocktail sausage, messages full of secret little in-jokes and innuendo, messages that didn't seem to hint at a quick fuck that had happened and been discarded, but something much, much more dangerous. They hinted at trust.

*

A week later, Stella was sitting in the corner of the café she went to work in sometimes, a coffee in front of her, her laptop balanced on the edge of the table. The coffee was too weak and too expensive, but she found the background chatter and activity helped her concentrate; dead silence and quiet made her feel nervous, distracted. And she had a bit of spare money for once; she'd been paid the first part of what she would make from the ghost-writing project, so she could justify an overpriced coffee while she worked.

But today, the words danced in front of her eyes as she lost her focus, and she found herself staring past them. She was up to the point in the autobiography where her subject was taking their first steps into show business (the interviews for which had involved a lot of phrases like 'I knew I could do it – I just had to believe in myself' and 'it made it easier to step out on to that stage knowing that my nana was up there, watching over me, willing me to give my performance a hundred and ten per cent') but rather than concentrating on the reality-TV star, all she could think about was Johnny.

Specifically, Johnny and Delilah. Ever since she'd found the little cache of direct messages between the two of them, she had been obsessing over the girl, feeding her fixation by going on to her website and Myspace page, staring at photos of her. She was beautiful, no doubt, in an edgy, tattooed and showgirl kind of way. Not totally different to a look Stella herself might have played with, if she was honest, at one point. The main photo on her website was of her half naked, wearing sequinned nipple pasties and hot pants, a cowboy hat balanced on her dark hair and held on with one hand as she sat astride a carousel horse. 'Delilah Kitten's Fairground Fantasy' the page proclaimed, in old-fashioned circus-style lettering. 'Roll up, roll up!' exhorted the banner. She wore thick eyeliner and a jewel glittered in her belly button. She looked exotic, exciting and a bit wild. Stella could quite see the attraction. It was the same attraction that she and Johnny had had, once.

She let her fingers stray to the mouse pad and brought up her Internet browser, typing Delilah's Twitter handle into the address bar and waiting while it loaded. Delilah's background photo on Twitter was a different one – this one showed her wearing the scarlet jacket of a circus ringmaster, a long leather whip in her hand and a twinkle in her eye. Stella sighed.

I'll be there! Can't wait. RT @JohnnyA – Gigging tonight at the Half Moon, hope to see you all down there.

Stella read the message that Delilah had put up . . . when? She checked the time: 10.17 a.m., a couple of hours ago. Starting early, considering your nocturnal habits, she thought to herself. There was something about the woman retweeting Johnny's message to her followers that Stella found exceptionally irritating. More so than any of the rest of it, almost. There was something proprietorial in the tone of it. *I'll be there!* As though it were a given, as though it were her right.

It sodding well isn't your right, though, she thought, furiously. It's not your job to publicise his gigs and go along and support him. It's mine. And that's exactly what I'm going to do.

She clicked the little red cross to close the screen, and went to her email. She needed to call in backup. 'Izzy, Caroline, Harriet,' she typed, and their email addresses came up.

Her fingers whizzed across the keyboard. 'J's gigging tonight. Thought would get a little gang together to support. Has been too long. Fancy it?'

She clicked on 'send' and then shut her laptop. She put the computer in its case, and began to gather her things together. Work was over for today. She thought she would pop round the corner to the walk-in beauty salon and have her nails done. And get a wax. It was probably about time she reminded Johnny what his wife was made of.

The club was full, and Stella pushed and jostled her way through to the bar, where she could see Izzy waiting.

When she reached her, she took the bottle of wine Izzy was holding and made her way over to a table near the front of the room, with a Reserved sign on it. She had called ahead and told Johnny's manager that she'd be coming, asked him to save her a space, and not to tell her husband. 'I want to surprise him,' she'd said. And it had been true.

'Here they are,' Izzy said, as she caught up with Stella and put four wine glasses down on the table. She jerked her head in the direction of the entrance, and Stella turned. Caroline and Harriet were working their way towards them, Caroline looking awkward and out of place in the trendy bar.

'Caroline's lost lots of weight,' Stella said, thoughtfully.

'I know. I put on about a stone after I got married; she seems to have lost it. How annoying,' Izzy replied.

It was then that Stella saw her. She was standing near the back of the room, to one side, alone. Totally confident in her solitude in a way that Stella immediately envied. She wasn't playing with her drink, or her phone, or looking around willing someone to come and talk to her. She was just – there. Stella let her gaze remain on the girl she had spent so much time imagining, despite knowing what she looked like intimately from her photos. There was something about seeing her in the flesh that was immeasurably different. She had the same dark hair, shiny and almost black; tonight it was loose, with the front curled into a loop forming a fringe, and a polka-dot bow clipped above one ear. She wore a version of a sailor suit, retro, fifties, with a low-cut top and little shorts that sat above opaque tights and T-bar Mary Jane shoes.

Stella continued to watch her as Harriet and Caroline reached their table and Izzy kissed them both and poured out wine.

'Hi,' Stella said, 'I'm glad you came,' and she too kissed the girls in turn, still watching Delilah over their shoulders as she did so. Someone was talking to her now, some guy chatting her up, and she was listening to his lines with a tilted head and an amused smile on her red lips. Mac's Russian Red, Stella thought to herself; she wore the same one, and suddenly the thought made her feel sick. Or it might have been the cheap white wine. She drank more anyway, watching as Delilah dismissed the hopeful suitor with a shake of the head and a shrug of her shoulders, unbothered by his disappointment, her eyes returning to the stage. She hadn't noticed Stella. Was that because she didn't know what she looked like? Or didn't know she existed? No, she would know about her; Johnny never hid the fact that he was married, Stella knew, never removed his wedding ring or put the photo of her and Viking that he carried in his wallet behind a credit card. So maybe she just hadn't seen her yet. Did she want her to see her? To turn and look at her, be forced to somehow acknowledge her presence? Stella wasn't sure.

Caroline looked uncomfortable, she noticed.

'You OK?' Stella asked her, when Harriet and Izzy had become involved in a conversation about the reality show they were both addicted to.

Caroline shrugged. 'Yes. I . . .' She took a swig of her wine. 'I don't know what to do about sex,' she said, quickly, as though she had to get it out before she lost her nerve.

'Er . . .' Stella wasn't sure what to say. What was she being asked, or told? Surely Caroline and Bart had . . .

'I mean, we have sex. Obviously. And it's very nice.' Caroline blushed.

'OK. Well, good.'

'Oh God. Sorry. I shouldn't have said anything.'

Stella laughed. 'Cazza. It's fine. I'm fairly unshockable. And you haven't actually said anything yet, you know. What's the problem? Spill.'

Caroline sighed. 'I just . . . I don't know.' She took a deep breath. 'You know I'd only slept with one person before Bart.'

'BB – yes, I think I knew that. Timmy, or something, wasn't it?'

'Timothy, yes. Timothy Wilkinson.'

'OK. How was Timmy?'

'Timmy was – nervous.'

'Oh.'

'Yes. It was underwhelming, I suppose. But, you know. Fine.'

'God, Caroline, you're killing me. Fine. Sex shouldn't be fine. Sex should never be fine. Terrible, uncomfortable, amazing, breathtaking, funny, weird – any of those things. But never fine.'

'Breathtaking? I don't think so. His penis was like a chipolata.'

Stella snorted.

'We need to pour white wine down you more often. OK, so, you shagged Timmy with the chipolata cock. I take it Bart doesn't have the chipolata problem? Because, you know, there are positions you can—'

'No! It's not that.'

'Good. Didn't think so. He doesn't look like he's got a small cock.'

'Stella!'

'Who doesn't look like they've got a small cock?' Harriet leaned forward.

'Oh trust you,' Stella said. 'A sniff of cock and you're suddenly all ears.'

'Urgh. I don't want to sniff anyone's cock, thanks very much.'

'Oh God.' Caroline put her head in her hands, mortified.

'Come on, it's fine. It's fine! We're all listening. Bart's got a great cock, Timmy was nice in bed, now you're all caught up,' she said to Harriet and Izzy, who had abandoned their reality-TV gossip for good. This was much more interesting; Caroline never talked about sex.

'Why are we talking about Timmy?' Izzy looked confused. 'That was ages ago, wasn't it?'

'Not *that* long ago,' Caroline protested, then stopped. Was it worse to admit to having lost her virginity so late, or having had such a long gap between her only two lovers? She sighed and gave up. 'OK, yes, ages ago. The point is, I wasn't exactly experienced, and neither was Timmy – Timothy – so it wasn't as if I learnt loads from him. And then I met Bart . . .'

'No chipolatas there. More of a Cumberland, would you say?' Stella tried to keep the giggle out of her voice.

'Oh forget it.' Caroline pushed hair back from her face.

'Stella . . .' Harriet elbowed her. 'Carry on, darling. Ignore slaggy in the corner. She can't help herself. What's the problem – is it Bart?'

Caroline shook her head, and suddenly felt very wobbly.

'No, it's not Bart. It's me. We're trying for a baby, you know.' The women nodded. 'And I – I'm just really worried that he's bored. I mean, every time we have sex, it's because it's the right time. And, I don't know, I feel like I should be doing – other stuff. But I don't know what. And he's done so many things, and been with so many people, and I just keep thinking he must be so horribly, horribly bored with me, and maybe he's going to have an affair and I wouldn't even really blame him, because I probably give really rubbish blow-jobs and watching porn makes me want to be sick.'

And she burst into tears.

An hour and another bottle of Chilean Sauvignon later, the girls had mopped up Caroline's tears and convinced her that Bart would not have married her were she truly dull in bed, and that it was definitely not the reason why they had not managed to conceive yet. And Stella had promised to lend her her copy of a book that she said had taught her at least three things she had never heard of before and which had been surefire successes, which Caroline looked a bit nervous about but agreed to read. And then it was time for Johnny's band to come on, and they all realised that they were quite drunk and had better have some chips to soak up some of the vats of wine they had managed to get through while listening to Caroline's woes.

Stella went to the bar to order the food, and realised that while they had been talking, Delilah had worked her way forwards. Now she was nearly opposite their table, off to one side, perched on the wooden bar that ran around the room, one leg crossed over the other. She looked like a Vargas pin-up girl, Stella thought with a flash of envy.

Then Johnny emerged, and Stella watched as he stood in front of the microphone stand, arranging his guitar strap on his shoulder, settling into position. The room had gone quiet again, as it always did – he commanded attention when he walked on stage. He wore an old T-shirt and soft black jacket, and his jeans were faded and frayed, and no one could take their eyes off him, least of all the two women either side of the room, who he was, as yet, unaware of.

Then he raised his head and looked up and out into the audience, an easy smile on his face that faltered a little, and he saw, and he was aware. And it was then, in that instant, that Stella knew exactly why she had come, why she had set up this very moment. The spike in her heart as she saw the panic behind his eyes, as he took in the presence of both women, told her. She had done it to know for sure what she was dealing with; to see him struggle as he stood on display before these two women, blonde and dark, the wife and the mistress, in public, in a place where he was exposed and could not lie. He could not lie on stage. And she saw it. The division of loyalties, just for a moment, before his eyes returned to her, and he grinned a relaxed grin, and turned and whispered something to the rest of the band, who nodded.

'Ladies and gentlemen, thanks for coming tonight. Before we get going, I'd like to dedicate this first song to someone I love very much.'

Across the room, a tiny smile played on Delilah's red lips.

'My incredibly hot wife, Stella.' He lifted his arm and gestured to their table, and Stella raised her glass to him. 'Mother of my son, light of my life, best thing ever to happen to me,' he continued, and Stella laughed. 'This is a song I wrote for her when we first met.'

Stella sat back in her chair as the band played the opening chords to the song she knew so well, and Johnny blew her a kiss. He didn't look to the other side of the room as Delilah turned to leave. She didn't glance over at Stella. So she knew exactly who I was the whole time, Stella thought to herself. And she knew that she had won. For now.

The Lodge

It was cool inside the old, run-down shooting lodge, and the light was dim. The day was overcast, and the lodge was behind a cluster of evergreen trees. Anyhow, the only source of light was from the small window, which was half covered. That was fine by him. He didn't want it to be bright. Didn't want them to be able to see in. Didn't want the other man, who was propped up in the far corner of the space, to start spotting things that he might be able to use against him. Maybe he should blindfold him? He should have done so earlier, when he had tied his hands behind his back. He looked around for something he might be able to use.

There were some old sacks piled up on top of a wooden crate; he could use one of those. But to do that, he would have to go near him, into his space, and that would mean taking the gun to him. That, or putting the gun down as he tore off a strip of fabric and tied it around his head, or just slipped the sack over his head whole. No. Neither would be good. Neither would keep him safe.

He looked around the room. Maybe there was something else he could use. Some other way to stop his eyes resting uncomfortably, accusingly on him, like one of those portraits of women whose eyes followed you around the room. They had always given him the creeps.

The floor was grubby and dusty. The room hadn't been swept out for a long time. In the right-hand corner, on the other side of the room from his hostage, there were tools – a big pair of garden shears, rusted shut from lack of use, a ride-on lawnmower in a poor state of repair, a pair of small tin drums, an old gas canister. He mustn't let him get to those things. They could be used as weapons.

'Move further to that side,' he said.

The man looked towards the pile of clutter.

'No, not there. To your right. Further into the corner.' He waved his gun in the direction he was referring to, and the man made a muffled sound, his eyes wide. Then he shuffled awkwardly towards the very corner of the space.

That was better. He carried on looking around the room. Along the back wall there was a set of wooden shelves lined with dented paint tins. Farrow and Ball, dozens of shades of off-white called things like Elephant's Breath and Dimity that women spent hours poring over. No man could ever see the difference. Apple trays, broken and empty of fruit; an old rake, its wood split and warped; a bag of compost, split and mostly empty. Nothing of any obvious use to him. This was nothing like the outbuildings nearer the house, which were new and smelt of freshly sawn wood and tomato plants. They had been shown round those sheds when they had first arrived for the weekend, as part of the house tour. 'This is Spiros's command centre,' the owner had said, his arm holding the door open for them, 'and he rules it with an iron fist in a gardening glove. Steal his fruit and veg at your peril, though I couldn't blame you personally; he always wins something at the village fair, don't you?' The middle-aged Greek man had looked up from his trays of seedlings and smiled benignly. He was used to being shown off like one of his own prize pumpkins.

But no, this building was far from the house, an afterthought. It would have been used years ago, before the house had been opened up to the public, for repairs and storing unwanted stuff that no one could quite bear to chuck in the skip. He squinted in the gloom. Under the shelves lay the desiccated corpse of a rabbit, its legs wizened and its fur patchy. It was past stinking. That was about right, for this place.

This was the place where things came to die.

Chapter Five

September 2008

Something was up. James could feel it as soon as he walked into the building. There was an edge in the air, a sense that everyone was suddenly aware of every movement their body made, every word formed by their lips. They watched themselves as though on TV screens, letting no remark emerge unchecked and unverified.

Where would the axe fall first? There had been rumblings for a few weeks now, gossip passing between the traders that things were bad, worse than anyone was admitting. The run on Northern Rock had been a shock, but nothing that anyone thought was terminal. It was a minor stroke, that was all, requiring rehabilitation and some physio, but banking would be back on its feet again before long. Then Bear Stearns had started to struggle in the summer, and things had suddenly felt a lot more serious. Now Lehman Brothers had fallen, and people were rushing around trying to stem the flow of blood that suddenly seemed to be seeping from every orifice in the city, trying not to tread in it as they made their way to work, hoping that if they pretended it wasn't there, in great big sticky pools, it would somehow disappear.

He walked through the revolving doors and towards the lift

that would take him up to the fifth floor where he worked. Who would it be? Emerging markets, most likely; they had been on a downward turn recently. Debt, as well, was a perilous sector to be in at the moment; they could probably lose a couple of heads from there easily enough. They were going to have to be seen to be making cuts, that was the thing. Appearances were everything, and they couldn't afford to look as though they were sitting pretty while Rome burned around them. It wasn't just jobs, it was the whole culture that was changing. No more surprise appearances by Britney Spears at the summer party, no more weekend jollies to New York or Cape Town by private jet for the top traders.

He was lucky, he thought, as the lift pulled him up towards his office. In so many ways he was lucky. Lucky that his sector – commodities – had been doing so well recently, that his reviews were stronger than they had ever been, just when he needed them to be most. Lucky to have Pearl and Alfie, too.

The caffeine from the espresso he'd drunk before leaving home whizzed through his bloodstream, pushing him forwards. The Nespresso machine was one of the best things he'd ever bought. He loved the ritual of it, sliding the little coloured pods into their slots. Arpeggio was his current favourite, a strong, smoky roasted flavour that made him believe he could be outside a little café in Rome, rather than in his kitchen in south London. The image was an indulgence, but a harmless one.

'Morning.' Phil, one of the traders, was at his desk, phone to his ear as usual, hands hovering over the keyboard of his computer. He raised one hand in greeting to James as he walked past. Down the carpeted stretch of hallway, towards his office at the end. He picked up a bottle of mineral water from the stocked fridge on his way. Began to run through in his head what he needed to do first.

'James?'

He paused and turned. Parker was hanging out of his office, one hand supporting him on the door frame. 'Got a minute?'

'Always, always. Just let me . . .' James motioned to his briefcase and bottle of water, indicating that he wanted to drop them in his own office first. Parker looked awkward. He hesitated. Then gave a short, small shake of his head. 'No. Right away, James, if you don't mind.'

And at that moment, he knew.

Parker couldn't do it, in the end. Had to hand the task over to his boss, Jeremy Howard, who was already in the room when James entered, his suit sharp and his tie covered in inappropriately cheerful-looking elephants.

Parker's face was a storm cloud, fury and embarrassment and frustration writ large across it. He could not meet James's eye as his friend stood before him, still holding his briefcase and bottle of water, both of which felt heavy in his hands now, cumbersome and difficult to manage. He did not put them down, didn't feel quite able to. It would have sent the message that he was expecting to stay. Take off your coat, sit awhile . . . He was not going to be here for long.

'Unpleasant but necessary . . .' Howard was saying. 'Unfortunate events . . . the firm must take immediate, clear action . . . Last in, on a team level, first out.'

James nodded. There was nothing to say. No case to be pleaded. It wasn't as though he had failed, they told him, it wasn't that he had done anything wrong. 'On the contrary, you've had a good run recently, and we'll be recommending you in the highest possible terms going forward.' Going forward to where, though? They all knew there would be no new openings for traders floating about at the moment; everyone would be battening down the hatches. Digging their heels in, as James had thought he had dug his in. But there was nothing to be done. Commodities was being shrunk right down to a skeleton team, who would be taking on more work in order to streamline operations, make sure they were running a tight ship. A ship that would not, it turned out, include James. Last in, first out. His recent transfer, the one he had been so excited about, because it had taken him away from futures and back to commodities, which he enjoyed the most, had left him vulnerable, despite his success there.

He nodded, and said he understood. They were travelling in difficult times, and they would all have to climb the tightrope together, and then he realised that he wasn't making any sense at all and Parker and Howard were looking sympathetic, and he couldn't bear that, so he nodded once more and turned away.

'James?' Howard said before he reached the door. 'Take the day off, why don't you? Go and enjoy the Indian summer.' James paused, his hand on the door handle. There was a silence. Parker and Howard waited to see if he would take the proffered hint, the dignified option that allowed them all to pretend that he really was just taking the day off, that he wasn't to all intents and purposes being thrown out of the building so that his computer could be secured and his office cleared. Disgruntled ex-employees causing trouble were a very real risk, and one that the famously circumspect company did not take.

James nodded, his eyes towards the floor. 'Sure. I'll take the day off. Take the kids to the park, maybe.'

'Good. Jolly good.' Howard was visibly relieved. There was to be no unpleasant scene. Security would not have to be called. Things could get back to normal quickly and without fuss.

James pulled his tie off as he walked down the street, and stuffed it into his pocket. The air was warm, and he undid the top button of his shirt. That would be something, at least. No ties and polished shoes for a while. No five-thirty alarm. No client dinners that went on until the early hours when he was exhausted and desperate to be curled around Izzy in bed. No schedule that he had to keep to, because he was a responsible grown-up member of a high-flying investment bank and that was just what you had to do. No – no anything, really.

No salary. He took a deep breath. That was the big one, wasn't it? No nice tidy package of money dropping into his bank account every month. For as long as it took him to find another job, they would be relying on the redundancy package that he knew he would get and – what else? The café that Izzy was about to open, in just a few days, that was the most urgent and obvious problem. They couldn't back out of it now, they'd already sunk far too much money into it to consider doing that; they were committed. Contracts had been signed, staff employed . . . The thought made his gullet lurch. There might be nothing coming in. And there were a hell of a lot of things going out. The mortgage, the nursery fees, the car payments, the credit-card bills. All the weekly and monthly expenses that seemed to be involved in running a middle-class family. The twice-a-week cleaner, the once-a-week gardener. The children's shoes, their haircuts, the man who came to clean the oven and the one who came to clean the windows. The broadband and cable TV, the magazine subscriptions and organic veg box and deliveries of carefully butchered cuts of free-range chicken and grass-fed beef. The French-conversation lady who came to expose his children to a foreign language every Wednesday after school; Izzy's leg and bikini waxing and eyebrow threading and his own sports massage; the membership to the Bovingdon club and the personal-trainer sessions. The loan. The large, unwieldy loan that Izzy didn't know about. That he would have to continue to service in secret.

James felt faint as he ran through the list in his head and realised that he had never before thought about the sheer amount of *maintenance* that his family seemed to require on a day-to-day level. So many people employed just to keep them trundling along. And they were hardly unusually profligate or extravagant. Panic began to well up inside him and the responsibility of being the main wage-earner hit him for the first time ever. How would he keep the machine moving forward? How would he make sure his family did not suffer because of his failure to keep his job? Pearl, Alfie, Izzy – they did not deserve to have their lives turned upside down because of what had happened.

His mind flitted from possibility to possibility, racing forward like a child running downhill. He could wait it out. Get another job as a trader. He'd pick something up, he was sure. But did he really want to? That was the thing. Now that he had jumped ship, or been pushed overboard, maybe he should carpe the diem, take the opportunity that had been pushed on to him, and do something different. He'd been saying he felt trapped and bored for long enough, hadn't he? Maybe this was the blessing in disguise that he had secretly been hoping for.

He pulled his BlackBerry out of his pocket and, as he walked down the street, tapped in the first few letters of Will's name. W . . . I . . . L . . . His email address popped up and James selected it.

News, he tapped into the subject line. *Got some for you*, he continued in the message box. *Lunchtime pint/sarnie? Need to . . .*

Without any warning, the screen went dark. James stared at it. Tilted the device towards the light in case he was imagining it. Pressed the on/off button. It remained stubbornly, resolutely shut down. For a moment he wondered what had happened, though he knew, somewhere in the recesses of his brain, exactly what the reason for the shutdown was. But for a few brief seconds it was as though his synapses were refusing to retrieve the information, refusing to join the dots. Protecting him from the knowledge that the sudden blankness that had overtaken his screen was the technological incarnation of his banishment from the embracing arms of his company. His job. His identity. He stared at the screen for a second longer, as a pigeon pecked at some chips scattered on the pavement near his feet. Then he turned his face to the sky, letting the sun warm his skin. He dropped his BlackBerry into the bin next to him, and heard it fall down through layers of drinks cans and cigarette packets and other unnamed and unknown substances, before settling. He was free. Or maybe it was freefalling.

'Hello, James,' said a voice in front of him.

His heart thudded, and his feet ground to a halt. Oh God. Oh dear God. He looked up, though he didn't need to do so to confirm what he already knew.

Amanda Fairlight. The very last person he had expected or wanted to see right now. She stood there, her eyes cold, and her expression unreadable, at least to James.

'Not now, Amanda. Not today.'

He carried on walking, too numb from what had just happened in his office – in what had been his office – to be shocked by her appearance. It was inevitable anyway, he supposed.

'Yes, James. Today.' She picked up her pace to keep up with him as he strode towards the tube station. Her voice was just as he remembered it. Clipped, in the manner of a 1930s film star, upper class and husky, with slightly jagged edges from the years she had spent living in the downmarket bit of Notting Hill trying to pretend she was poor. It looked as though she had got over that phase now. She was dressed as eccentrically as ever, but in a glossy, groomed way, not the straggly boho style she had favoured before. She wore a vintage beaded chiffon tea dress, with shiny red patent shoes and a cream fur coat. It looked real to James, but what did he know? She had cut a sharp, straight fringe into her blond hair, and a patterned Hermès scarf was tied around her head. In her left hand she held a cigarette holder, a long, engraved silver one, with a black Sobranie cigarette in its grasp.

'I got your email,' she said.

James nodded. 'And the money?'

'Yes.'

He carried on walking. 'Good. There's nothing for us to discuss, then.' His voice sounded cold, even to himself. But it was necessary. Now more than ever, he had to protect his family.

'I've been waiting outside your building. I thought I'd have to be there until lunchtime. I didn't think walking into your office would be very – politic. And I hate those places. Full of men in suits and too much aftershave.'

James sighed. Of course she'd waited. Amanda was nothing if not determined. 'There are laws against stalking people.'

'Not very easily enforceable ones, take it from me. Where are you off to, anyhow? I thought I'd be waiting far longer than this. Got a high-powered meeting, I suppose.'

'Something like that.' The woman was impossible. He slowed as he reached the tube station, and a man shoved a copy of the *Standard* into his hands. He took it automatically and rummaged for some change. Amanda held out her pack of cigarettes to him.

'Do you want one?'

James shook his head. 'No. I gave up.'

She raised an eyebrow, and exhaled smoke into his face. He willed himself not to cough.

'Of course you did. So sensible.' She smirked, and James fought the desire to defend himself. There was nothing wrong with being sensible, dammit. But that was the thing about

Amanda. She always made you feel as though doing anything other than what she wanted was to be boring, horribly square. That was the reason he was in this situation at all.

'Leave me alone, Amanda. I gave you everything I could, there isn't any more. Especially not . . .' He stopped himself. 'There's no more.' He felt panic rising in his chest and he knew he had to get away. 'Just leave me alone!' And he turned and ran, shamefully, into the thick warmth of the underground, as Amanda stood on the pavement and watched him go.

Izzy sat at her kitchen table surrounded by the paperwork of her life. To her left, a stack of bills for the café, which was opening next week. A box of flyers, designed by a guy in Will's office who was a whizz with Photoshop, sat to one side, ready to be delivered to the surrounding houses and businesses, offering a discount on lunch for the opening week. They were smart, black and white with a slightly retro look, and Izzy felt a little shudder of excitement and nerves every time she looked at them. Next to them was a file full of household admin, sorely neglected recently, that she had to attend to – boring things like a parking permit that needed renewing and the contract for the new kitchen that had been installed in their place in the country. Izzy thought for a moment about all of the money that this paperwork required to service it. To keep the machine whirring along. How would they manage if James didn't get another job soon? It had only been a few days and already she was fretting.

She pushed the worries aside, and finished writing the card that would go with Harriet's sister Em's wedding present, signing it from 'James, Iz, Pearl and Alfie', and sealed the envelope. When she had first been married she had left a space for James to sign his own name on birthday cards and thank-you letters and all the other domestic correspondence that somehow, mysteriously, seemed to fall to her, even those for his side of the family, but nowadays she didn't bother. Didn't have the energy to chase and keep reminding him to do it.

She had never worked out how that had happened, she pondered idly. It was almost as though it was part of the marriage vows. 'With my body I honour you, all that I am I give to you, and all of your Christmas cards I write for you.' Though if she had been forced to admit it, she would have said that she liked, really, having control over what they gave and to whom, enjoyed the compliments that came her way about how well she selected gifts and the unusual cards she found (she picked them up as and when she saw them, keeping them in an old cigar box on a shelf). Wouldn't have trusted James to know whether a bride and groom were a White Company decanter kind of a couple (elegant and classic, as she had decided Em and her fiancé Henry were) or a John Lewis goose-down pillows kind of a couple (practical, but still desirous of luxury), or an antique salt cellar kind of a couple (quirky, less conventional). The differences were subtle but important, in a way that she would never have been able to explain to her husband. Well. He would have time now, wouldn't he? To help around the house, with the children. Though she was not sure how much 'help' he would be.

She scribbled a note to herself to ring Harriet before the wedding at the weekend and make sure that she was OK. She knew her friend had been dreading the thing for months, not least because of that vile dress that she was being made to wear and that Ginny had been so tactless about, and Izzy thought she could do with a bit of moral support.

'I'm seriously considering not going,' Harriet said to Izzy later that evening, over a large glass of Chablis outside the little wine bar halfway between their two houses. 'Just not turning up. What could they do? Nothing.' She tapped the ash off the end of her cigarette.

Izzy nodded. 'It's an option. Not exactly politic, but . . .'

'Fuck politic. Seriously. I'm sick of pandering to the little cow.'

'You don't mean that.'

Harriet sighed. 'Probably not. Ugh. I don't know.' She shook her head, and when she spoke again, her voice was angry. 'This is what I hate, Iz. This is not the kind of person I am. I love my sister. I want her to be happy, even though she is a pain-in-the-arse prima donna at times. But I'm becoming one of those hateful, bitter . . . spinsters.' She shuddered.

Izzy shook her head. 'You are not a spinster. Spinsters are at least forty.'

'Great. Only a few years to go.'

'Oh stop it, you're only just past thirty. Stop feeling sorry for yourself.' She took the bottle from its cooler and refilled their glasses.

'Sorry.'

'Don't apologise. Just don't be so sad. I don't like it.'

'I'll try.'

They sat in silence for a second.

'Seriously, though, lovely, what are you going to do?'

'I don't know if there's anything I *can* do.'

'You can't carry on like this.'

'No. No, I can't. We can't. We're making each other miserable. Will knows I'm not happy and it puts him on edge. I know I'm making him nervous and I can't help it, and then I resent him for making me feel like that in the first place, all jealous and bitter, and then I feel bad for that, because it's not really his fault, after all, and the whole thing's a big mess.'

Harriet's face was glum.

'Come on, whose fault is it? He's a grown-up, Hats, and he's not really acting like one.'

'Why, because he doesn't want to get married?'

'Yes.'

'That's not really fair, though, is it? Who says everyone has to want the same thing? The two-point-four-children thing isn't for everyone, you know. I know it makes you two happy, and that's great, but maybe Will just isn't the marrying kind.'

Izzy pursed her lips shut and left a pointed pause before she spoke. Harriet could be bloody impossible sometimes; as argumentative as Pearl. Izzy picked a bit of nail varnish off her thumbnail.

'Marriage isn't some sort of panacea for all ills, you know. James has just lost his job. Right after I opened a café in the eye of the biggest recession since God knows when. Marriage might be great, but it can't fix that. I don't know if anything can.'

Eventually Harriet groaned. 'See? I'm a fucking nightmare. I don't know why I'm defending him to you. I'm sorry. I know you're having a shit time as well. Sorrysorry. Any news on a new job?'

Izzy smiled and shook her head. *Don't want to talk about it*, her face said, silently. 'I'm sure something will turn up. We'll be fine. We don't have much choice, do we? Have you spoken to Will's mum about it, ever?'

Harriet snorted. 'The Iron Lady? Hardly. She only stopped calling me "what's her name – oh, Harriet" two years ago. She's probably forbidden him from marrying me; told him I wouldn't make a suitable lady of the Highland manor. She's probably right. I'd be dire at it.'

'Don't exaggerate. She's nice enough. And their place is amazing.'

'If you have a thing for week-old pheasant terrine and having to sleep under five blankets and some dogs, yeah, it's great.' Will's family home was a stone castle in the Highlands, fearsomely cold in winter, in the middle of nowhere. Izzy and James had been up there for a week in the summer once, a few years ago, with Will and Harriet; they had taken over half a wing on the east side of the castle, where they had spent the week fishing and eating massive roasts and sitting up watching the sky never getting quite dark till what would have been dawn. Izzy remembered it as a week full of laughter and red cheeks and woodsmoke.

'I'm a misery, I know,' Harriet finished, draining her glass. 'I'm going to go.' She got her wallet out.

'I'll do it,' Izzy said, waving her hand. 'I'll see you at the weekend. Go home to that boyfriend of yours. Remind him of the girl he fell in love with. You never know what might happen.'

Harriet looked thoughtful. 'Darling, even I can't remember the girl he fell in love with, it was so long ago.'

It had been a throwaway remark, but the next day, when Harriet was at work, it came back to her. It was a slow day. All her clients were being unusually quiet, there were no crises to deal with, no urgent projects to pull together, no events scheduled for the next week or so. She was half-heartedly catching up on some emails and other admin, but her words kept on coming back into her mind. *Even I can't remember the girl he fell in love with, it was so long ago.*

Maybe that was the problem, the reason why Will hadn't proposed, why they were just drifting along aimlessly. Maybe she had changed, become someone else, without either of them really noticing?

'Do you think I've changed?' she asked Tara, her business partner, when she took her her lunch.

Tara raised her eyebrows, a forkful of couscous on her way to her mouth. 'Changed? How?'

'I don't know.'

'Since when?'

'Whenever. In the last few years.' Harriet waited.

'You're not really helping me out here, Hats. Have you changed, in some unspecified way, at some point since I've known you, is that what you're asking? No.'

'Are you sure?'

'Do you want to have changed? You've got a bit older. Does that help?'

Harriet sighed. 'I don't know. No. Yes. Thanks.'

She went back to deleting unread junk mails from her inbox.

Maybe it wasn't that she *had* changed, but that she hadn't. Maybe Will had changed and left her behind. Maybe he was just bored. They didn't go out much together any more, it was true, not on dates. It was all to see friends and work stuff. She couldn't remember the last time they had been out for dinner, or to the cinema, for no particular reason, just the two of them.

She picked up the phone.

''Lo?' Will sounded distracted.

'What are you doing tonight, Will?'

'Hi. Um. Not sure. Rugby's on.'

Harriet nodded. 'Want to go to the Crown?'

'To watch the rugby? I don't think they show it.'

Harriet tried not to sigh. 'No, not to watch the rugby. To have dinner, with me. Your girlfriend. A spontaneous date.'

'Oh.' Will's voice was wary. 'Am I in trouble?'

'Will!' Harriet groaned. 'No. You're not in trouble. I just . . . I just thought it would be nice. Never mind.'

'No, wait, it would be nice. Sorry. Course it would. Can I meet you there?'

Harriet smiled. 'Yes. Course. See you there about half seven. Love you.' She put the phone down and checked her watch. She had time for a quick trip to Selfridges.

*

In the Crown, at eight o'clock, Harriet waited, a glass of Pinot Grigio in front of her. She had almost finished it, but she was damned if she was going to buy another one. She wanted Will to see that she had had time to drink a whole glass of wine while she waited for him. She checked her phone again for a text. Nothing. Across the room, a man was watching her, glancing across at her from where he stood with his group of friends. She shifted in her seat, aware of his attention. At least the new Marc Jacobs top she had bought earlier wasn't going completely unappreciated, even if it was by some random office boy rather than her boyfriend.

She picked up her mobile and texted Caroline. *How's that book Stella lent you?!* After a second, her phone buzzed with a reply. *Um. Enlightening . . . ?* Harriet smiled to herself. Caroline was so uncomfortable discussing sex that Harriet could think of only one other occasion during their near-twenty-year friendship that she had done so, and she had been so prudish at school that she had been unable to countenance the use of tampons as she thought it would mean losing her virginity. The thought of her reading one of Stella's explicit volumes of advice and instruction made Harriet giggle. Lucky old Bart *was* in for a surprise, she thought, if Caroline took any of it up.

'I wish it had been something I'd said that put that beautiful smile on your face. But maybe if you let me buy you a drink, it will be?'

Harriet looked up. The man from the other side of the room was standing next to her table. Up close, he was still good-looking, in a waxy sort of a way, but his suit was shiny and he smelt of crisps. She grimaced. 'I don't think so, sweetie. But thanks.'

'Come on. You're almost out. And it doesn't look like he's going to show up, does it? Seems a shame to waste that lovely new top.' He raised an eyebrow, and pointed to the Selfridges bag sticking out of her handbag.

She rolled her eyes. 'Very smooth, Poirot. But I'm not waiting for anyone, actually.'

'No? Then there's no reason not to let me buy you a drink.'

'Sorry. I was about to leave. Just stopped in on my way . . . to dinner.'

The man nodded, a smirk on his face. She was fooling no one. She stood up to leave, picking up her bags. As she did so, her phone buzzed. It was Will.

'Sorry, darling. Got caught up. Going to have to postpone dinner. Sorry. I love you.'

She sighed. The man waggled his eyebrows, annoyingly. 'Sure you don't want to change your mind?'

Harriet looked at him. He was standing in front of her, and for a moment she considered it. Considered saying fuck it, and putting her things back down, and letting him buy her a drink, and letting him spin her cheesy lines and pretend to laugh at his jokes. After all, Will wasn't here, was he? Why shouldn't she enjoy herself as she had set out to do when she left the office?

Then she shook her head, and pulled on her jacket. 'I don't think so. Have a good night.'

He shrugged, and went back over to his friends, who laughed and clapped him on the back and teased him about being turned down.

'What are you doing?' Harriet whispered to herself, as she pushed the swing door of the bar open and began to search the street for a taxi. Will stood you up, he's busy, work's busy, he wouldn't have done it if something important hadn't happened. That doesn't mean you need to start considering every offer from a slimy stranger as a great alternative way to spend the evening. Jesus.

But she didn't want to go home. She hovered outside the pub

for a minute in the cold, her breath thick in front of her and the air damp with unfallen rain. For a second, she thought she might cry. Where *are* you, Will? Why couldn't you just have come, on time, and sat with me, and made me feel like we were a proper couple who were going to be OK?

She took a deep breath. Then she took out her phone, and rang Stella. The man in the pub had been right about one thing. She was fucked if she was going to let a new top and a full face of make-up, complete with eyelash extensions courtesy of the beauty bar in Selfridges, go to waste.

On the night Izzy's café was due to open, she sent her two recently hired members of staff home to change before the evening shift, locked the door, and stood behind the counter. She had half an hour of peace in the newly finished shop before everyone started to turn up and the evening, and the next phase of her life, began.

She couldn't quite believe that she had done it. What had started as a whim, a question asked without really thinking, had turned into – into this. Izzy looked around the room. The old oak tables were scrubbed and lined with tea lights. The menu boards that she had scoured eBay and repossession companies for were up on the walls, neatly lettered with the special menu of canapés she had created for the party. Kedgeree arancini, courgette flowers stuffed with herbed goat's cheese and drizzled with honey, little mugs of chilli-spiked gazpacho, hot twists of olive-studded bread, pots of summer pudding made with brioche and laced with elderflower liqueur. She had called the café Pearl's Place, and the awning above the door proclaimed its name proudly.

And she was proud, she realised now, for the first time in ages. It was a job well done, so far, and though it had ended up costing her more than she had bargained for, and more than she had even admitted to James, she felt sure that it would be worth it.

The white-tiled space buzzed with Izzy and James's family and friends, and she felt pink-cheeked and wide-eyed with the effort of making sure that she spoke to everyone, thanking them for coming and checking that they had had a drink and something to eat, and keeping an eye on Petra and Dan, reminding them to see that everyone got one of the little boxes of home-made chocolate and salted caramel sweets covered in pearlised powder as they left, and looking to see who was coming through the door now – oh good, it was her Pilates teacher, she'd hoped she would come, she knew everyone and was a good person to have on board, as was Tasha James, who was one of those women Izzy tried to avoid having to talk to but who she knew could make a huge difference to the success of the café.

'Tasha! I'm so glad to see you.' Izzy kissed her on both cheeks, noticing that Tasha held her slightly at arm's length as she did so.

'Managed to squeeze you in between Tom's Mandarin and Dora's harp. Have half an hour. I'm so jealous of you. I'd never have the spare time to set something like this up, but then you're so wonderfully laissez-faire when it comes to your two.' She smiled, and they both knew she wasn't jealous at all, simply pleased with herself for being fertile enough to bear four children and fit enough to still be a size eight afterwards, and Izzy bridled at the implication that the café was just something she'd slotted into her incredibly laid-back life as the mother of only two, fairly inadequate children, and forced herself to resist throwing the plate of food she was holding down Tasha's permanently sun-kissed cleavage. Instead she said sweetly, 'Gazpacho? It's dairy-free – practically calorie-free too!' and laughed falsely, hating herself. But she so wanted her little café to work that any amount of sucking up to Tasha James was worth it.

From the other side of the café, Stella caught her eye and winked at her, raising her glass in a toast and then making a 'smug cow' face in Tasha's direction. Izzy grinned. The little party felt a bit like her wedding had done, in that, at that moment, she could reach out and touch all of her favourite people in the world. Her children, her husband, her friends. Stella in the corner, bitching about everyone and cracking through the booze. Harriet next to her, pulling her cigarettes out of her bag, about to drag Stella outside for one, elbowing Will to tell him where she was going and reaching her face up to his for a kiss as she went. Will deep in conversation with James, the two of them looking relaxed and happy. Her in-laws, Ginny beaming with pride, Julian as easy and comfortable as ever, chatting to her guests and making them feel welcome. Caroline and Bart just arriving, Caroline looking flustered but smiling and mouthing 'sorry' to Izzy from across the room. Everyone who was important to her right here, in one place, eating the food she had cooked and enjoying themselves. And Izzy knew that she had done the right thing.

'Are you Pearl?' Izzy stopped loading empty soup mugs on to the tray she was holding to look up at the man asking the question. He was tall and tanned, with blondish hair that was slightly scruffier than his beautifully cut suit would lead you to expect, and surprisingly dark eyes.

'Pearl's my daughter,' she replied. 'I'm Izzy.' She wiped her hand on her apron and held it out to him. 'I'm sorry, we haven't met.'

'No.' He continued to stare at her, and she had to force herself to hold his gaze, because something in it made her want to look away. 'I'm afraid I wasn't invited. I came with a

102

– friend.' He gestured somewhere outside. 'I seem to have lost her. But I must find her and thank her – this is the most wonderful place.'

'Oh.' Izzy smiled. 'Thank you.' She shifted on her feet, unsure of what to say next.

'The area's been crying out for somewhere decent to eat. For those of us who would otherwise be thrown on the mercy of the Tesco ready meal, I think it's going to be a lifesaver.'

He returned her smile, and her discomfort disappeared. She couldn't work this man out at all. His clothes said grown-up, success, polish. But his hair and his demeanour and that smile – they said something else entirely. And she wasn't at all sure they said anything she should be listening to.

She cleared her throat.

'Well, you're very welcome. Do you live nearby?'

'Yes. Quite.' He tilted his head to one side and didn't say anything else. Izzy began to feel uncomfortable again. The man could hold a silence like a monk. Suddenly her mouth seemed to have gone dry. It was hot in here. She must go and prop the door open.

'Right. Well, it was nice to meet you. I'd better . . .' She gestured to the room, thinning out now but still busy, and full of the detritus of the evening.

'Of course. Thanks for letting me crash.' He turned, and walked to the door, hands in his pockets, and strolled over to the other side of the room.

'I'd just like to raise a glass, and say bloody well done to Izzy. She's worked her socks off on this place and I think we can all agree it's paid off. Darling, it looks fantastic; I'm so proud of you. To Izzy, and to Pearl's Place!' James led the toast, and kissed Izzy on her blushing cheek as everyone joined in.

'God. I'm terrible at this,' she said, when it had quieted. 'But just to say – thanks so much for coming. It's free tonight, but it won't be as from tomorrow, so I hope this isn't the last I'm going to see of you load of liggers.' Laughter. 'Seriously, come back, bring your friends, tell everyone you know. Please. Or the kids are going to have to live off the sawdust from the rabbit hutch, and that would be really sad.' More laughter, and a little squeeze of her hand from James.

As Izzy finished her speech, he hugged her, and kissed her head. 'I mean it, you know,' he said quietly. 'I am proud of you. I know I wasn't that supportive to start with . . .' She coughed, and raised her eyebrows.

'Do you now?' she said. 'Can I have that in writing, please?'

He kissed her again. 'I know, I know. I was a bit of a wanker when you first mentioned it. A lot of a wanker. But seriously. You've done a bloody good job.' He faltered momentarily, his voice becoming strangled, and suddenly he sounded as though he was going to choke. She raised her head and looked at him quizzically. He was staring across the room at the man who had come over to her earlier, who was deep in conversation with a blonde woman.

'What is it? Do you know him?'

James smiled at her.

'Yes. Yes, he's a big trader actually, Stephen Garside. I'd heard he was moving to the area. I'm going to go and say hello. You OK? Happy?'

'So happy. Thank you, my darling. Yes, go and talk to him. Sounds like he might come in useful.'

'Exactly.' James looked at Izzy.

She did look happy. Her eyes sparkled, and she glowed with satisfaction. It was worth everything to see her look like that. He smiled.

'Good. You deserve to be. Well done.'

'Thanks, darling. Now all we need is a nice stream of

customers to come through those doors, and you might not have to worry about getting a new job at all.'

James nodded. And went over to talk not to the man who had caught his eye, but to the woman with him. Amanda Fairlight.

This time he accepted the cigarette she offered, as they stood around the corner from the café. He needed it.

She tapped the packet and he took one, and she lit it for him with a tortoiseshell lighter. Her lipstick was red, he noticed, when she was up close, very, very red, and her perfume was thick and spicy in the air around her. He leaned back against the wall. Like a teenager, he tried not to cough when he inhaled. Failed.

'You never gave up, then,' he said.

Amanda exhaled. 'Never. I'm dedicated. Well, I did for a while, of course. But I started again. Stupid really. When did you?'

'When Izzy was . . .' He stopped. Amanda grimaced.

'When Izzy was pregnant?'

He nodded.

'Very responsible father-to-be,' she said quietly. There was a silence, and then she laughed. 'Thank God you did give up. You always were rubbish at smoking.' There was affection in her voice, and James softened. It was true.

'Remember Calais?'

She snorted with laughter. 'I've spent the last fuck knows how many years trying to forget it, but yes, I do remember Calais. You and those ridiculous Gitanes.'

'I thought I was so sophisticated. Taking my girl to France.'

'I know. Shame.'

'Oi! It was romantic.'

'Oh yes, very. Especially the food poisoning.'

'In that awful hotel.'

'Mm. French loos.'

'God. Sorry.'

They both stared ahead, not looking at one another.

'How did you know to come here tonight?' James couldn't quite decide whether to be angry or impressed.

'I know what questions to ask. And to whom.'

'What does that mean?'

'Does it matter? I'm here now. You and me. Just like old times.'

'Not quite like old times.'

'No.' She ground her cigarette out beneath her shoe. 'OK. Chat time's over. You need to get back inside before that lovely wife of yours starts wondering where you are.'

'She's busy,' he said, and then, 'Look, Amanda,' but he ground to a halt. She waited. He had no idea what to say.

Amanda lit another cigarette and watched him search for words that would not come. Eventually she rolled her eyes and took pity on him.

'Oh for God's sake, James. You are crap, you know that? You always were.'

'I know. Believe me, I know.'

'Listen, I'm not here to ruin your marriage. I'm sure Izzy is lovely—'

'She is,' James said fiercely. 'She's amazing.'

'Calm down, darling. Like I said, I'm sure she's lovely. I'm sure your child – children?' She tilted her head to one side.

'Children. A boy and a girl.' James felt reluctant to tell her their names, for some reason that he could not quite fathom.

'I'm sure your children are adorable. I'm sure you're quite the perfect family.' And there was just a hint of an edge of ice in her voice now.

106

'I'm pleased for you, James, I really am. But here's the thing. Cass is lovely too.'

Her name jolted him, and Amanda took advantage of his discomfort.

She sighed. 'You know what I want, James.' She reached out and touched his arm. 'I don't want your money – not that I don't appreciate the gesture,' she added quickly, in case he demand back what he had already given her, 'but it's not why I'm here. I just want you to see your daughter.'

His daughter. His firstborn, the girl he had only discovered existed a few years ago, when she was already half grown, the girl he had been able to pretend didn't exist until now. Now, it seemed, he could bury his head in the sand no longer. Cass. He had known her name of course, since the day he had first found out, but hearing it again now brought her into focus, suddenly. This Cass, his daughter who had been christened Cassandra by her mother, had a nickname. She was a real person.

It had been five years ago that he had found out. Amanda had emailed him, on his work email, out of the blue.

Sorry to spring this on you, darling, [she had written, with typically infuriating insouciance] but here's the thing. I know it's been an age – more than eleven years, to be exact, if you remember. You probably don't. But I know just how long it was, because, darling, I have a permanent reminder. She's called Cass (Cassandra, but it's a bit of a mouthful, and Cass has just always suited her), and she's eleven in May. You can check the dates, if you feel so inclined and if you still keep a diary of those days or anything. You can check mine, if you want to. Anyhow, she's been asking about you recently – well, not you, as such, of course, she doesn't know who you are. But about her daddy, about where she came from, all that kind of stuff. Children ask so many questions, don't they?! Well, you may not know, I don't know if you have any of your own now or not. Any *more* of your own. But I'm not married – any more, long story – and I think it would be good for her to have a man in her life. And, as her father, I'm afraid you're the obvious choice for that role. Let me know how you want to play it.

Best love, Amanda

He'd been numb with shock, at first. A child. An actual child. Not just a baby, but an eleven-year-old girl, old enough to ask questions about him and go to school and – everything else that eleven-year-olds did these days, whatever that might be. He'd walked around the common for ages, after work, thinking and remembering and wondering, until Izzy had phoned him and he'd gone home, telling her he'd been out for a drink with Will. It hadn't been long before the shock had turned to anger. How dare Amanda? How dare she keep it from him, for all these years, for over a decade, for God's sake, and then just reappear out of the blue with an email that might have been written to a casual acquaintance telling them some bit of news of no importance. It just wasn't on. Well, she could fuck herself if she thought he was going to just jump when she told him to. He had Izzy now, he was marrying Izzy, and he would not jeopardise that for anyone or anything, let alone Amanda bloody Fairlight and her child. Her child, not his, he told himself; it probably wasn't even his. She had never been exactly pious; who knew how many others there had been? He hadn't thought she was sleeping with anyone else at the time, but why would he? He had been twenty and full of the arrogance of youth. Who was to say how many others she had considered landing this on and rejected them as being too irresponsible, or not earning enough, or impossible to contact. He was a convenient target, he was sure, and he wasn't bloody having it.

So he had deleted her email, married Izzy, and pushed the whole thing to the back of his mind. She had continued to send him messages, though. Six months passed before the second one. *Darling James*, it had started. *I know my last email must have been a bit of a shock, so I thought I'd give you time for it all to sink in.* A bit of a shock, he'd thought, furiously, typical. Talk about understatement of the year. *Anyhow, you've had a chance to think it all over now, so please let me know what you'd like to do next. We're in the States at the moment, but I'll be over in the summer. My numbers are . . .* There hadn't been any room for the possibility that James might not want to see Amanda and Cass; she just assumed that he would call, it felt like. Well, she could assume away. He wasn't going to call, and he wasn't going to be pressured into doing so by the little details she dropped in about the girl. *Cass is doing so well at school*, she added near the end of the email. *She loves art and geography and numbers. Funny combination, but then I suppose that's no real surprise. She's getting so tall, as well, she can nearly wear my clothes, which is an absolute bugger for me. I'm sure she's going to look better in all of it than I ever did.*

'She's stunning,' Amanda was saying now, 'I mean, really properly beautiful. I always thought I scrubbed up OK' – she winked at James, and he looked away, uncomfortable – 'but she's something else. Honestly, you'll just die when you see her.'

There it was again, that assumption. That confidence. James looked her in the eye. 'Amanda, listen . . .'

Amanda's voice was suddenly steely. 'No, James. No. You listen. You've ignored me and fobbed me off for five years. I've tried to play nicely. I've tried to understand. I know I should have told you to start with, and let you decide what you wanted to do then, but you were twenty, we were both twenty, for God's sake, and I was scared and bolshie and too damn independent and bloody-minded for my own good, and I was sure I could do it all by myself. And you know, I did. I did it by myself, I looked after her and I raised her and I did quite a good job actually.' She stubbed out her cigarette and lit another one. 'And it's fine that you don't want to have anything to do with me, and reject me and make excuses to me, because frankly, darling, I don't give much of a shit. But it's not fine that you do that to her. She's sixteen now, and she wants to know her father, and if I can't make it happen she'll come looking for you herself, and if you disappoint her or reject her then you know what? I'll destroy you. I will destroy you if you hurt her. She deserves better, James. She deserves better than me, and she sure as hell deserves better than you, but we're what she's got, and we're all that she's got, and she . . . she deserves that much.'

'All right,' he said, after a long silence. 'Yes. You're right. She does deserve it. And I'd like to meet her. I'd like to meet my daughter.'

Chapter Six

October 2008

Will sat across from the group of men, leaning forward, elbows on his knees and fingertips together, talking passionately and with conviction as he came to the end of his spiel. 'The credit industry and the economy itself is struggling. Consumers are frightened. There's no denying that. But with hardship come opportunities; where weak men falter, brave men can seize the day and rise to the top. I believe wholeheartedly that there is still money to be made, and made well. Which is why I hope that you will decide to support Henry Butler's in the next phase of its development.'

Several of Will's applications for mortgages to fund his holiday properties plan had been turned down. Henry Butler's was already carrying a considerable amount of debt, and the looming recession was causing the usual lenders to tighten their belts. The business was growing, but it was still relatively young, and there was a wariness in the air now. Banks weren't willing to sign away hundreds of thousands of pounds on the basis of a quick meeting and a sketch of a business plan, as they had been not too long ago. So Will was going down the private investment route. Bart and Julian had pledged investment in the scheme already, and had recommended it to friends and acquaintances. He had approached some individuals he had met at various events who had expressed interest in his company. He was, as they say, 'putting feelers out', and was optimistic that he would get the cash he needed, and be able to have his plans ready to go by next summer. But then it was rare that Will was anything other than optimistic, about anything. It was in his nature to expect the best, and he was usually rewarded by having those expectations fulfilled.

After the hand-shaking and the thank-you-for-comings were all over with and the men had gone, Will allowed himself five minutes of staring out of the window. His offices were in Mayfair, not too far from the gallery where Caroline Rathbone worked, and he sometimes popped in to say hello to her if he was out and about at lunchtime, or walking back from a meeting. Maybe he'd go and see if she was free for lunch, he thought. Why not? His big meeting was over and he felt it had gone well; he deserved a nice lunch. He could always have phoned Harriet, but she'd probably be busy, he told himself, not examining too closely the reasons why he didn't call to check. Harriet and his love for her felt complex at the moment, bound up with expectation and decisions and somewhat fragile as a result. Caroline was a straightforward girl. Always had been.

'I really think he's going to ask her,' Caroline said breathlessly down the phone to Izzy, from the gallery. She kept her voice quiet so that the couple in the corner of the space couldn't hear her gossiping. But she had to tell someone.

'Caroline . . . hang on . . .' The noise of the bustling café faded as Izzy took the phone outside. 'Look, are you sure?'

'Well, I saw him today, he came to the gallery. We had lunch. No big thing, we just went round the corner to Langan's.' She gave herself a mental tap on the wrist. *You don't always need to justify seeing Will. You're doing nothing wrong.* 'He said he had something special planned. He seemed really excited about it. What else could it be?'

'All sorts of things. I don't think you should jump to conclusions.'

'Come on. It has to be that. It's her birthday, he's planning a surprise . . . Izzy, it's so exciting. But do you think I should tell her?'

'No! Christ, Caroline, don't say . . .'

Caroline kept an eye on the couple. The woman looked over, and she smiled warmly at her. Damn, she was going to have to go and talk to them.

'OK, all right, I won't say anything.'

'Promise? It may not be anything at all . . .'

'Got to go, bye!'

And she put the phone down and clipped across to the couple. 'Good afternoon. Are you interested in the nineteenth-century watercolours in particular? Because we have some lovely . . .'

'Happy birthday, darling.' Will handed Harriet a cup of tea, and she propped herself up on her pillows to take it. 'It's going to be one to remember.'

'Lovely. Thanks.' What did that mean? She pushed her hair away from her face and reached for Will's hand. 'Get back in.' She pulled the duvet aside for him. 'Come on. It's my birthday, you have to do what I say.'

'Don't you want your presents?'

'Yes. But I want this present first.' She grinned, and drew him towards her, sliding his dressing gown off his shoulders as he got back under the covers.

*

The pile of gifts that sat on the tray he brought her, handing it to her with a flourish, was satisfyingly intriguing, with different-shaped packages and a handful of cards next to them. Some from Will – for a man, he was surprisingly good at finding cards, always giving her more than one, with silly messages inside; one from her parents, her mother's careful handwriting on the envelope instantly recognisable; one from James and Iz, even though she would see them tonight. That one was handmade, by Pearl, a folded piece of paper with a wonky crayon drawing of a sunflower on the front, and a scrawled 'Happy Birthay Arntie Hareit' inside. She smiled and put it on her bedside table. Nothing from Ginny and Julian, which was odd. They'd sent her a card every year since she had known Caroline. Ginny used to send her parcels when they were at school as well, after Caroline had told her that Harriet's own mother never sent her anything. Post was a big event at boarding school, and the arrival of a parcel, especially a surprise parcel, was the sort of thing that made life bearable. Ginny had been brilliant at them, stuffing shoeboxes full of treats: chocolate bars and cheap sparkly rings and trendy stationery of the sort that teenage girls mooned over for hours.

But this year, nothing. Probably stuck in the post some-where. Harriet's eyes ran over the various shapes of her presents. Something soft and flattish, a cashmere sweater maybe, Will was good at choosing those; a rectangular parcel, probably the box set of the new season of *24*, which they were both addicted to and spent hours bingeing on at weekends, giving themselves adrenalin headaches; a couple of book-shaped packages, one of which was hopefully that Richard and Judy one she'd been wanting to read; and one or two smaller ones. One of which was square and solid-looking. Harriet deliberately didn't pick that one up first. *It's going to be one to remember*, he had said. And he had told Caroline that he was planning something special – she had let it slip when they had been on the phone the day before. That had to mean . . . didn't it?

'Any particular order?' she asked, sipping her lukewarm tea.

'No. One or two are pretty obvious what they are, I'm afraid. There's only a certain amount of disguising you can do with some shapes.'

She smiled at him. She hadn't wanted to hope. But maybe it was . . . She reached for one that was clearly a hardback book.

'Ah, that I think you'll like.' He winked at her. Oh? Maybe it wasn't a book after all. She'd read about men who'd hollowed out hardbacks to hide rings inside. Would he have done something like that? *Stop it, Harriet, It's just a book*. But she couldn't entirely smother the little flutter of hopeful excitement that flickered inside her. It was her birthday, after all. What better time to choose?

She unwrapped the copy of *Nigella Express* and flicked through it. 'Oh, wow, looks fab.' *You're ridiculous*, she thought to herself, *you're actually obsessed. I can't believe you're disappointed that a book, a book that you wanted, doesn't have a fucking engagement ring somehow hidden inside it. Dangling from its spine or something*. She laughed at herself.

'What?'

'Nothing. Just – how fat would I be if I ate like this every day? Caramel croissant pudding, though. Yum.'

'You could eat so much of that you turned into a pudding, and I'd still think you were hot.'

'Hotter than Nigella?'

'Ooh. That's pushing it, to be honest.'

Harriet bashed him with the book and reached for the small, possibly jewellery-box-shaped package. 'This one next?' she asked, lightly.

'Sure.' His face gave nothing away. She picked at the Sellotape, unwilling, somehow, to tear it open. If it was what she was hoping it might be, then she'd want to keep the paper. A memento.

She slid the paper off, uncovering the box. Amarinth Jewels, the script on its lid read; the name of the small local jeweller into whose window Harriet had gazed so often. Her mouth felt dry.

'Oh, Will.' She gave a little sigh. She almost didn't want to open it and break the moment of anticipation. What would it be like? A solitaire, or a trilogy ring, maybe? She pressed the little button and felt it click and give, and the lid rose up.

It was a pair of diamond earrings. Silver hoops, with baguette-cut diamonds running through the centre. She took one out, and it caught the light, reflecting a rainbow on to the bedroom wall. She didn't think she could speak, but she had to say something.

'Oh, Will,' she said again, and she thought she might burst with the disappointment of it, and the guilty ingratitude that she was suddenly overwhelmed with.

'They look beautiful on you,' he said later, as they got in the cab to go to James and Izzy's. 'Just the right size for your sweet little ears.' He leaned over and bit her right ear lobe, and she squealed. The cab driver looked in the rear-view mirror and caught Will's eye.

'Stop it,' she whispered. 'Poor man, don't embarrass him.'

'It's fine,' Will said, 'he knows it's a special occasion. The address I gave you earlier, mate, yes?' He raised his voice to talk to the driver, who nodded and pulled away from the kerb.

'Why does James need to borrow your suitcase again?' Harriet checked her lipstick in her compact. 'Surely they've got masses of their own.'

'Nothing big enough, apparently; Izzy had a big clear-out and chucked a couple away. By mistake, she said, but James reckons she just didn't like them. Anyhow, now he's going to visit some friends in Wales and he needs to take them – um, some stuff.'

'Why can't he just buy one?'

Will thought quickly. 'No time. He leaves tomorrow.'

'Oh.' Harriet shrugged. 'Weird.'

Will put his arm around her shoulders. 'Mm.' She'd realise soon enough that they weren't going to James and Izzy's. But he wanted to keep the surprise intact for as long as possible.

'I can't believe it,' she kept saying. 'I can't believe you did it. You've never done anything like this. Never.'

The train was whizzing through the tunnel, on its way to Paris. It hadn't been till they'd gone through Battersea that she'd looked out of the window and said, 'Hang on, we're going in completely the wrong direction, Will, tell ... 'Scuse me, you need to turn around.' The driver had grinned widely, relieved that the subterfuge was finally over and he could relax. 'No, madam, quite going in right direction, sorry for untruth,' he said, and put his foot down a little harder on the accelerator.

'Will?' She'd turned to him, her smile uncertain. 'What's going on? Where are you whisking me off to?' Babington, she had thought, maybe, or Whatley Manor? A night away, how fab. It had been absolutely ages since they'd been away together, just the two of them. Will wasn't one for big romantic gestures, not like Caroline's Bart. Harriet had felt, since he and Caroline got together, a little jealous of the gifts he lavished on her and the trips he booked. She knew she shouldn't feel like that – god knew Caroline deserved to be the one in the spotlight for once – but somehow the balance of things between the two women had shifted when Bart came along, and Caroline's new-found love life had brought out unworthy, prickly feelings in Harriet.

'You'll see,' he had said. 'Patience.'

She had kissed him, hard, and the cab driver had giggled mischievously. 'And don't look in the suitcase for clues,' Will warned her, through her kisses. 'There aren't any bikinis to give the game away, so don't get too excited. All the relevant info's in here,' and he patted his breast pocket, reaching his arm out and fending off her attempts to slide her hand in. 'Back off, you hussy. Off! Or we're going nowhere.' And he had laughed and winked at her.

'Paris!' she'd shrieked as they rounded the corner by St Pancras. 'We're going to Paris, aren't we? Oh Will. Oh my God. OhmyGodohmyGod. I can't believe it.' That was the first time she said it.

She was still saying it when they checked in at their hotel, and Will told her to shower and get changed for dinner, that he'd booked somewhere already, and that they'd have a drink beforehand in the bar downstairs, and then had changed his mind, and had waited until she was in the shower and then got undressed and got in with her, making love to her from behind as she held her hands flat against the glass walls, the hands that, despite her earlier disappointment, were sure to be adorned somewhat more impressively than they currently were by the end of the weekend. 'Screw cocktails in the bar,' he had said as he pushed inside her. 'I need to fuck you, very urgently.'

'Oh God,' she had murmured again, 'I can't believe it. Oh Will . . .'

They'd still made their dinner reservation, even if Harriet's hair was slightly damp and she was a little flustered and flushed as she ordered them a platter of seafood to start with in perfect French, which had made Will raise an eyebrow lasciviously.

'You'd better watch out, Miss Bailey,' he had said in a low voice, 'or you're going to turn me on so much I'll be forced to do something unmentionable underneath this starched white tablecloth.'

She'd raised an eyebrow, and said, '*Je suis désolé*, Monsieur Erskine,' and he had groaned.

A stiff-looking Frenchwoman with a severe haircut at the next-door table had looked appalled at her accent, but she didn't care. She didn't care about anything, because she was here, with Will, and he had planned it all and he was so gorgeous, and she was so happy, and by the end of the weekend she would be engaged to be married, engaged to be the future Mrs William Erskine, she was sure of it, because you didn't take someone to Paris on their birthday when you had been together for as long as they had and not propose, did you?

'I can't believe it,' she said to Caroline, on the Tuesday after they got back. She had emailed and demanded Caroline meet her for a drink after work, and Caroline had realised from the terse brevity of the message that it would not be a celebratory one. They met at a bar near Harriet's office, behind Selfridges.

'I can't *fucking* believe it. What sort of a man takes his girlfriend to Paris, on her thirty-first birthday, when he is well aware that she is hoping he will shortly pull his fucking finger out, and *doesn't* propose to her. I mean, really?'

'Oh darling. I'm so sorry. It must have been so disappointing.'

'It was! All weekend I was waiting for him to do it. Thinking, is he going to take me to the top of the Eiffel Tower and ask there, is he going to go down on one knee in a restaurant, will he ask when it's just us, in the hotel? And then getting to the end of the weekend, and the train journey home, and he was all pleased with himself and full of it, and I had to pretend to be so happy and say what a wonderful time I'd had, and all I could think was you shit, you absolute shit.'

Harriet reached the end of her sentence, and her tether, and burst into tears. Caroline held her hand as she sobbed.

'I'm so sorry. Oh Hats, I feel awful.'

'It's not your . . . fault . . .'

'But I totally jumped to conclusions. I shouldn't have said anything. Izzy was right.'

Harriet stopped sobbing for a second. 'Izzy?'

Caroline looked guilty. 'I told her what Will had said.'

Harriet moaned. 'So everyone knows. Caro*line*.'

'I'm sorry. Stella doesn't know.'

'Great.'

'Hats, Izzy loves you. She's sad for you.'

Harriet's face was sulky. 'I know. Ugh. I'm being a bitch. But – she's just so perfect, you know? I can't bear her feeling sorry for me. I'm such a disaster compared to her. Compared to all of you. Even Stella.'

Caroline raised an eyebrow, and Harriet laughed. She had calmed down now, and she lit a cigarette.

'Sorry. Sorry to go on. It's not your fault, darling. I would have assumed the same thing, and I probably wouldn't have been able to keep my big mouth shut either. How's Bart?'

Caroline smiled. 'He's fine, thanks. We're fine. But Hats, listen, have you talked to Will? Have you told him how you feel?'

Harriet shook her head and wiped her eyes with her napkin. 'How could I? "Thanks so much for these amazing diamond earrings, and a trip to Paris, both of which must have cost you a bomb, and all my other presents, but actually it's not good enough, I wanted a ring." I couldn't. I'd sound like such a spoilt cow. Who am I kidding? I *am* such a spoilt cow.'

'You're not. Don't say that. You're just . . .'

'Desperate. A desperate cliché.'

Harriet inhaled a mouthful of smoke and looked away as

she exhaled it. On the other side of the table, Caroline took a deep breath.

'Well, if you are, I am as well.'

Harriet glanced at her, cynical. 'Why?'

Caroline's eyes rested on the glass in front of her for a moment before looking up at her friend. 'Because I've done seventeen pregnancy tests in the last three months. Because . . .' she lowered her voice, 'I've given my husband thrush, we've been having sex so much over a few days when it's the right time. Because I haven't had a proper coffee since March, or more than one glass of wine at a time, and I've spent hundreds of pounds on vitamins and acupuncture and reflexology and I've even considered going to see a psychic healer who claims to be able to unblock negative energy around your ovaries, and I'm still not pregnant.'

'God, Caz, I'm so sorry. I didn't know. Well, I knew, of course. But I didn't know it was that bad. Jesus.'

Caroline nodded. 'It's bad.'

'Have you had, you know? Tests?'

'Bart won't. Don't . . .' She held up her hand to silence what she knew was a tirade of defensive anger about to gush forth from Harriet. She didn't have the energy for it. 'Don't, please. I know, I know. But he won't. I'm working on him.' Harriet bit her tongue.

'And it feels like there are pregnant women everywhere I look, all waddling and uncomfortable and happy, and I want that so much, and women pushing babies around in buggies and meeting up for coffees and they're everywhere, I can't go anywhere without looking for them, now, it's mental. I get on the tube and I used to do that thing where you scan the carriage and work out how much fatter you are than the other women?' Harriet nodded in recognition. 'Now I scan the carriage and see how many women are standing up holding their hands over their stomach or with a baby in a sling.'

'I look for engagement rings,' Harriet said, laughing sadly as she lifted her glass to her mouth.

'Christ,' Caroline said. 'We're tragic. How did this happen?'

Harriet shrugged, glumly. 'Bloody men. Bloody love.'

Chapter Seven

November 2008

Izzy stood behind the counter of Pearl's Place, pouring home-made lemonade into glass milk bottles with tops like Kilner jars, before sealing and labelling them. They were part of a new children's lunch-box deal she was trialling – a bottle of the sweetly sour drink, a sandwich, a squidgy brownie or flapjack and a little bag of crudités with a pot of hummus, for a snack. She was selling them in old-fashioned brown paper bags covered with stickers. She hoped they worked. The carb-free lunches were going quite well, certainly helped along by the rave review in the local glossy mag that was delivered to all the houses in the area, but the takeout side of the business was slow to get started. She was trying to think of more ideas, new ways of enticing not just her friends but real customers in away from the Tesco Metro around the corner and the bakery down the hill. She'd been wondering about a breakfast delivery service on weekend mornings, taking bacon and sausage doorstep sandwiches and fresh coffee and juice to those who were too hung-over or child-beleaguered to make it out of the house. The problem was getting someone reliable enough to do the early morning shift and take charge of the food at that time – she couldn't do it herself; that, she thought, really would be a deal-breaker for James, whose patience for lying next to her in bed while she scribbled out new menus and went through wholesale order forms was beginning to wear a little thin.

Mind you, so was her patience for coming home to find him sitting in front of *Neighbours*, eating bags of crisps like a student, with his laptop perched on his knee. Oh, it wasn't his fault that he hadn't found a new job yet, 'in the current climate' and all that. But she couldn't help but blame him a little. Surely it couldn't be *that* hard to find something? Even now, people must still be hiring. What was he doing wrong?

Izzy sighed. Best not examined too closely, she thought, scrunching the tops of the paper bags up, like much of the vagaries of marriage that resided in the saucepan-grey area between happiness and boredom, contentment and irritation. Best to just get on. It weighed on her, though. James took care of the money, but she was sure that they couldn't have too much more in the way of savings, what with the amount she'd ploughed into the café, and everything else. She wiped the counter down with a J Cloth and began stacking the bags into a plastic crate, ready to carry out to the car.

'I'll take that for you.'

She looked up, although she didn't really need to – she knew perfectly well who the voice belonged to. Standing in front of her was confirmation. Stephen Garside. Despite herself, she blushed, and then silently cursed herself for doing so. He smiled a little, and she knew he had noticed the rush of blood to her cheeks that his presence had sparked.

'There's no need, thanks.' She busied herself lifting the crate and walked over to the door, passing by him as she went. He smelt of expensive cologne and new cars.

He shrugged, and opened the door for her, following her as she headed towards her Volvo. 'I was going to email your husband,' he said, walking alongside her, hands in his pockets. She didn't reply. 'And invite the two of you over.'

'I'm sure he'd like that. You've got his email address, I assume?' she replied. She felt uncomfortable, aware that she was being short, rude even. She couldn't help it. She couldn't say anything else, because something inside her didn't trust herself to do so.

'I thought maybe Will and his girlfriend as well.'

'Harriet.' Izzy nodded briefly and balanced the crate on top of her car as she clicked the button on her keys that controlled the central locking.

'Ah yes. Harriet. I've been thinking about investing in Will's company. He's pretty sharp.'

Izzy turned. 'How do you know Will?'

'We went for a pint the other day. He and James and I. The City's a small place. We know lots of the same people. Bumped into one another. James was having some meeting.'

A meeting, Izzy thought. An interview? She didn't know. She was trying not to ask James too much; about his job search; she could see his defences rise every time she did. Well. Maybe he had got an interview. Maybe there would be good news.

As she went to open the boot of the car, leaving the crate on the roof, Stephen Garside grabbed her wrist. She stopped. 'I didn't want to email your husband. I wanted to see you.'

Izzy paused for a moment. It was the first time they had touched. And there was a heat to it that whispered to her: *This is the first time, not the only time. This is the start of something.* She pulled her arm away as though she could quiet the voice by doing so. Her hand shook as she slid the tray of bags into the back of her car and shut the boot on them.

'Well, I'm very flattered,' she said, determinedly keeping her voice light. Don't make a big deal out of this. He probably does it to every slightly bored-looking married woman he comes across. Don't make it into a big thing when it isn't.

She began to walk back to the café, forcing herself to think of work, not the feeling of Stephen Garside's eyes on her as she went. She had to lock up and then take the sandwich bags to the party one of her neighbours was having for one of her four children – she'd agreed to provide them as a sort of market research, see how they went down with the kids and hope that, if they liked them, she'd be able to build on that with their parents. If it went well, she planned to bring in a system where people could order the lunch bags in advance for the coming week, for however many days they liked; she had a rolling menu of fillings so that they didn't get the same things day in, day out. She thought quite a lot of the mothers would welcome the opportunity to stop making sandwiches every evening, and remembering to get lunch-box treats delivered with the weekly Ocado order.

As she opened the café door and went in through it, Stephen Garside touched her again. This time it was his hand on her shoulder, and she wanted to jerk around and tell him, indignantly, not to touch her, but she couldn't. She couldn't move. So she just stood for a few seconds, not turning, not speaking, not even breathing, just feeling the weight of his hand through her cotton sweater, and wishing, despite herself, that it was on bare skin.

Eventually she turned to him and he let his hand fall to his side.

'So. Will you come to dinner? Or am I going to have to have some boring email conversation with James about work before asking him instead?'

His expression was determined, his eyes clear in their intention. Izzy's loyalty to James finally sprang up inside her.

'It wouldn't need to be boring,' she said. 'My husband is

actually a very entertaining correspondent.' The words sounded ridiculous as soon as they came out of her mouth. Stephen Garside raised his eyebrows in amusement.

'Well I'm sure he is, ma'am,' he said, in a drawl, and doffed an imaginary cap at her.

'He is! He's clever man. And funny. And very good at his job.' Oh God, Izzy, shut up. You're not his personal PR girl, you're his wife.

Stephen Garside held up his hands, acquiescing. 'All right, all right. I'll email James. The boys will correspond. You never know. Maybe something good will come out of it for him, job-wise.'

Izzy didn't reply, but she said a silent prayer. *Please let James get a brilliant job, and please don't let it be working for this man*, she wished, as she nodded and tried to look pleased. *I don't think I could bear it, the thought of it.*

'I'm glad I saw you,' he said, quietly. Then he leaned forward and she wondered if he was going to kiss her. And was terrified by the realisation that she wanted him to try, even as she took a step backwards and turned her head away.

'Yes, it was lovely to see you again as well,' she said brightly. 'I must get on. But I look forward to dinner.' She gave him an impersonal smile. The one he gave her in return was knowing.

Eventually he turned and walked out of the door, raising a hand in farewell as he went, without saying another word. And finally Izzy could breathe again.

When she got home, James was there, a bottle of wine open, a smile on his face. That was a pleasant surprise.

She dropped her gym bag by the washing machine in the utility room and gave him a quick kiss. 'I've ordered the curry,' he said. 'Will's getting here in quarter of an hour.'

'Great.' She poured a glass of wine for herself and topped

him up. 'I'm going to take this up to the bath,' she said, holding her glass in the air. 'You guys can have a bit of time together first. I'll be down soon. You seem chirpy. Good job news?' She crossed her fingers automatically. Please let him have got an interview, she thought as she walked down the hall towards the stairs.

'Maybe. Just maybe. Stephen Garside emailed me. He's asked us to dinner in a couple of weeks. Said he's having some people round: us, Will and Harriet, a few others. Bit of a pre-Christmas do. Great, huh?' His voice was excited, and Izzy stopped in the hallway. She had already kicked her trainers off, and her feet were bare on the cream carpet. She dug her toes into its thick fibres as though it would somehow ground her. Of course. She had known the email would come. Stephen Garside was obviously not a man who didn't follow through with what he said he was going to do. But somehow it still felt like a shock, still discomforted her. Stephen Garside had never stepped foot inside their home, and yet somehow he was here now, inside the walls. Inside their marriage.

'What did you say?' she asked, lightly, her hand on the banister.

James stuck his head around the corner. 'I said we'd love to, of course.'

'I don't want to go.'

'What?' His expression was incredulous. There was no note of suspicion in his voice; no reason had occurred to him why they should not go and worship at the court of Stephen Garside.

'He's brash. Arrogant. I don't like him. I don't think we should make friends with him.

James shook his head. 'He's one of the best traders in London – in the world, maybe. He's a big deal.'

Izzy shrugged. 'Doesn't mean I have to like him.'

James looked confused, hurt even, and Izzy's heart contracted.

'You don't have to. But we're going to dinner. I already said yes.'

'Right. Make sure you put it in the diary, then,' she said as she went upstairs, her heart thudding.

'Iz. What's the problem? Come on. You know we have to go. I need a job. He could help me. Maybe even offer me something himself – you never know what might happen, right?'

James's voice was so hopeful, so desperate for her approval. She couldn't bear it. She turned at the top of the stairs, and pursed her lips into a kiss. 'Don't worry. I know. We'll go, I'll be nice. You're right. You never know what might come of it.'

James had agreed to meet Cass at the Oriel, by Sloane Square station, at five o'clock. He'd arranged for Pearl and Alfie to stay at their nursery until seven, rather than picking them up at three as he usually did now. Izzy's nanny-share idea had been shelved, and James was a full-time parent. He wasn't mad about it – could see now what Izzy had meant about the tedium of looking after small children all day, even with the break that the nursery provided him. But they couldn't afford to do anything else, so that was what they had decided. They could afford even less than Izzy realised. James was struggling to keep the dire state of their finances from her, so every saving counted. They couldn't really afford the nursery, either, but Izzy hadn't wanted to disrupt the children's routine any more than necessary, and it meant that James had time to look for jobs and go to interviews.

Not that there were many of those around. He had been searching and searching for a new job, calling in every favour that he could think of, asking friends and old colleagues and people he had met at dinner parties who hardly remembered him. It was humiliating, and worse, it was futile. A few of them had sounded positive to start with, had asked him to send his CV over. But none of the openings had come to anything. He couldn't understand it. 'In the present climate,' people said, apologetically, 'we just can't overstretch ourselves . . . take any risks at all . . . So sorry, sure you'll find something soon.' And he would smile, and say he understood, and go away and wonder what it was that he had said or done that had put them off, or whether there really were simply no jobs to be had. His confidenece was shot.

Still, the nursery was coming in useful today, and the manager had happily extended the hours for him at short notice. 'Always a pleasure, looking after your two,' she had said, smiling her wholesome smile. 'Especially Pearl, she always makes me laugh. I remember when she first came in here. Charged straight up to me and demanded that I play ring-a-ring-a-roses with her, because it was her favourite, and she wasn't staying unless I could do it properly. She's a caution, your eldest.'

His eldest. It was strange how the re-entrance of Amanda into his life, bringing with her Cass, had realigned how he had to think of his family. Pearl was no longer his eldest child, his firstborn; Cass had taken that title from her, without her even knowing. She was no longer his only daughter; Izzy was no longer the only mother of his children. Not that she knew that, of course, and not that he meant for her to find out. He couldn't bear for her to have that knowledge ripped from her. It would matter to Izzy, very much, he knew that. That she had not been the first to bear his child, not the first that he had created life with. It mattered to him as well, of course, but not in the same way. It was different for men.

It had been two months since Amanda had followed him from work that day. Getting on for six years since he had first heard from her, and learned of the existence of Cass. He felt a bit ashamed of himself that it had taken so long to get to the point where he had agreed to meet her. But no, he had not been ready to do so before. Hadn't been able to get his head around the idea. It was better, for everyone, that he had done exactly as he had done, and waited until now. Cass was older, she would be easier to talk to, she would understand the pressures he had been facing and the reasons why he had not been a part of her life until now.

He walked up the escalator and out into the street. The news-stand to his right held rails of thick glossy magazines, their headlines designed to appeal to teenage girls like his daughter, and he paused and looked at them: '101 ways to wear the new citrus brights', '32 reasons why he didn't call', '99 things you can do to look slimmer NOW!' What was it with magazines and numbers? Everything could be turned into a list. He looked at the covers again. He should take her a gift, he thought. He had time – he was early, as usual. That was what he would do. He would go down the King's Road and get her a present, something pretty to be wrapped up in tissue paper and a little bag that he could give to her. She would like that.

'What is it?' Cass asked, looking at the bright pink Whistles bag that James had placed proudly on the table in front of her. He was pleased with his purchase: it was a soft cotton scarf in a sharp lime green with a sequinned and embroidered trim that the assistant had assured him would be perfect for 'a trendy teen'. Or he had been pleased with it, at least, till he had seen Cass, dressed in a black leather biker jacket and leopardskin leggings, and big work boots that looked like something a scaffolder would wear, rather than a Bambi-legged teenage girl. Her eyes were aggressively lined with kohl and her hair was big and unruly, despite being straight. It had the attitude of curls without the ringlets. He was rather scared of her, he realised, as he put the bag between them, grateful for something to do with his hands, and pulled out the chair on the other side of the table. *She looks older than she really is*, Amanda had warned him in her email. *She's all bolshie and independent on the outside, and scared little girl on the inside. Look after her.*

James tried to remember this as Cass stared uncompromisingly at him from across the table. 'It's – it's a scarf,' he said. 'I think you'll like it. You can change it, of course, if you don't.' Thank God he'd got the gift receipt; there was no way she was going to wear the one he'd picked out. He'd seen an animal print one of some kind, though, he thought; maybe that would be better. 'Anyhow. It's just something small.'

'Why?' She sipped her coffee, which she had already ordered when James arrived, and continued to gaze at him. She hadn't got up to greet him, yet. He sat, and looked around for a waiter. He noticed she was drinking it short and black. When he was her age, he had only just graduated to milky tea, he thought, then stopped himself. Saying, or even thinking things like 'when I was your age' was a surefire route to sounding like an old git.

'I just thought you might like it,' he replied. The girl's cool, even cold gaze was making him feel distinctly uncomfortable.

'But you don't know what I like. What made you think I'd like this?' She deigned to peer inside the bag, and as soon as she caught sight of the scarf's bright fabric, one side of her mouth lifted in a sneer, as though an invisible wire had tugged it from underneath her skin.

'OK, it was the wrong thing to choose.' James attempted a smile. 'I'm not up on what the young are into.' The young. Christ, he sounded like his father. He'd be telling her about what it was like before the Internet or something soon, just to bang the final nail into the coffin of their relationship before it had even begun.

'A scarf doesn't make you my dad, you know,' she said quietly, as she stood, pulling her jacket around her.

'Don't leave,' he said quickly. 'God, Cass, I'm sorry, I've got it all wrong, I know, but give me a chance, eh? I am trying.' He stood before her, useless, panicked. Amanda would kill him if she found out that he'd screwed up their first meeting so badly that his daughter had left after only five minutes.

Cass gave him a scathing look. 'I'm going upstairs, for a cigarette,' she said, the top lip curling upwards again, but this time with a hint of amusement behind it. A challenge, maybe? Was she pushing to see whether he would try and stop her?

I'm not falling into that little trap, young lady, he thought to himself. I may seem like a past-it old twat to you, but I'm not as stupid as I look.

'OK. I'll order more coffee,' he said casually. 'Want some chips?'

Her eyes flicked back to him briefly. Ha. Cake or ice cream she would have refused, spurned as being sugary, bad for you, childish treats. But chips, no teenager he had met yet could refuse. She shrugged.

'Whatever.'

James watched her leave, and smiled. OK, he thought, I do know something about you. You're like your father. Can't say no to chips. And that, he thought to himself, was a start.

'I saw her today.' James spoke quietly into his mobile as he stood in the kitchen back at home. Izzy was upstairs, bathing the children. He went to the fridge and took out a beer. Will was the only person he had told about Cass. He'd had to talk to someone about it, and if it couldn't be Izzy, which it couldn't, then it would be Will.

'And? How did it go?'

James stood by the French windows and looked out into the garden. The magnolia that they had planted when they moved in was flowering, and Izzy's herbs were lined up in terracotta pots near the doors. Chives, thyme, coriander, parsley. A rosemary bush and a bay tree. She used something from the garden most days, when she was making dinner.

'Don't think we're going to be doing any father–daughter three-legged races any time soon. She . . .' James paused. 'She's kind of terrifying.'

Will laughed. 'She's a teenager.'

'Yes, but she's my daughter. Surely there should be some sort of . . . I don't know. Amnesty?'

'What, after you haven't been around her whole life? Yeah, right. You must remember how long teenagers can hold a grudge for.'

'I guess so. Anyhow. I'll see you later at Stephen's.'

'Yes. The big dinner. Could be good for you. Jobwise.'

'And you? Maybe he'll invest a pile of cash in your timeshare swindle.'

'Ha ha. Yeah, well. Let's hope the golden boy takes a shine to us all, eh?'

I saw her today. Izzy had been at the top of the stairs when she heard. About to get in the shower, get dressed and ready to go out. She was taking her earrings out, dressing gown around her shoulders, padding silently along the landing. She only heard because James was standing near the kitchen door as he closed it. 'I saw her today.' And then the click of the door shutting.

A lump began to form in her stomach, a hard lump of disappointment, mostly, and anger, and sadness, and humiliation. He wasn't referring to a friend, or a random colleague, she could tell. There was an affectionate and, also, a confessional tone to her husband's voice that she knew well. It was how he had sounded when he had admitted to her that he had lost a load of money on some stupid investment in a llama farm a few years ago; it was how he had sounded at the Eurostar when he had told her he'd forgotten his passport just before they were all due to go to Disneyland Paris. It was how he sounded when he knew he was in the wrong and was anticipating admonishment.

I saw her today. Will, of course he was telling Will. The keepers of one another's secrets. God only knew what little lies and not so little ones the two of them had hidden for each other over the years. And now. The worst sort. Oh God. Oh GodohGodohGodohGod. How far had it gone? It might not be a full-blown affair, she told herself, it might be something he was putting a stop to. I saw her today to call it off? To tell her no? If only she had stayed and listened for longer, but she hadn't been able to, had instinctively turned away and rushed back into her bedroom as soon as she had heard those words. *I saw her today.* When, when had he seen her? At lunchtime? After work? At the office – was she someone he worked with? Shit. Shit, shit, shit.

'All I'm saying is, don't jump to conclusions.' Stella handed Izzy a joint. 'And smoke this.' They were in the alley behind Izzy's café, leaning against the wall like truanting teenagers.

'Stell, I can't, I have to go home and get ready for this dinner.'

'OK. But you're got five minutes. So. You think he's been having an affair.'

Izzy shrugged and took a drag of Stella's joint. 'I don't know. What do you think? It doesn't really sound like James, does it?'

'No. But then . . . you never know. People do all sorts of things that you wouldn't expect.'

Izzy laughed. 'Thanks a lot. I feel so reassured.'

Stella made a face. 'Sorry, lovely. But it's better to know. Take it from me.'

Izzy nodded. 'What's happening with that?'

'It's still going on.'

'What are you going to do about it?'

Stella looked pained. Izzy had never seen her like this before.

She and Johnny's relationship had always been unconventional; Izzy and the girls had never understood it. But it had always appeared to work for them, so she had stopped herself from passing judgement on Johnny's dalliances. This was different, though. Stella was different.

'I don't know. Nothing, at the moment. There's no point backing him into a corner.' She shook her head.

'Have you talked to Harriet about it?'

'No. Well, yes, of course, but not recently.' She blinked. 'Let's not discuss it. You need to decide what you're going to do, more urgently.'

'Try and find out what's going on? I don't know, Stell. What should I do? What *can* I do? If he is having an affair, I mean. What are my options?'

Stella looked at Izzy and held the joint out to her once more, but Izzy shook her head. 'OK. You want to know, really?'

Izzy paused. 'Yes.'

'It's like when something catches fire on the stove. You can wait for it to burn out, and take the risk that it might not. That it might get bigger, and burn the kitchen down. Or you can do something to try and put it out yourself. And take the risk that you might get burned.'

Izzy and James stood on the steps of Southern Lodge, listening as a set of footsteps tapped down the hall towards them, behind the large, heavy black front door. James held a boxed bottle of Veuve tucked into the crook of his right arm; Izzy wore a black wrap dress with a heavy silver necklace and slim-heeled shoes. She took a breath. Suddenly, she felt nervous. James reached for her hand, and she let him take it. He gave it a squeeze, and her a little smile. 'All right?' She nodded.

She hadn't said anything to James about what she had overheard. Had just returned home, showered, and let the water wash her tears down the plughole. She hadn't spoken to Caroline, because she was James's sister, and she didn't want to force her into a difficult position. And she hadn't spoke to Harriet, because she was Caroline's best friend, and always had been, and Izzy never quite trusted that Harriet's loyalties were as evenly distributed between the four women as she claimed. Stella had been the right choice. Stella understood.

She had gone through her usual ritual of make-up and hair and dressing. But she had attended to every stage of it with slightly more care than usual. Had changed the dress she was going to wear at the last minute from a plain silk tunic to a wrap dress that hugged her curves, its fabric clingy and soft. Harriet and Will were running late.

'Welcome!' Stephen Garside stood before them, and she noticed his eyes take her in.

'Lovely, thanks so much for the fizz,' he said, putting the box down on a side table and leading them through a door to his right. 'Come through, there's a couple of chaps I'd like you to meet.'

James bounded forward, keen to be launched into the group of movers and shakers. Izzy watched him go. As Stephen led her husband up to a corpulent American man, he looked back towards her, and, his hand on her husband's shoulder, winked at her. She stared back at him, unsure how to respond. Was it a wink of complicity? A promise? A threat? She couldn't be sure. But something about it – about him – made her nervous.

The food was unlike anything Izzy had seen for a long time. Garside had obviously chucked some serious cash at the evening. Who was he trying to impress? She was desperate to make notes, but had to settle for trying to fix each course in her memory as it was placed in front of her. It was all whimsy and invention, a procession of dishes that showed off the skill of the chef. At the expense of the satisfaction of the diners? she wondered. Each was beautiful, exquisite, comprised of the finest ingredients, but was it somehow all a little lacking in soul?

Still, she gazed at the elegant plate that was arriving in front of her now – a rich man's cheese on toast, a small lump of truffled Brie melting enticingly on a small square of brioche, served with a little checked paper napkin underneath it. Izzy picked it up and popped it into her mouth in one. The woman sitting across from her, on the other side of the table, raised her eyebrows in surprise, or would have done had her brow not been so frozen by Botox that it would not move, and covered her portion with its napkin. Izzy contemplated reaching across and swiping it from the superior cow's plate, but the table was just too wide. Instead, she smiled and pretended to listen as her two next-door neighbours continued to talk across her about some American bank. Izzy caught Harriet's eye over the table and suppressed a giggle.

She was a little drunk, she realised, as she watched the waiter replace her glass with a fresh one to go with the next course. Matching wines for each course, fancy fancy. Anger flared inside her as she looked over and saw James in deep conversation with Botox lady. Who did he think he was? How dare he be cheating on her? How sodding dare he? If anyone deserved to be having an affair, after five years of marriage, two children and countless sacrifices made, it was her. If she had had to place bets on either of them being the one to cheat, hand on heart, she would have said it would be her. She was the one who still got attention from other men, with reasonable regularity; she was the one who had been bored, at home, for years, and who still hadn't been bored enough to stray. She was the one who had remained loyal while he had weakened. If he had. Maybe . . . No. Don't kid yourself. Don't make excuses for what you heard, try and explain it away.

She pushed her chair back and excused herself. She needed some fresh air.

From the terrace, Izzy could see into the drawing room, where dinner was taking place. Candles flickered, glasses glowed, guests laughed. It was the perfect image, in the perfect setting. Protected and privileged. The outside world could not touch them here.

She really was drunk. She lit her cigarette and listened to the fizz of paper crackling as she inhaled. Behind her, he came out on to the terrace, as she had expected he would.

'That is one seriously ugly shirt,' she said, without turning round. Her words were rude but her voice was light Anyhow, it was true. His shirt was vile. Shot silk, a nasty shade of mauve. Green piping at the cufts. Flashy.

He laughed, softly. 'I don't have a wife to vet my wardrobe for me,' he said. 'That's the problem. James is lucky. Does he know it?'

She shrugged. 'Does anyone?'

'I would.'

Izzy didn't move. She could feel him coming closer. The air changed, very slightly, as he moved to within a metre of her, and then stopped.

'No you wouldn't,' she continued, keeping her voice amused. 'Not after a few years, a few hundred petty rows about loading the dishwasher, a handful of excruciating Christmases with the in-laws. You'd forget, in the end, that feeling of excitement, that certainty that you are in just the right place with just the right person, that rush of blood to your fingertips that makes them tingle when you're near them. You'd stop seeing the beauty of them and start to notice the crow's feet and cellulite; you'd stop thinking that everything they said was fascinating and funny and start to groan inside when they told the same joke for the fiftieth time and looked pleased with themselves as they did so. You'd get old. You'd be married. You'd be just like the rest of us.'

'And I'm not now?'

Izzy laughed, and sucked on her cigarette again as she turned to face Stephen. He stood, hands by his sides, lit up by the flares that stood in large pots around the terrace. 'No, you're not like any of us. You're separate. Can't you feel it?'

He nodded, slowly. 'Of course I can.' He paused, and reached out his hand. 'Got a spare one of those?' he asked, gesturing to her cigarette. She delved in her bag and handed him one. He lit it, staring at her all the time. 'Of course I can.'

'So why don't you do something about it?'

'There's only a certain amount I can do. Lots of people around here are going to see me as the hedge-fund guy who's swept in and bought a big house, and I can't really change that. I'm certainly not going to live in some little flat just so no one sees me as different to them. But I don't want to go and live in a mansion miles from anywhere where the only people you see are your staff. So I do what I can. Hold dinner parties, be nice to people, make friends . . .'

'Chat up their wives.' She bit her lip. She shouldn't have said that. He laughed.

'Mm. Maybe not so sensible, I admit. But I don't make a habit of it.' He had admitted it, then. Wasn't going to play dumb and pretend he wasn't making a play for her. Izzy breathed. She was on dangerous ground here, and she knew it.

'So why me, then? Do I look – what, available?' She turned away from him.

'Far from it.'

'A challenge?'

'Maybe. I don't know, Izzy, to be honest. I can't really tell you what it is.'

Now he was behind her, and his hand was very lightly touching her arm. 'But I can tell you that I want you. That I haven't been able to stop thinking about you since we met. That you're in my head, under my skin, in the back of my mind all the time. I want you, Izzy.'

'I'm happily married,' she said. But a shiver ran down her spine all the same.

He paused. 'You're certainly married,' he said. 'But are you happy? The café makes you happy, I can see it in your eyes. When you're there, when you talk about it. You fizz. It's – joyful.'

She blushed, without knowing why.

'But you don't have that same energy when you're with James, when you talk about it. You don't have that light in your eyes, and it's sad. And all I can think about, all I've been able to think about, is how happy I would be if I could somehow put that light into your eyes during the rest of your life. Not just when you're in the café, or thinking about the café, but maybe ... just maybe, when you were thinking about me.'

Izzy shook her head. She could not admit how much she had already been thinking of him. Not to anyone, and certainly not to him. She wanted to tell him, wanted to confide in him. Wanted to step closer to him and slide her hands under his jacket, and breathe him in. But she did not. And suddenly she felt angry. Who was this man to step into her life, uninvited, and start stirring it up? What right did he have to do this? She had no doubt that he had a string of women ready and waiting for him – why was he taunting her?

'Don't play games with me,' she said, sharply. 'You know, flirting is one thing, getting us over for dinner, putting on the charm, making James think he's in with a chance. I'm sure that's just how you operate, the world you live in. I know how you all think when you work in the City for long enough. People become commodities. Their lives are just numbers. Things to trade. But I don't live in that world. I won't live in it. So . . .' and her voice was trembling now, 'don't play with me. It's not fair. And it's not . . . it's not very nice.'

Stephen waited until it was obvious that she had finished her speech. Her breath was coming fast and hard. She felt as though she might cry. And when he finally spoke, his voice also had an edge of anger to it.

'You should know something about me, Mrs Rathbone,' he said, and she winced at the sound of her married name coming from his lips. 'Actually, two things. You should know two things about me.'

He took her hand in his. 'One, I don't play games.' And then he lifted it to his lips, and held it there.

'But I always win them.'

He kissed her fingertips, and let her hand drop. And then he walked away.

Chapter Eight

Christmas 2008

It wasn't the same. Christmas for Caroline was the family home. It always had been, and it always would be. Ginny still filling stockings for her and James, and then Izzy when she had come on to the scene, little presents wrapped in crunchy coloured paper – chocolate bars and novels and lipsticks, calculators and gadgets from the pound shop and those bath bombs that dissolved in the water and left a ring of sticky pink froth around the edge of the tub. It was champagne in front of the fire, which her father guarded like it was a newborn baby, constantly prodding and poking it whenever it looked in danger of settling down to some level less than raging. It was trays of Marks and Spencer's canapés, mini quiches and prawn wontons and smoked salmon pinwheels. It was being allowed to open one present on Christmas Eve, because that was tradition, one from under the tree, that you had to choose really carefully, because even if it was a disappointing one, you could not have another until the morning. It was her dad's bread sauce and her mum fretting about the roast potatoes not being crisp enough and there not being enough to eat, even though she had bought enough food to feed a hundred and they would be finding Stilton in their supper for months to come. It was the candles that

Ginny bought in bulk that smelt of oranges and cinnamon, and the children watching *The Snowman* on Christmas afternoon while the grown-ups dozed. It was walking Mr Butterworth on the Common wearing the new collar that he was given every year, it was crackers and sitting up late with James drinking port (him) and amaretto (her), it was squealing, wriggling children and leftovers and family.

That was what she had always known, what she had done every year for the last thirty-one years, that was just what Christmas was. Except this year, it wasn't. This year, Christmas was a smart hotel in the Alps with just her and Bart, and no stockings, because they were giving one another just one proper present each, and one small one; they had agreed weeks ago that that was what they would do, and it had seemed all very sensible. 'We don't want to lug a load of crap over there that we just have to bring back again,' Bart had pointed out, and Caroline had agreed, and got him a new watch, and a book that she knew he had been wanting to read, and resisted the urge to buy him a smart navy blue handmade felt stocking that she had seen in Liberty and fill it with treats. She looked at his expensively wrapped presents now, nestled in the drawer she had taken over in their hotel room for her underwear, and thought sadly how joyless they looked compared to the pile of brightly, tackily wrapped gifts she would have got him had they been at home in London.

The hotel was doing a special dinner as it was Christmas Eve, and that was when the main celebration was here. All the children staying had been on a snowy moonlit walk through the woods to find Father Christmas, and as Caroline looked out of the window she could see them tramping back through the snow, their way lit by lanterns, their bodies solid in snowsuits and mittens that grasped their gifts, little puffs of excited breath bobbing along before them. In an hour there would be drinks downstairs, champagne cocktails and canapés in the drawing room, and then dinner, a thirteen-course banquet that the owner of the hotel had told her the chefs had been working on for weeks. Caroline had smiled politely, and said that it sounded wonderful, and it did: she had seen the menu, and it was all very impressive. But it wasn't home. It wasn't Christmas.

She picked up the phone and dialled her parents' number. Bart was in the sauna downstairs, sweating off a hard day's skiing and preparing for a long evening of eating and drinking. She hadn't seen him all day; he had been skiing the black runs at the top of the mountain with a group of men he'd made friends with, while she had been with a private instructor on some of the easier trails. Caroline was a perfectly good skier, but a nervous one – she had found herself getting more and more anxious as she got older. She sighed as she watched the children make their way indoors. This was a place to stay with a family, really. Maybe they would come back in a few years with their own children, when she could take little people tobogganing and enrol them in ski school, when she could watch her own son or daughter's face light up as they discovered 'Papa Noel' in the woods with a pile of gifts and a real reindeer . . .

'Hello?' Caroline pulled her attention to the phone.

'Hi, Mummy. It's me.'

'Darling!' Ginny's voice got quieter as she turned away from the handset and called the others. 'Darling, James, it's Caro. Pick up the other extension.'

Caroline could hear Pearl in the background. 'I most definitely will not have a bath because I might miss Father Christmas and then I would cry and cry and it would ALL BE YOUR FAULT, Mummy, and you would have RUINED CHRISTMAS . . .'

'What are you doing?' she asked, knowing what the answer would be.

'Oh, the usual. I'm peeling the veg for tomorrow while your father tries to beat Izzy at Scrabble. He's doing appallingly and being a very bad sport about it.'

Caroline grinned. Her father was a terrible loser.

'We're having lasagne for supper.'

'*Really?*' Caroline joked. They always had lasagne for supper on Christmas Eve. But her mother didn't get it.

'Yes, it's so easy, because I can make it in advance and freeze it – I made this one in November!' She sounded pleased with herself.

'Well done, Mum, sounds great.'

'Never mind all that, what are you doing? Are you having a wonderful time? It must be so romantic.'

'All right, sis?' James picked up the other extension. 'Can't believe you've forsaken the delights of watching Iz kick Dad's arse at Scrabble for some poxy five-star hotel. Foolish.'

Caroline laughed, but as she did so, tears came to her eyes. 'Yes, I'm having a wonderful time,' she said, trying to sound sincere. 'It's the most beautiful place, and yes, it's terribly romantic.' She looked around the hotel room, with its four-poster bed and overstuffed chairs, and wished she was curled up in her usual armchair in the corner of her parents' living room.

'Magical, really. Yes, wonderful food, I've eaten much too much. Diet starts in January.' Her voice sounded forced and overly jolly.

'Look, I must go,' she said. 'I have to get ready for dinner. I just wanted to say hi. Give the littles a kiss from me.'

'They're opening your presents tonight,' James said. 'Pearl insisted. They miss you.'

Oh God. That was it. She couldn't help herself. 'I miss them, as well,' she said, bursting into tears. 'I miss all of you.'

Just then, the door opened and Bart appeared, his face pink and damp from the steam rooms.

'Darling? Are you all right?' Her mother sounded concerned.

'I'm fine, fine, having such a lovely time. I'll see you in a few days, we'll call tomorrow, bye, bye.' She hurriedly put the phone down and wiped her face with her hand, but it was too late, Bart had seen the tears.

'Caro? What's the matter, angel?'

She stood, snuffling the tears away, and went over to him. 'Just being silly. Nothing, I'm fine. Good sauna? We should start to think about getting dressed.'

Bart took her by the elbow. 'There's no rush. What's the matter? Why were you crying?'

His voice wasn't as sympathetic as Caroline might have expected, and she looked up at him, wanting his approval and comfort. 'I said, just being silly. Sudden attack of homesickness. That's all.'

She kissed his neck, but he pulled away.

'Bart? What?'

He shook his head. 'I can't believe it.'

'What can't you believe?'

'How . . . I should have known. I should have known nothing I could do could ever be good enough.'

'Bart, baby, what are you talking about? I don't—'

'I planned everything. I paid for everything. I brought you here, to the best hotel in the Alps, an award-winning hotel, and you're homesick. You'd rather be back in London.'

Caroline wrapped her arms around her waist. 'I wouldn't rather be in London, I wouldn't rather be anywhere,' she protested. 'I just had a moment of feeling – sad. That's all.'

She stepped forward and put her hands on his shoulders. They were stiff and unyielding.

'I miss them, that's all. It's Christmas. They're my family. It doesn't mean I wouldn't rather be here . . .'

Caroline stopped in mid-sentence, and it took her a moment

to realise why her words had stopped forming. Then her mind caught up with her body, and she took it in. It was because Bart's hand had struck her, across her face, across her mouth, and her head had turned to the side, into her shoulder.

'Oh,' was all she could say. And then, 'Oh dear.'

There was a loud smack, as Bart's hand slammed into the wall, and she winced and stumbled backwards. But it was not her that he had hit this time. Just the first time. Just the once.

'Fuck,' he shouted, and she whimpered. 'Fucking hell, Caro. Why did you have to do that?'

She didn't say anything, and he groaned. 'Why did you have to do that?' he said again, quietly this time, as though he were talking to himself. And then he pulled her towards him, wrapping his big arms around her and stroking her hair, muttering, 'I'm sorry, I'm so sorry, angel, my angel, I just wanted everything to be perfect,' and she found herself comforting him, and kissing his arms, and whispering, 'It's all right, I'm fine. I'm fine, I love you, I love you,' and letting him kiss her face, her eyes and cheeks and then her lips, his tears falling like an absolution on to the place where his hand had landed and then his lip seeking hers, hot and urgent, and she let him kiss and stroke her and take her, on the edge of the bed, his need for forgiveness so great that she could do nothing other than give it, give him what he needed, give him herself, give him everything. And afterwards she let him run her a bath, and fill it with scented oil, and wrap her in a hot fluffy towel, and call her his angel. And it was all right again, because he was her husband, he was the one she had chosen, and she had to make it all right, because who else was going to? And she knew that he loved her. All the time, as he was bathing her, and getting her dress out of the wardrobe, and giving her her Christmas present early, a pair of beautiful diamond earrings that he wanted her to wear that evening, he was telling her that he loved her. He loved her.

Christmas Day for the Rathbones was quieter than usual. Ginny was distracted, not entirely there. Julian assumed that she was missing Caroline.

But they both jollied things along, for the sake of the children, whose Christmas was already looking a bit thin on the ground, present-wise. Julian and Ginny had bulked out their stockings, despite protests from Izzy. 'Christmas isn't just about presents, Ginny, they must learn that. Things are difficult at the moment. It's just the way it is.'

'Yes,' she had said, 'you're quite right, they must learn. But in time. They're still so tiny. Let me spoil them. Please.'

Izzy had given in, and Ginny had gone shopping, stocking up on treats.

Ginny wasn't the only one who was distracted, though. James and Izzy were walking on eggshells, both treading around one another. Both keeping their own counsel, their own worries. Their own secrets.

In the morning, after Pearl and Alfie had torn open their stocking presents and eaten chocolate coins for breakfast before collapsing in front of one of their new DVDs, Izzy had snuck out of the house, on the pretext of taking Mr Butterworth to get some fresh air. It was stuffy inside, Bart and Caroline weren't there to provide distractions, Ginny was fretting in the kitchen, and James was skulking around looking like a spare part. Probably adding up the cost of everything, she thought.

But really, she went outside so that she had an opportunity to open the little package that had arrived for her at the café, wrapped in beautiful thick paper, a small card attached to it, and which she had hidden in her jacket pocket as she slid the lead on to Mr Butterworth's collar.

Happy Christmas, Izzy, the card read. *I tried to find something beautiful that you could wear that wouldn't look like an expensive bauble and attract attention. The subterfuge of it all was quite exciting. I hope I've succeeded, and that you like it. Love, SG.*

She opened the box. Inside was a plain ring made from a silver-coloured metal. It was chunky, and the top of it was thick. She ran her thumb around it, and found a small hinge on the inside. She pressed on it, and the top of the ring clicked open. It revealed a secret compartment, like an Elizabethan poison ring, though this ring did not contain belladonna, but something far more exquisite. The secret compartment was lined with diamonds. She slid the ring on to her right hand, and tilted it so it caught the sunlight. A shower of tiny rainbows reflected off the car window, and she smiled. Then she clicked the ring shut. From the outside, it looked like a plain silver ring again, the sort of thing you might find in hundreds of little boutiques, the sort of thing she might easily have bought for herself. But like her heart, it held a secret. Izzy Rathbone was falling in love.

James took the opportunity provided by Izzy's departure to go and text Cass. It had become the way they communicated, if you could call it that. She wouldn't speak to him on the phone, and he had only seen her twice since that first awkward coffee in the Oriel, but she would accept and sometimes reply to texts. He was learning that they went down better when he didn't write in full sentences, or try to approximate her teenage text speak (the one time he had tried that, it had been an unmitigated disaster) but messaged her using his own shorthand. It seemed to amuse her.

Happy Xmas, he typed out now. *Hope u're having gd day! & that present is not too sad.*

The reply beeped back more quickly than usual. *Present fine. Thx. Colour not totes tragic. C x*

James read the message with pleasure and a little pride.

Colour not totes tragic – this was high praise indeed from the usually intractable Cass. And an 'x' at the end. It was more than he had dared hope for. He felt a sudden rush of affection for his children, all of them. And went into the den to watch *Pingu* with Pearl and Alfie.

Christmas at the Rathbones' might have been quiet, but in the Bailey household, where Harriet was with her family, it was a boisterous affair, involving a three-bird roast ('A chiturken, or whatever he calls it, that Hugh Fearnley-Whatsit,' Harriet's dad had said, his glasses steamed up from distressing the potatoes. 'A turducken,' Harriet's brother-in-law had corrected, bossily, 'as in a *tur*key, a *duck* and a chicken,' and Harriet and her father had shared a look a solidarity, as she sat at the kitchen table shelling the chestnuts for the sprouts with a sharp knife), the nine of them – Harriet, her parents, her sister Em and her husband Henry, her brother Mark and his wife Anna, and their twins, Tiggy and Molly – and three randoms. Often there were more, but this year Harriet's mother had been relatively restrained and only invited the strange woman from down the road who smelled of mothballs, a recently widowed friend who kept having to go off to the downstairs loo to weep at the sight of anything, from crackers to the carving knife, that reminded her of her late husband, and her golf instructor, who wore a toupee that Harriet thought must surely blow off in the wind when on the golf course. Finally, thankfully, there was Harriet's adored godfather, Harry, after whom she had been named and who she loved more than almost anyone in the world. He owned an antiques shop in Brighton, and for Christmas presented her with a beautiful art deco cocktail cabinet, complete with cut-glass cocktail glasses and a silver shaker and cocktail picks, all of which had their own special places within the polished walnut case. It lit up when you opened the top, and had mirrors on the inside of the doors, and it was the most beautiful and utterly impractical thing she had ever seen.

'Oh Harry,' she had cried when he had wheeled it in, 'I love it, it's heaven. *You're* heaven. But where on earth will I put it?'

'Get rid of something. That useless and absent boyfriend of yours, maybe, to make room,' he'd replied, winking. She rolled her eyes at him.

'Will's very lovely,' she said, but not crossly, 'and you know we have to spend Christmas apart. Will's family . . .' and she made a face. Harry had nodded and said yes, he was lovely, and he understood, but did Will have a special compartment for spirits, and hand-carved legs?

Harriet had insisted on sitting next to Harry at dinner, and she busied herself serving him now, piling his plate high with the turducken, which had taken her father half an hour to carve and so was rather on the cold side of tepid, and roast potatoes and parsnips and buttered carrots and sprouts with chestnuts and Harriet's bread sauce, and he drank red wine and told her scurrilous tales of his adventures in the gay saunas of his home town.

'I'm sure you're not meant to be telling me all of this,' she said, when she finally got a word in. 'Aren't you meant to be my moral guardian?'

'Indeed I am,' he said, proudly, 'and I can think of no better way to protect your charming lady-morals than by warning you of what absolute reprobates men are. I sacrifice myself, dear Harriet, to show you the desperate consequences of living a life of moral turpitude, and urge you to take the path of virtue.'

He looked pleased with his speech, and ate a forkful of turducken. 'It's faintly obscene, this, isn't it?' he pondered. 'Shoving birds up each other's arses. Not that I have anything against that, in principle, of course. I'm an equal-opportunity gay.'

Harriet snorted.

'Yes. Now you put it like that, it is. Thanks.' She put her fork down. 'You didn't mean that about Will, did you?' she asked quietly.

Harry looked at her. 'What, about him being useless? Of course I did. He's very beautiful, wasted on a woman,' he said, his voice intentionally light.

'I'm serious.' She took a deep breath. 'I'm going to give him – well, an ultimatum, I suppose.' Her voice was so quiet she was almost whispering, not that she needed to – any chance of her being overheard was fairly impossible, due to Tiggy and Molly's furious row over the necklace in their grandmother's cracker, Tara's futile attempts to referee, and the golf instructor's booming voice telling the recent widow about nine irons.

'We're going to James and Izzy's for lunch the day after Boxing Day. I'm going to go home tomorrow and talk to him.'

'Oh dear. Are you sure?' Harry put his knife and fork down and picked up his glass. This was clearly not a moment to focus on the turducken.

Harriet shook her head. 'No. Not really. It's fairly desperate, isn't it? But I can't think what else to do.'

'Darling one. Does it matter to you that much?' Harry's face was full of love and concern, and it made Harriet want to cry. He had always been the person she could rely upon to put her first, more so than her parents, even.

'Yes,' she replied, and as she said it, she felt the truth of it. 'It didn't used to. I wanted it, but I didn't *have* to be engaged, you know? I just thought it would be nice. But now . . . after Paris . . .'

Harry winced. She had told him all about Paris over a long lunch at Café Boheme, and he had almost cried for her over his French onion soup, and berated himself for his choice of restaurant. 'I should never have brought you here,' he had muttered. 'So insensitive – forgive me, darling Hats,' and she had blinked, not realising what he meant at first, until it dawned on her that he was talking about the Parisian-styled venue, and laughed and hugged him for his sheer wonderfulness. 'Why can't everyone be as thoughtful as you?' she wondered, and he had recovered himself, and smiled, and said yes, it would be desirable, and why didn't they have chocolate mousses for pudding?

'Now I feel like we can't go forward unless something happens. *I* can't go forward. Will doesn't really seem to be able to tell the difference.'

'Are you sure there would be a difference? Marriage isn't a magic potion, you know. It doesn't make it all better. Sometimes it can make things very much worse. I should know.' Harry's smile was wry. He had been married once, to a wealthy American woman, with predictably disastrous consequences after she had found him in bed with the interior designer she had hired to redo her orangery, though she was so appalled to have made such a catastrophically poor choice of husband that she had set him up with his antiques shop and a tall thin house in Brighton that he owned outright on condition that he never return to the state of Oregon again. 'No loss,' he had said breezily. 'I'd swear never to go back there for a coffee eclair, between you and me, but I didn't let her think that,' and Harriet had told him he was wicked and he had agreed.

'I know. Of course I know that. But – look.' She gestured at the table. The three couples – Anna and Mark, Em and Henry, her parents. And then the three waifs and strays. 'Which camp would you rather be in?'

Harry shrugged. 'Neither. My own camp camp. You don't have to be like everyone else, sweet cheeks. Sod what they think.'

'It's not what they think, though. It's how I feel. And I can't ignore that any more.'

He shook his head. 'No. I suppose you can't.' He reached down by the side of his chair and picked up the bottle of red wine he had stashed there, refilling Harriet's glass and then his own. 'Don't want to let them get their hands on the good stuff,' he said in a low voice, and she giggled.

'Just a word of warning, darling. Give Will your ultimatum, if you must. But only do it if you're prepared for the answer. Because it might not be the one you want.'

Harriet nodded, and sipped the wine he had poured for her. He was always looking out for her, Harry. Always thinking of her. But she was sure that this time he didn't need to. Will loved her, and she knew he wanted them to be together. He just needed a little push, just needed to see how much this meant to her, and it would all be fine. Suddenly she felt more positive about the future than she had for ages.

'Thanks, Harry,' she said, squeezing his hand affectionately. 'You always make me feel better.'

'Good,' he said, but his face was worried. 'Just take care of your heart. Because you've only got the one, and sometimes when it gets broken, it just doesn't mend in the way everyone says. Time doesn't heal all wounds, Hats.'

'Don't worry,' she said. 'Don't be sad. It'll be fine.' She lifted her knife and fork again. 'It's all going to be fine. Eat your turducken.' And she smiled.

She was nervous, as she put the key in the front door, and her hands were cold, and she fumbled and dropped the key on the ground. 'Damn.' She reached down to pick it up out of the muddy pile of leaves next to the doormat. The cocktail cabinet was in the back of the car – sometimes Will's four by four was useful – and it was going to have to stay there until he got back from the airport in the morning.

'It's you,' Will's voice said, as the door opened in front of her. She looked up from her position bent over, muddy fingers holding the key. 'Thought you were a fox trying to get into the rubbish. Need a hand?'

He was standing in front of her, wearing his old uni rugby shirt and a pair of frayed jeans, his hair a mess, a piece of the thick Marmite toast that he was addicted to in one hand, and he grinned at her and then looked beyond her to the car. 'Got a lot of stuff? Hang on, I'll put some shoes on.' He craned his neck. 'Bloody hell. What on earth is that?'

Harriet had stood up by now, and she wiped the key on the bottom of her parka and put it in her bag. 'Art deco cocktail cabinet. Obviously. Harry's Christmas present.'

'Where on earth . . .'

'Are we going to put it? Good question.' As she spoke, Harry's words floated back into her head. *Get rid of something*, he had said. *That useless boyfriend of yours, maybe, to make room.* She didn't want to get rid of Will, though. Quite the opposite.

He was pulling on a pair of Hunters that he kept by the front door with one hand, finishing his toast with the other. 'Want some?' he said, waving it at her.

'How come you're back?' she asked, shaking her head. 'I thought your flight was tomorrow.'

'Changed it. Couldn't bear another night of Mrs Maclaren trying to get me to chat up her boot-faced daughter. You know the one . . .'

'Aisleen? With the nose?'

Will snorted. 'That's the one. "You're a fine-looking single man," she kept saying. "Ye should return to your inheritance and claim your birthright." ' He took his Barbour from the peg and shrugged it on.

His mimicry of Mrs Maclaren's Highland brogue was accurate, and Harriet remembered the disapproving looks the woman had always given her. A southerner, waltzing in trying to steal the heir to Erskine Castle, the man she had pinpointed as a future husband for her unfortunate-looking daughter practically from birth? Mrs Mac, the Erskines' nearest neighbour, was having none of it, and so chose to simply ignore Harriet's existence, referring to Will as single whenever necessary or possible. On the odd occasion that Harriet went up there and Mrs Mac was forced to confront the reality of her, over the inevitable drinks, she simply referred to her as Will's 'friend', and pushed her embarrassed daughter's many countryside accomplishments to the fore at every opportunity. 'Aisleen plucked fourteen brace of pheasant single-handedly this morning, and not a feather left on them.' Or, 'Aisleen pulled a breech lamb out with her own hands, that was stuck, and when its mother died she fed it from a bottle by the range for weeks.' Pointed looks at Harriet, who would never be able to match such achievements, would follow, until Will appeared to take her hand or put his arm around her shoulders, whereupon Mrs Mac and Aisleen would suddenly find themselves in a hurry to leave.

A fine-looking single man. Harriet couldn't stop herself.

'I want to get married, Will,' she blurted out, her breath visible in the cold air, and then watched as her words dissolved in the space between them. Will stood, his hands by his sides.

'Oh,' he said. 'Right.'

'Don't say anything. Or I won't be able to finish.'

He nodded, obedient, and just furrowed his brow. Harriet was cold on the doorstep, her toes hurt with it, but she couldn't move inside, couldn't do anything. If she did, if she started the normal pattern of unloading Christmas presents and laundry from the car and hearing about how his mother had served turnips instead of roast potatoes on Christmas Day and telling him about the horrors of her nieces, exaggerating to make him laugh, then it would slip away, this chance, this moment, and she would lose her nerve and stay in this limbo of frustrated, sticky impotence for ever, or so it felt. So she stood on her own doorstep, like someone selling cheap tea towels and chamois cloths, her hands shoved into her pockets and the man she loved so much in front of her, and she said the words that she had been afraid to say for so long.

'I want to get married, and I don't want to wait for years for you to propose. I don't want to have another summer of going to weddings and everyone avoiding me, or giving me sympathetic looks when all the single girls have to catch the bouquet, and know that the bride is positioning me so she can try and make sure I get it. I don't want to be the odd one out with all our friends, and have Izzy and Stella and Caroline all feel like they have to watch what they say around me, when they moan about their husbands or talk about anniversaries or in-laws. I don't want to have to keep wondering whether we're just going to keep going like this until we eventually break up and I'm too old to find someone else, so I'm left trawling through the divorcees for someone who might marry me to have children, someone with children who'll hate me and an ex who'll resent me; wondering whether, every time we go out for a special dinner or away for the weekend or whatever, you're going to propose, and then being disappointed.'

Will looked stricken, and opened his mouth to speak, but didn't.

'I don't want to spend Christmas apart again, you at your parents' and me at mine, because we're not married, or engaged, and so everyone thinks that it sort of doesn't count and we should just go on acting like we're still single, and I get treated like the nanny when Anna's sick of looking after the kids and Auntie Harriet will just do it because it's not as though she's got anything better to do, poor single thing.' (That wasn't fair, she knew it wasn't fair; she loved her nieces and Anna never assumed that she would take them off her hands, but she couldn't help it, it was all coming out now in a big snotty stream.) 'And coming back to London and everyone wondering whether this New Year's Eve will be the one, and nothing changing, at all, ever.'

She took a deep breath and tried to get herself back under control. 'I want to get married, Will,' she said again. 'And you need to decide.' She looked at him and saw in his eyes that he knew what she was about to say, what she was about to do, and was willing her not to, but she had gone too far now and she could not turn back.

'Either we get engaged, soon. In the next month. Or—'

'Don't,' Will said, shaking his head, 'please don't do this, Hats.'

'Or it's over,' she continued, unable to quite believe she'd said it. 'I can't do this any longer, Will. I just can't. You don't have to decide now, of course.' She made a useless gesture with her arms. 'Sorry. Bad timing, bad moment probably. Think about it, whatever.' She felt horribly, hotly ashamed, wanted to turn her back on him and run away, but she couldn't.

'No,' he said, softly, 'I don't need to think about it.'

She sniffed, and felt her body judder with relief. Thank God. Thank God she wasn't going to have to wait any longer. It was all going to be OK.

'I'm sorry, Hats.' The tone of his voice made her jerk her head up to look at him, and when she did, she saw that he was crying. 'I'm sorry, but – fucking hell.' There was anger in his voice now, and she stared at him. Oh no. Oh no, no, no.

'I said don't, but you didn't listen. I – I love you. You know that. Always have done. Always will.' He shook his head. 'Shit. I can't believe you made me do this.'

She held out her hand to him. *I take it back*, she screamed, silently. *I take it back, don't say it, don't say what you don't want to say, like I did, don't say something you can't take back.* Because she knew she couldn't.

Will took her hand, holding her fingers loosely. His thumb rubbed her ring finger. 'It didn't have to be all or nothing, you know? I would have . . . I think I would have got there.' You think. But you're not sure, she thought. And that's why. Because *I think I would have got there* isn't good enough. Not any longer.

He let go of her hand and it dropped to her side. 'But I won't be fucking well held to ransom, Hats. I won't walk down the aisle with a fucking gun to my head. If that's how you want to . . .' He paused, calming his voice. 'If it's marry me now or it's over . . . then I guess it's over.'

He didn't meet her eye. 'Shit,' he said, and kicked his boot against the door frame. He walked past her and went out to the car. 'I'm going for a drive. I'll see you later.'

As he got behind the wheel, he looked back at her as though he were going to speak. And then he shook his head and drove away.

Harriet leant against the door frame, and wept and wept. Harry had been right, of course he had been right. She had only been prepared to hear one answer, the one she wanted, the one she hoped and hoped she would get. Why hadn't she just listened to him? She could have kept her mouth shut, and she would have been indoors now, making more toast for Will and herself, a pot of tea, a fire to sit by and, later, make love in front of, instead of standing out here, crying alone, on Boxing Day, as the wind whipped her hair around her face. A car drove past, and from inside she could hear the Pogues singing 'Fairytale of New York'. It had always been her favourite Christmas song, the one she had played over and over again, Will groaning and putting cushions over his ears as she sang drunkenly along to it. Now she knew that she would never be able to listen to it again without remembering this moment. It was ruined for ever. She had spoilt everything.

It was too late, and it was the worst feeling in the world.

The Lodge

They sat, for a while, in silence. They had been inside the lodge for almost an hour, by his watch. He looked at it now, at its round face with its perpetual calendar and night and day dials. A symbol of success? Of wealth, at least. Material wealth. How important it had seemed to him. He smiled to himself.

A grunt came from the corner, and he turned his head quickly in the man's direction. He was still, his face angry. Had he been trying to loosen his bound wrists, was the grunt an escaped sign of exertion? They stared at one another.

'Don't,' he said to him, quietly, the gun slightly raised. 'Don't try and do something stupid.'

The man looked away, banging his head back against the wall in frustration.

He moved a little closer to the window, gun outstretched in front of him so that those outside could see it, keeping his head and shoulders low. There they were. A huddle of armed police, their snipers in position. They weren't far from the town here, despite the remote feel of the house. He shouldn't have been surprised that they had got here so quickly. He supposed that when guns were involved, everything moved fast. Somehow, though, the whole situation was a surprise to him. It wasn't as though he had planned it, after all. Come away on the weekend thinking that by its end he would be – would be what? Dead? Imprisoned? Still here, sitting, waiting? No. It would have to end sooner rather than later, he knew that. He had no supplies, no water. Would fall asleep, eventually, if nothing else. How long could the human body physically stay awake for? He wasn't sure, but he knew that adrenalin would only go so far. At some point, exhaustion would set in and his reactions would become slower, he would lose focus.

He had better come up with a plan before that happened.

Chapter Nine

January 2009

Stella sat at the kitchen table, her laptop open in front of her, providing a blue glow. The light was on in the hallway, and it shone through into the room, which was otherwise in darkness. On the hob sat the remains of her dinner, a pan of chicken soup. She had eaten only a few mouthfuls.

She typed. Her wrists ached, the familiar bone-weary ache that made her wish she could open them up and massage the tendons. Instead, she reached for the razor blade that sat on a piece of paper to the left of her MacBook Pro, and pushed a pile of coke into a slim line. She leant down, and snorted it. It was past three in the morning, and this was her fourth line of the night. It should be her last, she knew, or she would never get any sleep. She glanced at the clock. Three fourteen. Who was she kidding? She wouldn't sleep until he came home anyhow. Gone were the days of being able to go to bed when Johnny was out, and not think about what he was doing or who he was with.

Since the night at the gig, when she had felt so triumphant about what she had thought was a win against Delilah, things had got worse. Johnny was out constantly. His band was going well, they were showcasing a lot and there was suddenly quite a bit of interest in them from some of the big labels. He was excited, kept telling Stella that 'This is it, this is what we've been working for. It's all happening.' His manager was taking him out to parties, private members' clubs, industry drinks dos, telling him he needed to be seen in the right places, with the right people. Was Delilah 'the right people'? Was he taking her along to the things he told Stella she would be bored by? 'Full of musos, talking about amps and the best way to record stuff. You get enough of that rubbish at home, surely, babe?'

Stella typed on. The good thing was that she was writing, a lot. All at night, pretty much, in the quiet, moonlit hours when the rest of the world was asleep and there were no emails or friends on Facebook popping up to distract her. She would sit here at her kitchen table, and drink a couple of glasses of wine, and write. Her novel was growing, slowly, surely; it was up to seventy thousand words now. Soon she would send it to Benjy again, the next chunk, for his approval. It was a coming-of-age story in a way, a psychological thriller in another. It mixed genres, Benjy had said, which could be a tough sell, especially at the moment, but could also be 'brilliant, diamond, the next big thing. All depends on finding the editors who'll fall in love with it. Which is what you pay my good – don't laugh – my good self fifteen per cent for.' But she had to write more of it before he would send it out. It was a massive gamble, in terms of time spent working on it and potential return. Which was another reason why she was writing the thing in the middle of the night. She couldn't justify giving up working hours to something that might turn out to be a total indulgence, a waste of time. And she had the autobiography to finish, during the day, and her usual freelance work. She clicked over to her iCal. Damn. She was interviewing a singer tomorrow, a guy who was known to be a complete prima donna, more than most, even. Right now, the thought of going into town and sitting listening to him wank on about 'the music' was more than she could bear. She got enough of that at home, as well, she thought unkindly.

The bad thing about Johnny's absences, she knew, apart from the obvious, was the amount of coke she had found herself doing. And the wine. They balanced one another out, though, so she never felt drunk or out-of-control high. But it helped her stay awake, into the small, quiet hours, it helped the words flow, it helped – it helped his absence take up less space in her house and in her head as she sat there and typed her story, the story of a lost girl who had to struggle to find herself in her own past, the story that had been bubbling in her head for so long and which she was finally letting spill on to the screen.

The baby monitor sat before her, and she glanced at it, automatically, but all was calm. Viking slept like a boxer knocked out for the count; arms flung where he fell, face serene and clear of any expression whatsoever, his blond curls slightly too long around his neck. But Stella couldn't bear to cut them. He was upstairs, in his little box room with its Tintin wallpaper, hundreds of sheets torn from old copies of the books that she and Johnny had spent hours scouring eBay for and then plastering the walls with. 'So he'll always have something good to read if he wakes up and gets bored,' Johnny had said when they were doing it. 'He's only six months old,' Stella had reminded him. 'He won't be able to read for months. Years.' 'Pfft. Your son? Child of the bookworm? He'll be eating those words up by the time he's walking.' Stella had laughed, and thought indulgently how nice it would be if he was right.

He wasn't, of course not, but Viking loved looking at the pictures on his walls, would say hello to Tintin and Snowy when he came into the room and good night to them before he went to sleep. They had become his friends, his companions. It had been a good decision, a good idea of Johnny's. He did have them.

Stella rolled her shoulders back and looked at her novel, her fingers resting lightly on the keyboard. She was at a tricky bit, a section of plot that required her to tread carefully through. She couldn't just let her fingers run away with her, she had to make sure she laid the trail and put the signposts up in the right place, or she knew the whole thing would turn into a confused jumble. She needed clarity. She needed . . . She gave in, and did another line. Just a small one. Just to kick-start her tired brain.

It was four o'clock and the bottle of wine was finished by the time he got back. She had stopped writing, and was sitting on the sofa, laptop on her knees, reading an old interview with the singer she was to meet tomorrow. In it, he had uttered the immortal words, 'Music is my muse, my master and my mistress, my passion and my tragedy.' Christ. What an arse.

She made a note to ask him about the tragedy of music. Hopefully she could get him to say something even more pretentious that they could use as a pull quote. She would make him believe she was enthralled by him. She was used to doing that with musicians.

'Stell? You still up?' The front door shut gently behind Johnny as he crept in. He appeared in the doorway, his parka slouched around his shoulders.

'What time do you call this, then?' she said, in a mock-stern voice, as though she were joking. They both knew she was – and she wasn't.

'Yeah. Late. You must be shattered.' He stepped forward and touched her cheekbone. 'Working?'

'Working. Waiting.' Their eyes met. She looked away.

'How was tonight? What was it again?'

'Dinner with Max.' Max was Johnny's manager. Johnny kept his eyes on Stella. Not averting his gaze; did that mean he was telling the truth?

He looked over to the kitchen table. 'OK. Bedtime?' He went to turn the lights out, holding his hand out to help her up from the sofa.

'Wait a minute.' He paused.

'What?'

'Tell me the truth, Johnny.'

'Always.'

'Do you love her? Do you love her more than me?'

'Stell . . . don't do this.' Johnny's face was sad, and the sight of it almost made Stella give in and take his hand and let him lead her up to bed. But only almost.

'I've never asked about any of them before, have I?' She never had. It had been her unspoken rule. But now, emboldened by the wine and the coke and the coming dawn, she was asking.

'You've always known . . .'

'Yes. Which is why I haven't asked. I never needed to. You always came back.'

'I still do.'

'It's different.'

Johnny sighed and leant his head on his hand as it rested on the door frame. 'I'm not going anywhere, Stell.'

She stood up, putting her laptop down on the sofa cushion and heading for the fridge.

'Do you want a drink?'

He looked at her in surprise. 'Now?'

'Yes, now. We've started, so we might as well finish.' She pulled out a bottle of supermarket Chablis and opened it. Johnny shrugged.

'You started.'

'Beer or wine?'

'Wine. Have you been doing charlie?'

'Only a line. I had to work.' It wasn't true, of course. She had done a lot more than a line. There had been two more after the 'last' and fourth line, and she had only stopped because she had noticed with alarm that there was only a small amount left. She couldn't finish it all in one evening. That would be . . . bad.

'You've been by yourself with Viking. Sure that's a great idea?'

Stella spun around, the bottle in her hand. 'Don't. Just – don't. I've been by myself with him because you've been out shagging Delilah!'

She shut her mouth in surprise. She hadn't expected to say her name. Hadn't wanted to. Somehow, as long as she didn't acknowledge her, didn't say her name, didn't speak the words, it wasn't quite real still. She could pretend she was just like all the others, the faceless, nameless girls who floated through Johnny's life and whose beds he passed through, who were no threat, no danger, made no impact.

Johnny ignored the glass of wine she had poured for him, and took a tumbler and the bottle of Jack Daniels out of the cupboard.

'OK. I guess we're doing this, then.'

'I guess we are.'

'You've never minded before.'

Stella tilted her head to one side. Was it true that she had never minded? She had never said anything, no. And he had obviously taken that to mean that she didn't care. Was that the case? Not quite. It wasn't that simple. When it came to her and Johnny, it seemed nothing ever was.

'I knew it was what you needed,' she said, carefully. 'I would have preferred it to be different. In an ideal world, you would have been satisfied by just me.'

'You do—'

'Not completely.' Stella's voice was firm, and Johnny quieted. 'Not entirely. You couldn't be. You were like a kid – like Viking in the sensory place we took him to, all wide eyes and looking around like he couldn't believe his luck.'

Johnny smiled at the memory. It had been an exhibition, with a mirrored pod that children could crawl around in. Every so often coloured lights would pulse gently, or a twinkling sound would ring out from different corners of the space, and Viking would turn his head towards them, swivelling his body around cumbersomely after him, transfixed.

'Yeah. He loved that.'

'Could you have pulled him away from that? From that joy?'

Johnny shook his head. 'Course not. It was bad enough when it ended.' Their slot had lasted for half an hour, before the lights and sounds gradually slowed to nothing, and Viking had looked up and to both sides and around himself, waiting for them to start again, until the door slid open and the world outside spilled back in. There had been tears, and then cake, to soothe.

Stella crossed her legs. 'That's what it was like. What it's always been like. I could no more have made a fuss about the other girls than you could tear Viking away from that. It was you. It was part of who you were, and part of who I'd fallen in love with. I didn't want to try and change you. You were you.'

'I still am.' Johnny walked over and sat facing her on the other end of the sofa, pulling one leg up on to the cushion and underneath his body. His hair was scruffy, it needed a cut, and the tuft of what was almost a Mohican on top was askew. Stella stopped herself from reaching forward and tweaking it with her fingers. Outside the French doors, a cool light began to seep in and a bird chirped.

'You might be. But . . . this. This is different. It's different with her.'

Johnny didn't speak. He didn't deny it. Couldn't. They both knew she was right.

'Stell. I don't know what to tell you.'

'Tell me I'm wrong.' Her voice was almost a whisper. 'Tell me she's like all the others. Tell me she's going to melt away, like they all have. Tell me she doesn't have any claim on your heart.'

It was the final line that got him. She could see it. As she spoke those words, he seemed to crumble a little inside. Soften in on himself. He drained his glass. In the background, Stella realised that the CD she had put on earlier was still playing. Alanis Morrissette. She'd been listening to it for the first time since – God, since she was a love-tortured nineteen-year-old, probably, lying on her bed scribbling angry poetry. 'Head Over Feet'. They both listened as Alanis thanked her unnamed for his patience, and Johnny smiled wryly.

He didn't need to say anything else. But he did. 'I can't. I'm really sorry. But I can't tell you that.'

Stella got up and shut the door to the hall, before taking a cigarette from the packet on the bookshelf and lighting it. She never smoked inside. Spent hours pacing up and down the garden, cigarette in her hand, phone wedged between her head and her shoulder, cup of tea in her other hand, in the big fisherman's jumper she often wore to work in and her at-home uniform of leggings and thick sheepskin Ugg boots. A parka in the winter. Come snow or hail or bronchitis she would smoke just outside the French windows, keeping her cigarette out of Viking's view. 'I don't want him to grow up thinking that's what Mummy and Daddy do,' she told Johnny. 'That it's normal, that he should imitate us.'

She needn't have worried about that, she thought now. Nothing Mummy and Daddy did was normal.

'I guess it was always going to happen,' she said. 'Sooner or later. I just told myself that it wouldn't.' She was standing by the fireplace, into which she flicked her cigarette ash. 'I told

170

myself it would just continue as it always has, and we would stay the same. But it's a numbers game, really, isn't it? You fuck enough nameless, faceless girls and eventually one of them sits up and holds on, and tells you her name. Makes you look at her face.'

A note of bitterness had crept into her voice, and Johnny heard it. He looked up at her, his face expressionless. 'Maybe.'

'Don't you want to . . . I don't know.' Stella touched her fingers to her forehead. She was so tired, and her head hurt. It was the lack of sleep that made comedowns feel so awful, she knew. She had realised that when Viking had been a baby, and she had been sleep-starved for the first three months, falling on it like a clucking junkie when Johnny took over from her and she could crawl into bed and shut the door. The feeling was the same, almost, as the feeling the day after a long night, or long lost weekend. Minus the burning sinuses and the faint, lingering, Ecstasy-induced nausea that was strangely pleasant. But the rest of it – the heavy, aching limbs, the muscles that throbbed and blazed, the dull headache and the thick, porridgy brain? That was all familiar ground that she was covering. In a way it was a comfort. She knew this land. Everyone had told her, before she had given birth to Viking, that she would not know what had hit her, that motherhood and all it brought with it would be both more and less than she could ever have imagined, ever have conceived of being possible, even. She had bristled, at this, silently. She had an imagination; it was what she made her living out of. She had empathy, she had sensitivity. Did they think she was stupid? So when it had happened and she realised that they were, in part, quite right, it had been comforting and somewhat satisfying to know that there was at least one respect in which they had not been right. 'The tiredness,' they had said, 'there's nothing like it.' But there was.

'Don't you want to pretend you're going to end it?' she continued. 'Tell me it doesn't mean anything? That you won't see her again? Isn't that what people usually do?'

'What's the point? You know it wouldn't be true. You know me, Stell. You always have done. You probably knew before I did that . . . that this was different.'

'When did you know?' Stella waited for the answer. But she already knew it would be some time after she had known it. After she had read the messages between Johnny and Delilah on his Twitter feed. He was right; she had known him for too long for things to be otherwise.

'I don't want to hurt you with this.'

'I need to know what I'm dealing with. If this is different . . . I need to know.'

And Johnny took a deep breath, and told her. They had met after one of his gigs; the drummer had brought her along. They'd been drinking in the Horseferry, Johnny and his manager and the rest of the band, along with a few of the hangers-on that tended to gravitate towards them. She'd met the drummer, Hal, the night before. 'Met being a pretty loose way of putting things. I don't think it was exactly a meeting of minds.' Stella couldn't help but smile at the incongruous image of the beautiful, stylish Delilah with the sweet but frankly dense Hal, whose only thoughts were for his beloved drums.

Had she gone there with Hal for a reason, a reason of her own, planned and prepared for? Stella wondered now, as Johnny told her about the evening they had all spent together, drinking whisky and eating the pub's famously disgusting burgers ('I still don't understand why you go there,' she said. 'What must Delilah have thought? It's so – relentlessly grim.' Johnny nodded. 'The grimness is the point,' he said, solemnly.) Had meeting Johnny been her endgame all along?

If it had been, he wouldn't have seen it. Men never did. It was the women who saw the triumphant flick of the eyes, the tiny curl of the edges of the lips that told the story of a battle won and a conquest made, a long-nursed desire satisfied. Hal, sweet, leather-clad Hal, with his forehead thick as a boulder, had probably been the grateful recipient of a night that was simply a stepping stone into Johnny's bed.

It was heavy with half-light outside, and Stella knew Viking would soon be starting to chunter to himself and the time for story-telling would be over. 'Go on,' she said.

'We hung out that night and then I didn't see her for a while after that.' Stella knew that 'hung out' meant 'slept together'. It was what she would have expected. 'She wouldn't see me again. I asked her to come to watch us play a couple of times, on Twitter. She said she was busy.'

Clever girl, Stella thought; by doing that, Delilah had set herself apart from the groupies who thronged around the bottom of the stage, all big eyes looking up at Johnny and tops that they tugged down to give him a better view. She had done the one thing that would guarantee Johnny noticed her – she had said no. Johnny wasn't used to girls saying no. Stella had to admire her for it.

'And we just started chatting, on Twitter, you know? We follow quite a few of the same people. I mean, not all, obviously. She's into a lot of the vintage scene as well, but she's got loads of friends in bands . . .' I bet she does, thought Stella. 'And she's a good writer, too. Sharp.'

'Have you written songs together, then?' Stella asked, and she had to swallow in order to get the words out. She reached for her drink but then thought better of it. It was too light outside now to keep pretending it was night-time. She padded over to the hob and turned the gas on to boil the kettle. 'Do you want tea?'

'Yeah. I mean, yes, thanks, tea, not yes we've written together. I wouldn't write with another girl. I don't think I could.' Stella smiled to herself as she put the tea bags in the mugs and got the milk out of the fridge. Small triumphs. She would make pancakes, she thought, suddenly feeling the gnaw in her stomach and the need for warmth and comfort. They were Viking's favourite, and Johnny loved them as well, drowned in a syrupy puddle of lemon and sugar. As the kettle began to steam, she got out eggs and flour and a jug to make the batter. It would have time to sit before Viking woke.

'So. Then what?' She poured the water into the mugs. They might have been discussing the supermarket shop for all you could tell by their voices. Someone looking in through the window would have seen a picture of domestic bliss – Stella at the stove making pancake batter, Johnny on the sofa, mug of tea in his hand, now, that she had brought him. It was only if you looked closer that the cracks appeared in the picture: the half-full glasses only just abandoned, the tremor in Stella's hand as she beat the eggs into the mixture, the shadows under Johnny's eyes and the way he clicked the cap of his Zippo open and shut with one hand.

'Then we met for coffee. We went to the Tate. We went to look at guitars. We just did . . . stuff. We became friends.'

Stella sipped her tea. 'But not just friends.'

'I thought it was . . . you know, at first. I thought that first night had just been . . .'

'Like the rest.'

'Yes.'

'But it wasn't.'

Johnny took a deep breath. He chose his words carefully. 'It was, then. The first time. But then we spent all this time together, and we talked online, and she was at some of the same parties – not planned, but just because . . .'

'Because you know lots of the same people?' Stella knew how this story went.

'Yes.' Johnny looked over at her. 'What?'

'Nothing.' She shook her head. She wasn't going to tell him that the reason they had found themselves at the same parties would not have been because of some extraordinary coincidence, but because Delilah, beautiful Delilah with her dark hair and her quiet determination, had made sure of it. Oh, she knew this woman well. 'Go on.'

'It was the second time that I realised.'

Stella felt her head nod, automatically. Suddenly it all felt real again. She gave the batter a final stir and slid it into the fridge to rest, reaching for her cigarettes in the same movement. She went outside this time, though, pulling the cardigan that had been on the back of a chair on over her jumper and standing in the doorway, her hand out to one side so the smoke didn't float back into the room. She needed the distance that standing here gave her, the bubble of protection that surrounded her when she was smoking a cigarette. She did not have to deal with the real world, with the present, the now, in the same way; she could watch it as though from one remove.

'Why was it different? How?' she asked, but she didn't need to. She knew. Delilah had worked her way under his skin, she had seen it when she had found those first messages between them. They had laughed together, got drunk together, walked through London in the rain dodging cycle couriers and pigeons, stood side by side waiting for buses, their shoulders touching, their hands brushing against one another as they reached for their Oyster cards. She had become real to him, had come into focus.

Johnny looked uncomfortable. 'It's weird.'

'The whole thing is weird. Tell me.'

He nodded, and looked at her. 'I knew it was different because it reminded me of us. Of when we first met. Of you.'

Caroline had been on her way to her parents' for tea, a box of blackcurrant tarts from the smart patisserie up the hill in her hand, when she saw the police car in the driveway. She had got the bus and walked rather than driving, because Bart had gone off on some work trip. A meeting out of London, she thought, though he'd been vague about the details. And these days, she didn't like to push.

She dropped the pink-ribboned box of tarts when she saw the car, and ran, her legs awkward and stumbling, across the road and through the gate and up the steps, her fingers fumbling with her key, dropping and scrabbling for it on the porch floor until the door opened and she found herself looking into the face of a policewoman, who said, 'It's all right, it's Caroline, isn't it? No one's hurt, your parents are fine. Why don't you come inside?'

'What on earth were you thinking?' she asked Ginny, once the shock had subsided enough for her to speak and she had her hands wrapped around a mug of hot tea that the policewoman had made. She had put too much milk and sugar in it and she had used the wrong sort of mug, the chipped and old ones that Ginny saved for builders and the gardener, but it felt like the most comforting thing in the world at this moment.

'I don't . . . I don't think I can have been, really.'

Ginny sat before her, a handkerchief in her lap, pale-faced and cowed. She was wearing a tweedy skirt the colour of the Scottish highlands, greens and heathers, and a grassy-coloured jumper, a string of pearls at her neck. The police had left, having warned her that 'If the shop owner hadn't known you and been so understanding about it, we may not have had any choice

176

than to arrest you.' Ginny had nodded, obediently, fearfully, sitting quietly in her chair like a child.

Julian, who was standing by the kitchen window looking craggily baffled at the scenario that had just unfolded in his house, shook his head once more. 'Ginny. What came over you?'

She turned the hanky over in her hands. 'I told you. I don't know. I just . . . I just lost myself, for a minute. Lost control.'

'But *why*, for God's sake? You have plenty of money, don't you?' Julian paced, the sleeves of his shirt rolled up and his tie hanging on the back of one of the kitchen chairs. 'Or has something happened? If you've got into a mess with your account and you need more money, you just have to ask me, you know that.'

Ginny nodded. 'I know. I have plenty of money, darling, thank you, you're very generous.'

'I don't want you to thank me.' Caroline watched as her father knelt down in front of her mother and took her hands in his. 'I want to understand. Why did you take the necklace? Why didn't you just buy it, if you wanted—'

Ginny leapt to her feet with a sob, pushing his hands away. 'I don't know! I don't know, I told you. I just – oh I don't know anything any more.' She ran from the room, dropping the hanky on the floor as she went. Upstairs, they could hear her crying.

Julian leaned down and picked up the square of cotton. It was still wet with Ginny's tears, and he sat for a moment, holding it between his palms.

'I don't understand,' he said quietly to Caroline. 'I just don't understand.'

And she sat down on the chair next to him, and leant her head on his shoulder, as though somehow, by doing so, she could pull all of them back in time, to the days when her daddy could solve any problem and her mummy could heal any wound.

*

'I don't know why you've asked him round,' Bart said, crossly. Caroline continued to lay the table. Three places, for her, Bart and Will.

'No. I know you don't,' she replied. 'It's perfectly clear that you don't understand. He's an old friend, and he needs our support. He's your friend as well.'

Bart shrugged. 'He's the one who didn't want to get married. She's your best friend.'

'Yes, she is. But believe me, you don't want Harriet round for dinner at the moment. It's best that I see her by myself, with the girls. She's in a terrible mess.'

Caroline sighed as she thought of Harriet. She really was in a bad way. She was hardly eating, she was drinking too much, and Caroline was sure she'd been going out and – doing God knows what. Other men, she suspected, and she did not approve. Stella might have joked that the way to get over a man was to get under another, but she knew Harriet, and she knew her heart was broken and would not be mended by sex. Not that anything was.

'And it's important that we don't take sides, as a couple. I don't get you,' she said, as she folded a napkin and laid it on top of a side plate. 'You're friends with him, you've invested in Henry Butler's, we see him all the time. Suddenly you're being all – weird.'

'I just think it's fairly patronising, the way everyone's getting him over for dinner, like an exhibit, as if you're expecting him to have some kind of breakdown at the supper table.'

'He may not have wanted to get married, but that doesn't mean he wanted to break up with Harriet. He didn't. He's terribly upset about it. I can tell.'

Bart raised an eyebrow at her. 'Because of your "special relationship"?' he asked.

Caroline threw a napkin at him. 'I knew it. There it is.'

'What?'

'You're jealous.' She put a hand on her hip.

Bart scoffed. 'Don't be so daft . . .'

'Yes you are, I can tell. I knew that was what it was. You're jealous because you know I used to . . .' She paused.

'Be in love with Will.'

'Have a crush on Will,' she admitted. 'It was a teenage crush, that's all. And he was always in love with Harriet.'

'Which you couldn't bear. You were always jealous of them,' Bart said. His voice was cold.

Caroline took a breath and turned away from him. 'What a cruel thing to say,' she said, and her voice wavered. How could he say that to her? It was true, of course it was. But the tone of his voice – it scared her. And it reminded her. Of another time, recently, when he had sounded like that. At Christmas.

'I just wonder whether you're pleased they've broken up,' he continued. Caroline gave a little yelp, and glanced up at him. His face was cold, and his body language stiff and unforgiving. He looked angry with her, properly angry, and she didn't understand why. She shook her head, and busied herself getting wine glasses out of the cupboard and putting them on the table, to hide the fact that tears had rushed to her eyes. She was scared, and desperate to make things right again.

'Of course I'm not. I'm sad for them both. They're two of my best friends.'

'Mmm.' Bart's grunt was sullen, and Caroline slammed the wine glass that she was holding on to the table.

'I don't want to fight with you about it, darling. It's not worth it. It's not important.'

'I thought it was. They're our friends, you said, we must support them. Now you've changed your mind. Which is it?'

Caroline stood in front of him. 'Sorry. Forget it,' she said, and now the tears that had been building fell on to her cheeks.

Bart waited. And then he smiled.

'It's all right. I know you didn't mean to upset me,' he said. His face was his own again now, where before it had looked not like him at all. Such anger.

'I love you,' he said now, and she smiled. They were in tune again, and the world felt right.

'I love you too,' she murmured, 'I love you and I'm sorry.' And as she said it, she tried to remember what it was that she was apologising for, again.

It was insecurity, plain and simple, she knew it was. He'd been hurt so badly by his ex, so betrayed by her. What damage we do, what casual damage, she thought, as she slid the fish pie into the oven and shut the door on it. Their kitchen was small and square, with sunny yellow walls and white tiles around the worktops. The Cath Kidston apron Caroline was wearing always made her feel like a fifties housewife, and her collection of blue and white striped Cornishware sat in a glass-fronted dresser, wholesome-looking, ready to be filled with creamy porridge and jam, and hearty stews. She longed, though, for a big kitchen, like James and Izzy had, with doors out on to the patio, where she could grow herbs and Bart could barbecue, and a big range cooker on which she could make soup and roasts and fairy cakes. She started to wash the spinach. What she wanted wasn't so much the kitchen as the family inside it, the children to make fairy cakes with, showing them how to run the spatula around the inside of the bowl and slot the paper cases into the tin, a family kitchen in a family home, there for Bart when he got home from work, the children ready to welcome him and to sit on his lap and chatter away to him about their day while he smiled, indulgently, and Caroline brought him a whisky and soda.

That would finally erase the ghost of the woman who had hurt him so much, who had left these traces of betrayal that still

180

cast a shadow over him sometimes, like tonight. He had told her all about it when they first got together, how they had been living together, happily or so he thought, for a year, how he had been planning to propose to her, had even picked out the ring and planned how he was going to put it inside a cracker for her to discover at dinner. How one day, a few weeks before Christmas, he had come home early from work, to surprise her. She worked from home, as a graphic designer, and he had thought he would take her out for lunch, bunk off for the afternoon, make love, watch a movie, maybe. He had come in through the front door, and known, immediately, he had said, that something was not right. That it wasn't just her in the flat. His brow had creased as he told Caroline this, and she had wanted to reach up and smooth the furrow with her finger, wipe away the memory of it. But she could not, so she had just squeezed his hand and listened as he told her how he had walked down the hallway towards the living room, and seen a shoe on the floor, just one shoe, that had destroyed his life. 'I had never considered how a single object could carry such weight,' he had said, 'until that moment.' It was an old brogue, a brown suede brogue, worn down at the heel. He had picked it up and held it in one hand. 'Unfortunately it didn't carry as much literal weight as it did figurative,' he had said, wryly, 'when I threw it at the bastard's head.'

The shoe had belonged to his best friend, who had been, at that moment, 'fucking my fiancée on the sofa. My sofa. I remember that seemed really significant for some reason. He was on my sofa, pumping away at her. Hadn't even managed to get all his clothes off in his hurry. He was still wearing his shirt. Stupid, the little things you remember.' He had looked up at Caroline then, his big dark eyes soft and vulnerable. 'Sorry, darling. Sorry. It just hurt so much. I haven't been quite the same since, to be honest. I'm afraid you're taking on someone rather battered.' She had wept for him, taken him in her arms and covered him in kisses. 'I love you,' she had whispered. 'I'm never going to hurt you. I'm always going to be here.'

How could she have done it? It made Caroline furious on his behalf to think about it. She finished rinsing the spinach and put it in the big stock pan to wilt. She filled another pan with water and put it on to boil for the peas. Will was insistent that you could not have fish pie without peas, and she agreed with him. Hateful, selfish bitch, did she even have any idea of the harm she had done to her beloved Bart? Of the actual, real consequences of her actions? Probably not. People like that never did. They just wandered through life leaving a trail of destruction behind them, oblivious to the damage they had done. He hadn't even got all of his belongings back, poor thing, had turned around and left the flat immediately after throwing the shoe, not stopping, not pausing to be drawn into explanations or apologies, and had had another friend go back and pack up his things for him. Inevitably, some had been left behind. 'Nothing irreplaceable,' he told Caroline with a sad smile. 'The only irreplaceable thing was my heart. My ability to trust. But you . . .' He had stroked her cheek. 'You, my angel, are mending me. Making me whole again. I was living a strange sort of a half-life, until I met you. Like a sleepwalker. And now I'm awake.'

Dinner was fine, in the end, despite what had happened earlier. By the time Will arrived, everything was all right again, and Bart was the Bart she loved so much; welcoming and generous, clapping Will on the back when he got there and taking his coat, topping up his glass, getting out the good brandy for him after dinner, telling stories about the guys at work and asking about Henry Butler's. He was, Caroline thought, his best self, and she allowed herself a small moment of pride as she washed her hands in the bathroom after supper, because it was partly down

182

to her. She was getting the hang of being married, maybe. A year ago she would have made a huge thing out of his earlier comments, there would have been proper tears and recriminations and she would have felt like it was the end of the world, that the unkind words that had passed between them were symptomatic of a bigger problem, a permanent one, that their marriage was doomed. Ridiculous.

She could hear the two men talking now, from her position in front of the basin, and she paused for a moment and allowed herself to listen. Bart's deep voice was murmuring something, she couldn't make out what, and then Will's chimed in in response. It was strangely comforting to hear the two of them talking so easily. Not something she would have thought she would be listening to, even a couple of years ago. She could admit it now; that Will's voice had struck a twinge of pain into her heart whenever she heard it, until she met Bart. It was only then, when she fell so deeply in love, that she was able to see him without having to pretend. How life changes around us, without us even being aware of it, she thought. And then she remembered the pregnancy test that she had put down on the basin surround, not even picking it up, so used was she to peeing on the little white sticks, and glanced down at it. Then she did pick it up, oh damn, it was still wet, and now she had pee on her hands, but she didn't care, she would wash them again in a second, but for now she just wanted the line that she was wishing for so desperately to appear and answer all her prayers. She wiped the test stick with loo roll and washed her hands with Molton Brown liquid soap, then looked at herself in the mirror above the basin. She tried to see if there was any difference in her face, but she couldn't spot anything. She didn't feel any different, not really. Though she had got so used to looking out for the signs, and misreading them, over the last thirteen months that she had stopped looking. Had had so many disappointments, months when she had felt sick and her breasts had been tender and she had been convinced that this was it, only for it not to be, again, that she had purposely switched that part of her brain off. Now, though, maybe she had been feeling different recently. A strange, slightly metallic taste in her mouth when she woke, a sleepiness that didn't disappear with an early night. Hardly anything. She lifted the stick and stared at it, and willed it to reflect what she so wanted to be true. Come on, she told it, come on. Give me the right answer, the only answer. Come on!

But when the single line appeared, they told a different story, one that she didn't want to hear, couldn't bear to keep hearing. Not pregnant. The words taunted her. Not pregnant. And she threw the stick into the bin.

Chapter Ten

July 2009

The hotel where Julian Rathbone was to celebrate his sixtieth birthday, surrounded by a small group of family and friends, was a medieval-style building with mullioned windows and flagstone floors. The reception area contained an arrangement of soft rust-coloured sofas covered in cushions, into which James and Izzy were sinking as they waited for Julian and Ginny to complete the checking-in process, and trying to stop Pearl and Alfie trampling all over them. Mr Butterworth sat looking morose in his travel basket. Harriet had travelled down with James and Izzy and the children. She was better, a little, Izzy thought. At least she was getting dressed and going to work now, which she hadn't been for almost a month during January. But she was far from the old Harriet. Izzy was worried about her. She was out all the time, sometimes with Stella, the two of them partying like eighteen-year-olds. Sometimes Izzy suspected that Harriet went out alone, picking up men, maybe? Or just drinking by herself. 'I do have other friends, you know,' Harriet had said indignantly, when Izzy had called her on it last week, asking who she had been out with the night before. 'Just because I'm not with one of you lot doesn't mean I'm sobbing into my pillow all night. I was out with Tara, if you must know.' Izzy had apologised, and nodded, and hadn't told Harriet that she had spoken to Tara earlier and discovered that the two of them hadn't been out for weeks. 'I'm really worried about her, Izzy,' Tara had said. 'She's not herself at all. It's hit her so hard, and she won't admit it.'

Harriet wasn't the only one Izzy was worried about. Stella was off the radar half the time as well, and had shrunk significantly last time Izzy had seen her. She was doing too much coke again; you could see it in her eyes and in the judder of her fingers as she held her cigarette, as well as in the jut of her cheekbones and the chatter that often went nowhere. Then there was Caroline, who seemed – sad. Not ill or heartbroken, and there was no way she was hitting the booze or drugs too hard, but there was a sadness about her that made Izzy fear for her. It was the baby thing, no doubt. Izzy remembered how hard it was, and she and James had hardly had to try for any length of time. It was taking its toll on Caroline. And if she was really honest, Izzy was worried about herself, as well. About her marriage. She and James were cordial but distant. She and Stephen Garside emailed and spoke on the phone regularly now. She hadn't slept with him yet. But she had let him kiss her. And she knew that if things didn't change, if something didn't happen soon, sex was only a matter of time. She was heading into a place where she was going to cheat on her husband, something she had never thought she would do, and she didn't know how to stop it. Or whether she even really wanted to stop it. Most of her wanted it to happen, most of it was desperate for it to happen. But there was something holding her back, some loyalty, some love, some propriety. She just didn't know how long it would hold for before it gave way and she fell into the abyss . . .

'Shall we give them lunch now?' James interrupted Izzy's thoughts as Alfie climbed up his torso, heading for the summit of his shoulders like a mountaineer. 'We could order some sandwiches here. Then they might have a nap in the room.'

'I don't want them to have a nap now,' Izzy said, removing a dried flower arrangement from Pearl's reach, 'I want them in bed at a reasonable time tonight so we can enjoy dinner.'

'Don't WE get to enjoy dinner as well, Mummy?' Pearl pouted. 'Aren't we allowed dinner. Are you going to STARVE us to death like the orphans?' Her plaintive voice rang out loudly across the hallway area, and an older couple passing by looked down at them disapprovingly. Izzy wasn't sure whether they were glaring at Pearl for making a noise or her for being a cruel mother, or both, so she smiled as charmingly as she was able to at them and said, 'She saw an Oxfam advert on TV. Hasn't stopped going on about the starving orphans ever since. Such an overactive imagination!' The woman sniffed, sourly.

Mr Butterworth whimpered gently as Alfie pulled his ears out like wings and made a 'neeeeoowwwwww' noise.

'Alfie, *don't* do that, poor Mr Butterworth . . .' Izzy hoiked her son up off the ground. 'I'm going to take them outside, before they destroy the place. Come and find me when we've got our rooms sorted.'

James nodded.

'Take Mr Butterworth with you, will you?'

'Oh . . .' Izzy looked mildly annoyed. 'Can't you come, then, if he needs to go? I don't really want to have to wrangle all three of them.'

James looked apologetic. 'Mm, I'd better wait and find out where our room is. Help Dad with the bags. Sorry, darling.'

Izzy rolled her eyes, and picked up Mr Butterworth's lead from the floor. 'Come on then, Mr Butterworth. Come on . . .'

Mr Butterworth reluctantly got to his feet. He was not an energetic dog.

Excellent. James sat back in the sofa. His phone beeped and he pulled it out of his pocket. 'It's Will,' he called to his mother. 'He'll be here in half an hour.' Ginny smiled, and nodded.

'Lovely, darling.'

He could sneak in a quick gin and tonic while Izzy and the children were gone. He looked around to attract the attention of a passing hotel employee, and ordered a double. He didn't mention, because he was so used to seeing the words, and because he wasn't really paying attention, that the exact wording of Will's text had been slightly different from what he had reported. It had read: *Hey mate, we'll be there in half an hour or so. Just stopped for petrol. W.*

'It's just what I need,' Harriet said to Izzy as the two women walked across the green-striped lawn. 'This weekend. Fresh air, a massage, good food, good friends.' She slipped her arm through Izzy's. 'Get out of London, out of the flat.'

'How is the flat?'

'Hateful. You were quite right, I shouldn't have taken it, not then, not straight away.' Harriet had rented a small flat immediately after her break-up with Will, in the acute fug of grief and regret and misery that she had been flooded with, and it had been a bad decision. The place was dark, apart from the bedroom, which had a street light outside the only window that shone just at the wrong angle, so that when you slept you were flooded with orange light; it was boxy, with none of the slightly haphazard charm of Will's little house on Mortimer Street, and the bathroom smelt of mould and fusty damp towels however many Jo Malone candles Harriet burnt. It was a gloomy place, though to be fair, she knew that she would have made the most sunny, charming apartment feel miserable at the moment, such was her permanent mournful mire. But now she was here, in the sunshine, away from the horrid little flat, and she could relax.

'You could have stayed with us for a bit, you know.'

'I know. Thanks. But you've got so much going on. I'd have felt like a burden. The flat'll be fine. I just need to get my head together and get it sorted out. Paint it and . . . you know. Stuff.' Harriet waved her hand in the air. 'It's a good shopping opportunity at least, I suppose.' She pulled her jacket off and dumped it on the wooden bench nearby. 'It's warm.'

'Beautiful.' Izzy handed Harriet Mr Butterworth's lead. 'Hang on to him, will you? Pearl, DON'T poke the peacock, get away from it RIGHT NOW.'

Harriet snorted as Izzy raced across the lawn to catch Pearl, who was chasing the poor bird into the bushes. It clucked along, its head bobbing in alarm as it tried to escape her determined clutches. Harriet adored Pearl, but she did remind her a little of a miniature dictator. A mini Pol Pot, issuing orders. No wonder Izzy looked so drawn these days. And her arms were so thin. Having children did seem to be better than a thousand tricep dips for keeping bingo wings away. All that lifting. She, on the other hand, hadn't lifted anything heavier than a bottle of wine for more than three months, and it showed. She must go to the gym. It was just so much effort. But here, she felt like making a new start. When she got back to London, she was going to sort herself out. She'd go to the gym, book a session with one of the trainers, even. Paint the flat. A nice dove grey for her bedroom, she thought, one of those dusky colours that Will had always said would look gloomy but which she knew would look lovely and classy. Buy some new bedlinen, something girlie. Make it look nice, like somewhere she wanted to be.

A new start. She took a deep breath of blossom-scented air and stretched her shoulders. It was a glorious day. She looked back towards the hotel building. In the window, she could see James, standing talking to his father, a glass of something in his hand. She waved at him, feeling a sudden rush of affection for the Rathbones. They were her second family, really, closer in some ways than her actual family felt. They were tightly woven into the fabric of her life.

'Who else is coming?' she asked, as Izzy returned with a rebellious-looking Pearl.

'I just wanted to take one of his feathers,' the girl said furiously, 'but Mummy is too mean to me as usual.'

'Yes, horrid Mummy.' Izzy let go of her daughter's hand. 'If you're not careful, horrid Mummy will put you on Mr Butterworth's lead, so you can't run away. How would you like that?'

'Yes!' Pearl squealed with delight. 'I would like that, go on, Mummy, I be the puppy.'

Pearl dangled from Izzy's legs. Izzy and Harriet shared a look. 'She's certifiable,' Izzy said. 'Um, sorry, who else . . . The Cartwrights, the Sinclairs, Julian's brother and his wife . . .'

'The one with the nose?'

'Yes. Bart and Caro, of course, they're coming a bit later. Think that's it. Should be quite fun. Assuming I can keep the brats under control.'

'Oh.' Harriet's voice was low, and trembled as she spoke.

'What?' Izzy was holding Alfie, who was sucking his thumb and looking as though he might fall asleep. 'Alfie, darling, we're not having a nap now. Why don't you go and play with Pearl?'

'Sleepy,' he replied, resting his head on her shoulder.

'Oh no. Why . . . Izzy, why didn't you tell me . . . I wouldn't have come, I can't . . .'

Izzy turned. 'What is it?'

Harriet was standing, sunglasses held loosely in her hand, staring at the gravel turning circle in front of the hotel, at an old, battered four by four.

'Will.'

He stood next to the car, looking up at the sky, stretching

190

his arms out as he always did after driving to loosen his back.

'Oh, bloody hell.' Izzy watched, appalled, as Harriet stared at her ex stretching, smiling. And then continued to stare as the passenger door opened and a very small blonde girl got out. She had hair that shone in the sunlight, and was immaculately dressed in the sort of pale peach that showed every mark and highlighted the golden softness of her skin. Her hair was held back with a navy headband with a flower to one side, and her large sunglasses and handbag underlined the slightness of the rest of her. She was like a little doll, in patent navy ballet pumps.

'Oh fuck.' Izzy didn't know what else to say. 'Fuck. Hats. I'm so sorry. I had no idea.'

Harriet nodded. She could not speak. She couldn't make a sound, as a hundred questions with only one answer rushed through her mind. She watched, helpless, paralysed, as Will came around to the girl's side and slipped his arm around her waist, laughing easily as he kissed her head, then pulled an overnight bag – just one, shared overnight bag – out of the back of the car and shut the door. They walked towards the hotel together, her steps small and his strides long but somehow fitting together, Will raising an arm in greeting to James, who was staring out of the window at them, and then, clocking the bemused and open-mouthed expression of his friend as he took in the scene before him, making a face that said 'What?' and a shrug of his shoulders. And then he turned, following James's gaze, towards the lawn, where Izzy and the kids and Harriet were all standing, and his eyes met Harriet's as the girl looked on, confused, and asked him something to which he clearly had no answer.

'What. The. Actual. Fucking. Fuck, James?' Izzy hissed at her husband in the hallway by the hotel reception. Around the corner, a whispered conference was going on between Will and the tiny blonde girl, who, it turned out, was called Colette. Harriet had rushed to the loo, where she had locked the door and was currently sobbing. Izzy had been to check on her once, and would go back and attempt to coax her out as soon as she had figured out a) how this had happened and b) and more importantly, what they were going to do about it.

'I've got no idea. I didn't even know Harriet was coming.'

'I didn't know *Will* was coming.'

'Well, yes.' James scratched his head. 'Mum asked him ages ago.'

'Why didn't you tell me? You never bloody think to tell me anything, and look what happens.'

James shrugged. 'I just assumed you knew, I suppose. Mum said . . . she said she'd asked Will, and he'd said that they'd love to come.' Light began to dawn on James's face.

'They. He said they'd love to come. James, did you know Will had a new girlfriend?'

'Um. No?'

'It's not a multiple-choice quiz, darling. Don't sound like you're guessing. Did you know or not?'

'He might have mentioned something. I didn't think he was going to turn up with her, though.'

'And you didn't tell me.' Izzy sighed.

'No, I didn't tell you. We haven't exactly sat down to chat much recently. You haven't really been around, you know.' James's voice was full of anger, a level that surprised both of them. Izzy silently backed off. They were on dangerous ground.

'What did your mum say?'

'Why don't you ask her?'

Izzy turned. Behind her, Ginny was approaching, looking worried. Julian followed her, thunderous.

'Oh dear. This is all a bit of a to-do, isn't it?' Ginny fiddled with the locket around her neck. Next to her, Mr Butterworth belched gently.

'It's a bit more than that, Gin. Harriet's inconsolable. Sorry, but what on earth were you thinking, inviting both of them, without telling me?' Izzy paused. 'Or not just me, anyone. Without telling *them*?'

'Yes, what were you thinking?' Julian's voice was impatient. He couldn't be doing with all of this drama. It was delaying his lunch.

Ginny looked from her husband to her son to her daughter-in-law, her fingers working still at the gold links of her necklace, her mouth open as she searched for the words to explain her mistake.

'I ... I don't know,' she said eventually. Julian snorted, donkey-like.

'For God's sake, Ginny, what do you mean, you don't know? You invited both of them, yes? What did you think was going to happen – they'd see each other and realise their mistake and everything would be fine?'

Ginny looked at the ground in panic. She didn't know what to tell them. They were all so angry with her. And they had every right to be. She'd got it all wrong, and she was going to have to work out some way to put it right. Tell the truth, her mother had always said, when she had made a mistake, or broken something, when she had been a little girl. Just tell the truth and you won't be in trouble. She couldn't tell the truth now, though, she knew, as she looked up at the angry faces of her family. Couldn't tell them that the reason both Harriet and Will had turned up was that she had rung Will's house, and invited him, and he had said yes, they'd love to come. Couldn't tell anyone that she had clean forgotten that Harriet and Will had split up, so when he said 'they' it hadn't registered at all, because of course he would say 'they'. She had emailed Harriet the details, knowing that Will would lose track of them, had thought it was a bit strange that Harriet had replied saying something about it being lucky that she was free at such late notice, but had assumed that Will had maybe forgotten to pass the invitation on. Men were always forgetting things. Not that she could complain about that, now. She couldn't tell them that she had only remembered they had split up a few minutes ago, when the whole drama had begun to unfold as Harriet spotted Will and Collette outside, but that she still had no recollection of when or how the split had happened. She was desperately trying to grasp it, pull the memory that she knew must be there from the recesses of her brain, and trying also to hide the fact that she was panicking, completely frozen with fear, because she knew that something was very wrong with her, and she had no idea what it might be.

She turned to James, and held out her hand to him. She couldn't tell them – but she could tell him. Could ask for his help. She would tell Julian after the weekend, talk to him then. But for now, she just needed to smooth things over and get through the weekend without any more calamities.

'James, darling. Can I have a word in private, please?'

'It was all a big cock-up, apparently, not intentional at all.' Izzy stared at the white-painted door of the toilet cubicle. 'Ginny said she sent you the invitation, yes?'

'An email,' Harriet snivelled. 'Yes.'

'Well, James says he asked Will. I don't know if he thought Ginny wanted him to, or whether he just went off-piste or what, but that's how it happened. I'm married to an idiot, darling, and I'll bollock him later and find out exactly what happened, but for now, will you just come out of the loo?'

There was a long pause, and then the cubicle door opened.

Harriet's face was pink and her eyes were puffy. She held a wad of ragged loo roll in her hand.

'Good. That's a start. Now, let's get you to your room and make you a stiff drink, and I'll run you a hot bath. Cure for all ills.'

'I'm not *staying*, Izzy. I can't sit around all weekend watching him fawn over that little twelve-year-old. Who is she?'

'She's called Colette, apparently.'

Harriet snorted. 'Of course she is. Colette.' She stared at herself in the mirror as she ran cold water over her wrists. 'Fuck.' She exhaled. 'Did you know?' Her eyes caught Izzy's.

'No. Promise. I would have told you.'

'Would you?'

'Probably.' Izzy perched on the edge of the basin unit. 'Yes. If I'd known it was something serious.'

'Is it?' Harriet's eyes widened. Izzy shrugged a shoulder. She couldn't say what she was thinking. But Harriet said it for her. 'Of course it is. He wouldn't bring just some fling on a weekend like this. Shit.'

She reached into her bag and began tapping concealer around her eyes. It was a bit of a losing battle against the raw red that her crying jag had inflicted on her skin, but one that she fought valiantly. She sniffed, and rummaged for mascara. Fucking Will. Fucking James. Fucking, *fucking* Colette. Colette. What sort of a mimsy, prissy, whiny name was that anyhow? The sort of name you couldn't say without simpering girlishly. The sort of name whose owner would have a proper, practised signature all curlicues and twiddly bits. She probably did little hearts over her 'i's and put smiley faces at the bottom of notes.

'What's that ring?' She nodded to Izzy's right hand. 'It's nice.'

'Oh . . .' Izzy splayed out her fingers. 'I got it a while ago.'

'Really? I haven't seen it before.'

'No. I only started wearing it again recently. Felt like my hands could do with a change, you know?' She smiled, and then rested her hand by her hip so the ring disappeared.

'So. Have you . . . been out with anyone, since Will?'

'Ha. You can say "fucked", you know, Izzy. Yes, course I have.'

'Who?'

'Oh, no one.' Harriet ferreted around in her make-up bag, avoiding Izzy's eyes. 'Just some guy I met in a bar. A couple of guys. You know.'

'Anyone nice?'

Harriet nodded. 'Yeah. I've been having fun, don't you worry.' She grinned at Izzy and hoped that her expression conveyed the right amount of mischief and single-girl-around-town raciness that she knew her friend was looking for. There was no way she was going to admit that she hated it, hated being single, hated the men she met and the nights she spent with them. Hated herself for still doing it.

The first one had been the guy from the Crown, the man who had chatted her up when Will had stood her up. She had gone back there a few weeks after New Year's Eve, in the depths of January, when most people were dieting or detoxing or broke. She had had a feeling that he would be in there. And he had been. His eyes had caught her as soon as she entered the pub, and she had gone straight over to him, knowing that if she wavered she would lose her nerve. 'Still want to buy me that glass of wine?' she had asked, and he had looked as though he couldn't believe his luck, though he quickly tried to cover it with a veneer of cool insouciance, and steered her towards the bar and a bottle of white. It had been less scary, somehow, with him than it would have been picking up some total stranger. He felt familiar, a little. After him, it was easier. She went out every couple of weeks by herself, picked someone up, had sex with them, left. She always went to their house, so that there were no awkward moments if they didn't leave. And it was – fine. She didn't come home and shower for hours or lie awake hating herself, nor did she find any of them attractive or interesting enough to want to see again. She was bored, and miserable, and spending a few hours with a man made her forget, for a while, how miserable she was, and she could play the part of a good-time girl and then go home and go to sleep. In the morning she would wake up, and for a moment she would be fine, because she would be half asleep still, and then she would come to properly and open her eyes and the room in front of her would not be the familiar bedroom that she had shared with Will for so many years, the window would be in a different place and the air felt different, and she would be spread-eagled across the bed instead of lying neatly on one side of it, and she would sigh and wish that she could just go back to sleep again.

But she was not going to tell Izzy any of that.

Izzy picked at the corners of her nails. 'So, any of these men look like they might become, you know – something more?'

Harriet shook her head. This she could be honest about. 'No. I don't want another relationship. Not now.' I want Will, she said, silently to herself. I just want Will.

'It was much simpler when we were dating, wasn't it? I can't imagine what it must be like now. I mean, if you did want a relationship, what would you do – Internet dating, I guess. Everyone seems to do it now.'

'We didn't date. That's the point. We just shagged our friends. But at some point, you run out of friends.'

Harriet paused. 'You know, sod it. I'm not going home. I don't want to spend the weekend in that horrible flat, staring at the walls and eating a whole M and S meal deal for two. Why should they get to have all the fun? I'm going to stay here, and I'm going to have a facial, and a glass of

197

champagne in the bath, and a nice dinner with my friends, and celebrate Julian's birthday. And I'm going to look awesome, and little Miss Colette can stick it up her tiny twenty-three-year-old backside.'

Izzy held her hand up, and Harriet clapped hers against it in a high five. She pulled her shoulders back and gestured to Izzy. She looked and sounded confident, but she sure as hell didn't feel it. 'Come on. Come and find my room with me before I change my mind.'

She was glad that she had packed more than one outfit, and that she had had that little shopping accident in Westfield on her way down here. She had meant to be just picking up a birthday present for Julian, but had got waylaid by Reiss and Whistles. Which she had been feeling guilty about – living by yourself was expensive, she was discovering – but was now relieved about. She stood in the centre of her bedroom, a chintzy but comfortable room with its own fireplace, all of her clothes on the bed, her hair damp, and her skin soft from her facial, and assessed her outfit options.

There was a dark blue dress made out of a slightly shiny fabric that was clingy and sexy. Maybe a bit too sexy? She didn't want to look like some slutty auntie next to Colette's fresh youthfulness. How old was she, anyhow? Twenty-three, twenty-four, maybe? It was embarrassing really. Onwards, onwards. There was a black-skinny-jeans-and-jacket option, with the sleeves rolled up to her elbows, possibly, and the silky beige top underneath. Killer heels, natch. Or there was a second dress, not a new one, a black shirt dress made of washed silk that looked like not much off but that on, with a belt, and the top buttons left undone, made her look and feel dressed up in an almost wanton way. That was the one. It had to be. She took off her towelling dressing gown and put the dress on, buckling a skinny patent-leather belt around her waist and pulling it in tight. Red lipstick, bare legs and high heels, and she would be good to go.

Will had bought her the dress, she remembered now. They'd been in Bangkok, stopping over before flying down to Phuket, and they'd been walking past a dressmaker's when he had spotted it. He hadn't bought it then, but had sneaked back and left it, wrapped in purple tissue paper, on her side of the bed that evening. She'd worn it and worn it, and he'd always loved her in it. Had always loved her. Until she had ruined it all.

Stop it, stop it. She looked in the mirror as she applied a thin line of black liquid eyeliner, winging it out from the corners of her eyes in little flicks. Colette was younger than her, and smaller, and blonder, but she was sexier, she felt sure of it, as long as she kept her confidence up. And Will was a man who appreciated women, who had a high sex drive and whose sex life with Harriet had always been excellent. They had never turned into one of those couples who didn't do it any longer, whose lack of sex had become a joke that neither of them found funny. She was the one everyone knew, she knew all of the family's private jokes and stories, all of the subjects to steer clear of and the anecdotes that got wheeled out at every get-together. She was an insider, and Colette, blonde little perfect little Colette, was not. Harriet might have lost Will, but she was not going to lose her place in the group and in the family, the place that she had held for so many years, as Caroline's friend and Will's girlfriend. She might not be one of those things any longer, but she was still the former. And she was going to make sure Colette knew about it. Harriet smoothed the skirt of her dress down over her thighs, and went down for dinner.

*

'And then I started working for Daddy,' Colette was saying, at the other end of the table, 'and I've been there ever since. I'm in charge of most of the interior decorating now,' she finished, proudly.

Will leaned forwards, his arm slung over the back of her chair. 'It's how we met. Colette's father owns the property company I've bought some of my holiday houses for Henry Butler's through.'

'Cosy,' Harriet muttered under her breath, from her place at the far end of the dining room. It was a long, rather narrow room, papered in a cream and sand-coloured stripe, with watercolours of the hunt that Harriet had seen Colette look at with distaste when they came in for dinner. She was going to have to get over *that* if she wanted to stay with Will. They had reached the main course; the starter, a wood pigeon and mushroom terrine that Colette had turned her ski-jump nose up at, had just been cleared, and a trio of waiters were filing in bearing plates of beef Wellington and silver dishes filled with baby vegetables. Harriet smiled at one of them as they carefully put her plate down in front of her.

'How's that going?' Andrew Rathbone, Julian's brother, was asking Will. He was a pompous sort of a man, director of a medical supplies company, plump around the waist where Julian was slender and trim, with bifocal glasses that made him look a little toady, and dandruff. 'Julian told me he'd invested in this new scheme of yours. Sounds all a bit like a con to me. Persuade me otherwise.'

Instinctively, from force of long habit, Harriet bristled on Will's behalf, and almost spoke to defend him. But he was unbothered by the dig, laughing and shrugging. 'I won't need to persuade you of anything, Andrew. The pots of money I'm going to make for your brother will do that.' He looked Andrew in the eye and tilted his glass towards him. 'Cheers.' Andrew harrumphed, and turned his attention to Colette.

'And you think this is all a good thing, do you? Eh? I suppose you do, if he's going to get rich from it.'

'Andrew!' His wife, a solid, matronly woman, admonished him. 'So rude. Poor girl's only just met everyone. Ignore him, dear. He thinks everyone in the world is as cash-fixated as he is.'

Colette smiled at her, then at Andrew. 'I don't need a man to support me, Mr Rathbone. My father provides for me very generously.'

Andrew Rathbone grunted. Harriet glanced over at Caroline and crossed her eyes at her in frustration. Caroline giggled, and put a bit of pastry in her mouth. Bart leaned over and whispered something in his wife's ear, and she nodded, a little smile on her lips as she listened to him. Harriet looked away. It was moments like this that made her wince. The little fragments of easy intimacy that couples had; the way their hands would gravitate towards one another's as they walked along the street, even as the rest of their bodies and brains were otherwise engaged with gesturing or bag-carrying, as though magnetically linked. The way that, even from across a room, they could glance over and attract the attention of their other half with an almost imperceptible movement, a tiny tilt of the head or twist of the mouth that meant 'come and rescue me, this guy is boring me to tears', or 'get me a top-up', or 'I told you we had to leave by ten and it's almost half past, I have to be up early in the morning even if you don't'; the silent language of their relationship secret and private. The way she had been able to look at any menu in a restaurant and know exactly what Will would order from it, and he her. Those were the things she missed.

She sighed, and looked up, back towards the far end of the table, and found that Will's eyes were on her, intense and serious. She didn't move. Just looked back at him. Across the table, Caroline shifted uncomfortably in her seat as she clocked

201

the silent exchange, and hoped that there wasn't going to be a scene.

Harriet held Will's gaze for a moment longer, then looked away, tilting her head back and letting her dress fall open at the neck as she turned to talk to James. Let him look if he wanted to. Let him look.

He hadn't spoken to her since they had all come downstairs, gathering in the hotel drawing room for drinks before dinner, their party taking up much of the small room. Bottles of champagne had been opened and bowls of olives laid out on the polished side tables, and the atmosphere had been politely awkward, in the main, as the older generation appeared and took in the unusual selection of younger guests for the first time. Harriet had dealt with it by sticking firmly on the other side of the room to Will, and making sure she was near either Izzy or Caroline all the time. 'I'm Harriet, Caroline's friend from school,' she reminded the Cartwrights and the Rathbones' other friends, aligning herself with Caroline so there would be no confusion, and watching the expressions on their faces as they nodded and accepted drinks and then went into a little huddle. 'I'm sure that she used to be with that nice Will . . . Well he's holding hands with the other girl, so I assume not . . . Pretty little thing, isn't she . . . I'm just saying, dear . . . Well, it's all very modern . . .'

It felt strange, though, being in the same room as him for this amount of time and not talking to him, not sharing a joke about how Ginny was fussing over the butter being unsalted or a look of wry amusement when Izzy got all defensive about being a working mother to one of the Rathbones' more traditional friends. Strange not to be the one by his side.

Don't be morose, she told herself. It's not sexy. Be relaxed, unbothered, confident. But it was harder than it looked, keeping up the appearance of not caring.

She looked to her left and then her right for someone to talk to, but both James and Stewart Sinclair were involved in other conversations. Instead, she caught Izzy's eye, and nodded her head towards the door. The main course was over; they could nip out for a quick cigarette without being rude. Izzy nodded in response, and held up her finger. One minute.

As Harriet walked out into the hallway, she paused. Ginny was standing in front of her, facing the wall. She appeared, at first, to be staring at a small drawing, at head height or thereabouts, but something was not quite right.

'Ginny?' Harriet walked towards her. Ginny was standing, but all her weight was on the right side of her body. Her left side looked numb, frozen almost. Her hand was out in front of her, touching the wall, as if to keep her balance. She nodded, a small movement, without looking up at Harriet.

'Yes, yes, I'm fine,' she said, moving her left leg slowly backwards and forwards, still pressing her fingers against the wall.

'You don't look fine.'

'Just . . .' Ginny spoke slowly, her voice sounding slightly slurred. Only a tiny bit, not so as you would even notice unless you were standing close to her, listening carefully, as Harriet was.

'Just a bit too much excitement and champagne, I think. You go on.'

Harriet touched her shoulder. 'Are you sure?' She didn't want to embarrass her by treating her like an invalid, but something was wrong. But then Ginny straightened up, and took her hand away from the wall, turning to face Harriet and smiling. 'Oh Harriet, stop fretting,' she said briskly. 'I said, just a bit too much fizz and a rush of blood to the head. Let's get back in for pudding, all right?'

She bustled down the hallway towards the dining room, her

green dress modest and her low heels sensible, and Harriet shrugged. If Ginny said she was fine, who was she to argue?

The room was in full swing. Puddings had been delivered and abandoned, chocolatey spoons were scattered over the table. Everyone had swapped seats, gravitating towards the people they wanted to talk to, those they felt most relaxed with. Half-full champagne glasses were everywhere; people had got to the stage of the evening where they were losing them.

'Always a bit of an error to have a party like this over two nights,' Will said, next to Harriet. 'People tend to get carried away on the first night. I remember James's stag. We were all so wrecked on the Friday night that half of our number didn't even make it back to the hotel. Saturday go-karting was a bit of a wipeout. Or wipe-up, for the poor buggers working there.'

Harriet didn't turn. She was sitting at one end of the table, had been talking to Izzy about a new idea Izzy had for the café, until the baby monitor had flashed red and Izzy had whizzed upstairs to see what was happening. Harriet took a deep breath. She could smell his woody cologne and the unmistakable, indescribable scent of his skin. Her fingers tingled. She could feel the memory of touching him imprinted on them.

She picked up her almost empty champagne glass and drained it. 'Yes. I remember. You couldn't actually speak by the time you got back on the Sunday evening. You stank for a week. Of, you know. Death.'

Will laughed. 'I felt as though I was dead. Christ. Can't do it any longer. Too old.'

'Well.' Harriet looked around the room, at the Cartwrights and the Rathbones, fine wine in their hands, Jacques Vert jackets and pearls still immaculate. 'I wouldn't worry. I doubt this is likely to turn so raucous.'

'No.' He paused. 'Fancy a brandy?'

She took a breath. Brandy was what they had got drunk on on their first date, all those years ago, cheap cooking brandy, after they spent so long in the restaurant that everywhere had been closed. They had gone back to Will's, where it had been the only thing he had had to drink. 'Terrible planning,' he had apologised, pouring it generously into little tumblers. 'Can't believe I'm so rubbish. Hardly smooth, is it?' But she hadn't wanted him to be smooth. And they had drank most of the bottle and made cheese toasties at one in the morning and danced to Bon Jovi.

'Sure,' she said, then, 'What about Colette?'

He looked at her. She still hadn't met his eyes. 'She's gone to bed,' he replied, softly. 'She gets tired.'

Harriet bit her lip, bit back the instinctive dig about children having to be put to bed early, and looked up at him. 'OK.' She nodded. 'A brandy would be good.'

They sat in the corner of the bar, at a small round table, in two wing chairs, glasses of brandy in front of them. The rest of the bar was quiet. Chatter and laughter continued to float over from the dining room, where the Rathbones continued their celebrations. It was ten thirty.

'So . . .'

'How are . . .'

They both spoke at the same time. Harriet bit her lip. Will smiled and shook his head.

'Since when were we so awkward, eh?'

Harriet shrugged a shoulder. 'Weird, isn't it?'

'How are you, Hats?' Will stared intently at her. She took a deep breath. She wanted to touch him. To reach out and take his hand in hers, wind her fingers through his. She could feel it, the ghost of the memory of how his hand would feel, the pads at the base of his fingers slightly callused, his palms dry and warm. She looked over at him.

'OK. You know.'

'Not really. No one will tell me how you've been getting on. It's like they all think I stopped caring about you when ... when we broke up.'

'Didn't you?' Harriet held her breath.

Will looked sad. 'No. Of course not. I hope not. Hats, I'll always care about you. Always. I thought you would know that.'

Harriet thought she was about to cry. 'How would I know that? I haven't heard from you since I moved out.' There was a painful lump in her throat, and she swallowed to try and release it, but still it ached.

'I didn't think you'd want to talk to me.'

Now she did start to cry. 'I always want to talk to you. I don't want to talk to anyone else.' Christ, how undignified. She had been doing so well. A few words from Will and she was a gibbering wreck. 'I miss you so much.' Oh God, she had promised herself that she wouldn't say this, wouldn't even think it so she didn't give off weak 'missing you' vibes, if there was such a thing, and here she was, sobbing into her brandy.

Will looked at his glass, uncomfortable. This was it. This was the moment where he could say 'I miss you too', or just reach for her hand, and it would all be OK. They could go back to how it was, she knew they could. He could get rid of Colette and she could move back in, move home, out of the flat of doom, and they could go back to hanging out with their friends and bickering about what film to watch and the last few months would melt away.

'I'm sorry,' he said, and could not meet her eyes. *I'm sorry.* In response to 'I miss you so much', that was on a level with telling someone you loved them and them saying 'thank you'.

Harriet felt like crawling under her chair and rolling up into a ball. Instead, she downed her glass of brandy and looked around for the barman to order another one.

'Oh God,' Will said, rubbing his face with his hands. 'I'm cocking this up, aren't I? I didn't mean I don't . . . Of course I miss you, in a way . . .'

Harriet heard herself make a strange yelping sound. 'In a way. Right.'

'No, I mean. Look, of course I miss you. It's strange not having you around. We were together for so long, weren't we? It's difficult to get used to. But . . .'

She took a deep breath. 'But now you have Colette.'

Will paused, and nodded. 'Maybe we hung on to it for too long, you know? Maybe it's a good thing that you pushed for me to decide.'

Harriet didn't respond.

'I've met someone, you know, and you will too. You're amazing, Harriet. You're an incredible woman. Someone's going to be very lucky to have you.'

I don't want someone to be lucky, you fool, she thought. I want you. I have only ever wanted you. And now I've lost you. She pushed her chair back. 'I'm going to take this up to bed,' she said, as the barman brought her second brandy over. 'I'll see you tomorrow, I guess.'

She felt utterly exhausted. Drained of all energy. She couldn't even be bothered to cry. She just wanted to get away from Will, from the pity she felt emanating from him, from his sympathetic face, and crawl into bed.

Will stood up, pulling his trousers up at the same time. As he always did. The familiar habit bit into her heart.

'Night, then,' he said, and went to kiss her on the cheek. She lifted her face to him, without thinking, and looked him in the eyes. He paused. From over by the private dining room, she heard a noise, a scuffle, but ignored it. She leant forward, quickly, before she could stop herself, and kissed him on the lips, pressing her face to his, inhaling and breathing him in. She felt him respond, naturally, automatically almost, and then stop himself, stiffen and move his face away slightly. 'Not a good idea,' he whispered, but his body said otherwise. He squeezed her elbow. 'Not a good idea,' he repeated.

'Who are you telling?' she asked, quietly.

'Hats . . .' He looked at her. His breath came in a judder. 'Are you sure . . .' He lifted his hand to her face, and touched his thumb to her lip. 'I do miss you, you know,' he whispered.

Harriet nodded. 'I miss you,' she said. Her hands went to his waist. She could feel his breath on her cheek.

'Oh God.' Caroline's voice rang out from the other side of the room, and Harriet jumped back, guilty. Ready to explain, defend herself. 'I was just . . . We weren't . . .'

But Caroline wasn't looking at them; she was looking at the floor, where her mother lay, her green jacket rumpled and rucked up around her and her neck rigid as her body convulsed. 'Oh God,' she cried. 'Someone call an ambulance. Someone help!'

Chapter Eleven

August 2009

They were going to have to tell the children. James, and Caroline. Best to tell them together. Then there would be the grandchildren, eventually. They were so small, though. Ginny couldn't bear the thought of it.

She hadn't been able to take it in, when they told her. It didn't feel real. 'You have a brain tumour, Mrs Rathbone,' they had said, and the first thing she had thought was that if they were telling her that, they could at least call her by her own name, not that of her mother-in-law. For a moment she was a newly-wed again, still unused to her name, finding it hard to get her fingers to make the letters when she had to sign a cheque. Of course she was Mrs Rathbone now, had been for decades. She was a mother-in-law herself, twice over. She hoped that she was a good one.

But it was hard – no one told you how hard it was – to see your children with people who didn't always do things properly. To suddenly have to restrain that maternal impulse that you had always been able to give in to, from the days when you leant over the table to cut up their roast potatoes, or reached for their hand as you began to cross the road. She had done that with Bart once, not so long ago – they had been out for lunch, the four of them, on a Saturday, and on the way to the local French bistro that they were heading to she had pressed the button and automatically reached for his hand as she stepped into the road. He had let her take it, as well; it was rather sweet. Hadn't wanted to offend her by pulling away, had let her lead him across the road, like an overgrown child, until Caroline had turned her head and spotted them and laughed. 'I think he can manage by himself now, Mother,' she had said, and Ginny had felt silly, and blushed. She had dropped his hand, embarrassed, and apologised to him, but he had patted her on the shoulder and said he wasn't at all sure that he could manage, had almost been run over on Piccadilly the other day because he was crossing the road without paying enough attention. 'Staring at the BlackBerry, as usual,' he had said with a wink, and she had been grateful to him for what she knew was a deliberate kindness.

Still. They could not all be deliberately kind just so that she felt useful and necessary, in the way she always had done when the children were small. It had been one of the things she had liked most about being a mother, that feeling of purpose, of being necessary. Necessary to the running of the house, to her children, to Julian. There was a point to her. Well, there had been then. Not any longer.

She sat in the chair, facing the doctor, in his small consulting room. Julian was in the seat next to her, his chair turned towards hers, his hands encasing hers in his. She remembered now. Of course she was Mrs Rathbone. That was her name. She blinked, and waited for the doctor to continue. The room was square, and he sat behind a smart mahogany desk. There were photos in silver frames on the bookshelf next to him, of him with a pretty woman who must be his wife, at a party, and one of them skiing, their sunburnt faces crunched up happily as they squinted in the direction of the camera. There was a wedding photo of a girl in her thirties, wearing one of the strapless dresses they all went in for now that she thought made them look as though they had a towel wrapped around their torsos, but that were all the rage. Then one of the same girl holding a little baby, a girl, by the looks of things, though she wouldn't have wanted to put money on it. You had to be so careful. People really didn't like it if you got it wrong. Still, he had a family, children, grand-children, that was good. Why was it good? She didn't quite know, but she was sure it must be.

'. . . The frontal lobe,' he was saying, quietly and calmly, 'in a rather tricky position, I'm afraid . . .' She forced herself to focus, and concentrate. She must pay attention. It sounded important, what he was saying, but she couldn't quite place why, exactly, couldn't work out its relevance to her. Maybe she should be taking notes. She reached for her bag to get out her notebook and pen, so she could write down what he was telling her. She could look it up then, later, when they got home.

She couldn't reach her bag, though, something was stopping her. Holding her back. She tried to move her left arm again, to stretch it down towards the floor in what she knew must be a simple movement, but she couldn't. It was like that time at the hotel, she thought vaguely, when everything went stiff on one side and she had pretended to Harriet that she was tipsy and looking at the picture on the wall. It was as though the messages wouldn't work – as though there were a jam in the signalling department. She stopped trying.

'Are you all right, Mrs Rathbone?' the doctor was saying.

'Yes, yes. Quite all right,' she said. Her voice sounded a little strangled, and she sat still. She didn't want to draw attention to herself and make a fuss. The fuzzy stiffness would go away soon, she was sure. Anyhow, there was a more pressing problem for her to deal with, and that was Julian. He was still grasping her hand tightly with one of his, and his face was wet with tears. Why was he crying like that? Her heart broke for him. Julian

211

never cried. Or hardly ever. He had shed a couple of restrained, manly tears when James and Caroline had been born, as well as a few when she had lost the baby she had been carrying in between them; one or two when he had given Caroline away. And a fair few when there had been that awful business with his – friend. So what – half a dozen occasions, in forty-odd years?

Now, though, he did not hold back. He sobbed, his shoulders jerking up and down, and the hand that was not holding on to her was covering his face. She could just see his eyes, under his heavy, greying eyebrows, in such distress that she could hardly bear to look at him.

'Shh,' she whispered, 'don't cry, darling. It's all going to be fine. Isn't it?' She looked towards the doctor for reassurance. He would tell Julian. It would all be fine. The tingling numbness in her right side was fading now, and she felt more herself again. She couldn't remember what the doctor had told her, but she would just get him to go through it again. She gently let go of Julian's hand and managed to pick her handbag up with no problems now, taking out her small leather-covered notepad with the little pen that slotted into its side.

'Now, I'm sorry, Dr . . .' She looked at the nameplate that sat at the front of his desk, helpfully positioned. 'Dr Gardiner. If you could just run through that again. What is it that Julian has?' It must be Julian, that must be why they were here and why he was so upset. Poor chap, he never had been much good with blood and things. Hadn't been able to cope when she had to have stitches when she cut herself that time chopping leeks, had had to sit outside the room and wait while she was . . .

'Julian's fine, Mrs Rathbone,' the doctor was saying, though. 'Julian's fine, don't you worry. I'm afraid it's you that's unwell.'

'But . . . no . . . don't be silly,' she said, almost laughing. 'I feel perfectly fine. I've just had a bit of a summer cold, that's all. It really isn't anything to make a fuss about.' She turned to Julian.

'Come on, darling, let's go, shall we? I do appreciate you taking so much trouble over me, but it really isn't necessary. Let's go home and we can get fish and chips for supper, as a treat.'

Julian took a deep breath. 'Yes. Yes, that sounds lovely.' He wiped his hand over his face. He had stopped crying now, but he looked weary and his skin was slightly grey. Drained, that was how he looked. She reached forward and touched his cheek. 'You're good to me, darling. You're a good man.'

They stood, and Julian shook the doctor's hand.

'I'll put everything we've talked about in a letter, and send it to you tomorrow,' Dr Gardiner was saying. 'I know it can be hard to take a lot of information in all at once. The shock of it . . .' Julian nodded.

'Thank you. Yes, thank you.' He shook the man's hand again.

'Come along, darling. I'm sure the doctor's got far more important patients to see. We mustn't take up any more of his time . . .' Ginny started saying, and then stopped. It came back to her, all of a sudden, in a rush. He had said something about her being unwell. What was she doing chatting about fish and chips? She stopped, and turned slowly to the doctor.

'Did you . . . did you say – I have a brain tumour?'

The doctor looked at her kindly. 'Yes. Yes, I'm afraid so. Would you like to sit down again?'

Julian drove them home slowly, carefully, steering them through the traffic of central London and down towards home in his big silver estate car. He had always driven an estate car, for as long as they had been married. He liked the stateliness of them, somehow. They seemed to glide. Ginny had always had something smaller, nippier. These days it was a little Polo, navy blue, covered in Mr Butterworth's silky, Werther's Original-coloured hairs, with a soft padded basket in the passenger-side footwell for him to curl up in on their occasional trips out together.

Not that Ginny drove much any more. She had stopped taking the car out regularly some time ago, Julian thought as he drew up to the traffic lights by the corner of the common. Mr Butterworth was getting old and stiff and didn't like to walk far, so she usually just took him on the lead to the bit of the common nearest their house, where the duck pond was, cajoling him all the way as he loitered and dragged on his lead, keen to be allowed to return home.

Maybe that wasn't the only reason she hadn't been driving, though. Maybe the excuses about wanting to lose a bit of weight, stretch her legs more, had been just that – excuses. Had she been suffering in silence, and if so, for how long? Should he have noticed earlier, done something? Guessed?

The answer, he was forced to admit, was almost certainly yes. He should have opened his eyes to her, should have spotted the signs and realised that was what they were – signs. Not just become frustrated with her and grumpily retreated to his study, shutting the door behind him. Literally and metaphorically.

The shoplifting, that had been a sign. He had asked the doctor while Ginny was in the loo, where she had gone to collect herself after the news had finally sunk in, whether it could have been related, and he had said yes.

'It was so unlike her,' he said, his elbows resting on his knees and his fingers interlocked. 'She's always been such a – such a good girl. Stickler for the rules, for doing things properly. Always kept the children spick and span. Kept *me* spick and span, come to it.' He sighed. 'I just thought she was . . . bored, I suppose.'

Dr Gardiner's face was kind, in a distant sort of a way. 'The area of the brain where your wife's tumour is located is responsible for impulse control. In part – that's not its only function, but it is one of them. This is what probably caused the shoplifting. She did not experience the same level of impulse control that she usually would. Wasn't able to regulate her urges. Some patients overeat, compulsively. Others experience sexual disinhibition. Behave in ways that would usually be unthinkable to them.'

He spoke in these strange, slightly truncated sentences that set Julian's teeth on edge and made him feel nervous. Still, he was a good doctor, Julian knew. The best in his field, or so he had been told. That was the important thing. Ginny deserved the best.

Julian glanced at her now, surreptitiously, as he turned the car into the driveway and let it slow to a halt. She was silent. Still. She had not cried at all yet. Had it really sunk in? The doctor had explained everything to her, how the tumour was in a part of the brain that was difficult to get at, how they did not think they would be able to operate in order to remove it, but that they felt the best course of action was a course of radio-therapy to shrink it and, as he put it, 'lessen the effects of the symptoms you have been experiencing as a result of its persistent presence'. Its persistent presence. It made the tumour sound like a toddler, a naughty toddler who kept demanding his mother's attention, nagging, whining, whingeing. Knocking things over and getting into places it wasn't meant to. A toddler called – a toddler called Paul. James had had a friend from playgroup called Paul when he was two or three, one of those difficult toddler ages, a difficult, permanently snotty little boy with a whine in his voice and a nasty habit of pulling things off ledges and on to the floor on purpose when he thought no one was looking. Julian had put his foot down eventually, and told Ginny she wasn't to invite Paul round to play any longer, after one afternoon when he had kicked James in the shin, leaving a big bruise with a graze at the centre, and broken one of Ginny's favourite vases by elbowing it off the kitchen table. Paul. That was what he would call the tumour, this uninvited, unwelcome visitor to their lives. Paul.

215

He felt a little better once he had thought of that, and he patted Ginny's hand as he put the handbrake on and started to get out of the car. He would deal with this Paul just as he had dealt with that little bugger. Firmly, decisively. No negotiations, no messing around. They would be fine. Ginny would be fine.

'Come on, darling,' he said, unclicking his seat belt and opening his door. 'Let's get you inside and put the kettle on. Then I'll go and pick up those fish and chips. We could have them in bed, if you like. Wasn't there an episode of *Casualty* on the recorder that you wanted to watch?' He stopped himself. Of course she wouldn't want to watch *Casualty*. Stupid of him. Insensitive fool, it was the last thing she'd want to do. 'Sorry, not that.'

Ginny remained in her seat, not moving. He went around to her side of the car and opened the door for her. 'I could stop by the video shop . . .'

'I'm not having the treatment, Julian,' she said, as he held it open for her to step out of. 'I know what you're going to say,' she continued, firmly, before he could speak. 'You're going to say "we can think about it" and "we don't have to make any decisions just yet" and you'll have that determined look on your face thinking that you'll be able to persuade me otherwise later so it doesn't really matter what I say now.'

Julian kept his mouth shut.

'Well, I don't want to think about it. I've thought about it as much as I need to. And I've made my decision. I don't want to spend any more time or energy thinking about it than I have to. I'm not going to spend whatever time I have left . . .'

'Ginny, don't . . .' He couldn't help himself from exclaiming at that. The mention of time left, as a finite, immovable goal-post, was too much for him to allow to pass by unchallenged.

But she carried on, determined and undaunted by his distress.

216

He knelt down so he was at her level, and gently reached over to undo her seat belt.

'I'm not going to spend that time going to and from that hospital. Sitting in traffic, you taking up all your time driving me there and back. I know you'll do it, and you'll do it uncomplainingly, but it's not what I want. I don't want the children to have to do it either, come and pick me up from appointments when you can't, wonder and worry whether the next round of treatment will be the one that does the trick either way, spend hours waiting for the verdict outside the doctor's rooms. They don't need it, they've got their own lives.'

'They love you,' Julian said, helplessly.

Ginny smiled at him, and reached out her hand. He took it in his and brought it to his lips, kissing it. He looked at her. Her eyes were clear, and bright. You would never have known there was anything wrong with her; that just an hour ago she had been told of the severity of her illness, had been so confused and forgetful. There was no confusion in her face now, none of that uncertainty. Just clarity, and resolve. 'I know they do, darling,' she said gently, 'and that's why. One of the reasons why. They don't need to suffer through that.'

'We'll all get through it together, we'll fight it together,' Julian said, and he could hardly get the words out. 'We're a family, Gin. We're a family.'

She shook her head. 'We won't fight it together, darling one. No I'm not fighting this. This is my decision. Mine. I've spent all my life doing things for other people, putting them first. You, the children, the grandchildren. And I've been glad to do it. It's what I enjoy, and I've done a good job, haven't I?'

Julian nodded. It was undeniably true.

'Then you owe me this,' she said, and now her voice did waver and tears sprang to her eyes, but she held them back, with sheer force of will. 'This is what I want. I'm doing it for me. And if you love me and if you're any kind of husband, you'll support me.'

Julian did not reply. He knew what she was referring to, in her silent, unspoken way. That one awful year, the year when he had almost lost her, had thought he had ruined everything, destroyed all that they had worked for and all their happiness with one bad decision, one short period of weakness and submission to temptation.

'How could you?' she had screamed at him, really screamed; he'd never heard her make a noise quite like it before, not even when she'd been in labour. 'How could you, Julian? After everything, after all these years?'

He had sent the kids to friends in the afternoon, when he had got home and known by the look on her face as she sat silent, white-faced at the kitchen table, refusing to say a word; had called up Harriet's mother and told her there was a family emergency – 'My mother's rather unwell, I'm afraid, we need to go and see her and I'm worried it'll be too upsetting for the children' – and she had sounded concerned and said of course, she'd pick them up straight away, and the kind look on her face when she came to the door had made him feel like even more of a heel. When, a few months later, his mother really did become suddenly ill, and die, he had remembered that day, and that lie, and felt sure, though he was not a superstitious man in the slightest, that he had brought it on himself, that he had tempted fate and it had answered him.

'Granny will be OK, won't she, Dad?' James had asked as they left, fourteen and trying to be a man, his teenage back determinedly straight but his eyes like a child's still. Julian had clapped him on the shoulder and said yes, she would be fine, he was sure, and had astonished himself with the ease of his lies.

He had not, it seemed, astonished Ginny in the same way. As soon as the front door was shut and the children were safely out of earshot, she had flown at him, full of rage and hurt, pounding at him with her small fists. 'You liar, you vile, vile liar. God, I can't bear to listen to you lie, it just comes so easily to you, doesn't it? You've been lying to me for months, for years maybe, how could I know how long? How many lies have you told, Julian, to me, to your children? How many? How many?'

He'd had to hold her wrists, in the end, to try and stem the flood of blows raining down on him, but still she fought and pummelled until eventually she stopped and just cried, which was worse. She wouldn't look at him; no matter how hard he tried to get her to talk to him she would not, just sat and wept and wept. In front of her was an envelope, an anonymous letter, and a photograph. A photograph that Ginny was staring at, disbelieving, as though if she looked for long enough it might turn into something else, something less devastating. Eight weeks of stupid, stupid weakness, that was all it had taken to break the heart of the woman he loved so much and to strike what he feared would be a permanent blow to their marriage; eight pointless weeks that he wished he could tear up and throw away just as he was tearing up the letter. 'Look,' he'd shouted, 'it doesn't have to spoil everything, it doesn't need to. We can go on, Ginny, we can go on as before. It's over already, I promise. I swear, it's over, it was over before it had even really begun.'

She had looked at him then with a cry of rage, a squeal almost, and crashed her hand down on the table. 'Don't lie to me! Stop lying!' And she had walked quickly out of the room and slammed the door, and he had heard her go into their bedroom and had known that he should leave her alone, for now.

The lie became truth shortly afterwards. He left the house, rushing down the steps without bothering to put a jacket on, and half walked, half ran to the phone box at the top of the street. He wanted to put things right, and he could not make this call from his home. When she answered, he realised that this woman, who had so entranced him only weeks ago, now seemed as repellent to him as rotting meat. 'I will never see you or speak to you again,' he had said, calmly and with no emotion in his voice. 'If we should bump into one another I will not acknowledge you. There is nothing between us. There never was.' He had listened to her weep and apologise, and had felt nothing.

'I'm sorry,' she cried. 'He hired a private detective. I didn't know he was going to write to her. I wouldn't have let him, I promise. Is she—' He had hung up. He would not discuss his wife with this woman.

When he had returned to the house, he had ventured upstairs, and had found Ginny packing all of his clothes into a suitcase. It was the characteristic neatness and care with which she was doing it that had got him: no throwing things in any old how for her; she was carefully folding shirts and balling up socks so that they slotted into the gaps formed by his shoes, wasting no corner of space. He had watched her for a moment, and then had sat down on the edge of the bed and wept himself, his forehead in his hands, his shoulders juddering, unable to raise his head and face her, so ashamed was he.

'Don't cry,' she had said, not soothingly, as she might have done to a child waking from a nightmare, but impatiently, crossly. He shook his head. He couldn't stop. 'Don't cry!' she'd said again. 'You don't have the right to cry. You don't have the right.'

She had thrown a china cow at him then, an ornament that he had bought for her on their honeymoon in Scotland, and it had broken and she had wept and wept, kneeling on the floor and picking up the pieces gently as though they were the pieces of her broken heart, and eventually he had stumbled on to the floor and shuffled towards her on his knees, still weeping himself, and held her and she had let him now, and they had stayed there, crying, for what felt like hours, until their joints ached and their heads pounded with the effort of it, and their tears had been staunched by exhaustion.

In the car, Ginny closed her eyes for a moment, tired by her speech. She was quite right. He did owe her.

She allowed Julian to help her out of the car, smoothing her skirt down as she gathered her things and headed for the house.

'Now,' she said, as he walked her, arm loosely around her shoulders, up the steps to the front door. 'How about that fish and chips?'

'You can't,' Caroline said, when they told her. Her mouth was set in a line, straight, solid, her jaw clenched as she tried not to cry. They had rung and asked her and Bart to come over for supper, and James and Izzy, and to leave the children at home. They had known as soon as they had done that that it would be bad news. 'Tell me now,' James had said on the phone to his father. 'Just tell me.'

But he and Ginny had agreed that they would tell them all together, in person, that was what they had decided, and so he simply repeated that he would see him at seven that evening, and gently said goodbye. Ginny had done a couple of roast chickens with bread and salad, and there was cheese and tomatoes from the garden.

'You can't just decide that,' Caroline continued. 'It's not – it's not only up to you, really, is it, Mummy?' She was dressed in her smart work clothes, and she looked elegant and chic, but her face was that of a scared child. Bart held her hand and remained silent.

'I mean, I know you're the one that it's bad for. Who's going to have to go through it. But we'll all be there, we'll all help you. It's just the shock of it. That's what it is.' She nodded, as if to reassure herself. 'Just the shock of it.'

James cleared his throat, and then spoke.

'I think it would be better if we discussed treatment options another time. When we've all had a chance to let things sink in.' He looked pale and shaken.

'No.' Ginny shook her head, firmly. 'No, I'm sorry. I really am sorry. I know it's an awful lot to take in and absorb all at once. But you must listen to me and understand. It's important that you understand. I'm not going to have any treatment. I'll have painkillers, and anything like that that the doctors think will help me cope with it. And I'll use whatever complementary treatments make me feel better. Acupuncture's supposed to be very effective for some of the symptoms. But I'm not going to go through months of chemotherapy and radiotherapy, when we know what the outcome will be. I'm not going to do it.'

'But you don't know!' Caroline's voice trembled and she stood and walked over to the window. 'You can't know, no one can! You don't know what they'll find out, they're doing more research all the time. And doctors get things wrong – you know they do. How can you be so – so selfish?'

Ginny smiled at her daughter. 'I know,' she said, 'it's quite a thing, isn't it?' She didn't deny her self-centredness. Didn't feel the need to. It was curiously uplifting.

Caroline sighed in frustration and turned to her father. 'Daddy. Tell her. You have to tell her.'

Julian spread his hands out in front of him in a gesture of helplessness. 'Darling. I know. I know it's hard to hear. And I struggled with your mother's decision at first. But . . .'

Caroline shook her head and refused to listen. 'No. No, no, no. You can't support her, support this. You just can't.'

Julian took a step towards her and she pushed her arm out in front of her as though to ward him away. 'My darling girl. Don't upset yourself. Don't.'

Caroline began to sob, deep, heart-wrenching sobs as he walked towards her and took her in his arms. She collapsed into them, leaning against his chest and soaking the front of his striped shirt with her tears.

After a while, he motioned for Bart to come to them, and passed his weeping daughter gently into the arms of her husband. She allowed herself to be transferred without complaint.

'I do wonder whether you've thought all this through, Ginny,' Izzy said, carefully. 'Have you considered the implications for Julian? When you get . . . weaker?'

Ginny straightened her back. 'Of course I have, thank you, dear,' she said, and a moment of electricity passed between the two women. 'There's a wonderful hospice not too far away. We went to see it yesterday, didn't we?' Julian nodded. 'It's really very peaceful. There's a lovely garden.'

'Oh God,' Caroline yelped into Bart's shoulder. 'A lovely garden. Well that's just fucking perfect, isn't it? As long as there's a lovely bloody garden.'

'Try and understand, darling heart. I want it all to be as easy for you as possible. That's why. Partly why.'

'What would make it easy for us, Mama, would be knowing that you – that we – were doing everything that could be done to fight it,' James said quietly. 'Speaking for myself, at least.' Caroline nodded tearfully.

'Exactly.'

'Well, I can see that. From your point of view. But I'm afraid there's something that you're just going to have to accept. This isn't happening from your point of view. Not first of all. Not foremost. Yes, it'll affect you deeply, horribly, and I'm sorry for that.'

Ginny took a deep breath, and looked around at her family. Her gaze was kind but determined. 'But this is happening to me. And I shall cope with it in the way that I see fit. The way I am able to. I want my death to be some reflection of the way I have lived. And I am not going to die fighting.'

Caroline and Bart didn't stay for supper. Caroline was too upset, too tired, she said; she just wanted to go home and have a bath and get into bed. 'All right, darling.' Her mother had nodded. 'I'll call you tomorrow.' Caroline hugged her, but could hardly look at her. In the car she was quiet as they reversed out of the drive and down the hill.

'I can't decide whether I'm furious with her or – I don't know what,' she said eventually. 'I can't believe Daddy's going along with it. We have to do something, Bart. We have to make her see.'

They had taken a taxi home, as they had gone to the Rathbones' straight from work, and Bart reached into his pocket for his wallet. Caroline took the house keys from her handbag and stopped on the steps that led to the front door of their apartment building. It was a tall redbrick Victorian house that at some point had been divided up into flats, one on each floor. The windows were large and the ceilings high. But really, Caroline longed for a house. Maybe when she eventually got pregnant.

'I don't think we do, though, darling.'

'What?' She turned to him in surprise. He raised his hand to the cab driver in thanks as he pulled away, and then jogged up the steps behind her.

'I know how sad it is for you. For all of us. But she's right, you know. It is her choice.'

Caroline slid the key into the front-door lock, her fingers trembling as she did so. 'I don't believe it,' she said. 'Bart, you can't possibly be saying we should just let her do this. Just let her . . . die.' The door opened and she walked quickly up the stairs, finding the key for their flat as she went. She had to get inside, had to be in the safety of her own home. Her mother, her beloved mother who had always been there for her, always looked after her. Caroline and Ginny had been close since forever. They'd never had the teenage fallings-out that lots of her friends had had with their mothers. Caroline had never really rebelled in that way, that was partly why. Ginny had never given her any need to. She had always been calm, and kind, and generous, and reasonable. And now she wanted to do this awful, selfish, utterly unreasonable thing. She wanted to throw it all away, everything. Her marriage, her children, her grandchildren, both existing and unborn . . . her very life. She was prepared to leave it all behind, and for what? So that she did not have to go through some unpleasant treatment? What sort of attitude was that? What sort of example, coming from the woman who had always told Caroline to 'stick at it, darling, keep going. You can make almost anything work if you just keep trying.' And now she wasn't even going to try at all. Caroline couldn't comprehend it. It was as though her mother had already died, already gone, and left someone entirely other in her place.

As soon as she got inside, she shrugged off her jacket and hung it up on the peg by the door, kicking her ballet pumps off and walking barefoot across the carpet to the kitchen. She needed a glass of water.

'You sound terribly casual about it,' she said as she let the water from the tap run cold over her fingers before putting the tumbler underneath it. 'As though she were deciding which supermarket to do the shopping at or whether or not to get a new haircut. This is her life, Bart. She's going to die if she doesn't have the treatment. She's going to die soon. And no one seems to really give a shit. Least of all her.'

She drained the glass of water in a couple of long gulps and refilled it.

'Don't say that,' Bart said from behind her. 'Don't make it sound like I don't care.' He was facing away from her, resting his hands on the edge of the kitchen worktop, and his face was

225

in profile to her. He didn't look at her, but his voice was quiet and warning.

'Well, do you?' Caroline's voice was high and taut, in total contrast to his; hysteria was seeping into it. She could hear it herself, like an elastic band stretched too far, but she couldn't help it. Panic was rising up in her chest like water in a blocked drain, and she couldn't stop it. 'Because it doesn't sound as though you do. If it was your mother, we'd all be having to run down there to pay court at her bedside; if it was your mother, you'd be flying her to some expensive specialist on the other side of the world because God forbid she should suffer an ingrown bloody toenail for more than five minutes. But when my mother is dying, when she has a tumour in her head, Bart, if you can even understand that, then we're all supposed to just say, oh well, never mind, she had a nice life, bye bye, Ginny . . .'

He turned towards her, quickly, and she was shocked by a look on his face that she had never seen before, a look that made him ugly and frightening.

'Don't talk to me like that. Don't say I don't care. I'm not some idiot. I won't have you make me out to be the bad guy, all right?'

'I'm sorry.' She was shocked by his anger. 'I'm sorry. It's just with all of this happening at home . . .'

'What do you mean, at home? *This* is your home. That's not your home, not any more. Unless you want it to be.'

She looked down. Her wrist was in his hand, she saw. That must be why it hurt so much. Her skin was turning red underneath his fingers, the flesh twisted and her arm bent in towards her. She tried to move it but his grip was tight and held fast.

'Bart, let go. Let go!'

He continued to hold on to her arm, and she could hear his breath, fast and regular. 'Would you rather be back there, with Mummy and Daddy? You think I don't understand anything,

226

don't you?' he said, ignoring her pleas to let her go. 'Why did you marry me if you think I'm so stupid, hmm? Why didn't you marry someone who would agree with everything you said, some sheep who would follow you around like a little lapdog? Why?'

'I didn't want to marry someone else,' she said, her voice a wail. 'I wanted you. I love you. Bart. I don't understand. I'm sorry. Bart, I'm sorry.' Not now. She couldn't bear it. She needed him now, needed his comfort. 'I'm sorry,' she said again. But this time her apology was not enough, did not have the power to soothe and calm him. He raged on, his voice getting louder, his body closer to hers and harder, more full of angry blood that swirled through him.

'You didn't marry them, because they wouldn't have you. You married me because I was the only one on offer.'

'No.' She shook her head. It wasn't true. She loved him with all her heart, she did. But there was the tiniest bit of truth to what he was saying that meant her denials sounded false even to her. It wasn't as though she had been overwhelmed with proposals of marriage, or even dates. But that didn't mean she had settled for Bart – far from it. She hadn't been able to believe her luck. 'Why would you think that? Bart, please let go, you're really hurting me.' He loosened his grip a little, but kept hold of her arm.

'You've hurt me, Caroline. You've hurt me very much.'

'I've hurt *you*? How? Bart, my mother . . .'

'Yes, I know. She's very unwell. But I can't support you if you don't trust me. You don't trust me, so what's the point? What's the point in carrying on?'

'Baby, what are you saying? Don't say that. I trust you. Of course I trust you.'

'I don't think you do. You say I don't understand, that I would put my mother before yours, you don't listen to what I'm trying to say to you . . . I know you're very upset, but it doesn't mean you can take it out on me.'

His voice had softened, and his eyes were sad. The sight of them broke her heart.

'Bart, listen to me. I would still have married you if every man on earth had proposed to me. I would have married you if you had nothing, if you were a beggar on the street. I would follow you anywhere.'

'Because you want a baby. And I'm the only one that's going to give it to you. That's all you want.'

She looked at him uncomprehendingly. She almost laughed, it was so ridiculous. She could not love Bart any more than she did. His presence was like oxygen to her, she craved him. And here he was suggesting that she wasn't bothered whether he was here or not, that she just wanted his sperm, like some kind of crazed hormonally fixated madwoman. OK, she was desperate to conceive, and maybe she had pushed him a bit with the scheduled sex, but she was doing it for them. For the family that she was trying so hard to create. Trying, trying. Her whole life was spent trying.

'I . . .' She couldn't speak. Her head hurt, and her back ached. She was exhausted. Didn't understand how all of this had happened, what it was she had said that had made him like this. But then . . . she had been hysterical, had accused him of some things that weren't true and which were unfair. She had obviously hurt him more deeply than she had realised. She must learn to keep her temper, even when she was upset. It didn't really matter now, anyhow, how she had started things off; it mattered that she make them right. And then she could go to bed, and sink into sleep, and everything would be better in the morning, it always was, and she and Bart would cope with what was happening at home – with her parents – together.

'It's not all I want. It's not.' And a sudden rush of anger filled her chest. How dare he? How dare he say that? 'If that was all I wanted, then don't you think I'd have looked elsewhere for it by now?' As soon as the words were out of her mouth, she gasped with the horror of them.

'Oh no, Bart, I didn't mean . . .' But it was too late. He hit her, once, hard, in the stomach, and she doubled over as the air shot out of her body. She hadn't meant it. It wasn't his fault that she hadn't got pregnant, there was no reason to think that it was his fault. She had just been so angry, so upset, so hurt. And now she had ruined everything. Tears fell from her eyes and hit the floor. A strange, long squeaking noise was coming from her mouth and she couldn't stop it. Couldn't move. She looked up at Bart from her position bent over by the wall, and their eyes met for a moment. He paused, looking deep into her eyes, and shook his head, then took another step back and turned away from her.

He walked down the corridor and opened the front door of their flat, grabbing his jacket from the peg by the door as he did so. She could breathe again now, and she straightened and followed him.

'Bart – don't go, it's silly . . .'

He spun around and his eyes were blazing. 'Don't call me silly. Don't ever call me silly!'

'I didn't! I didn't mean you . . . Bart, I'm sorry, come back.'

But he was gone again, moving forwards, moving away from her. Out of her reach. Through the door and on to the landing, shrugging his jacket on as he went, his face thunderous and his shoulders stiff with anger.

'Bart!' She heard the shrieking, hysterical desperation in her voice and hated herself for it, but it was everywhere inside her and she couldn't stop it flooding into her mouth like bile. Still he kept moving, his feet thudding down the stairs.

She couldn't bear it. He mustn't just walk out like this, in such anger; he mustn't be allowed to. She ran down the stairs after him, her feet padding lightly, making a faint echo to her husband's footsteps.

'You can't leave. You can't leave, I won't let you. We're married, we have to talk things over.' Her voice was a high-pitched whine, and she thought somewhere in the back of her fear- and grief-addled brain how slappable she sounded. She had always hated women who whinged.

'We have to try. We have to try harder.' She reached forward and took hold of the collar of Bart's jacket, tugging on it. She would stop him leaving. She just had to make him see how important it was. She had to get through to him.

She pulled on his jacket and her hand was damp with the tears that she had wiped from her face. As she pulled, he turned – 'Get off – get OFF me' – and swiped her arm away with his, as though he were swatting a fly. She had already been moving faster than was sensible, in shoes with a skiddy base down worn carpets, and the motion of avoiding his arm sent her off balance. She grasped with her fingers, uselessly, for something to hold on to once more, but there was nothing; her feet had slipped out from under her and her coccyx landed painfully and jarringly on the step as she hit it, and then slid down the flight of stairs. Her top was pushed up as she went, and she could feel the synthetic fibres of the ugly patterned carpet scraping and grazing her back.

By the time she reached the bottom of the stairs, her arm was twisted underneath her where it had got caught as she tried to save herself, and her wrist was throbbing and painful. Bart reached her just a second later, his breath coming fast, his eyes terrified as he knelt in front of her, afraid to touch her. 'Caroline? Oh God, my darling, stay there, stay still, it's all right, I'm here . . . You silly thing, how did you trip like that?'

He pulled his mobile phone out of his pocket and tapped 999 on to the screen. Caroline closed her eyes. She couldn't bear to keep them open and see him, see herself. 'Caroline.' His voice was serious and kind now. All the anger was gone. She opened her eyes again and looked into his. He blinked. She was so confused. More than anything, she felt relief that he was not angry with her any more, that he was taking care of her. That was all she wanted. So when he looked down at her and said, quietly but firmly, 'I didn't mean it. It wasn't my fault,' she simply looked up at him and shook her head. 'No. No, my darling, of course not. It wasn't your fault.'

And he held her hand, gently, and kissed it, as though rewarding her for her complicity.

James and Izzy and Pearl and Alfie were decamping to Cornwall for August, the four of them. A family holiday. Izzy had closed the café for the month, putting a sign up on the door saying that they would reopen in September. She hoped that was true. In the last couple of months it had been harder going than she could ever have imagined. The initial flush of enthusiasm had worn off, and people weren't quite as interested in the place any more, had got used to it being there; it had become part of the furniture. Izzy knew this was the danger time – restaurants and cafés opened and closed within a few months all the time. She had to make it work, though. She had too much invested in it, personally and financially, for it not to. They could not afford for it to fail. But staying open all through the summer when there were no customers to justify the overheads could be financial suicide, so rather than limp on through August, she decided to close, decisively, and think through her plan of action for the autumn. Everyone was away, anyway, in their holiday houses in Tuscany and the south of France, or, like them, by the seaside in England.

They hadn't been going to have a holiday at all this year. Couldn't afford it, not while James still hadn't got a sniff of a job – and it had almost been a whole year – and they were worried about leaving Ginny and Julian if they went abroad. But this way they could come as well, were planning on driving down for the second week. 'The sea air will do you good, Gin, it can't not,' Izzy had told her mother-in-law, who had demurred when she had first suggested it. 'I don't want to be a burden, darling,' she had said. 'I want you to get a proper break, you deserve it.' She wasn't being a martyr, Izzy knew; she really meant it. 'We want you to come. Please? For the children, if no other reason. They love you so much. I'd love them to spend some proper time with you.' She didn't say 'while you still can', but they had both known it was what she meant, and Ginny had agreed.

James had protested at first. 'We can't possibly afford it,' he had said when she had shown him the brochure, panic and irritation in his voice. 'For God's sake, Iz. Don't you get it? We don't have any—'

'Money, I know that. I get it, James. We don't have to pay for it.'

'What?'

She grinned at him.

'I know. Amazing, isn't it? Sarah Lowther's offered it to us.'

'But why?'

'She's my friend.'

'I know that – actually, do I? Who is she?'

'From the gym. She and her husband Tim came to dinner last year. He's tall, round glasses. You talked about Nintendo.'

'Oh, right.' James looked vague.

'Anyhow, it's their house. Well, hers, really, she inherited it. They can't use it, they're in the States for the summer, and she doesn't want the hassle of renting it.'

'But she could make a fortune!' James was right. It was a prime Cornish holiday rental. They went for thousands a week.

'She doesn't need the money. She doesn't want loads of people she doesn't know staying there, and she knows we're having a tough time.'

James's face went into a pout. He hated the fact that not only their family and friends but random acquaintances knew that he hadn't yet found a new job.

'Well. How generous of her.' He sounded slightly sour, but he couldn't say much else. He could see that Izzy was determined. And she was right. Some time by the seaside, away from London, would do them all good.

'Fantastic. I'll go and text her now. How exciting!' And she had kissed him, and run off upstairs.

Blue sea and crabbing on the beach. It would be perfect.

I don't need to use it, Stephen had written, *and I think your children would have fun there. There's plenty of room and it's quite comfortably fitted out. Please say yes – I don't want to advertise it, for various reasons, and I hate the thought of it sitting empty during the best month of the year.*

Quite comfortably fitted out, indeed, Izzy had thought when she had pulled up to the house after a long, wearing drive down with Pearl torturing Alfie by taking his toys from him and then dangling them in front of him, just out of his reach, and Alfie demanding to be fed every half an hour. They had stopped five times, and got through three CDs of stories and to the end of Izzy's tether. James was no use at all; he had slept through the first three hours of the drive and then snapped at the children for the second. Izzy had no idea why he was so tired. It wasn't as if he was working. Nor was he even really looking after the children; they were still going to nursery as they always had. He needed the time to look for jobs, he had said; he didn't want to disrupt their routine when he would probably only be out of work for a few weeks, he had said. A few weeks. That had been wildly optimistic, hadn't it?

She looked at him in the rear-view mirror. His head was resting against the window and he was staring out of it. Was he thinking of *her*? she wondered. Was he missing her already? She chewed on the bit of skin next to her thumbnail.

'*You have reached your destination*', the sat nav told her, bossily, and Pearl piped up from the back, 'Does that mean we are there now, Mummy, at very long long last?'

'Yes, darling. It means we're there.'

'Well why doesn't she just say you're there? Instead of you have reached your destination? Why can't she just—'

'Look, Pearl. Look at the lovely house.' James pointed to distract her. 'Look, I bet there's a special room just for you.'

Izzy tuned out and let Pearl's chatter fade into the background as she stopped the car in front of the property. It was a big slab of a building, with a path that led down to its own beach. Already she could hear Pearl craning forward, dying to be let out of her enforced entrapment to go and explore, but Izzy turned to them and said, 'Wait a second, darlings, Mummy just needs to . . . let the car cool down.' She got out and shut the door firmly behind her. Just one minute. She wanted one minute to breathe in the air and let her shoulders settle back.

The house was painted white, its front older, from the twenties maybe, but its back something else entirely, she discovered as she walked around the side of the building. Like a hen concealing its finest, softest feathers, the rear of the building was a great expanse of modern glass, all light and clean lines. Limed wood decking led straight on to the sand, with big wooden tables and chairs, and outdoor heaters for chilly nights, just in front of the glass doors. Izzy turned, shielding her eyes from the sun, to check that the children were all right. Pearl was bashing Alfie with her recorder.

'Pearl! Stop that now . . .' She had better go and let them out. But first, she slipped off her shoes, and let her toes sink into the cool, dry sand. Heaven. She was in heaven, and she silently thanked Stephen Garside. Because James might or might not be thinking of whoever this woman was who had been distracting him recently, but she was certainly thinking of Stephen Garside. She missed him.

Was it silly to miss someone she saw as little as Stephen Garside? Stephen Garside, who she could not think of by his first name, only his full one. Stephen Garside, who sent her gifts, small, easily hideable gifts that she could secrete in a pocket of her jacket or inside her purse or at the back of a drawer. It had become something of a game, for him, the finding and sending of these tiny tokens. A shiny penny, with a red ribbon tied around it, left on the doorstep of the café, a tiny scroll of paper tucked inside the ribbon that fell out when she unfurled it. *Find a penny, pick it up, all day long you'll have good luck*. A pack of campanula seeds in 'Isabella Blue'. A tiny vintage glass bottle engraved with the letters 'I. G.' in curvaceous script on the side, a note rolled up in the neck that read simply, *In Hope* . . . A stream of little things that kept him in her mind, that made her heart beat faster, that made her aware that he was thinking of her, always, ardently. And alongside the lethargic, sluggish presence of her husband, who was snappy and closed off, who hardly said two words to her when she came in from the café, who was so bound up in his own impotent misery that she did not know what to say to comfort him any more, they had the desired effect – they turned her head and her heart towards Stephen.

She felt guilty about James. Of course she did. He was unhappy, he was ashamed that he was still out of work, he was desperately worried about his mother. But he wouldn't talk to her about any of it, wouldn't let her help him. Just shut her out, pushed her away, until she could not bear to keep trying. The rejection stung, and she pretended it didn't, and he was hurt that she stopped trying, and pretended that he wasn't, and so they continued on, limping towards some future point in their marriage where they would have to face up to what had happened to it.

She still had not taken that final, irreversible step into infidelity. Stephen Garside had kissed her, and she had returned the kiss, yes. But as for the rest . . . it was oddly chaste. Part of her was grateful for this. She did not have to feel pushed into making a decision that she was still not quite ready to make, despite everything. And yet part of her was frustrated by it. She almost wanted him to push her, to insist that the tension between them be acted upon, to stand in front of her, close to her, so that she could taste the tang of his aftershave, and so that she could not escape. To take the decision away from her. Was that unfair? Maybe. She was the one with the most to lose, so she should be the one to take responsibility for the choice. She knew that. But it was always her taking responsibility, it felt like. Always her leading the way. It had been her who had suggested that they start to try for a baby when they had been married for a couple of years. She who had pointed out that the studio warehouse flat they had been living in would not house a baby, when she had got pregnant. She who had booked holidays, and planned outings, and planned their wedding, and taken charge of almost all of the decisions that made up her and James's marriage.

And she wasn't sure whether she could be the one to take charge of the ending of it as well.

It was like letting the trap up on the greyhounds, unleashing her children. Pearl wriggled down and free of her straight away,

and Alfie toddled off after her. 'This way. Inside first, please.'
Izzy herded the kids to the front door. She didn't want them
racing into the sea or head first into a sand dune or something.

Inside the hall, she found an envelope.

I've had Elsie make sure the place is as child
friendly as possible, but do let her know if there's
anything else you or they need. I think the only thing
I haven't fenced off or put a safety catch on is
the sea itself, which unfortunately, I am unable to
tame. Though if I could... Make yourself at home,
and enjoy. PS Please don't worry about any
breakages/marks on walls, etc. It's all much easier
to clean/mend than it looks.

The note was unsigned. Nothing in it to indicate who had
written it. She lifted it to her face. It smelt of nothing but paper,
and she felt foolish. She slipped it into her pocket.

As she might have expected, her definition and Stephen
Garside's definition of 'quite comfortably fitted out' were somewhat different. The house was immaculate; full of light and
white walls that she was already terrified the children would
mark, despite Stephen's postscript. There was a huge open-plan
living room that led out on to the garden, and the kitchen doors
opened on to the decking area that she had seen from the back.
A massive range cooker and an array of gadgets faced her on the
work surfaces. She could have some fun in here.

Upstairs, the place was just as luxurious. The bedrooms were
all large and airy, with en-suite bathrooms containing big free-
standing baths that faced the sea, and wet-room areas to rival
any chichi boutique hotel. Izzy felt her shoulders unknotting as
she padded around the rooms.

'This is my bedroom, isn't it, Mummy, a princess room?'

Pearl said, as soon as she saw the little room with sloping ceilings and a canopied bed that Izzy suspected might have been brought in recently and especially, just like the smaller one shaped like a train carriage that Alfie had seen and grinned at with such glee.

'Yes, darling, this is yours. Shall we go and get your things so you can put them away in the drawers all nicely?' Izzy asked, optimistically. However nicely Pearl's things were put away, they would be on the floor in seconds as she rifled through them to choose her outfit of the moment. Pearl changed clothes like she changed her mind – frequently, and without a backward glance.

Izzy and James unloaded the luggage from the car, and she made Pearl and Alfie cheese on toast from the basket of supplies left by Elsie, the housekeeper. There was another note tucked into the hamper, which contained piles of local goodies – fresh bread and a dressed crab and a big slab of Cornish Yarg and a round of St Endellion, the soft Brie-like cheese that Izzy could already envisage baking with wine and garlic; clotted cream and a paper bag of scones, a little cardboard container of blackberries and raspberries, and a bottle of sparkling wine. This note told Izzy that Elsie would be in three times a week, to clean and change linen, and bring more coal for the barbecue and other supplies if needed, and could be booked to cook 'if required, with twenty-four hours' notice. Baking a speciality, no more than twenty for dinner.' Afterwards she took the children out on to the beach, to let them run off their pent-up energy from the car and fill their lungs with sea air – better than Calpol for knocking them out. Then, when they had gone to sleep, she would make crab linguine for her and James with fresh pasta and plenty of chilli and olive oil. And she would open that bottle of wine, and they would sit and eat on the deck, watching the sun set over the sea. She couldn't wait.

If it hadn't been for the nagging feeling of guilt, the prospect would have been even more thrilling. She shook herself. She was going to have to get over this, otherwise she would ruin this perfect opportunity with fretting.

She wasn't used to it, this ever-present feeling of unease. Until now, her marriage had been unblighted by the infidelity and untruths that seemed to characterise so many of her friends' relationships. Stella and Johnny with their frankly bizarre, in her view, status quo, which seemed to involve Johnny shagging anything that fluttered its eyelashes at him and Stella pretending not to notice. So passive for someone so strong and fiery in all other areas of her life. Harriet and Will with their apparent inability to move forward, whether together or apart. Caroline and Bart with their hunger for a baby that would not take root.

Until recently, she and James had been the ones who no one worried about, who seemed all right. Solid, dependable, the couple you could look towards and think, 'See, marriage isn't all bad, they've been together for, what? Ten years at least, and they're doing OK, aren't they?' And they had been. They had been content, comfortable, if not wildly happy all of the time. But who could hope for that? They supported one another, they trusted one another, they were a team.

Izzy stood up from where she had been kneeling at Alfie's bedside, and gently moved Babbit, the filthy grey bunny that Caroline had given him when he was born and which he had clung to determinedly ever since. As she did, his fingers loosened on the toy, and, seeing her opportunity, she lifted it out. He murmured in sleepy, unconscious protest, and then stilled. She breathed a sigh of relief; she could wash it and it would dry overnight, and by the time he woke in the morning, it would be back in his arms. He would be suspicious of it for a while, as it would smell of washing powder rather than God knows what scent it usually had to him, but that wouldn't last long.

Alfie's memory for disappointment or hurts was fleeting, unlike Pearl's; that girl could harbour a grudge for longer than the proverbial elephant.

She looked in on Pearl as she passed her room; she was fast asleep, burrowed under her quilt like a worm working its way into the ground, her cheeks flushed. Izzy pulled the covers back from her face. She would overheat otherwise, she always did; she would tunnel into her covers until she was deep inside them, then wake up in the night, florid and damp with sweat. Izzy leaned over and cracked the window open to let some air into the room. The house was air-conditioned, of course, but the panel for it was complicated and Izzy didn't have the energy to figure it out tonight. And she didn't really like it, anyhow. She'd rather let the sea air sweep the cobwebs away. She inhaled, and leaned out of the window for a moment. The air had that glorious fragrance of seaweed and fresh salt and that indefinable something that would have told her they were by the beach even if she had been blindfolded. She looked up. The sky took her breath away. You didn't get skies like that in London – just the permanent greyish-orange glow of street-lit smog, the occasional glimpse of the moon trying to poke through its choking scarf of cloud. But here – it was a thick embroidery of stars that glittered at her, lighting the pathways that ran around the house and the white stones of the driveway with their white embers, and the air felt soft against her skin.

Izzy looked down. It wasn't, she noticed, just the moon and the stars that were lighting up the stones of the driveway. She could hear the low rumble of a car, the wheels crunching over the stones as it slowly turned down the lane and made its way towards the house. She glanced at her watch. It was nine o'clock. It couldn't be Stephen Garside, could it? No, he wouldn't. Surely he wouldn't. With a tug of nerves in her stomach, she turned away from the window, and went downstairs.

*

Izzy didn't recognise the car that was pulling up to the house. It was an old Mercedes, one of the ones with a long bonnet and a low-slung body. It was a metallic pistachio colour, and it shone silvery green in the moonlight. Izzy stood in the porch and watched as it trundled to a halt. It wasn't James, obviously, and she was certain it wasn't Stephen. That was a woman's car, not a man's, no question about it. Was that a sliver of disappointment she felt in her stomach?

If it was, it was quickly overtaken by surprise, as she watched two women get out of the car and begin unloading themselves and piles of bags on to the drive. Actually, it was a woman and a girl, she realised, as she looked more closely. The woman was blonde, her hair set in the sort of waves that women had their maids do for them in the twenties, soft and deceptively simple-looking. She was wearing a military jacket, with epaulettes that stuck out from her narrow shoulders and big sweeping lapels, over what looked like a satin nightie. Lace-up Victorian work boots and woollen tights completed the ensemble. The girl was in a similarly eclectic outfit – this time an orange-lined bomber jacket of the sort that Izzy remembered wearing in the nineties to go clubbing, with a leopardskin tea dress underneath it, and Doc Marten boots. Overall, in fact, something Izzy could have seen herself in, fifteen or so years ago.

She continued to watch, unsure of what to do, as, in a move akin to Mary Poppins and her carpet bag, the older woman wrenched an old steamer trunk out of the back of the car, and then leapt back as it almost fell on her feet. 'Bloody hell, Cass, what on earth have you *got* in there? Oh well, there's plenty of room.'

The younger girl shrugged, and looked towards the house. As she did so, her eyes met Izzy's, and she gazed at her, neither speaking nor moving, until the woman who Izzy by now assumed was her mother, though she didn't really look old enough to be, looked up from her struggles with the luggage.

'Oh! Hello,' she said, flashing Izzy a wide, deep-plum-lipsticked smile. 'You must be Izzy.'

Izzy stepped forward, finally jerked out of her paralysis. 'Um. Yes.'

The woman raised her eyebrows. She was clearly expecting her to say something else. 'Well,' she said, rummaging in the pockets of her coat before eventually finding a pack of Vogue cigarettes and holding it out to Izzy, who took one, in a daze of confusion, and allowed the woman to light it for her. 'Maybe you could give us a hand. When we've finished these. Have you eaten? We stopped for a Burger King on the way, but it was fairly ghastly, so it didn't really hit the spot.'

Izzy shook her head. 'No, not yet. Look, I'm sorry, but . . .'

The woman looked up at her through thick eyelashes that must surely be false. 'Yes?' A rope of paste diamanté glittered around her neck.

'Who *are* you?'

The woman stared at her, and then burst out in a hoot of laughter that was so infectious Izzy almost joined in. Almost.

'Oh darling. I'm Amanda, of course. Amanda Fairlight.' She held out her hand, and gave a little bob of a mock curtsey. 'And this is Cass.' She motioned towards the girl who was perched on the bonnet of the car. 'Darling, don't sit on Maisie there, you know she's a fragile old thing, and you're not as birdlike as you used to be, you know.' She cast a pointed eye at the girl's slim thighs, and then rolled her eyes at Izzy. 'Teenagers. Ridiculous vegetarian diet seems to mean she lives off coffee and doughnuts. It's not good for the cheekbones, all those carbs.'

Izzy nodded. 'Right. But . . .' She hesitated. How to tell these people, who were clearly expecting her to be expecting them, that she hadn't a clue who Amanda Fairlight and Cass might be? In the event, she didn't have to. Amanda Fairlight got there by herself. She turned away from chastising her daughter, and looked back at Izzy, her eyes fixing on her, making Izzy feel a little as though she couldn't breathe. The woman was over-whelmingly glamorous, in the sort of way that made Izzy feel like a little girl, tagging along on the heels of an impossibly chic godmother.

'Oh dear,' Amanda said, slowly, 'oh dear me. You haven't got a clue who we are, have you?' She smiled and shook her head, tutting under her breath.

Izzy heard the front door open behind her, and James's feet on the gravel behind them take a few steps, and then pause. The woman looked over her shoulder, towards him, and smiled, shaking her head.

'Well, well, well. What a naughty boy you've been.'

Izzy spun around, frowning. James was standing, hands in his pockets, his threadbare jumper stretched out of shape, looking ashen and about twelve years old. Like a schoolboy who had been caught playing truant. Oh God. Was this her? It had to be. This was the woman. Well. She was different from what Izzy would have expected. More flamboyant, more outrageous-looking. Still. She supposed he wouldn't be likely to have an affair with someone just like her, would he? What would be the point?

'I never said that I'd . . .' James trailed off.

'Told your wife about us? No. I suppose you didn't. I just assumed that you had.'

'You didn't assume anything. You knew.' James stepped forward, his face pale and taut with anger. 'You're just here to cause trouble. You fucking thrive on it. You always have.'

Amanda lifted a perfectly arched eyebrow an inch. 'I don't think that's terribly fair, James. But I did think it was time everything was given – a bit of an airing. That much is true.'

James's fist punched down by his hip in frustration and he turned, hands grasping his head. 'Damn. Fuck and damn you.'

'Are you . . .' Izzy wasn't sure she could bring herself to say it. But she had to. 'Are you sleeping with my husband?' Her voice shook and she steeled herself for the answer.

The teenage girl groaned. 'Oh God, GROSS.'

Izzy shot her a look. She shouldn't have asked that in front of the child. But what was the girl doing here at all?

'Right, please go inside. You . . .' she pointed at the girl with a wavering finger. 'Cass. Please go inside and help yourself to a piece of the cake that's on the side. Your – your mother and I need to talk.'

Cass rolled her eyes and ignored her, but she did put her headphones on. Izzy returned her attention to the woman, who was still standing in front of her, a slight smile on her lips. James had not come any closer. That seemed to be all the confirmation she needed.

'Please tell me what you're doing here. Right now. How dare you come to this house, where my children are asleep in bed? If you think that you can sleep with my husband and just waltz in here and no one will say anything, then you are very badly mistaken.'

'Well, darling, it's not exactly just waltzing in, is it? I left it sixteen damn years.'

'What? What are you talking about?'

'Oh God. Izzy . . .' James seemed to come to life now, taking a step forward and grabbing her elbow. 'Listen . . .'

Amanda gave a little laugh as she exhaled a thin plume of cigarette smoke. 'Yes, brace yourself, darling. This is obviously going to come as a shock.'

And Izzy listened, open-mouthed, as James told her exactly who the two women were.

'Your *daughter*? Your fucking teenage *daughter* is here, with her mother, looking like they've walked off the set of a photoshoot for *Vogue* or something, and all you can say is "Oh shit"? Oh shit is right, you absolute fucking cunt. Oh shit. Yes, actually, I'd say oh shit does just about cover it.'

'Darling—'

'Don't. Darling. Me. I can't believe it, James. I really can't believe it.'

Her voice had changed now. The anger that had been pushing it forward had dissipated, and she sounded lost and frightened. 'How long, James?' she asked. 'How long have you known? How . . .' She trailed off, but he could hear all the unasked questions bubbling up and filling the miles between them.

'I don't want you to stay here,' she said. 'Get out. I want you to get out.'

'Where do you want me to go?'

'I don't care. I just don't want to look at your face.'

'What about . . . you know. My . . . Amanda and . . . Them?'

James wished that he could reach out and gather his wife up into his arms. She looked so young, so fragile, and so desperately hurt. If only he had told her. If only he had been braver, trusted her more. He could see now that he should have done. How stupid he was. Of course she was always going to find out somehow, and finding out like this . . . He cursed Amanda, but even as he did, he knew it was not her fault. Not really. She had always been disorganised, impetuous, liable to make impulsive decisions without any warning. It didn't occur to him, just then, to question how she had known where they were.

It was his fault, anyhow. If only he had told Izzy . . . If only, if only.

'Oh, they can stay. I think Amanda and I have plenty to talk about.'

A sliver of fear ran down James's gullet. He didn't have time to consider the prospect of Izzy and Amanda discussing him for long, though, because a second later there was a coat and a set of car keys being chucked in his face. 'Get out!'

Izzy stood in the hallway and leant her forehead against the wall. It felt cool and reassuringly solid. Maybe she could just stay here? Rest here, against the wall, and just let it all swirl around her. She felt as though she were at the centre of a tornado, a whirling dervish of a cyclone that had taken all the elements of her life that she thought were solid and fixed – her marriage, the trust she felt within that marriage, the certainty of the family she had created, her very sense of who she was and her place in the world – and let them fly around her, disparate and impossible to grasp hold of suddenly.

How quickly it could all start to fall apart, she thought now, and with such small, individually quite insignificant events. An overheard conversation, a cigarette on a terrace, a sentence unspoken. An invisible but seemingly impermeable barrier had worked its way between her and James and she didn't know how to break it down again, or whether she even could. What scared her most was the thought that maybe that was because she might not want to.

She had worked so hard to make her family, to create something out of the nothing she had come from. When she had met James, she had been estranged from her parents, and though she had seen both of them in recent years, they were not experiences she was in any rush to repeat or relationships she wished to rekindle. 'He's not a bad person, my father,' she had told James eventually, having avoided the subject of her family for as long as she could in the early days of their relationship. 'Just – weak. He left my mother when I was three, just walked out one day. He told her he was going to the shops. Never

246

came back. Ran away with the woman down the road, who'd been after him for years. God knows why.' They'd been lying in bed. James had stroked her shoulder with his finger, and she had nuzzled into his neck. 'He's still with her, anyhow. They never had any children of their own. She's got a couple. I don't know. I'm certainly not welcome there.' 'How about your mother?' James had asked. 'You'd think him leaving would have made the two of you pull closer together.' 'You'd think.' Izzy had turned over on to her back and let her arms flop behind her head. 'I tried to pull closer to her, certainly. It just made her pull back further.' She'd closed her eyes. It wasn't a time she enjoyed remembering. 'She didn't neglect me. Not physically. There were always meals on the table, I always had clean clothes, I had everything I needed. Apart from a mother who loved me.' She shook her head. 'I don't want to talk about it. I don't want to spoil our weekend.' James had slipped his arm underneath her and pulled her back in towards him, kissing her and looking into her eyes. 'We'll make a new family,' he had whispered, 'one of our very own. That no one can touch. I'll be your family.'

That was the night she had told him she loved him for the first time, she remembered now, so overwhelmed had she felt by his determined dedication to her. And they had done it. They had become one another's family, and created their own. It had been unfashionable, at the time, to take your husband's name when you married; it was supposed to be emancipating to retain your maiden name rather than subjugate yourself by changing it, but Izzy had never felt freer than when she signed her new passport and driving licence and credit cards 'Isabella Rathbone' and could finally cast off the memories and everything else associated with her family. It hadn't been quite that straight-forward, of course it hadn't. But still, Rathbone she had become, for better or worse, but mostly for better, and she had produced two Rathbone children to add to the line-up, and she had felt a sense of completeness that she had, when she was younger, been sure she would never achieve.

Now part of that completeness had been erased by the arrival of Cass and Amanda. The part that had been the unbreakable (or so she had thought) knowledge that their children, Pearl and Alfie, were something that she and James had done together, for the first time. It had been so precious, that part of her. Those memories, of them finding out she was pregnant with Pearl, her waving the little white stick at him excitedly and getting a splash of pee on his dressing gown by accident. The first scan, when she had been white and shaking and sick with nerves and morning sickness, all of which had disappeared with the sight of Pearl's fat little tummy and long, frog-like legs on the monitor. The way they had called her 'frog' after that, all the way through the rest of the pregnancy. The way James had looked at them both when Pearl was born, as though they were the most precious creatures in the world, as though he could not believe what Izzy had made. They had done all of that together, and she had been first, she had been the only one who could ever have given him those things, whatever else might happen. And suddenly, she wasn't the only one any longer, and she wasn't even first. All of those times she remembered were actually the second time, for him, whether he had known it or not. Had he known it? She hadn't given him a chance to tell her. Had he known, even as she was pushing their baby out into the world, that Amanda had already done the same thing, with another little girl, in some other hospital room? Had he even been there, by her side, as she did so, whispering the same words of determined encouragement into her ear? The thought of it pierced her heart far more sharply than any sweet nothings he could have whispered to a lover. A child was a far greater betrayal. 'There's nothing worse than having an affair, than giving your heart to someone else,' she had said to him once, when she had been young and passionate and idealistic. Now she knew there was a far more treacherous gift than your heart.

She felt a presence in the hallway with her, and opened her eyes. Amanda stood, unlit cigarette in her hand, in what Izzy did not yet know was one of her habitual poses; arm containing the hand that held the cigarette raised so that her fingers framed her pretty chin, arm without the accessory to hold bent at the elbow, hand resting on her waist. She had taken her coat off, and was wearing a long man's cardie over her dress. The dress that was, now Izzy had the chance to get a closer look at it, most definitely a nightie.

'It hasn't been going on for long, you know,' she said, her blue eyes blazing, intense and searching. Then she laughed. 'God, sorry. Making it sound like an affair, aren't I?'

'It's what it feels like.' It was what she had thought it was.

'Mm.' Amanda put the cigarette between her lips, and didn't say anything else.

Izzy didn't want to talk to this woman. She was gallingly self-assured, and with good reason. She was beautiful and confident and she had a past with James that Izzy knew nothing of, and she was everything Izzy didn't want to face right now. But more importantly than any of those things – she was here. And she could give Izzy the answers that she so desperately needed, and which she couldn't yet bring herself to ask James.

Izzy moved her body so she was leaning back against the wall, let out a long, slow breath, then turned her head towards Amanda.

'Do you like crab linguine?' she asked.

They sat outside, the three of them, wrapped in thick cardies against the cool evening wind. It might be August, but as soon as the sun went in, the salt in the air turned to what felt like sharp little crystals that whipped against your face. Izzy turned the patio heaters up, and lit big candles in hurricane lamps, and handed round glasses of wine (Cass's against her better judgement, but Amanda said she could, so Izzy poured her a half glass with a light hand and a slightly raised eyebrow. Still, what did she know about teenagers, and how to parent them?). Eventually, though, she ran out of diversions, and was forced to sit down and face Amanda's amused gaze. The woman missed nothing, clearly.

'Have you finished?' she asked, a smile on one side of her mouth, as she scooped up a huge pile of linguine and wound it around her fork with one hand.

'Sorry,' Izzy said, a little more sharply than she really meant to. 'I wasn't expecting company.'

Cass made a noise that was something between a snort and a grunt, a particularly teenage sound that set Izzy's teeth on edge even as she remembered making similar noises herself. It was the sound of dissatisfaction. She could see why her mother had hated it so, she thought; it was a spoiled, sulky sort of a noise – and then she bit back the feeling. The last thing she needed now was to start seeing parallels with her mother, especially in regard to this girl who was not even her daughter.

'Cass was eleven by the time I told him,' Amanda said, out of nowhere. It was another of her habits that Izzy had not yet had a chance to become used to. She blurted out statements and questions as they came to her, with no regard for her audience. 'He knew nothing about her before then. Didn't see her for years after that. Ignored half my emails, the git.' She took a gulp of wine. 'So it hasn't been some long-running deception. Really, I should be the one that's furious with him, for not seeing her for so fucking long. If you think about it.'

Izzy looked up in surprise, as Amanda popped another mouthful of pasta into her mouth. 'This is really good. I'm a terrible cook.'

'Shouldn't we wait until . . .' Izzy looked over towards Cass, who rolled her eyes.

'It's nothing I don't know already,' she said, impatiently. In contrast to her mother, she was eating her pasta a single strand at a time, using her fork and a spoon to roll it up in neat spirals before putting each one in her mouth. It was going to take her a very long time to finish the bowl at that rate. Maybe that was the point.

'Oh,' said Izzy. 'I see.'

'We don't have any secrets, me and Cass. When you're a single mother as young as I was, you – well, you grow up together, really.'

She stared at Izzy, that unflinching, uncompromising stare again, and Izzy felt a strange impulse to defend James against the unspoken accusation. It was hardly his fault you were a single mother if you didn't even tell him you were pregnant, she thought. But she said nothing.

'Don't say we're more like sisters,' Cass said, through gritted teeth, and Izzy had to stop herself from laughing at Amanda's wounded expression. Amanda shrugged.

'Fine. I won't say a word,' she said. Izzy doubted that.

'The point is,' Amanda continued, and Izzy did allow herself a smile this time, 'that you shouldn't be too angry with him. He was trying to do the right thing – by you. He ended up doing the wrong thing by us. By Cass, mostly, of course. I don't matter.'

Cass rolled her eyes. Amanda's self-deprecating martyrdom was obviously a familiar pose.

'You were the one he was thinking about. You were the one he was protecting.'

'He lied to me.'

'Only by omission. And that doesn't count.'

'It counts.'

'Not really—'

Izzy cut her off. 'It counts to me. The point is, he knew he had a daughter. For the last five years, he's known. And he said nothing. Gave no clue. It's like – it's like I've been living with a stranger.'

Amanda shrugged. 'I think that's a bit melodramatic, darling.'

Fury ran through Izzy. Melodramatic? Christ, the woman was impossible. She was beginning to see why James had kept his daughter at arm's length. Acknowledging her would have meant dealing with her mother. She itched to say this. But, in the end, 'Right,' was all she could get out. 'I'm not sure it is.'

'Well, it's up to you, obviously.'

'Yes. It is.'

'I'm just saying . . . don't punish him for loving you. You've got a good man. You should make sure you hold on to him – or someone else will.'

Izzy stared at Amanda in shock. What was she saying? That she would make a play for James if Izzy wasn't careful?

'Oh God,' Amanda laughed, and for the second time that evening Izzy felt as though the woman could see inside her mind. 'Not me! Darling James. No, he's far too . . .' She caught Izzy's eye, and stopped herself. 'Well, we're not really suited. Never were. There's a reason it didn't last beyond a few months with us. Sex can't hold you together for long, however good it is.'

'Mum!' Cass threw her cutlery down in disgust. 'I'm *eating*!'

'Well, hardly, darling.' Amanda poked her fork at Cass's plate. 'You're getting through it so slowly, you're practically going backwards.'

Cass sighed, loudly. 'If I eat too quickly you tell me I look greedy and will get fat. Now I'm eating too slowly. What am I meant to do? Use a stopwatch so I can time myself and make sure I'm eating at the perfect pace?'

'Don't be silly, sweetheart. Just eat normally. It's not complicated.'

Cass glared at her mother, before getting up from the table and stalking off towards the beach, hands thrust deep into her pockets. 'You're always telling me what to do!' she called out over her shoulder. 'I can't wait for you to leave me alone.'

'Not long now, darling. Not long now,' Amanda called, throwing Izzy a wink as she did so. She pushed her empty bowl away and refilled their glasses. 'Soon you'll be gone and I'll be all alone, and you'll miss me nagging you.'

'Yeah, right.'

'Until then, if you've finished, you're excused. Go and listen to your me-me-me-pod.'

'You're not funny, Mum. Just sad.'

Cass was heading back towards the house. Izzy watched her go. Could she see James in her? It was hard to say. Maybe. Something about the eyes, the set of her nose.

Amanda watched Izzy watching her daughter. 'She looked terribly like him when she was born, you know,' she said. Izzy turned. The woman seemed to have a sixth sense for what she was thinking. It was infuriating. 'They say babies do, some evolutionary thing, don't they? So the father knows they're theirs. Not that that was relevant, in my case. I was the only one who was there with her to see what she looked like.'

Despite herself, Izzy felt a pang of sympathy for Amanda. She remembered those first, precious moments as a new family so well. The thought of doing it all by herself – she couldn't imagine it.

'I'm sorry,' she said, a little stiffly. 'It must have been very difficult.'

'Oh, don't feel too sorry for me.' Amanda's voice was breezy. 'I made my own bed, after all. I could have told him back then. I'm sure he would have "done the right thing", as they say.'

'Why didn't you?'

'Because I knew he'd want to do the right thing. And I didn't want him to. He wasn't in love with me. I was in love with someone else. I liked James too much to want him to screw up his whole life by marrying me.'

Izzy's face must have betrayed her surprise.

'I know. Mature, wasn't it? I'm not a total bitch, you know, Izzy.'

'I never . . .'

Amanda lit another cigarette, and Izzy took one too. Amanda waved her hand in the air. 'I don't blame you for hating me. At first, at least. But here's the thing. You're going to have to stop it.'

Izzy inhaled and shrugged. 'I don't see that I have to do anything.' She sounded sulkier than Cass. But she couldn't help it.

'No. But you will.' Amanda was firm, self-assured. Her voice was that of a woman who knew she held more cards than Izzy might have imagined.

'Go on.'

'I want Cass and James to have a proper relationship. I want her to spend some time with him – with all of you. To know what it's like to be part of a normal family.'

'I'm sure that eventually, she and James will see each other regularly. But you can't force—'

'Not eventually. Now. You're the one that has to make it happen. You know what James is like. He'll um and ah and stall and it'll be six months down the line and they'll have been for one cup of coffee. It's the woman who makes situations like these work. It always is. We both know that.'

She was quite right. But why should Izzy simply step aside and make room for Cass in her family? Make the sacrifices that it would involve, explain the situation to all of their friends and family, clear a space for her. She hadn't asked for any of this.

The resentment must have shown in her face, because Amanda continued, and her next words hit home.

'Haven't you wondered how I knew you were all here, Izzy? James isn't the only one who's been keeping secrets, is he?'

Izzy looked sharply at Amanda. What . . . ?

'Stephen's an old friend. I asked him a while ago if I could use this place for a week. He told me he'd already lent it to someone else, for the whole month.' She leant forward on her elbows. 'Well, I can tell you, Stephen Garside doesn't just "lend" his properties to people for weeks on end. There's usually a reason rich men are rich, and it isn't because they're generous.'

Izzy shook her head. She should never have come here.

'So I knew it must be someone he'd fallen for, fallen hard. And then I remembered seeing him looking at you at your opening party . . .'

'What? You were at my party?'

'Darling, I'm the one who brought Stephen. Like I said, he's an old friend. You've got me to thank that you met him.' Amanda looked pleased with herself. 'I got it out of him. And so I thought I'd pay you all a visit. How was I to know James hadn't told you about me and Cassie?' Her eyes were all innocence.

'You did know, didn't you?' The knives had come out now. There was no pretence between the two women any longer.

'I suspected.'

'Didn't you care? Didn't you think about what you were doing?'

Amanda nodded. 'Yes. I cared very much. About my daughter. Our daughter. I knew I was going to have to do something to get James to stop being such a bloody wimp. Get it all out in the open. But I don't think you want *everything* out in the open, do you? I don't think you've told James that this is Stephen's house, for instance, have you?'

She blinked, slowly. Izzy took a deep breath.

'No. No, I haven't.'

'Exactly. So why tell him? Why rock the boat? You've got the moral high ground, nice and secure. You don't want to lose it, do you?'

'It's hardly about the moral high ground,' Izzy snapped. But a bit of her whispered, 'Liar.'

Amanda smiled. She knew she had won. 'Whatever. Like I said, Izzy. It's always down to the woman.'

'I can't believe it.' Caroline looked genuinely shocked, Izzy decided. She had been watching her carefully as she told her girlfriends about the discovery she had made. Or, rather, the discovery that had been forced upon her by the arrival of Amanda and Cass. She had been wondering whether James had confided in his sister, though he had sworn he hadn't. But then Izzy wasn't inclined to believe much that James said just now.

'I'm sorry,' he had said, over and over again when he'd arrived back at the holiday house the next morning. He looked terrible, with a grey face and huge thumbprint-like bruises of tiredness under his eyes, and Izzy had felt spitefully pleased to see him in such a state. At least he felt bad, really bad. 'I'm sorry, I'm sorry, I'm sorry. I've been such a bloody fool, Iz.'

She folded her arms, and just stared at him. He held his hands out to her. 'I can't bear it. I can't cope with you being this angry with me. Tell me it's going to be OK, Iz. Tell me *we're* going to be OK.'

Izzy shrugged and turned away. 'I don't know,' she said, calmly. She put the kettle on to boil, and started thinking what she would make for breakfast. In times of trouble, menu planning was Izzy's rosary. Soft-boiled eggs squished on to toast, crisp bacon, coffee and plenty of it. Later, she'd get smoked haddock and make a big vat of kedgeree. She felt the need for its soothing, chilli-spiked carbiness. 'Have you got any more teenage children squirrelled away?'

James hesitated. She could feel his uncertainty as she pulled eggs out of the box and rested them on a tea towel. Unsure whether the sliver of light he thought he could hear creeping under the door of her voice was really there, or whether he was imagining it. Afraid that if he risked laughter he would be bawled out for not taking the situation seriously enough; afraid that if he didn't laugh at what had been intended as a conciliatory joke, she would be upset. She knew the thoughts that were clicking through his brain. Years of marriage gave you that power, if a power it was. She sighed, and turned back to face him. She would put him out of his misery; she didn't have the energy to rage at him much more.

'For God's sake, James. Am I so – hard? Am I so difficult to talk to that you couldn't tell me?' His face furrowed, and he shook his head.

'Of course not.'

'So why? Why the secrecy? We always used to be able to tell each other things.' Izzy glanced out of the window as she spoke. There was a reason she had used the past tense; it wasn't only James's secrecy that she was referring to.

'We still can.' James crossed the kitchen and held her, gently. 'Nothing's changed, sweetheart. Nothing between you and me is different. I fucked up, and I know that, but I promise you, nothing is going to come between us, and our family. You're my number one, you and Pearl and Alfie. No one else.'

'But you can't say that,' Izzy said quietly. 'Not any more. Whether you like it or not – whether I like it or not – it's not just us any more. Is it? And I don't know . . .' She took a deep breath. 'I don't know whether I can carry on like that.'

'Izzy. Don't say that. You mustn't say that.'

She shook her head. 'Come on, James. We may as well be honest. It's not just Cass and Amanda turning up, is it?'

James folded his arms. 'I don't know what you mean.'

'Things have hardly been brilliant recently.'

She was doing it, then. She was pushing it forwards, to this dark place.

'Things will be fine. When I get a job, when Mum's better . . .'

'Oh James!' she cried out in frustration. He stopped. 'James,' she said again, more quietly this time. 'Your mum isn't going to get better. She's not. She's accepted that. And you have to. You just – have to.'

He wouldn't hear it. 'I can't. I can't let her die without doing anything.' His eyes were wet, and she felt like the cruellest person alive. There was no way she could raise the rest of it now. No way she could tell him that they were in Stephen Garside's house, that he wanted her to leave James for him, that she was thinking about it. Because she was. If she was really honest, in the middle of the night, when she woke up, she was considering it. Imagining what it would be like, how it would work. She was thinking about leaving her marriage, and although the thought terrified her, with every day that passed, every conversation that went unspoken between her and James, every bitter remark that slipped out, it became a little less so. And now this . . . She didn't know if they could come back from this. She didn't know if she wanted them to.

She resisted the temptation to put her arms around James, who was leaning against the kitchen worktop, one hand over his face. That would not solve anything. She could give him comfort, tell him it would all be OK, that she could forgive and forget, that the two of them could get through anything together. And once, it would have been true. But now? She couldn't say it.

'I think you should go back to London,' she said, quietly. 'I think you should leave.'

He nodded, slowly. 'Right. What about Cass? Amanda's buggering off. Do you want me to take her with me?'

'Yes. Spend some time with her. Poor girl looks like she could use a bit of attention.'

'And you? What are you going to do?'

Izzy thought. 'I'm going to call in the cavalry,' she said.

It had felt a bit like summoning a council of war. Caroline had piles of holiday to take, she always did; she was so conscientious, her boss practically had to beg her to take days off, and Harriet and Stella were both self-employed, so suddenly, the next day, they were all there, arriving in Caroline's car with quickly packed holdalls and piles of magazines and bottles of wine and cigarettes.

'So. Are you OK?' Caroline asked, her voice quiet, once they had dumped their stuff in the hallway and headed into the garden with drinks and a big bowl of pistachios to pick at. Izzy shook her head.

'No. I'm not OK, Caroline. Not at all. James lied to me. Your brother lied to me, for years. He had a child with someone else and he didn't tell me. You know, I'm just not sure I can get past that.'

Caroline looked away, and Izzy regretted her sharpness.

'No. I bet.'

Stella smoked. 'Why did James not tell you before now? I mean, it's not as though he got this woman pregnant when you were together, was it? It doesn't have to be a deal-breaker, surely? If he'd told you, it would have been fine. Obviously I do see that it's an issue that he didn't.'

'Yes, it is a bit of a fucking issue, Stell, as you put it.' Izzy stared at her friend. How did Stella cope so equably with

259

Johnny's infidelity? She had never understood it. 'I don't know, really,' she replied. 'He didn't find out about her till five years ago, or something. He said he wouldn't see her. Was scared, I suppose.'

'It's not as though he'd done anything wrong though, is it? It could happen to anyone,' Stella continued. 'In a way, it's almost more surprising that it hasn't happened before now. It's not as though any of our men were saints in their youth. Or since then,' she added quietly.

Izzy bristled a little inside. *It's hardly a big deal*, Stella seemed to be intimating. *What are you making such a fuss about?*

'Anyhow, why has he buggered off back to London? Shouldn't he stay here and face the music?'

'I told him to go. I don't . . . I don't want him here, apologising, looking all sorry. I just needed some space to get my head around it. Work out what I'm going to do. What we're going to do.'

'But you're not . . .' Caroline looked terrified. 'You're not going to split up or anything, are you?'

The girls waited. Izzy shrugged.

'I don't know. I honestly don't know.'

'Wow.' Caroline took a sip of wine.

'Come on, Iz, you can't be serious.' Stella tutted. 'It's not worth chucking a marriage away over, surely?'

'It's not just this . . .' Izzy started to say, and then stopped herself. Close as she was to all three of the women sitting in front of her, she wasn't going to tell them everything else that had been going on recently. 'It's not just Cass existing, I mean. It's the dishonesty that I'm fucked off about, Stell, not the fact that it happened. Though I'd rather he didn't have a teenage daughter; it's not exactly ideal.'

'No, well, life isn't, is it?' Stella's eyes met hers, and Izzy bit.

260

'I'm quite aware of that, thanks. My life isn't as perfect and rosy as you seem to think, you know.' The silence crackled.

Eventually Stella shrugged. 'No one's is.'

It wasn't really the apology Izzy had been angling for. But it would have to do.

'Don't I know it,' Harriet added gloomily. Izzy stopped herself from snapping at her too. But Harriet really was going to have to pull herself together at some point. What was the statute of limitation on break-up angst? A month for every year the couple had been together? That seemed reasonable. Which meant that Harriet should have started to sort herself out by now.

'What's the latest?' Caroline asked Harriet, kindly.

Harriet shrugged. 'You tell me.'

Caroline's mouth opened, and then closed again. 'I don't . . .'

'You've seen him recently, haven't you?'

'Well, yes. I had a drink with him earlier in the week.'

'Of course you did.'

Caroline went pink. It was her body's default reaction whenever she felt accused or on the spot. It all showed in her cheeks. 'What are you suggesting exactly, Hats? That I'm doing something wrong by seeing one of my oldest friends?'

'No. Oh no, of course you're not doing anything wrong. Sorry. I'm sorry.'

Caroline nodded. 'It's OK. I understand,' she said, primly.

'You don't, though.' Harriet picked at the skin around her thumbnail. 'I'm not being weird, but you don't. You've never been dumped by anyone.'

This was true. You couldn't be dumped if you never had proper boyfriends.

'He didn't exactly dump you, though, did he?' Stella pointed out. 'You kind of pushed him into it.'

'Stella!' Izzy shot her a look.

'What? It's true.' Stella got up from the table.

Harriet's eyes filled with tears. 'Thanks for that,' she said.

'For fuck's sake, Stella.' Izzy took Harriet's hand.

Stella rolled her eyes. 'Come on, darling, I'm sorry,' she said to Harriet, 'but everyone's thinking it. It's been over six months. He's with Colette. They're living together. He's not coming back. You need to move on.'

Harriet let out a yelp of pain and turned to Stella, her eyes flashing with fury. 'I need to move on? Right. Excellent. Sorry, forgive me if I don't take relationship advice from the woman whose husband's never gone a month without cheating on her.'

Stella chucked her cigarette into the ashtray and reached for another one. 'It's not cheating if I know about it,' she said, but the hurt was audible in her voice. 'Don't judge, you know, Harriet? It works for us.'

Now it was Caroline's turn to scoff. 'Oh, really? How does it work for you? So you're drinking a bottle of wine every day and doing drugs while you're meant to be looking after your child because you're so blissfully happy, is that right?'

'Darling. Don't be bitter. I know it must be hard to see people with children, but, you know. No need to take it out on me just because hubby's not coming up with the goods. Or maybe it's you?'

'You bitch.' Caroline looked to Izzy for support. Izzy just sat, unable to speak.

'Jesus. Stop it. All of you. Please stop it,' she said eventually, looking around at them, her voice softer and feebler-sounding than any of them were expecting. Shamefaced, they fell silent.

Izzy put her head in her hands and cried. What was happening to her friends? What was happening to her life?

Chapter Twelve

She didn't know how it had happened. Well, she did, of course. 'When Mummy and Daddy love each other very much . . .' Except in her case, there was no Mummy and Daddy who loved each other very much. There was a mummy, so it seemed. There was very much a mummy. She stared at the pregnancy test in her hand. There was no mistaking it. There was a mummy, or rather in anything between five and eight months there would be. And, by extension, that meant that there would be a daddy. But not, she feared, one who loved Mummy very much. Not right now, at least, and certainly not when she told him the news.

Harriet flopped back on her bed. She had imagined the moment that she found out she was pregnant many times, but she had never imagined that it would be like this. In her fantasies, which she'd allowed herself to indulge in from time to time over the years, in idle moments when one of her friends announced a pregnancy, or when she saw a pregnant woman around her age on the tube, the scenario might change in its details, but the atmosphere was always the same. Sometimes she saw herself sneaking into the bathroom in secret, presenting the positive test by simply putting it in front of Will as he watched TV and letting him slowly realise what was going on. Sometimes she thought that they might have planned it together, and that he would be pacing outside the bathroom like the expectant father he would shortly be, and she would emerge, shyly smiling, and he would lift her up into his arms, joyous, before carefully putting her down again; her and her precious cargo. The way she found out might have been different, but there were constant features – her, and Will, and their mutual happiness.

She had never thought this would be how it would happen. Never thought that she would be alone, in a poky flat, lying on her bed, unsure when the thing inside her had actually been conceived. *The thing.* Not the thing. The baby. But she couldn't think of it as a baby. Not yet. It would make it too real, too terrifying. A whole other person, inside her? No. It was, at the moment, simply a collection of cells. Maybe. Or it could be an actual baby. A small one, yes, but shaped like a baby. Depending. If she had got pregnant that first time, it could be – she counted – fifteen weeks in. She opened her laptop and Googled 'fifteen-week-old foetus'. She was going to have to find out how pregnant she was, and soon. There were things she would have to do, surely. Like – go to the doctor. That was the first step. That was what you did, wasn't it? Go and register the fact that you were pregnant with them, get on some kind of list? Was there a list?

It could fit in the palm of her hand, still, if she were fifteen weeks pregnant, the website said. Harriet held her hand up in front of her face and tried to imagine it. God, that was – that was bigger than she had thought. She would probably start to feel it moving soon, if she was that far along. She couldn't be, though. Surely if she had something that size inside her – the size of a small avocado, as the site pointed out – she would know about it? Something that was about to start swimming around – did they swim? Or was it more like floating? – she would have been aware of that before now, wouldn't she? If not, what did that say about her maternal instinct? The poor little thing. Stuck with a mother so useless she didn't even know how old her own child was. The thought brought tears to her eyes, and she smiled. Maybe she did have some maternal instinct after all.

It wasn't just telling the father that she was pregnant that Harriet had always imagined; it was telling her own parents. She'd thought about that, too, over the years. Envisaged waiting until the first scan, maybe, then sending them a photo printout of the baby, all blurred and alien-like, inside a card. One with something about grandparents on the front, maybe. That was the sort of thing Caroline would do, all perfect and neat.

Caroline. Oh God. That was another problem. Harriet stared at the ceiling. How was she going to tell her? Caroline could hardly walk past a pregnant woman or someone pushing a pram in the street without tears filling her eyes. How would she cope with Harriet getting pregnant when she wasn't even with anyone, hadn't even been trying? It seemed carelessly cruel.

In the end, she went to the person whom she had run to with so many crises in her life, though none as big as this. She had gone to him with exam failures and boyfriend dramas, when she had been suspended from school for getting drunk and passing out in the loos during the summer concert, and when she had had her first bit row with Will. She went to Brighton, and to Harry.

She didn't tell him she was coming. She should have called, she knew; Harry's life was erratic and colourful and there was no way of predicting whether he would be there when she turned up, or, if he was, whether he would be alone. But she couldn't bring herself to speak to him on the phone. He would know something was wrong, that this wasn't just a random desire to spend a weekend by the seaside with her beloved godfather, and he'd try and winkle it out of her (he was impatient and incorrigibly nosy, and would not be able to contain his curiosity were she to give him prior warning) and she would end up telling him, and she didn't want to tell him on the phone, standing there alone in her flat without him to hold her hand. She just didn't want to be alone.

His shop was down a small side road off the main drag of Kemp Town. It took up the ground floor of a tall Regency building that had seen better days but that retained an air of its former grandeur. Harry lived on the top three floors of the building, and there was a separate flat in the basement that he rented out to a female taxidermist who wore her work: fox furs and hats with little stuffed birds perched on top of them. Harry had once given Harriet a handbag with a handle made from a stuffed snake that he had bought from the woman. It had given her the creeps, and she kept it in a box on top of her wardrobe. She should sell it on eBay, really; the woman had become quite famous recently. Harriet could see her through the railings as she walked up the steps to Harry's shop; her mink-covered shoulders were moving around as she manipulated some poor stuffed animal into surreal poses. The thought turned Harriet's stomach and she thought for a moment that she might be sick right there on the street. She looked up at the sky and held on to the railing, taking deep gulps of sea air until the feeling passed.

'Hats? Hats, darling, what on earth are you doing here?'

She looked up, and there he was, standing in the doorway of his shop, leaning against the frame, arms crossed, glasses on a chain around his neck. He wore a primrose-yellow cashmere jumper – she didn't need to touch it to know it was not wool, it was always cashmere – grey trousers with a natty blue pinstripe, and highly polished brogues, and something about the familiar, completely Harry-like outfit made her burst into tears.

'Oh dear. I see. One of those visits, then,' he said, and, taking her arm, led her inside the shop, and turned the sign on the door around so that it read *Closed*.

'Who have you told?' he asked, when he had taken her coat off and sat her down and got her to tell him what was going on, through snotty gasps. Once she had started crying, it had not been easy to stop, and she had found herself breathless and hot-cheeked, sobbing so hard that she began to worry that she would hurt the baby, and it was that thought that shocked her into a trembly calm.

'No one,' she said, wrapping her hands around the gold-rimmed cup of camomile that he had made her, wishing that instead of a delicate porcelain antique it was a thick, clumsy mug of builder's tea, heavy with sugar, but grateful for the warmth and comfort of being looked after.

'I couldn't. I feel – I feel like such a fuck-up.'

'Darling girl. Why? You're in your thirties. You've got a good job. You're not some wayward teenager, not any longer, much as I sometimes treat you like one.' She smiled. It was true. Harry never let her leave him without palming her some cash for the taxi home, or admonishing her that she wasn't wearing a warm enough coat. He was more maternal than her own mother like that. 'You're allowed to have a baby if you want to.'

She stared at her tea. 'That's the thing. Do I? Can I? Harry, I'm all by myself. I . . . I don't think I can do it on my own.'

Harry gave her a long stare. 'I'm not going to ask who the father is,' he said, eventually. She didn't reply. 'But I take it he doesn't know either?'

Harriet shook her head. 'Not yet. I can't . . . I just can't.'

'You'll have to tell him eventually. How pregnant are you? You have been to the doctor, or am I going to have to organise that as well?' His voice was sharp, but his eyes were kind as he winked at her to show her he was not angry.

'Yes. I went yesterday. I'm almost three months. He's pretty sure. I'm having a scan next week. They should be able to sort out the dates then.'

'You don't know the dates?' Harry raised an eyebrow. 'Darling. You have been busy.'

Harriet blushed. 'I haven't. Not at all.'

'Well, if you don't know . . .' Harry's voice was taut with the scandalous thrill of the conversation. There was nothing he loved more than being privy to a bit of gossip, even when it concerned his most loved godchild.

'Harry! Stop it.'

'Sorry.' He bit into a custard cream.

Harriet sighed. 'There are a couple of occasions when it might have happened, that's all.'

'But darling . . .' Harry paused. She could see that he was trying desperately hard not to be indelicately inquisitive.

'Wasn't I using anything?'

He nodded.

'Yes. I was on the pill. I have been for years. Didn't bother to come off it when Will and I broke up. Force of habit, I guess, rather than any particular optimism on that front. But . . .' She paused. She was such a fuck-up, whatever Harry said to the contrary. It was only him she could talk so honestly to; only him she could be absolutely sure would not judge her and think badly of her. Even so, she felt embarrassed telling him what a mess she had got herself into.

She took a deep breath. 'After Will and I . . . after I moved out, I had a difficult few months.' She stopped for a moment and bit her lip. A difficult few months was putting it mildly. Thinking back to that time made her feel sick. She had never before known such self-hating misery.

'I was drinking a lot. I wasn't in a very good way.'

Harry reached forward and took her hand. She gave him a

small smile. She felt duplicitous for receiving sympathy that she did not deserve.

'I'm not proud of how I behaved then. I don't really want to go into details.'

Was that a flicker of disappointment that crossed his face as she talked? No, she was being unkind.

'But the upshot of it all was that I got a bit erratic about taking my pill. Couldn't remember when I hadn't taken it, it would seem.'

'Well, really. Aren't they – don't they have the day printed on them or something? They should have. How in heaven's name is anyone expected to remember whether they've taken it or not?' Harry sounded outraged on her behalf, furious at the failure of the drug companies to make sure she didn't screw up her birth control, and she smiled. This was exactly why she had come to him first.

'They have days of the week on the packet. I wasn't – I wasn't exactly paying attention.' I was blacking out, was what she should have said, but could not quite bring herself to. I didn't know what day it was half the time. But that was something she couldn't say. Harry might be quick to defend her and slow to judge, but he was still her godfather, had still known her since she was a baby. There were some things he didn't need to know.

'So, you'll find out the dates next week. Then you can make plans. Tell your parents. Tell the father. You are . . .' Harry stopped himself. Reworded his sentence. 'Are you planning on keeping the baby?'

Harriet nodded. 'Yes. Yes, I am. Fuck knows how, or what I'm going to do, or any of that stuff. But yes. I'm keeping the baby.'

She folded her arm across her stomach, in confirmation, almost, of her statement. It was in there, somewhere, nestled deep inside her, growing even as she spoke. Its heart beating. It was part of her. There was no question in her mind – never had been – that she would be keeping it.

But there was a question about something else. Something she was keeping to herself for now. She could tell Harry almost everything, yes. Almost. But she couldn't tell him just how much of a mess she had been a while ago, and what it had been that had pulled her out of it. And she couldn't tell him that there was more than one candidate for the position of father.

Colette might look fragile and girlie, but she was determined. When she found something she wanted, she hung on tight until she got it. She had done it with the gold cup at the pony club – had clung on to Balfour's mane until she came in first, after he had tried to throw her off halfway around the course. She had done it with the nose job that she had nagged and nagged her father for until he had given in and bought it for her eighteenth birthday. And now she wanted Will. For keeps.

She loved Will, of course she did. He was funny, sexy, successful – on track to being really successful, she believed. But more than that, she had decided on Will. He was the kind of man she wanted to marry. He was posher than her, and had the easy Old Etonian charm that she had always found so attractive. Colette wanted her family life to be different to the one she had known growing up. She wanted her children to be part of the Establishment that she had felt herself ever so slightly not part of when she had been at school. She wanted them to instinctively know why fish knives were common and that no one ever said *serviette*. If they spoke with a hint of Estuary in their voices, she wanted it to be the affected vowel-dropping of the innately well-spoken, not the remnants of an accent they were trying to lose. She wanted to be able to turn up at school speech days and not feel them embarrassed by their parents for not quite fitting in (she was young enough not to have yet realised that all children were embarrassed by their parents; indeed, that was part of your role as a parent). She wanted everything that Will represented, everything that he took for granted.

And so, she would get Will. She would show Harriet, and all of the rest of them, who clearly saw her as a diversion, a silly little thing for Will to shag while he was on the rebound. James and his stuck-up wife Izzy, slutty Stella, her hot but lechy husband who shagged anything that moved, dull old Caroline. All of them.

All she had to do was work out how to get Will to propose.

In the end, it was pretty easy. Colette knew something Harriet had not known – that to get a man to do what you wanted, you had to do two things: make him think that it was his idea, and make him think that the prospect might be just ever so slightly out of his reach. Will was infatuated with her, she knew that. Everyone knew that. Men tended to be. It was a combination of youth and sex and an apparent innocence that drove them to want to protect her, and she was smart enough to know that its blush would fade before too long, and that she should capitalise on it while she could. Hers was not the type of beauty that lasted; by thirty-five, maybe earlier, she would be just another Fulham blonde in skinny jeans and big sunglasses.

They were at dinner with James and Izzy the first time she dropped it into the conversation – or didn't, to be more precise. It was a fairly miserable affair, with Izzy insisting that everything was fine and that things were carrying on as normal, serving beef Wellington in an obvious attempt to show them how unworried about money they were, and James frantically hiding the good wine at the back of the fridge and refilling their glasses with mean inches only when he had to. Poverty really did bring out the worst in people. Colette did count herself lucky that, thanks to the father whose manners and accent she found so appallingly humiliating, and his property empire, it was not something she would ever have to worry about.

'So pretty, wasn't she? Caroline, I mean,' she said, gazing at one of the wedding photos as Izzy served them canapés of smoked trout pâté in the living room. Izzy looked sharply at her.

'Yes. She is, isn't she?'

'She looks like Mum did when she was younger in that picture,' James said, his voice full of affection. 'At her wedding. I mean, different sort of dress and everything. But they do look alike. I'll try and find it after supper.'

Colette laughed. 'Oh, James, I'm sure she looked just lovely, but I think we're a way off mooning over wedding photos. Well I am, at least. I'll leave that to the old marrieds.'

Izzy raised an eyebrow, and stalked into the kitchen to check on the beef. Colette smiled at James, and slid her hand into Will's. Part one.

A couple of days later, she went on to Tiffany's website and signed Will up to their mailing list, making sure to tick the box marked 'engagement rings' when it asked what his particular interests were. He would think it was uninvited spam, and probably delete it as soon as it came in, but he would see it. He might even think it was a sign, she thought briefly, then dismissed the idea. Will was not a 'signs' sort of a person. But the idea would be planted, somewhere. It was all about opening his mind to the possibilities, making him realise the benefits of marriage. Part two.

She politely refused invitations from James and Izzy to get together for supper or a walk in the park with the kids, in favour of a couple of carefully chosen sets of her friends who appeared to extol the loveliness of the institution of marriage. One pair were newly married and so sex-crazed they could barely get through an evening in the pub without disappearing off to the loos for a quickie. This was nothing to do with the fact that they were married; indeed, Colette knew that it was not only one another that they were constantly shagging, but it served her purpose perfectly. Sex was important to Will, and the implication that it might stop or decrease in either quality or quantity as soon as the wedding vows were uttered was a common joke among his married friends and one that she was determined to squash. And James and Izzy were miserable at the moment, both separately and together. They were not a good advertisement for marriage.

The other friends she selected for them to spend more and more time with were privately miserable but masters at hiding the fact, and determined to present a united front to the world (she had married for money, he for sex and a social life, and as long as they were both getting what they wanted, they were as happy as they were ever likely to be). They were also members of Henry Butler's, which was even better, so Will and Colette went to private views and post-theatre parties with them, talking in the cab on the way home about how fun and lively they were, how they always had such a good time with the Beltrams (this calling of friends by their mutual surname was something Colette encouraged; it helped her cause to refer to people as a single, definable unit), while the Beltrams themselves rode home in complete silence.

She made sure that the evenings they spent with these friends, and any other happily married couples, were the most fun of the week. She dressed particularly carefully, in the demurely feminine but sexy little dresses that Will most liked her in. She was attentive, adoring and charming, and she made sure that the night was always rounded off with a particularly good fuck. Once she even gave Will half a hand-job under her coat in the taxi home, pausing and making him wait when they were three streets away, so that by the time they got in the front door he simply pushed her forward on to the stairs and took her from behind in a few brief thrusts, as she hung on to the banister and smiled, unseen.

When they went out, she flirted, while Will was in the loo or at the bar, with men who would then approach her, batting her eyelashes at them until they plucked up the courage to come and talk to her, usually managing to time it so that Will came back at just the right moment. Then she would act bemused and he was able to politely but firmly put the bewildered bloke off, by slipping his arm around her and saying, 'Sorry, mate, she's taken.'

But still he made no move. It was baffling to Colette. She had done everything she could think of. And she was quietly furious that her plan did not seem to be working.

And then, one evening, fate seemed to intervene. And she was able to seize the moment, in the way her daddy had always taught her.

Will had got in from work late. She never nagged him to come home at a certain time. She was calm, perfectly dressed as usual. She turned the heat on under the pot of moules marinière that was sitting ready on the hob. She wore a blue and white striped apron, tied tight around her waist, making it look tiny.

'Shit. What a day.' Will rubbed his hand over his face.

'Why? What happened?' She kissed him, and handed him a gin and tonic. Little things. But little things that made his life more comfortable. More pleasant.

He shook his head. 'My business is screwed, that's what. The whole thing could disappear. I don't know.'

'What?' She turned. The moules weren't going to spoil. 'Darling. What's happened? Will, what's going on?'

'It's all collapsing. The holiday properties – no one's renting them. Henry Butler's is ticking over – just. But lots of the smaller clients are cancelling.'

'Not the bigger ones, though?'

'No. But it's the small ones that we rely on to keep it pushing forward day to day. The big ones spend lots, but they need plenty of babysitting. The smaller ones are lower-maintenance. They're the basis of it. And I poured money into the holiday stuff. Stupid. Stupid, stupid, stupid.'

He slammed his hand against the wall. Colette jumped. She had never seen Will like this. His face was full of fury and frustration, his body taut, and the air around him thrummed with tension. It was unnerving – but it was also strangely appealing. Will, usually so laid-back, so charming, was showing his fight.

'I can't lose Henry Butler's, Colette. I can't just let it fall apart. It's the only thing I've ever really cared about. Not the only person . . .' He glanced up at her, a small smile backing up his words. 'But the one thing I've had to really work for. I can't bear to see it disappear. But I don't know how to save it. I don't know what to do.'

Colette moved between him and the kitchen worktop, then pushed herself up on to it so that she was sitting on its edge, facing Will, their heads level. She took his hands. Will was distraught, and a part of her hated to see him like this, but a larger part of her was thrilled. This was it. This was her chance.

'Darling.'

Will nodded. He wasn't meeting her eyes. She raised a hand to his chin and gently tipped it upwards until he was looking at her. 'That's better,' she said, gently. 'Listen. It's all right. It's going to be all right.'

Will puffed his breath out. 'Colette, I love you, sweet pea. And thank you for trying to make me feel better. But honestly, you can't—'

'Will, don't interrupt me, just listen.'

He fell quiet. Colette's voice was headmistress firm.

'I can help. I can. I know you think I don't know much about business. And that might be true. I don't have your flair. Everything you touch turns to gold.'

'Not this, it seems.'

'Oh, it does. It will. This is just a blip. Everything's gone crazy.'

'That's certainly true.'

'But it won't last. Not for ever. You just need to be able to hang on in there until the storm passes.'

Will shrugged. He couldn't see it, couldn't see a way through. But she could.

'I'll lend you the money.'

Will laughed, shocked. 'Baby.' He kissed her hand, still holding it in his own. Colette kept one eye on the mussels. They were almost ready. It should all be timed perfectly.

'You can't . . . I don't just need a couple of thousand. You're adorable.' He smiled at her. 'I adore you.'

'And I adore you, but please don't patronise me. I know we're not talking about a couple of grand here. You need a lot of money, fast, to prop the business up while you reconfigure, regroup, and while the worst of the recession passes. No bank is going to lend it to you. You don't have time to go through another round of venture capitalists, and you've exhausted all your private contacts for investment. Apart from me.'

Will stared at her.

'I have rather a large trust fund. I never told you about it. I don't like to talk about it.'

Will said nothing.

'I'll lend you the money.'

'Colette, I can't let you do that.' He looked shell-shocked.

'Why not?'

He shook his head.

'You love me, don't you, Will?'

'Of course I do. Of course.'

'You're not planning on dumping me any time soon?' She kept her voice light.

'What – no! Why do you . . .'

She squeezed his hand. 'Then there's no problem. If we're together, we're together. A team. And I'll lend you the money. What sort of relationship would we have if you were in trouble and I was able to help you, easily, and I didn't? Or you wouldn't let me?'

Will took her wrist in his hand and pulled her closer to him. She looked up at him, shocked by his passion, despite the fact that she had thrown in the firelighters and the match.

He stroked the tiny fronds of baby hair that surrounded her temples. They were so blond. So soft. They almost brought tears to his eyes.

'Darling Colette. You're right. We're a team. We are a team.'

As he gazed at her, he realised the truth of his words. No one had ever made a gesture like this, no one had so clearly put their faith in him, with no guarantees, expecting nothing in return.

'Thank you. Oh my darling girl, thank you.' He embraced her, and then pulled back. He was overwhelmed by it – by her. And suddenly, he knew.

'Will you marry me? I know I don't exactly look like a good bet right now. But I promise I'll prove it all to you. That I'll put you first. That I *am* a good bet. I promise. Will you?'

Colette smiled. She let herself melt into his arms, feeling her body lean against his strength as she looked into his eyes. It was everything she wanted.

'Oh Will,' she breathed, sounding surprised and over-whelmed. 'You don't have to . . .'

'It's not a thank-you. I'm not asking you because you're giving me money. God, what an idiot. You must think—'

Colette interrupted him. 'I think you're the sweetest man who ever lived. I think Henry Butler's is going to be a huge success. And I think I'm going to really, really love being Mrs William Erskine. Yes. Yes, I will. Yes!'

And she squealed and laughed as he lifted her up into the air and kissed her, and then gently placed her back on the kitchen worktop and carried on kissing her. She thanked Daddy, not God, for her smarts, and for her innate sense of timing, and, of course, for her immense trust fund. With one arm she reached out and turned off the heat under the mussels. They had had four minutes, and their shells had gently eased open. They would be perfectly cooked.

Chapter Thirteen

December 2009

Caroline sat with her legs pulled up to her chest, in hoodie and tracksuit bottoms, on her mother's bed. They were watching the DVD box set of *Dynasty* together, working their way through the trials and tribulations of the Colbys and the Carringtons, marvelling at the size of the diamonds and the hairdos, nibbling on Waitrose titbits that Caroline had picked up on her way over. Ginny couldn't face full meals, so Caroline and James and Julian had got into the habit of looking for little treats that they thought might tempt her – bits of smoked salmon and tiny cucumber sandwiches and macaroons. Izzy made her light mousses and roulades with extra eggs packed into the mix for nourishment. But Ginny only picked at it all.

'Look at that dress!' Caroline gasped. 'So eighties. I love it.'

'Darling, if you like that, there's plenty of similar monstrosities in my wardrobe. Take your pick.'

'You must have been very chic a few years ago, Mama.'

'Thanks very much,' Ginny said wryly.

'Oh, you still are, lovely Mummy, of course you are.'

Ginny smiled. 'Well. It'll be up to you what you do with it all when I'm gone, anyhow. Maybe you should have an eighties fancy-dress party before you get rid of it.'

Caroline frowned. 'Don't say that.'

Ginny looked over at her daughter. She reached for her hand.

'My darling. It's going to happen, you know. I'd feel so much better if you'd talk to me. If I felt that you were accepting it.'

Caroline's eyes filled with tears. 'I can't accept it. How can I?'

'I know it's hard. Of course I do.'

Caroline tried to breathe evenly. She wanted more than anything else to talk to her mother. To curl up in a ball next to her, snuggle into her side, and tell her everything. How unhappy she was, how bad things were between her and Bart, how she had made such a mess of her marriage and she didn't know how to fix it. Tell her that she was scared about what would happen when Ginny was gone, as she knew she would be before too long.

How would they all cope without her? Ginny was the glue that held the family together, she was the one who organised dinners and remembered birthdays and kept the present drawer full, who knew who didn't like tomatoes and whose favourite pudding was pavlova, who could get Pearl to eat her peas and Alfie to sit quietly with her and watch a whole episode of *In the Night Garden*. She was the only person who remembered how upset Caroline had been when her best friend at primary school had stopped talking to her for a week, or the fact that she had been the only girl at Brownies to get all of her badges, or what she was allergic to. Ginny was the keeper of the family history, and it felt as though when she was gone, all that would go with her.

'You will survive without me, you know,' she said now, as though she had read Caroline's mind. 'All of you. You'll help each other. Especially you, though.'

Caroline shook her head. 'What do you mean?'

'I mean that the others are going to need you.' Ginny turned to her, and looked at her with her clear pale blue eyes. 'You're a mum, my darling daughter. I know you haven't had babies of your own yet. And I'm so sorry for that. I'm sorry that I won't get to see them, and I'm sorry that it's causing you so much heartache.'

She squeezed Caroline's hand.

'But you will do, and when you do, you're going to be an amazing mother. Better than I ever was, I'm sure.'

Caroline sniffed. 'Not possible.'

'Sweet of you to say, darling. You look after people. You always have done. Ever since you were little, and lining up your soft toys in bed, making sure they all got the same amount of attention from you so none of them felt left out. You think about other people, you take care of their feelings. And that's what everyone is going to need in the coming months.'

Caroline couldn't bear it. Her heart felt as though it was going to explode with the need to tell her mother everything. She opened her mouth. She had to tell her, had to say something. 'Mama . . .'

Ginny leaned back on her pillows and let her eyes sink closed. The effort of the speech had tired her.

'I'm just so pleased you've got someone to look after you as well now. Such a relief. You go to your party, darling, I'm going to have a little sleep.'

Caroline stroked the back of her hand. 'Yes. You go to sleep, Mama,' she whispered. 'You sleep.'

New Year's Eve 2009

'God, Caroline, you're so thin. What are you now, a six?'

Caroline blushed as Harriet appraised her figure with a keen and slightly jealous eye, one hand on her bump. 'Your waist is practically the size of one of my ankles. Oh God. I'm enormous, aren't I? What if you haven't lost weight at all? What if you just look tiny compared to me because I'm such an elephant? Am I the size of a normal pregnant person, do you think? Is everyone this huge?'

Caroline smiled. 'You look lovely, you idiot. I have lost weight. I haven't been trying to. But it's been a bit full-on recently. Bart's happy about it, anyhow, so that's good.'

Harriet rolled her eyes. 'Oh well, as long as Bart's happy . . .'

'Stop it.' Caroline's voice was light, but there was tension in her eyes. Harriet knew that she shouldn't be going on about her pregnancy weight; Caroline would have loved nothing more than to be complaining of swollen ankles and heartburn. It was hard not to be self-centred, though, when your whole body had been taken over by a large, hungry, generally demanding passenger. It was astonishing that this baby managed to exert so much control over its mother's actions and emotions when it was still *in utero*. Not even part of this world yet, not really, and already it was making demands, making sure its needs came first. No, you can't have that glass of champagne, it had already said tonight. I don't like the bubbles and I'll make sure they give you painful hiccups. No, you may not sleep on your front any more, like you used to; you'll sleep on your side with pillows under me to cushion me. No, you may not eat those smoked salmon nibbles, the M&S ones that used to be your favourites; I don't like the look of them and I'll make them suddenly smell all wrong to put you off them. No, you will not watch an advert for a dogs' home without bursting into floods of tears, nor may you have a rational conversation with anyone for longer than five minutes without dropping me into the conversation, how-ever unnaturally. Yes, her baby was a demanding little bugger. And the really crazy thing was, she didn't mind one bit.

'There's Dimity. Or possibly Pointing. Which I think is a bit too bright. House white's too yellow; I want a greyish undertone.'

'What about Blackened. Too grey?' Izzy pointed to a small square on the paint card.

Stella wrinkled her nose. 'Maybe. I do like it, though. There's always Clunch. It's nice. I just don't think I can paint my hall in something that sounds like another name for minge.'

'There is that.'

'Fuck knows. I'll probably end up getting pissed and painting it orange or something in the middle of the night anyway.' Stella put the paint card back in her bag.

'So, how's everything with James? What's the story?' She opened the front door a few inches so that she could hold a cigarette out of it, and cold air funnelled in. Since the weekend in the summer when Cass and Amanda had appeared and the tensions that had been bubbling under between the girls had spilled over, Stella and Izzy had seen little of one another. They had both been busy, both caught up in their respective personal dramas. Theirs was probably the least close relationship of the four women. They got on well enough but did not have the shared history of Harriet and Caroline, or the familial ties of Izzy and Caroline, nor did they have the same appetite for nights out on the town that Harriet and Stella shared, or had done until recently, Harriet now being keener on nights spent with her feet up on the sofa than forced into uncomfortable shoes. So there was less to hold them together when circumstances began to pull them apart. And the four of them hadn't got together for a while. Caroline was distracted and distant, spending most of her free time with Ginny. Harriet was bound up in baby books and labour fears. Izzy was conflicted about almost every aspect of her life, and Stella was ignoring all of her problems in favour of the deep denial found in the bottom of a wrap of cocaine. They needed someone to pull them back together; they needed one of them to see that they were all hurting, and concealing their hurt, and ignoring each other's. They needed their heads knocking together, a mother might have said, but there was no mother around to say it, and so they trudged on, unable to see a way out of their private miseries.

'We're still together,' Izzy replied, waving Stella's smoke away and holding her hand out for a cigarette at the same time.

'For good? Or for now?'

'Who knows.'

'And Cass?'

Izzy lit the cigarette, shrugging. 'She's a sweet girl. She's staying, you know.'

'Mm. Caroline said. How's that?'

'Fine. The kids adore her. It's surprisingly – surprisingly fine.' It was true. Cass had slotted into the family more easily than Izzy would ever have imagined possible. It was almost as though she had always been there. And in spite of herself, Izzy had grown to feel an affection for the girl.

'It's not her fault, after all,' she said now, slightly defensively.

'Have you forgiven him yet?'

Izzy blew a stream of smoke out of the door. 'I don't know,' she said quietly. 'Not really, if I'm honest.'

Stella shook her head. 'So what's the point?'

'What do you mean?'

'Come on, Iz. Forgive him and mean it, or bin it. You can't play the martyr for ever.'

'Fuck off! That's not what I'm doing.'

'Isn't it?'

Izzy fumed. How dare Stella judge her? Oh, it was all right for her, she didn't seem to care what Johnny did. Not everyone had the same ability to just carry on as normal in the face of deception.

But she wasn't carrying on as normal, was she? Her thumb crept to the ring on her finger, Stephen Garside's ring. She had seen him only yesterday. His pursuit of her had not decreased in intensity; if anything, it had become more ardent, more determined. He was infiltrating his way into her life, his influence spreading slowly through it, like ivy working its fingers in between the bricks of a wall, and no one could see it but her. He was advising James on job opportunities, he was investing in Will's company; the three of them and Bart had even been to play golf together. She swung between finding it suffocating and reassuring. When she thought about it too much, it made her chest go tight. But with fear, or excitement?

She and the children had stayed on in Cornwall for a fortnight, James and Cass in London. She had told him to stay away, that she needed the space. It had just been her, Pearl and Alfie, and for two glorious weeks she had rejoiced in the solitude and the long evenings spent listening to the sea, but then she had become restless and bored, and realised that she must either return home or allow James to come back down, that she had to confront what was going on in some way. So she had packed up the car and taken the kids back to London, and after a long and painful discussion, she and James had agreed that they would carry on as before.

Only nothing was really as it was before. There was Cass, now, and the knowledge of James's past that hung around the house like a cloud, ready to catch her and rain on her at every turn. There were the lies he must have told, over the years, that kept on ambushing her – remembered snippets of conversation with friends about ex-girlfriends, or having your first child – things that she had taken at face value at the time and which now floated back to her, their duplicity obvious with hindsight. And there was Stephen Garside. She had called to tell him that they had returned to London early. 'I can drop the keys round,' she had suggested, tentatively, knowing that she was offering something more than his house keys as she did so. It had all spilled out when she had got to his house and he had opened the door and held his arms out to her, his feet bare on the marble floor, his eyes inviting her to come closer. And she had done. She had let him lead her inside, his arm around her shoulder, and she had only got a few steps into the house before she had blurted out, 'James has a daughter. An older girl, a teenager, and he never told me about her.' And Stephen had said nothing, just taken her hands in his, and before she could change her mind or think about what she was doing, she had leant up and put her hands on the rough, unshaven skin of his cheeks and kissed him, surprised at first by the unfamiliar feel of his lips and then excited by it, and then, just as quickly, aware that she must stop, had to stop or else she was not going to be able to. And she had pulled away, and apologised, and left his house, running to her car, chucking the forgotten-about keys behind her on to his driveway and driving off.

She had ignored his texts and messages after that, for two months. Had gone home, consumed by guilt, and made James his favourite dinner, stupidly, as though that would erase what she had done. And she had tried to put Stephen Garside out of her mind. To be a good wife, to forget about what had happened between them, to forget about what had happened between her and James, to forget about everything.

It hadn't worked, though. She had not accounted for Stephen Garside's persistence or for the depth of her own attraction to him, and a week ago she had agreed to see him, and he had laid his intentions out on the table. 'I love you, Izzy,' he had said. 'I don't normally pursue married women, and I don't normally keep pursuing someone after they've ignored me for two whole months. It's kind of a blow to the old self-confidence, you know?' She had sat far from him, at the other end of the park bench they were sitting on, her hands underneath her bottom, as though by sitting on them she could keep not only her body but her emotions under control.

None of it had worked, and she had left him feeling even more confused and conflicted than before. Which was to be expected, she supposed.

Stella was right, however, much as it might pain Izzy to admit it. At some point in the near future, she was going to have to make a decision.

She ground out her cigarette on the path and pushed the butt on to the pavement with her foot. 'Come on,' she said. 'Let's get back to the party.'

Stella grinned at her, and waved a little plastic bag containing a handful of pills. 'And I've got just the thing to make it go with a bang,' she said.

Later, from her position tucked into the corner of the kitchen, Harriet watched as Will and Colette made their entrance. She stood back from the group, hovering in the background. She wondered when he would notice. Will wasn't the most observant. And he wouldn't be expecting it. She had sworn everyone else to secrecy, made them promise they would not tell him. 'I want to tell him myself,' she'd said. 'I owe him that. He shouldn't find out from other people, as though it's just a bit of gossip. We were together for a long time, after all.'

They'd all nodded and said they understood, that she was quite right, of course she must tell him herself. Apart from Stella. Stella asked. Of course Stella asked. 'Whose is it?' she squeaked. 'Bloody hell, Hats, you're a fast worker.'

'I'm not telling,' Harriet had said. 'He doesn't want to be involved. And that's fine. I don't expect him to be. It's my responsibility, my baby.'

'But is it someone . . . is it Will?'

'Will's with Colette now, Stella. We broke up, remember?'

'Like that means anything. Colette.' Stella blew the air out from between her lips dismissively.

'It's not Will. It's not anyone you know. Not anyone I know really, even. Think of him as a sperm donor, that's what I'm doing. He's not relevant.'

Stella had narrowed her eyes and shrugged, and Harriet had been able to tell that she didn't quite believe her. She didn't blame her.

So she had promised everyone she would tell Will, and then she had gone to pick up the phone to ask him if they could meet, and she hadn't quite been able to do it. What had stopped her? The fear that he would ask if it was his? The fear that he would be angry, upset? She could have used it. She knew that. If she had really wanted to, she could have drawn him back to her with that one conversation.

It wouldn't have been fair. She reminded herself of that now. Forcing him to come back to her with the threat of possible fatherhood when she wasn't even sure whether the baby was his or not would feel like the worst kind of manipulation. And she still loved him too much for that. She'd learnt from her mistake of giving him the ultimatum.

They were in the doorway of the kitchen now, Will tall and towering over the rest of them, as usual, his curls bouncing as his head moved to kiss the girls and shake the hands of the boys. Colette tiny, hardly visible behind the others. Just a glimpse of pale blond hair, neatly swept back into a low ponytail. And the flash of something as she waved her hand in the air.

Harriet held her breath and tried to crane her neck without anyone seeing her. Oh God. It wasn't. Was it?

'Congratulations! What a surprise . . .'

Izzy's voice was a little sharp, and she inclined her head slightly in Harriet's direction. Oh no. It was. They were engaged. And they were announcing it on New Year's Eve. Just a year – almost exactly a year – after she had told him that he must marry her or leave her, he was here, with Colette, and they were getting married. This was all wrong. It was all wrong and upside down and it could not be happening. How had this happened? A little more than a year ago they had been together still, happy, at least if it weren't for Harriet's stupid obsession with getting married, the fly in the ointment that had blinded her, made her be stupid . . . And now he was engaged to this stupid little tart and Harriet was pregnant, and everyone was looking over at her, waiting to see how she would react, what she would do, and she didn't have any choice. She smiled, tightly, she was sure, probably more of a grimace, but she forced the sides of her mouth to point upwards, and, without moving from her position in the corner of the room, said, 'Congratulations, both of you. I'm sure you'll be very happy.'

The silence was heavy and awkward. Harriet watched as Will's face went from embarrassed, uncomfortable shame to shock as he let his eyes take in her new shape. No one spoke.

'Thank you so much, Harriet. I'm sure we will be as well.' Colette broke the silence. 'And goodness! It seems we aren't the only ones with news, are we?' She gestured to Harriet's belly, and for a moment, she looked as though she was going to head in her direction. Oh no. She wasn't going to touch her, was she? Harriet didn't think she could bear it if Colette started groping her stomach, or something. But she didn't. The moment passed, and Harriet was left standing there alone. She wished someone else would say something. She wished Will would say something. Or did she?

'Many congratulations, Hats,' he said, quietly. There was a question in his eyes. And it was one she could not answer.

'Are you sure you're OK?' Izzy's hand rested gently on Harriet's shoulder. Harriet was sitting on the edge of Izzy's bed, her hands folded underneath her bump. It was ten o'clock, and downstairs, everyone was drinking and laughing. The earlier awkwardness had been softened by champagne cocktails and wine and fondue, and for a brief period, no one was thinking about who was together or apart or who was out of a job or in trouble. It was just friends and family and laughter. Footsteps on the landing outside, stumbling slightly up the last couple of stairs. They listened. The stumbler paused. Then continued their journey into the loo next to Izzy's bedroom.

Harriet sighed. 'I'm not thrilled, Izzy, obviously.'

'No. I imagine not.' She sat down next to Harriet and pulled her feet up on to the bed. 'God. It's so weird, isn't it?'

'Yeah.'

The sound of something being dropped on the floor from the loo. 'Shit.'

Izzy and Harriet smiled at one another. 'Stella.'

'Yes.'

Next door, they could hear the *tap tap tap* of her chopping out a line of coke.

'Go, if you want . . .' Harriet jerked her head towards the wall behind which she knew Stella would be standing, leaning over the little pile of white powder.

Izzy shook her head. 'No. I can't be bothered. Tomorrow will be grim enough as it is. Too old.'

'Shit. Shit, shit, shit!' Stella's voice carried across the landing, and Izzy rolled her eyes.

'For fuck's sake. She'll wake the kids if she's not careful.' She pushed herself up off the bed, and went to the door.

Stella couldn't believe it. How, how, how could she have been so clumsy? She watched the wrap in horror as it floated, almost elegantly, off the side, and drifted, like a balloon that had slipped out of a child's fat fingers, towards the floor. Scrabbled to catch it, but it had flipped over when she had caught the edge of it with the silk sleeve of her kimono dress, and tipped its contents on to the carpet even before it had landed.

She knelt on the floor, and picked up the little square of paper. It was empty. She could have cried. 'Damn it,' she whispered, 'damn and fuck it.' No one else would have any; she discarded that possibility right away. They were all far too straight, or so they liked to think, to actually buy their own. Doing hers was fine; it was like giving up smoking and just bumming the odd one in the pub – it didn't quite count. They didn't have to actually dirty their hands buying the stuff, phoning up a dealer and going to pick it up themselves, carrying it around in the inside pocket of their handbag, its weight far heavier than it should be. They could just do the odd line of hers, at parties and nights like tonight, and pretend to themselves that she was a bad influence. She . . . she had to stop this internal rant and worry about how she was going to get some more.

She'd have to call Dave. It was New Year's Eve and he'd be busy, and probably on the other side of town at some club. How much extra would she have to pay him to come over here? She sat on the loo with the lid down and texted him. *Where are you? Need to see you. Can you come to SW6?*

Within a couple of seconds her phone buzzed his response. Dave's phone was an extension of his arm, always nestled in the palm of his hand. *No can do. In Manchester for the night. Have a good one. D.*

Stella threw the phone down on the floor in temper. Manchester. What the fuck was he doing in Manchester?

'Shit, shit, shit!'

She looked down at the patch of carpet where the wrap had fallen. It was scattered with flecks of white. She stared at it for a few seconds. And then stood up. Hey, what the fuck, right?

*

'Stella!'

'Jesus Christ.'

Stella turned her head and looked back over her shoulder. Behind her, in the doorway of the loo, stood Izzy and Harriet. Their expressions were disapproving, angry. They looked like two Victorian schoolmarms, with their arms crossed and their faces all stern and severe. The thought made her giggle. Just put them in a couple of – what were those things called – wimples! That was right. And they could be nuns. Well, not Harriet, maybe. A pregnant nun would rather go against the spirit of things, she thought. Even Stella knew that. But the idea made her laugh, and once she had started she found she couldn't stop. Tears rolled down her face as she crouched, rolled-up twenty-pound note in her hand, leaning forward on her haunches, convulsed with laughter.

'Stella. Stella, are you all right?'

Their concern made it worse. She waved her hand in front of her face. *Stop it, don't say anything*, she wanted to say, but all that came out was a strangled sobbing sound.

'Stella – your nose. You're bleeding.'

She paused, then, at last. Looked up at them, confused. What were they talking about? She wasn't bleeding. She was laughing. The wetness on her face was from her eyes. Tears of laughter. She was having such a good time. She shook her head, to show them she was fine. But as she did so, a drop of blood fell from her nose and down on to her dress. She lowered her head and looked at her chest. A thick red line had rolled down the patterned silk of her kimono, and merged with the print of green ferns and pink cherry blossom. Oh. Oh, they were right. As she stared, more blood fell, thick and fast; she sniffed, but it did nothing to stop the flow, just filled her throat with sticky clots, and she choked.

'Oh God. Harriet, get Johnny, will you?' Izzy stepped over and around Stella, reaching forward for a towel. Stella stayed on her knees, hands in front of her, covered in blood. She was quite unable to move. She just – couldn't. Izzy pulled the hand towel from its ring and went to hold it to Stella's face, but as she did so, Stella launched forward and vomited, retching the clots of blood that she had just swallowed, metallic and sticky as she spat them out.

Izzy reacted with the efficient calm of a mother who had spent long nights holding plastic bowls by small, fevered heads, steering Stella so that she was positioned over the toilet bowl in case of a second attack, and wiping the blood and bile from around her mouth at the same time. 'OK. You're all right, don't panic. Nothing's going to happen to you. It wasn't one of my good towels.' She smiled at Stella, who was chalk-faced and shaking. 'God, Stell. What are you doing? What on earth are you doing to yourself?' she whispered, pushing her bleached blond hair back from her face and stroking her cheek gently. 'Silly girl. Lovely, silly girl.'

Stella took a deep breath. She didn't understand. It had seemed so funny. It had all been so funny. She turned her face to the side and looked at her reflection in the mirrored cabinet next to her. She was kneeling on the floor, surrounded by fragments of coke that she had been snorting from the carpet, along with God knows what else that had been embedded in there. Her beautiful dress, antique, that Johnny had given her for Christmas and that she had been so touched by, covered in blood and spit and vomit. Her face smeared with blood, from before she had realised that her nose had started to bleed, drying dark red and crumbly on her skin. Her eye make-up messy and one of her best friends having to almost hold her upright. And it didn't seem that funny any more.

The house was dark when they got home. Johnny carried Viking's sleepy, warm body in from the car, the task providing a buffer between them. As long as Viking was there, they didn't have to speak, didn't have to look at one another. Didn't have to confront the wreck of their marriage. Johnny put him to bed. No discussion there, either. Stella knew she was in no fit state. Didn't want to touch her son like this; covered in her own bodily fluids, stinking and dishevelled. He should smell of sleep and milk and baby powder.

'And the prince rode all the way up the hill to the castle, carrying the princess on the back of his horse, and when they reached the top, there was an octopus guarding the gates.'

'An octopus?' Viking's voice was thick with sleep; he was battling to stay awake. Stella let her dress fall to the bathroom floor as she reached over and turned the shower on full.

'An octopus. And the octopus said . . .'

Johnny's voice faded as she put her head under the hot water and let it run down her face. She could feel the remains of her make-up sliding off. Her hair stuck to her scalp. The water was too hot, scalding; she could feel it turning her skin pink, but she didn't turn the temperature down. She needed the heat, needed it to cleanse her, purify her. The thought almost made her laugh. You're beyond purification, she told herself. You're too far gone for that. Purity is for babes and innocents. For people who wash in rainwater and walk barefoot through daisy-strewn grass, for people who float, not those who sink to the bottom, for people who . . .

'Stella . . . Stella, wake up. Wake up. Shit. Stella, come on. Come on.'

When she came round, the water had stopped running over her, but she was still damp. Her head hurt. She opened her eyes. Johnny was next to her, crouching on the bathroom floor. Why was she on the bathroom floor again? Twice in one night. That wasn't great. She smiled.

'Hi,' she whispered.

'What the fuck were you doing, Stella?'

'Taking a shower. I didn't want to be all messy.' Johnny sounded so angry. She knew why. He was cross with her.

'You had the water on full heat. You passed out. I think you're OK, you're not bleeding. I'm going to call an ambulance, though.' He spoke in short, clipped sentences, like someone in the army. Left, right, left, right . . . Angry Johnny. Very angry. Hang on, though. That wasn't right. He shouldn't be cross with her. She was the one who should be cross with him.

'I'm not going to the hospital. You have to go.'

'What?' A snarl, almost. His anger was only just under the surface. Prod him any more and it would all come spilling out. Like a sausage cooking in a pan. Ha!

'You can go to the fucking hospital. You can go. With Delilah.' She pulled her towelling dressing gown around her and stood up, shakily. She didn't need to go to any hospital. There was nothing wrong with her that couldn't be fixed by a husband who wasn't screwing someone else. Yes. That was it. That was the problem.

Johnny shook his head like a horse batting away a fly. 'You're not making any sense, Stella. Go and get into bed, OK? I'll ask the doctor to come here. Check you out.' He still wasn't looking at her.

'You can't just send me to bed. Send her to bed, send crazy Stella to bed, get her out of the way so Delilah can come instead, lovely Delilah.' She let the name trip over her tongue. 'Delilah. Del-iiiii-lah.' She was singing now. Why was she singing?

'Shut up, Stella. Go to bed, for God's sake.'

Johnny stood and walked out of the room towards their bedroom. Stella scrambled to follow him. 'Delilah, Delilah . . . Lie . . . lie . . . lieeee-lah . . .' She didn't want to carry on saying it, in this stupid sing-song voice, but somehow she couldn't stop. 'Lilah, Lilah May. Samson and Delilah. Are you her Samson, Johnny? Does she hold on to your hair, does she grasp on to it with her lovely long fingers? Is she sapping your strength?' Stella stepped towards him, her hands outstretched, fingers spread; she wanted to run them through Johnny's hair. He held his arm up, blocking her.

'Have I hit a nerve? Don't you want to talk about Delilah? Come on. Let's talk about her. Let's talk, Johnny.'

She sat down on the edge of the bed, arms crossed. She let her dressing gown slip down so her shoulders were exposed. He turned towards her, just briefly, and the look on his face was one of disgust.

'I'm not talking to you. Not when you're like this.'

'Oh fuck off. Just fuck off!' Stella threw herself face down on the bed, sobbing. She knew she looked like a child. She felt like a child. From behind her, after a long pause, Johnny spoke.

'I'm leaving, Stella.'

She held her breath. Didn't turn to look at him. Couldn't bear to.

'Not tonight. I can't exactly leave you in this state, can I?' He sighed. 'Jesus, Stell. How did we end up like this?'

She let out a jagged, juddering breath.

'Christ, what am I talking about? I can't leave.'

She sat up, wiped her eyes. Thank God. Thank God, thank God. 'Johnny, I'm sorry. I know I've been bad. I've been horrible to you. But it'll be OK. You'll see, we'll be all right.'

He sat on the edge of the bed. 'No. I don't mean we're staying together. Sorry. I can't.'

'What do you . . . I don't understand.' Sobbing again now, in gulps. How could he do this to her? How could he be so cruel?

'I meant I can't leave you like this. Not with Viking.' He thought. 'You need some help, Stell. Maybe we both do.'

Stella rocked. 'I need you. I just need you.'

'But we're not good for each other. Are we? Not any more.'

'We used to be. I can change. I can make it better.'

Johnny smiled, and pushed her hair away from her face. 'You always used to be able to. But I don't think you can any more. It's too late, Stell. I think it's too late.'

She shook her head. No. No, she wouldn't listen to this, she wouldn't let it be too late. But he was taking his hand out of hers, and kissing her on the forehead, and going to the door.

'I'll sleep on the sofa. We'll figure out what to do tomorrow. Get some sleep. OK?'

And as he went downstairs, it wasn't the anger that she'd heard in his voice earlier that pierced her heart as she cried herself to sleep, it was the distant kindness in it. And the knowledge that she had driven him away.

The Lodge

From outside the lodge, he heard a buzz of feedback from the loudspeaker. It crackled and squeaked. He held his breath. And waited.

He was tired now. Tired from keeping alert, making sure he watched his prisoner, paid attention to every rustle from outside or shadow that passed the small window. Tired from holding the heft of the gun, that weighed heavy in his hands and shoulders. The muscles across his back were tense and aching. He was thirsty, and he hadn't eaten since breakfast. Breakfast. It felt like another lifetime. The group of men, chasing away their hangovers with coffee and Bloody Marys, big plates of locally cured bacon and fried eggs from the chickens that pecked around the garden. A bucolic idyll, or it had been. Until he had shattered it.

'Darling? Darling, I need you to listen to me.'

Oh Jesus. No. No, no, no. Not her. They hadn't brought her. He could resist anything, anyone but her.

The woman's voice wavered. 'I know you must be feeling really scared. I know I am.' She swallowed, and paused.

'Baby. I need you to help me.'

He clenched his fists. He could feel his hostage's eyes on him. Questioning. Accusing. He had to stay strong. He had to block everything out. Her voice, his eyes. The voice inside his head that said, 'You're dead. You're dead if you don't listen to her, and you're dead if you do. This is it. This is where you're going to die.'

'I need you to do this, darling. For me. Please. If you ever loved me, if what we had meant anything to you, then you'll do as I ask. Please, my darling boy. Put the gun down. And . . .' Her voice wavered, there was a pause. She was conferring with the police, he imagined, asking what they wanted him to do. 'Please put the gun down, and come to the window with your hands in the air so that we can see that you've done it. Please, darling. Please!'

Chapter Fourteen

January 2010

'Most depressing day of the year, isn't it meant to be? The eighteenth of January? I can see why.' James sat at the kitchen table, a cup of coffee in front of him that he was turning around and around in his hand, idly. Don't *do* that, Izzy wanted to snap at him, but there was no good reason to do so and he would just look up, surprised, with that wounded puppy look, and so she kept her mouth shut.

'Things like that are just made up to give the papers something to write about,' she said, insistently upbeat. 'No day is inherently depressing.' She pointedly picked up his mug and wiped the table underneath it and around him, breakfast crumbs and splashes of the children's juice all satisfyingly sweeping up in the damp cloth so that she could run them down the sink and restore order, in this small way at least.

James shrugged. He was wearing an old uni hoodie over the T-shirt that he slept in, and ancient shorts, faded blue with frayed hems. Izzy snuck a glance at the clock. It was ten in the morning. He would be in the same clothes all day, unless she bullied or cajoled or sweet-talked him into getting dressed properly for some spurious reason or another. Persuaded him to go somewhere that even he could see he must not go wearing his

299

recently acquired second skin, though the list of places that he would not go dressed like that was shrinking by the day. So far he had been to the village, to pick the children up from nursery, taken them to the doctor, and to the supermarket in the clothes that she was growing to hate. The only time he changed and shaved without protest was when he was going to visit his mother. It felt like less of a battle to get Alfie dressed than James, these days.

'Come on. There are lots of reasons why they say that.' James was warming to his subject. 'Christmas and New Year are well and truly over. No forgotten presents still left under the tree. No tree, it's been taken down, so suddenly everything looks bare and you notice all the bits of scuffed paint.'

'Do you?' In which case, why don't you do something about it? she wondered. It's not as though you don't have time on your hands.

'But the tree's still mouldering in the front garden, all brown and a bit toothless-looking, because the council haven't come and picked it up yet.' You could take it to the tip yourself, she thought. It would only take half an hour. But then you wouldn't be able to complain that they hadn't done it.

'The weather's shit.' That, she could give him. The garden was bowed under the weight of the rain, and one of the fence panels had come loose in the wind and was rattling. Another job that wouldn't get done unless she paid someone to come and do it, which she couldn't afford. Oh God, we are getting old, playing our petty resentments out in our heads. All pursed lips and things left unsaid.

'And spring's still too far off to seem like it's ever going to happen. All the Christmas bills are in, the tax returns are looming, and for most people it's still not quite payday.'

Izzy rubbed her eyes with her fingers and wanted to scream. For most people at least there would be a payday. Something to oil the wheels, keep the machine rolling forward. For them there was just an abyss of bills and debt and relentless negotiations. Did they pay the credit card bill first or the car repayments? Did they sell the second car to plug the gap for a while or did they cut down somewhere else – God knows where, they were running out of things to cut and do without. Would it be worse to go to James's parents and ask for a loan or take the children out of the expensive private nursery that they went to in favour of the cheaper one, or staying at home with James trying to look after them and look for jobs at the same time. This, or that? One humiliation, or a different, but no lesser one? How quickly it all fell apart.

She forced herself to remain calm. It was Monday, her one day off, the one day that she did not have to open the café and sit behind the counter waiting for customers, knowing that every hour without them was another unpaid bill, another step further down into debt, another nail in the coffin of her dream. She would not let him ruin it with his misery.

'I thought we'd take dinner over to your parents' later. I've got all the shopping to make a roast. We can do it there. Your dad's looking a bit thin, I thought.'

James nodded. 'Sure. A roast. That'll make everything better.' He sipped his cold coffee.

Izzy sighed. 'Don't be like that.'

'Like what?'

'Like – *that*.' Like Kevin the bloody teenager, she was thinking.

'I'm not being like anything. I just don't see how going over there and making Sunday roast is going to help anything. I've got to go out with Will, anyhow.'

Izzy put the glass of juice that she had been holding down on the marble countertop, hard, and the glass sang out. 'You don't see how it's going to help? How is it *not* going to help, then?

How is taking food to your elderly parents who are going through absolute fucking hell, though you probably haven't noticed because you're too busy wallowing in your own vat of self-pity, showing them that we love them, that we want to look after them, giving them what might be their only decent meal of the week in between hospital appointments and microwaved ready meals because your mum can't cook any more and your dad never could – how is that not going to help? How can you not see that?'

She tugged off the striped apron that she had been wearing and tried to chuck it at him, but it just sank slowly and unsatisfyingly to the floor like a parachute. Her hands shook and her voice trembled with rage. He didn't look at her. Not even the wounded puppy routine this time. Just detachment. She wanted to hit him.

Instead, she picked up her bag and pushed her feet into the pair of Uggs that were by the kitchen door.

'Of course you can't see it,' she continued. 'You can't see anything. You can't see what's happening to us – what's happened to us. What this is doing to the children, to Cass. How much trouble we're in. You can't see any of it. Or you just don't want to. And I don't know which is worse.'

She was crying now, she couldn't help it, and without waiting for him to respond, she left the room and the house, letting the door bang behind her as she barrelled down the garden path in the pouring rain, her hands reaching into her bag for a cigarette. She was on ten a day now. Gone were the days of one secret, illicit sliver of pleasure from a single Marlboro Light. Now she smoked cheap, rough Embassys, in their red striped packet that looked as though they should have an old man's nicotine-stained fingers wrapped around them. The habit was a private one still, that was the only real similarity. Not entirely secret – she smelt of smoke when she came in from the garden, she knew it. But unacknowledged by her and by James. Another little lie that they had silently, wordlessly negotiated between them. She couldn't afford it, of course. But she couldn't see that it made much difference. They had no money, just bills. What difference did a few quid extra a day make? She understood, now, why the girls from the estate, who had nothing, spent their only spare cash on fags and bottles of cheap cider and tabs of Ecstasy. She had always looked at them, and wondered why they didn't use the money for something better, something more worthwhile. 'They could do a course,' she remembered saying, self-righteously, to one of her friends not so long ago, to her shame. 'There are all sorts of government schemes these days. They could better themselves. Get a job, stop living off the state. That's my tax money they're pissing away on drink and drugs.' She shuddered at the thought, now. Because now she understood. In a small, middle-class, embarrassingly belated way, she understood. When you had no hope, what was the point in looking to the future?

'It's a bit – flowery.'

'Are they flowers? I thought they were just, you know, swirls.' James examined the embroidered silk more closely.

'No, mate. Definitely flowers. Look. That bit there. It's a petal.'

Will's forehead furrowed. 'Mm.' He stared at the waistcoat. The background was cream, not that you could see much of the background, covered as it was with intensely coloured pink, lilac and mauve flowers. 'Maybe no one will notice? It could just be a pattern. A really *patterned* pattern,' he said, hopefully.

'You'll know. We'll know. Anyhow, forget about the flowers. Look at the gold trim.' He pointed at the bottom hem of the waistcoats in horror. They were trimmed with a lacy gold edging, a bit like something you might find around the base of an oligarch's lampshade.

Will sighed, and plonked himself down on the stool in the corner of the changing room. 'They're what Colette wants.'

James held two cravats made from lilac silk up in the air by his head, and they dangled there like the ears of an elephant. Will gave a small laugh, and then stopped, and shook his head. 'Fucking hell. Fuck. Fucking, fucking hell.'

He stared ahead, hand clenched around his pint glass.

'I can't do it.'

'To be fair, I'm not sure I can, either. We're going to look like right twats.'

'Not the waistcoats. Well, the waistcoats. But not just them.'

'Ah.' James let his hands, and the cravats, drop.

The two men sat, side by side, incongruous in jeans and embroidered waistcoats. 'What have I got myself into?' Will groaned.

'That bad, is it?'

'Yeah. Well – no. I don't know. I just … I just keep thinking how different it could be.'

'What, you and Colette?'

Will nodded. His chin rested on his interlocked fingertips. 'The whole wedding thing. Colette's great, she's really great. She's gorgeous, and young, and she loves me. She looks after me, and we do have a good time . . .'

'But?' James turned his head to Will. He sighed.

'But every time I have to look at a folder of stationery samples so we can choose the font that we're going to have on the reply cards, or spend six hours – six HOURS – walking around John Lewis deciding which coffee machine we want people to buy us, or spending forty quid on sugar cubes with hearts painted on them to serve with coffee . . .'

James raised his eyebrows.

'Exactly – I can't help thinking how different it would be with Harriet.'

'Ah.'

'Yes. Ah.'

James clapped his hand on his friend's knee. 'Come on. This is a conversation that needs booze.'

They ended up in a pub near the tailor's, a small, old-fashioned pub whose upholstered seats bore the patina of thousands of men's arses and the scent of decades of cigarettes smoked on them. Pints in hand, they sank gratefully into them, and gazed at the TV that was mounted in the corner of the room, showing a game of football.

'So. We need to get you a plan.'

Will shook his head. 'That's the thing, though. We don't. I'm marrying Colette. I've said I would – I asked her, for Christ's sake. So that's what I'm doing. There's no other plan.' He took a long swig of his beer. 'There can't be.'

'Mate . . .'

'I'm serious. Look, it'll be fine. It's not like I'm marrying someone terrible, it's not as though I've given up and gone back to marry Aisleen in Scotland and make my mother happy.'

'It's not like you're making yourself happy either, though, is it?' James let the slight irritation he was beginning to feel show in his voice. Will was being a wimp, and he couldn't understand why. He'd never been someone who just went with the flow and did what was expected of him – if he had been, he'd have been married to Harriet years ago. So why now? Why with Colette? Unless . . .

'Bloody hell. She's not pregnant as well, is she?'

'No. Not as far as I know, anyhow. And don't say "as well". Harriet's baby is nothing to do with me.'

James stared at Will. He was lying. Or at least, he wasn't telling the whole truth, James was sure of it. But he wasn't going to confront him about it. Not now.

'So . . .'

'So I'm not a complete shit, James. I'm not going to leave Colette standing at the altar.' Will sounded angry. James knew he was getting somewhere.

'Better than marrying someone you don't really love, isn't it?'

'Love. It's not all about love, though, is it? It's about settling down. Choosing someone you can build a life with.'

James thought back to when he and Izzy had first met. When he had proposed. Settling down, sensible choices – they had had nothing to do with it. She had been the person he had the most fun with. It was that simple.

'No, it is. It's all about love. It has to be. Because if it's not now, then it never will be. In a few years' time, when the shit hits the fan – and it will, believe me – when you've got a screaming baby and neither of you have slept for a week, and you can't remember what your wife's breasts looked like before they were covered in weird blue veins and leaking . . .'

Will winced. James nodded.

'Yup, veiny and leaking, mate. And everything the other person says makes you want to scream because you're so goddamned worn out by it all, and when you get home from work you stand outside the front door for one more minute, just to put off going inside and being handed a child that won't be put down without yelling the house down – then you'd better be able to remember why you're there, and how you got there. Because if you don't – if you can't remember just how much you loved her, how you were so crazy about her that you couldn't sleep next to her – then there's no fucking point. There's just no point.'

James exhaled, and then inhaled the rest of his beer, shaken by his speech. Will, next to him, said nothing.

It was true, thought James. He had loved Izzy madly,

feverishly. She had been the spike of passion in his life, had ignited feelings in him that he had never known existed, and had certainly never believed that he could feel. And still, there had been nights when the children were young when he had thought about just walking out of the door and never looking back. Still, they had ended up as they were now; an accumulation of terse texts and domestic arrangements and debt – not just financial, but marital. They each owed one another; neither was willing to write it off, or could not afford to. But once – once he would have given her the world. Still would, if she asked him to. He rubbed his face with his hands. He had to go home. He had started off trying to talk Will out of his marriage, and had ended up talking himself back into his own.

He stood up. 'I've got to go. I'll call you later, find out what you've decided. But for Christ's sake, Will. If you don't love her, if you love Harriet still – if you even think you might be in love with Harriet – you have to call the wedding off. And given that we're meant to be going on your stag weekend in four days, if you're going to do it, you have to do it soon. I'll need to start calling round the guys.'

James leant across the table and shook Will's hand, holding his shoulder. Will nodded, and said, 'Yes. Yes, I know. I'll think it over. I will. But no calling anyone. Whatever happens, I want to go on this weekend. We all need it. And everyone's looking forward to it. I spoke to Stephen yesterday. He's practically packed already.'

'Good call inviting him. I appreciate it. I really think he might be on the verge of offering me a job. I've just got a feeling.'

'Let's hope so. But I didn't just ask him because of you. He's a good bloke. And, you know, let's be honest. Being mates with him isn't likely to do any of us any harm, is it. Stop worrying. Go on. You get going.'

James hesitated, but Will waved him away. 'I'm fine. Could use some time to have a think. Go do what you need to do.'

Will watched his friend leave with something approaching relief. James was insistent, a dog with a bone when he got an idea in his head. He was right, as well, that was the difficult thing. Will could not argue with him convincingly, tell him Colette was the love of his life and that he couldn't live without her, that he didn't wake in the night and think of Harriet alone in her flat, with her bump, and wish she was next to him so that he could reach over and feel it. It was good that James had gone; he had enough to worry about without dealing with Will's messy love life. And it was good because it meant that Will could no longer let slip what he had almost told his best and oldest friend, could not tell him the truth about why he could not call off the wedding. Could not say, as he had been tempted to say as James was leaving, 'I can't. I can't not marry Colette, because if I don't marry her, I'll lose everything I've worked for, I'll have nothing. I have to marry Colette, because she's just lent me two million quid.'

Izzy sat on the park bench on the corner of the common outside Stephen Garside's house. It was cold, and the bench was damp beneath her jeans, and slick with lichen that she knew would leave a smear of green on them, but she didn't care. She just wanted to sit, and smoke, and not be James's wife, or Ginny's daughter-in-law, or Pearl and Alfie's mum or the woman who ran the café any longer. She just wanted to be Izzy, and this was the only place she could think of to do it. Yet something was stopping her going to the door and knocking. Something unnamed. It wasn't fear, nor was it girlish nervousness. She lit another cigarette.

In the end, she didn't need to go and knock on the door, because he came to her.

'I don't want to make any assumptions,' he said. 'I'd like to think that the fact that you're sitting outside my house in the pouring rain looking – well, frankly, looking less than completely happy and on top of things – means that you've decided to take me up on my offer and run away with me. Or just stay here with me. But . . .' He craned his neck under the bench, peering, looking for a suitcase that wasn't there. 'Nope, no bags full of children and shoes under there,' he muttered. 'However, my prior knowledge of women leads me to suspect that this may not be the case.'

Izzy didn't say anything. The reason that she had not gone and knocked on the door was clear to her now. It *was* fear – in a way, at least. She had been afraid that if she climbed the wide stone steps to that handsome black-painted door, and went through it, she might never walk back out again. That that would be the decision she could not unmake, the step she could not untake.

'I . . . I don't think it is,' she whispered.

Stephen shook his head. 'I thought not.' He handed her the towel that he was holding, and when she didn't take it, gently draped it around her shoulders, untucking her hair from underneath it so that it would not stick to her neck.

'Will you come in anyway?'

She didn't move. She felt very cold, and very, very tired. Stephen crouched beside her and took her hand.

'Izzy. As a friend. I promise. Nothing more. I swear I won't try to do anything other than help. So.'

He stood, and she let herself be pulled up by the hand, and led inside the house.

'How much?' he asked.

She was sitting at his kitchen table, a long, sleek slab of polished beechwood that dominated the centre of the room. It was a chef's kitchen, this, better than the one in his house in Cornwall, even, and normally Izzy's fingers would have been itching to cook in it. Now, she just sat, her hands wrapped around the mug of hot chocolate that he had insisted on making for her. 'It's my speciality,' he had said, winking at her. 'OK, it may not be as impressive as – what's your signature dish? Crab ravioli, something amazing like that?'

'Close.' She had smiled.

'Well, it's not Michelin-starred food, but it never fails to warm your belly and lift your heart. Especially with my secret ingredient.'

'Which is?'

He waved a bottle of cognac in the air before pouring a hefty slug into each mug.

'That's too good for hot chocolate,' she protested.

'Come on. I never did understand that. Wine too good to cook with? Balls. Why would you want to make something delicious and then slug cheap Pinot into it? Use the good stuff. It's no good to anyone sitting in the cupboard.'

Izzy's hair was damp still, pulled back into a loose ponytail, but she was warmer. Stephen had given her one of his jumpers, and made her hang her wet top on the towel rail in one of the guest bathrooms. She enjoyed the feeling of her body being much too small for it, her fingers poking out of the sleeves like a teenager's. It was reassuring.

'How much?' he said again, pulling out a bench and sitting down on the opposite side of the table. 'How much to get you out of this hole?'

Izzy laughed sadly. 'Don't be silly.'

'I'm not joking. I told you, the first time we met, didn't I? I don't play games, Izzy. You should know that by now, if nothing else.'

She looked up. 'I can't take your money, Stephen. Not . . .'

'What? Not what?'

'Not when you've made it so clear what it is you want from me.'

'Izzy. You think it comes with strings attached, is that it?'

'It always does.'

'Not with me.' He looked a little hurt.

'I don't mean that you'd mean it to. That you're proposing some kind of – deal.'

'I'm glad to hear it.'

'But you wouldn't be able to help it. Feel as though I owed you something. And even if you didn't feel like that, I would.'

Stephen shrugged. 'Well. I wouldn't want to stand in the way of your feelings of gratitude . . . I'm joking.'

'But that's just what I mean. Even if it's a joke, it would be there, wouldn't it. The expectation. The question.'

'I don't think it would.'

'I don't see how you can think that.'

'You don't need to. But you do need help.'

'Yes. But not from you.'

'Another man would be offended by that.'

Izzy dipped her spoon into her hot chocolate and sipped the foam from it. She could feel the alcohol glowing inside her throat. 'But not you.'

'No. I don't take offence easily.'

'Why do you want to help us, anyhow?'

Stephen sucked air in through his teeth. 'Jesus. What must you think of me?' He laughed.

'Not like that. But if you mean what you said to me before . . .'

He leant forward on his elbows. 'Of course I did. You know I did.'

'So why do you want to help my family?'

'Because I can't bear to see you in this pain. Because I'm not so selfish that I can't do something that's not entirely self-

311

serving. Because I love you, Izzy. And if you aren't going to leave, if I can't have you, then I want to know that you're OK. And at the moment, you're not OK. Are you?'

'No.'

'So?'

There was a silence. Izzy pushed her mug to one side, and reached her hands out across the table. She took hold of Stephen's fingers, holding them loosely. They felt cool and smooth. She took a deep breath.

'I don't want to take the money. Because I don't want you to think that it's because I'm grateful when I do this.'

And she leant forward over the table, half standing to reach him, and kissed him.

It was morning. Stella was not sure how it had got to be morning, as it seemed it was only a few minutes ago that she had been stumbling in through the front door, laughing and putting her fingers over her lips to shush the man at her side, as he kissed her fingers and moved them out of the way, pushing his lips against hers and his hips against hers as she half-heartedly pushed him away until she had paid the babysitter and seen her out of the door.

She rolled the cigarette she was smoking between her fingers, and looked in at him, asleep on the sofa at the far end of the kitchen. He wasn't a man, really. He had to be – what? All of twenty? He might even be in his teens. She chewed on the bit of loose skin by her thumbnail. She would have to kick him out soon. She checked her watch. Almost six. Viking would be awake before long. And she would have to get him up and dressed and give him breakfast and listen to him chatter on about whatever was in his head this morning and then put him in his buggy and take him to his childminder before she could crawl into bed and sleep a few hours of jittery, teeth-grinding sleep. And then . . . She didn't know what then.

iPhone, she should look on her iPhone, at her calendar. She would figure out what today was going to hold and how she was going to get her head around it. Soon. She would do that soon. She would just sit out here for a minute longer. She was tired. So tired.

Johnny was dreaming when the phone rang. Dreaming of an island, somewhere in the middle of an ocean, an island with pink sand and lapping waves, and mermaids that looked like Delilah and Stella, both of them, together, or next to one another, he couldn't be sure which, emerging out of the waves, all sly, seductive smiles and tendrils of wavy hair that merged with the sea foam and . . .

Mermaids didn't make that noise. They didn't shriek, shrill and insistent, they trilled gently . . . Johnny shook his head, still half asleep.

'Johnny. Phone.' An elbow nudged him in the side, and he grunted. The noise got louder, harsher. 'Johnny. Answer your fucking phone.'

He opened his eyes and took the phone that Delilah was holding in front of his face. 'Yup.' His voice was rough and he cleared his throat to try and make himself sound more awake.

'Mr Albright? It's Carol Lane here.'

Johnny pushed his hair back from his forehead and searched through his brain for a clue. Carol Lane. Carol Lane. He knew the name. He was sure he did. But it had been a late night, a long night, and he couldn't quite find it yet . . . Johnny's band had suddenly done what he had been saying it would, and what no one, including him, quite believed would ever happen, and taken off. They'd hit on that elusive combination of luck and timing and a good song – a great song – that captured and articulated something that people felt before they even knew they felt it, and they were in demand. Their gigs were selling out, record companies were asking to meet them, taking them to lunch at Soho House and Century, and, most significantly, their manger had started phoning them almost daily. 'Checking in,' as he called it. 'Touching base.' A couple of months ago he had all but stopped returning their calls. And then they had recorded 'Still Station', and released it on their own little label, for pennies, really, and now it was getting airplay on Radio 1 next week, just confirmed yesterday. That was what they had been celebrating last night. That was the reason he was struggling to remember who Carol Lane was, and why she might be phoning him at nine thirty in the morning.

'Your childminder, Mr Albright. I look after Viking?' Her voice was terse and impatient. In the background he could hear the sound of a child grizzling.

Johnny sat up. 'Viking. Is he all right? Is he OK? What's happened, has something . . .'

Carol sighed. 'Don't panic, nothing's happened. Well, as far as I know. I'm calling to find out whether you're going to be bringing him in or not, as I've got another parent wanting a last-minute place, and I need to tell them yes or no.'

Johnny let himself breathe out, slowly. The relief made his heart thud. 'OK. All right. Sorry, Carol. I'm not at home just now . . .'

Delilah opened one eye and glared at him out of it. She hated it when he referred to the house he had moved out of as home, still. 'This is your home now,' she said. '*Our* home. Unless you're not sure. Unless you'd rather go back to her.' She would turn away, her shoulders stiff and accusing, and he would have to kiss her neck and tickle her and flutter his eyelashes against her soft skin until she laughed and relented. He didn't want to go back home. He was sure he didn't. He missed Viking, and he wished he had been able to make the decision more gradually, in his own time, but he was better off here, with Delilah. He ignored her look, and squeezed her thigh under the duvet.

'What time was Stella meant to be dropping him off, again?'

'Eight thirty. As usual, on Wednesdays.'

'Right, of course. Well . . .' He looked at his watch.

'I can't get hold of your wife on either of her numbers. If you want me to say no to this other little girl, I'll need paying for today, whether Viking comes in or not.'

'I understand. I'll find out what's going on, and I'll phone you straight back, all right? I'm really sorry, Carol. Sorry.'

Sorry. How come he seemed to spend half his life saying sorry? he wondered, as he stormed down the road towards his and Stella's house. Sorry, Carol, I'll find out what my wife thinks she's playing at now. Sorry, Delilah, I've got to go back to my wife and find out why she hasn't taken my son to his childminder. Sorry, Stella, for shagging around for so long. That was one sorry he had never said. One sorry that he wished he had said, sometimes. In the cool darkness of four o'clock in the morning, when he lay awake, Delilah asleep beside him, restless and twitching as she slept, not still and calm in her repose as Stella always had been. It was strange the comparisons you made. Not about personality, or looks. Those things were obvious. So visible as to not be worth remarking upon. It was the little things. The way they washed up differently, Stella doing it as it was needed, keeping the tap running throughout as she couldn't bear the feeling of grimy water on her hands as she dipped them into the bowl, Delilah stacking it in teetering piles until the last bowl had been used and then leaving it to soak for hours. The way they brushed their teeth. Stella had to do it over the sink, spitting the paste out every few seconds because it made her gag otherwise, whereas Delilah would wander around the flat, toothbrush in her mouth, talking to him as she did so in incomprehensible sentences. It set his teeth on edge. It was stupid, to let it annoy him. It was such a little thing. It was always the little things.

'Stella?' The door was open, and her bag was on the floor in the hall. Half open, its contents almost spilling out of the top, it was so jammed full of stuff. Stella was constitutionally incapable of leaving the house with fewer than fifteen 'essential' items. Her notebook, at least one book, her phone, a pack of cigarettes, her lighter, her wallet (which, in turn, was stuffed full of cards, receipts, loose change, scribbled notes, and all manner of crap that he was always nagging her to clear out), a comb, lip balm, keys, her make-up bag, hairspray, sun block, moisturiser, perfume, spare earrings, spare tights in winter, a snack for Viking, one of his muslins, at least two pairs of sunglasses, a cardigan in case she got cold, deodorant in case she got too hot . . . He always used to joke that it would be easier just to carry her bedside table around with her on her back, like a snail.

She must have dumped it there ready to go out. She'd be in the loo, or feeding Viking yet another snack or something before leaving. Getting out of the house with Viking was always a pretty drawn-out process. 'Stella? Stell. Carol's been on the phone. Why are you so late?'

He walked through the hall, picking up the post that was lying on the doormat and leafing through it as he went. Mrs S., Mrs S., Mr J., Mr and Mrs J. . . . He might not be living there any more, but their lives were still tightly woven together.

'Stella?' His voice rang out through the house and he stopped in his tracks. It didn't feel or sound as though she were upstairs, racing around, running late, Viking tucked under her arm, hairpins in her mouth as she rushed to get ready. It didn't feel as though she were here at all. The house felt empty.

'Stella!' He ran through the kitchen, dropping the letters on the side as he headed for the door. The French windows to the garden were open, and a cold breeze was blowing into the house. An empty pack of cigarettes sat on the garden table, her lighter next to the full ashtray. Maybe she had gone to buy cigarettes. But her wallet was in her bag, he had seen it, and she wouldn't have left the front door wide open like that. Would she? He ran back into the house and upstairs.

'Stell. Where are you?' The bedroom was empty, their bed unmade, her clothes chucked around the room, and the sight of it stopped him in his tracks for a moment. Stella, despite her chaotic appearance, had always been almost obsessively tidy at home. He'd been the one who would chuck his things on the floor when he took them off before falling into bed. He tapped his knuckles on the door frame as he left the room.

Viking's room was empty, as was the bathroom. Johnny's heart was racing as he ran back downstairs, taking them two at a time, picking Stella's handbag up and turning it out on to the floor, unsure why he was doing so, just hoping that he might find a clue as to where they were. Viking's buggy was in the hall, folded up behind the door as usual. Stella's keys were in her bag, as was her phone. He clicked the button to bring it to life and saw the list of missed calls from Carol, but when he tried to unlock it to check any messages he found that she had changed her password and it remained barred to him. He sat on the bottom step of the staircase, and stared at the contents of his wife's bag – her life, as she always referred to it – spread out in front of him. And he wondered whether he was ever going to see Stella and Viking again.

Stella ran. She ran through the park, her feet sliding over patches of icy mud and grass still crunchy from the recent snow. She ran past the playground, aware of the stares of the two mothers who stood there, hands shoved into their pockets, cheeks pink from the cold, hoping that their toddlers would get bored of the swings soon so they could go and sit in the café and drink coffee. Their eyes judged her, though not as harshly as her own did. She wore last night's dress and tights, with biker boots that she was glad of as she ran, and the thick jumper that she had been wearing outside to smoke. It smelled of past cigarettes and cold air. It smelled of mistakes.

She ran. How could she have fallen asleep, at the garden table, in the freezing morning air that was now burning her skin? She hadn't been that fucked up, had she? So out of it that she could pass out in the February dawn. Whatever, she had never felt more sober now.

Where could they have gone? The guy didn't have a car, he hadn't taken Viking's buggy, her car had still been outside the house; she had had enough clarity to check that, in her panic, when she had come to, her fingers and lips blue, and stumbled inside to realise that they had gone. Why? Why had he taken him? What did he want with a little boy. He was a partyer, he was . . .

The truth was, she had no idea who or what he was. She didn't even know his name. He was just some guy. It hadn't mattered last night. He'd just been a friend of a – not even a friend, the friend of someone she knew by sight, someone who went to the same places she did, hung out with the same crowd, did the same drugs. She hadn't asked what he was called. It didn't seem important. He was beautiful, and young, and she could tell by his eyes that he wanted her, and that was all that had mattered. It was all she looked for, these days. She hadn't cared what his name was as they fell into the car, hadn't needed to call him anything at all. Hadn't cared as he fucked her on the sofa, on the kitchen floor, pausing only to do another line from the hollow of skin between her breasts and then kiss her, her tongue tingling as she licked the remnants of the drug from his mouth. Hadn't cared. And now . . .

318

She stopped running. What was the point? She had no idea where they might be, where he could have taken him, when they had gone, even. He could have got on a bus, hailed a cab . . . They could be halfway across London by now. And she would never see Viking again. Stella bent over double and pushed her hands against her knees to stop herself toppling over on to the pavement. She had reached the far side of the park and come out of the small metal gate by the newsagent. Pearl's Place was just over the road. The gift shop where she bought birthday cards and wrapping paper and emergency presents when she realised she had forgotten someone's birthday, the little off-licence that sold strange, dusty bottles of thick coloured liqueurs and where she ordered crates of Johnny's favourite beer from – where she *used* to order them from. Not any longer. Her world, her life, so familiar, and it was all broken and wrong and she had no place here, without Viking and Johnny, no place at all.

She remembered, now. Knew how it was that she could have passed out. She had taken a couple of Valium, after the boy had fallen asleep and before she had gone to sit outside and smoke. Had found them in his pocket, had swallowed them with a gulp of the vodka and tonic she had made him, before putting her big old jumper on and curling up on the bench to watch the smoke and hot air curl out of her mouth into the night, mindlessly. She had meant them to help her sleep, when she got to bed. But she had forgotten to do the going-to-bed part.

'Stella? What on earth's wrong? Jesus . . .' Stella straightened and turned and saw Izzy's face crumple in shock at her appearance. She spread her hands, which shook, either with fear or cold, or both, and the tears that she had not yet shed began to fall.

'He's gone. He's gone, and I don't know . . . I don't know where . . .'

Izzy took a step forward. She looked so clean, and together.

319

Her Pearl's Place apron neatly tied around her small waist, her hair all shiny and pulled back into a ponytail. She was everything Stella had failed to be.

'Stell, darling. Johnny went a while ago. He's been gone for a few weeks, remember? You wanted him to move out, you agreed. You remember. You said it was best for all of you, for the moment . . .' Izzy's face was concerned, full of trepidation as she moved slowly towards Stella, her movements gentle and wary, as though she were trying to calm a frightened and cornered animal. She made a soft hushing sound as she put her arms around her.

Stella shook her head, and when she opened her mouth to speak it took all of her strength to suppress the furious wail that threatened to emerge, and form it, forcibly, into words instead. She had to make Izzy understand. 'No. No,' she yelped, sounding like the wounded creature she must look like. 'Not Johnny. Viking. Viking's gone.'

He saw Stella and Izzy first. Went to them first. It was just chance, really, that had made him turn in their direction. If he had gone the other way, he would have seen the man walking towards him carrying his son. Just a turn of the head, a change of direction. Later, he wondered what would have happened had it been the stranger carrying his son that he had seen first. What would he have done? Nothing, while Viking was in his arms. But after? After he had made sure he was safe, and unharmed? Would he have launched himself at the man, beaten him, pinned him down? Called the police? Or made sure that the police were not called. Would he have acted first and asked questions later; would he have acted in a way he could not later take back? How far? That was always the question, wasn't it?

As soon as he saw his wife and her friend, he knew what at least half of the story would be. Stella was a mess. Her hair

320

pulled back into a chaotic bun, still backcombed and fluffy from the night before, half pinned up and half undone.

Stella herself was entirely undone. The upper half of her body was bent out of shape like a mangled paper clip, twisted and bound up with agony. Her eyeliner was thick and smeared, her face pale and her cheeks sunken. She had lost weight since he had last seen her. Her legs stuck up from her biker boots like punters' poles out of the river, and her hands and wrist bones seemed too big for her arms. She was not looking after herself. And she had not been looking after Viking.

The force of his hand on her shoulder knocked her off balance, and she almost fell to the floor as he shook it. 'What happened? Where is he? Where the fuck is our son? What have you done, Stella, Jesus, what have you done? What have you DONE?'

Stella stared at Johnny, her mouth open, her gut wrenching as she recognised the same panic in his face that she had felt when she first realised Viking was gone, the panic that was still there. They were united in terror and yet they had never been further apart.

'I . . . I don't . . .' She couldn't speak. Izzy put a steadying arm around her shoulder, propping her upright with a strong hold.

'Tell me. Tell me what happened. Tell me!'

Stella shook her head. Johnny's face was up against hers; he was shouting and raging at her. She felt the spit fly from his mouth and land on her face, and then she heard Izzy's voice near her ear.

'Johnny, Stella doesn't know where Viking is. She woke up and he was gone. We're going to have to call the police . . .'

'What do you mean, he was gone? He's a toddler, he can't have just opened the fucking door and walked out of it.'

Stella looked up at Johnny, desperately. She didn't know

what to say to him. How to tell him. And then – she didn't have to. Suddenly his face changed. Relief flooded over it like a wave.

'Oh God. He's there. There he is.'

Stella turned. Johnny pushed her to one side as he ran, ran over to the man who was carrying his son, who was chatting away quite happily as he chewed on a pain au chocolat. His face was covered in dark crumbs. 'Dada!' Viking grinned at the sight of Johnny hurtling towards him, let go of the man's hand and ran towards his father.

The man who Stella had spent the night with took in the sight of Johnny racing at him, Stella and Izzy not far behind. He held up a wary hand to ward off the blow that he thought might land on him, at the same time as he handed Viking over to his father.

'Jesus. Oh my little man. Hello. Oh thank God. Thank you, thank you.'

Stella reached them, her arms held out for Viking, but Johnny turned away, blocking her with his back as he kissed Viking's head.

'He woke up,' the man said. 'He was crying. I wasn't sure . . . He said he was hungry.'

'Johnny . . .' Izzy spoke quietly, her voice pleading on Stella's behalf.

'No.'

'Johnny, please . . .' Stella's own voice sounded alien to her, panicky and high. 'Please give me my baby, please. Give me my boy.'

The man carried on talking. 'You were out cold, he was upset. I wasn't going to do anything. I just thought I'd get him some breakfast, you know?'

'Shut up. Just shut up.' Johnny turned to face Stella. She had never seen such rage in his face before. It silenced her. She had never known that he could look like that.

'All right. I tell you what, my *wife*.' He spat out the word, as though he were trying to hawk a particularly nasty bit of phlegm from his lungs. 'I'll give you your baby.'

She held her arms out, grateful. All she wanted was to feel the warm weight of Viking in them, to hold his legs wrapped around her waist, his head resting, trusting, on her shoulder. Viking still trusted her. He might be the only one who did.

'I'll give you your son, if you can tell me one thing.'

She looked at Johnny. Anything. She would give him anything to have her son in her arms right now, and he knew it. But there was something in his expression that she feared. Something triumphant.

'Tell me the name of this man. Tell me what the man who's just wandered off with our child is called. Tell me!' He was yelling now, his mouth twisted.

Stella's own mouth gaped as her arms hung uselessly in the air. She stared at Johnny. Looked over at the young man, who was standing there, awkward, embarrassed. He opened his mouth. 'It's—'

Johnny spun around. 'Don't speak. Don't you say a fucking word, or I swear to God, you'll wish you'd never met my fucking druggie slag of a wife.'

The boy shut his mouth again. It was pretty clear to them all that he was already wishing just that. Johnny turned back to Stella, whose face was hot with tears of shame and sorrow.

'I knew it. You didn't even know his name.'

He didn't have to say anything else. There was no need for him to tell her how stupid she had been, what could have happened. The danger she had put her son in. The choices she had made.

'I'm sorry. I'm so sorry.' Half whispering, half sobbing, she held her arms out in front of her still, uselessly, pointlessly. Empty. She was empty.

'I'm going to pack Viking's things now. He'll stay with us. At least until you've sorted yourself out. Then we'll see. Get your shit together, Stella.'

She stared at Johnny as he turned away and walked back towards home, her home, that had been their home, Viking stumping along beside him happily. Izzy stood, silently, next to her. She said nothing. There was nothing to say.

Johnny's back was stiff, and he held Viking protectively, shielding him. From the cold. From hurt. And from her?

She had lost them. She had lost the only two people that really mattered to her. And she had no idea how they had slipped through her fingers.

Chapter Fifteen

March 2010

Thursday

Caroline sat at her desk, small plastic pack of sushi and an edamame bean salad next to her, and clicked on the icon for her Internet browser. Clicked on the bookmark that took her to http://benthamandcrowley.co.uk. It had become her lunchtime ritual, going out to get something to eat, coming back and scouring the websites of local estate agents for houses. Her boss tried to tempt her out, fretting that she wasn't getting a proper break, especially with everything that she had on her plate at present; on the days when she did leave the office, it was to go and eat lunch by her mother's bedside. He was a kind man, and she was lucky to have him for a boss, but he didn't understand. This was a proper break. This was the best break of all.

Bentham and Crowley was her favourite of the agents' sites; they specialised in the area she was most keen on. There were a couple of others, but this was the place that seemed to get the best properties. She knew just what she was looking for.

And today, it seemed that she had found it. It was a two-storey semi-detached house in a road not far from James and Izzy – but not too near, either. She didn't want them to feel – uncomfortable. Didn't want to be in their pockets. But it would be nice to be closer to them. Harriet's flat wasn't far either, though that was just a rental, obviously, and who knew where she would end up. In the meantime, though, when the baby was here, she'd need all the help she could get, and Caroline was determined to give it to her, no matter how painful it might be for her to do so.

She herself was still not pregnant. She was doing everything she could, not just to have a baby but to make Bart happy. Because she was sure that she could make him happy, that she could make the marriage work. She so wanted it to work, needed it to. She could not accept that it might not be the right thing; that would be giving up, it would be not trying hard enough, and she would never get over it, she was sure of it. And she needed Bart. She loved him so much. Anyhow, how could she go to her mother and tell her that she had failed in the only thing that had ever really mattered to her? Ginny would be so desperately disappointed in her. She could not do that to her, not now.

Her eyes teared up at the thought of Ginny, as they always did. She was so brave, so elegant even in her pain. She had gone into the hospice now, as she needed more intensive care than Julian could provide by himself, and she was unwilling to fill their home up with nurses and equipment. 'I want it to be my life that we focus on, *our* life,' she said when he protested. 'Not my illness, and not my death. This way other people can sort out the practicalities of it all, and you will know I am being taken good care of, and then when it's all over our home will still be home. I don't want it turned into a hospital ward.' She had brooked no argument, and so they had all agreed. Julian and James had gone with her, checking her in, carrying all her favourite things into her room – a cashmere blanket that would keep her warm without being scratchy, some spray that smelt of roses, photos of her children and grandchildren.

If only I could tell her I'm pregnant before she dies, Caroline thought now. That would be enough. That would make her so happy, make me feel like I have not been a disappointment to her. That would be enough.

She had been to the doctor, who had told her that many couples took at least a year to conceive, and that she was young enough and had plenty of time and should try and relax. She went for weekly acupuncture that was meant to help increase energy flow to the reproductive organs, she ate organic, she meditated. She wished she could convince Bart to have the quick, painless test that might explain why they were finding it difficult to conceive, but he would not. 'There's no need,' he said, when she raised it. 'These things happen in their own time, darling. There's no reason to suspect that there's anything wrong.' She didn't push it. She didn't want a row. Much of her life with Bart these days was spent ensuring that she avoided a row. It was essential.

Caroline returned her attention to the computer screen. The house needed some work, she could see that from the price, before she had even looked at the photos. Something that had been nicely done up in that road would go for three hundred thousand more than this was on for, easily. But it was at the good end of the street, near the bus stop and the gardens, easy walking distance from the C of E primary school that had such a tight catchment area that parents had been known to move a single road to get their children accepted into it. It was redbrick, with wisteria growing around the porch and bay window at the front. There were no photos of the interior, which wasn't a great sign. Caroline suspected that when she got there, she would find that it needed a lot more than 'some cosmetic updating' in order to turn it into the 'spacious and elegant family home' the agents promised it could be.

But she also knew that it had something special about it. She could tell, just from the one not very good photo, that she had to go and look at this house. *Her* house, as she was already thinking of it. She picked up the phone by her side, and dialled the agent's number.

They could show her around that evening; the house was unoccupied, they told her on the phone, and Caroline gave the house another mental tick. Unoccupied meant that the owner was likely to have died, or possibly been moved into a home – either way, whoever owned the house would probably want to get shot of it soon, and that was good for her. It would be unliveable in for a few months, she was sure; if the sale went through in two months, and she factored in four months of building . . . even if she got pregnant this month, that would still be OK, she wouldn't be moving in just as she was on the point of giving birth . . .

She stopped her mind in its tracks, and looked at the front of the house. This mental calendar was ever present, these days, the constant counting. If I get pregnant this month, it'll be born in December, a Christmas baby; if I get pregnant next month, I might have it on my birthday, that happened more often than you'd think, people giving birth on their own or their spouse's birthdays. She had to consciously not do it, or the calculations whirred away like ticker tape in the back of her brain.

The front door was painted a grubby white, and the paint was peeling and blistered. One of the window panes was cracked, and she peered through the grubby glass, but couldn't see much beyond a pile of unopened post in the hall.

'Mrs Beauman? Sorry I'm late, busy busy busy, know what I mean?'

She turned. The boy in front of her wore a sharkish grin, too knowing for his age. If he hadn't been wielding the key to a Mini Cooper emblazoned with the company logo, she would have wondered whether he was old enough to drive. She looked down at his shoes. There was something reassuring about the fact that they all wore the same too-shiny suits and awful shoes, slip-ons, with elongated, squared-off ends.

'Yes. It's all right.' She stood aside so that he could unlock and open the door. He chuckled as he saw her automatically go to wipe her feet on a doormat that wasn't there.

'You'll be wanting to wipe them on the way out, not the way in, know what I mean? Should've told you to wear one of them hazmat suits.' He laughed at his own joke as he led her down the hall, keeping up the patter all the way. 'Nah, it's not that bad, nothing a skip and a few Poles can't sort out for you easy enough. Right, living room, north-east-facing at the front, lovely morning light, innit. Original Vicky fireplace, and the moulding and that's original and all.'

She bent down and pulled up a corner of the carpet. It was covered with brown and orange swirls, and the underlay was plasticky and sticky. But underneath it were wide floorboards, dusty but solid-looking. The rest of the house was in a similar state. A combination of neglect and botched DIY jobs; Artexed bathrooms and a lingering smell of cat pee. But the windows were big, the ceilings were high, and the garden was long and walled on all three sides.

'Lovely outlook, plenty of space for the kiddies to run around, bit of a blank canvas. You green-fingered?'

Caroline ignored his remark about children and gave a little shrug. 'I'm not sure. I've never had a garden of my own.'

'You want to get your mum in to have a look at it. Mums always know about plants and that, don't they?'

She nodded. 'Yes. They do.' He was right. Ginny would cast her eye over it and be able to tell her in seconds what all the plants were, what should come out and what could be rescued. Oh, she missed her mama.

'So, why don't you give me a call tomorrow and let me know if you want to arrange a second viewing, bring hubby along to have a look.'

He handed her a business card.

'Has there been a lot of interest in it?'

He sucked air in through his teeth. 'Oh yes, lots of interest, always is in these doer-uppers. It's the thing these days, know what I mean, everyone wants to play renovator. Got another couple due to look around after you, as it goes.' He grinned at her.

'Right. And the vendor?'

'Old dear had to go into a home. Son's selling, and he's paying her medical bills until he does. He won't want to hang around waiting for the perfect buyer, put it that way.'

'How much to secure it, take it off the market, do you think?'

The agent raised an eyebrow at her, briefly, and then gave her a wink. The man might have been held together purely by his collection of facial expressions and clichés, she thought. What would happen if you took them away? Would he even exist any longer?

He shook his head. 'Couldn't say, Mrs Beauman, I'm afraid, couldn't say. Asking price is what it is, and he may be open to offers in order to get the sale to go through quickly. Of course, the better the position you're in, the better, know what I mean?' He looked at her as though he had just imparted some great wisdom, and she nodded.

'I'll ring you first thing in the morning. Nothing will be decided before then, will it?'

'Nah. You go home and sleep on it. Like I say, though, there's a lot of interest. A hot property, as they say in the trade.' He winked again, and she had to stop herself from wincing.

*

She picked up a rotisserie chicken from the place around the corner before she got home. There was salad in the fridge and a loaf of bread that she'd put in the breadmaker last night. Not her best ever effort, but it would do.

'Hi, darling.' She was in the kitchen chopping an avocado into chunks and dropping it into the salad bowl when he came in, a vinaigrette half made in a bowl next to her. 'Get you a drink? I've got a glass of wine.'

Don't chatter, she told herself. He can't bear being chattered at as soon as he walks in the door from work. It was one of the first things she had learned about living with her husband. Later. Let him relax, shake off the day, slip back into the mode he was in when he was with her. Talk to him later.

'I went to see a house today.' She was lying in the bath when she told him, pushing her cuticles back with the thumbnail of her other hand. Bart was brushing his teeth, ready for bed, in the white T-shirt and boxers he always slept in. He looked at her in the mirror, holding her gaze, expressionless, while he finished brushing and swilled his mouth out with water.

'I see,' he said. She looked down at her hands. 'Where?'

'Mencarthen Road.'

He nodded. She held her breath. Was he about to explode? She decided to carry on talking and hope for the best. 'It needs some work. Well, quite a bit of work. It's not been very well looked after. But it could be amazing, really amazing.'

'How much is it?'

She paused. Told him. He nodded again.

'All right.'

She stared. 'All right? What do you mean, all right? You'll come and see it with me? I'll have to ring the agent first thing; can you make time to go before work? I know it's not ideal, but I think we need to get in quickly if we want it, they're ever so popular, those roads, and the estate agent did say—'

'No, I mean, all right, get it.'

'*Get* it?'

He turned to her and smiled. 'Sure. Why not? It sounds like a good price. If you need to move fast, do. I've got Will's stag this weekend anyhow. I trust your judgement. I'd live with you in a ditch, you know that.'

She flicked water at him. 'Bart. You must see it.'

'Why? If you love it, I love it. I'll see it when it's ours. Phone him in the morning. Offer them the asking price. Unless you're not sure . . .'

She yelped, and leapt out of the bath, throwing her arms around him and covering him in kisses and soapy water. He laughed, and put his arms around her waist. 'No, I'm sure, I'm sure! Oh darling. Thank you. Thank you thank you thank you thank you. Oh God. I'm so excited.'

And she kissed his neck, and savoured the clean smell of his skin as she breathed it in. This was it. This was the new beginning for them, this was going to be the start of everything. The house was a sign that they would have a baby. They would move into the house with a baby inside her. She was sure of it.

Friday

'I can't believe we're on a minibus. I haven't been on a minibus since – I dunno. Primary school, probably.'

'I feel like we should be chucking crisps at each other and listening to a mix tape.'

' "Born to be Wild".'

'The Cure.'

'James. "Sit Down".'

'Ha. Do you remember? It was always played at balls . . .'

'And we'd all sit down, on the dance floor . . .'

'Which would be covered in cider and fag butts.'

'And we'd try to look up the girls' skirts.'

James looked over the back of his seat at the bus full of blokes, and laughed. Him, Will, Johnny, Bart, a couple of their old school friends, Stephen Garside, who James had suggested they invite, some of Will's mates from uni . . . They were all in their thirties, all grown-ups, with proper jobs and children, and and yet they could have been fifteen, all hormones and awkward elbows and bottles of vodka hidden in pairs of boxers at the bottom of their bags.

Well, most of them had proper jobs. Stephen Garside – his success was the most flamboyantly obvious. He'd offered to pay for champagne for the weekend, and James knew from his discussions with the Outward Bound centre they were heading for that he had politely refused their offer to supply them with a case of Moët in favour of having his own wine merchant deliver a particular vintage of Krug. James had been torn between envy, gratitude and a slightly snobby feeling that such a display was crass and not really in the spirit of things. Still, he wasn't going to turn the offer down. It wasn't just Stephen, though, whose achievements made his own look so lacking. Will had Henry Butler's, Bart was doing well, Johnny's band had taken off in a way none of them had ever expected. Pete, who had been known as Piggy Pete at school because he'd been able to put away a loaf of toast at teatime, owned a chain of sandwich shops that looked as though it was going to weather the recession; Graham, who had always been the quiet, geeky one in thick milk-bottle glasses and a Metallica T-shirt, had cashed in on all of those afternoons spent in the computer lab and created and then sold a website that had meant the recession was of little concern to him. And then there was James. OK, a couple of the other guys had lost their jobs as well, but they had found new ones, were back on the ladder. He had got nowhere.

Found nothing. And he couldn't understand why. He could see the pity creep into their eyes when they asked him about it, asked whether he had found something new yet, and when he said, 'No, actually, it's proving trickier than I'd hoped, still, I'm sure something will turn up before long,' trying to keep his voice buoyant and not let them see the despair that was ever-present but that he tried to keep damped down and hidden out of sight, they looked uncomfortable and embarrassed for him and for themselves. Their eyes would flick over his shoulder, searching for a way out while trying to conceal their discomfort, and they would underplay their own status, their own achievements, in that particularly British way. 'It's brutal out there,' they'd mutter, or, 'The right thing's just around the corner,' knowing all the while that it wasn't the right thing that mattered, it was anything that would pay the bills and keep the ship afloat, that the longer he was jobless, the more tainted he looked, the more he began to stink of failure. 'Why hasn't he found something else?' people began to wonder. 'What's wrong with him? There must be a reason, they must know something we don't.' And the doors would stay shut.

He shook himself. This weekend was for fun, not wallowing; his focus should be on Will, not himself. Snap out of it. He leaned forward and reached into the cool box by his feet. 'Fancy a beer, mate?'

Stephen Garside nodded and took the open bottle from him. 'Thanks. Should be a good weekend.'

James nodded. 'Yep. Should be.' He took a swig, and smiled at his new friend. He was right. He must try to forget about the job stuff, about the problems at home, about his mother. Just for two nights, he should let it all go, and enjoy himself. None of the others were sitting here fretting, after all, were they? He must make sure that he relaxed, joined in. It was Will's weekend, after all.

*

'I don't understand,' Caroline said to the woman on the other end of the phone. 'I don't understand why we've been turned down. I'm sorry, I know it's not just up to you. But please explain it to me again.'

The woman sighed a little. 'Mrs Beauman, as I have already told you, you simply don't meet the necessary requirements for a mortgage of this size.'

'But it's really not that large. We have capital – I have capital – and we can easily afford the repayments. It just doesn't make any sense. I had a mortgage on my old flat. My husband has a mortgage on our home.' As she spoke, she realised that she had no idea whether or not it was true. She had moved in with Bart, and assumed he owned the flat they lived in. Had given him the proceeds from the sale of her old place to make a dent in the mortgage, to make her contribution. But she had never seen letters from a mortgage provider, she realised now, bile rising in her throat. She swallowed it. Pushed on. 'The amount we're asking to borrow isn't much more than I owed on that property. But this time, the risk and repayments are to be shared between myself and my husband.'

'Exactly.'

'Exactly. What do you mean, exactly?'

There was a pause at the other end of the line. 'Like you said yourself. The repayments – and the risk – are no longer entirely yours. And you are no longer the only person that the bank would be lending money to.'

Caroline fell silent. 'What is it that you are telling me, precisely?' she asked, eventually.

'I'm not telling you anything, Mrs Beauman, other than the facts of your situation.'

'Right. Well thank you very much for your help.' Caroline couldn't keep the sarcasm out of her voice. 'I will, of course, be taking further advice. I've been with this bank for my entire life, and my father is an extremely valued customer of yours. And I'm sorry to say that when I reapply for this mortgage, it will not be with you.'

'That is, of course, entirely up to you, Mrs Beauman.' The woman paused. 'I would suggest, however . . .'

'Yes?'

'I would suggest that before you reapply for this loan, you obtain a credit report. For you both.'

'I'm surprised at Will, though. Not very bloody loyal, asking Stephen Garside, after everything.'

'What do you mean?' James said. He picked up the cut-glass decanter and upended it over his glass. They had eaten dinner in the large, wood-panelled dining room of the stately home where they were staying. A feast of steak and ale pies and sticky toffee pudding, smart nursery food, preceded by champagne on the lawn and accompanied by good red wine, had got the weekend off to a buoyant start. Now, full and slumped into their seats, they sat around the table, drinking and picking at plates of cheese. A trickle of blackened, silty claret dribbled out into James's glass. 'What everything?'

'Oh . . .' Piggy Pete's eyes narrowed so much that they almost disappeared inside his cheeks, and he reached for the bottle of port. 'You know. He's just got a bit of a reputation.'

'What for?'

Pete shrugged, and would not meet James's eye. 'Well. You don't get to the top by being a nice guy all the time, do you?'

James felt a lot more sober than he had a few minutes ago. 'No. But what's that got to do with Will? Or Will being loyal? Loyal to who, Piggy?'

'Don't call me that.' Piggy grunted, unaware of the irony of the sound. 'Look, forget it, all right?' He pushed his chair away from the table unsteadily, gripping his port glass in one hand. 'You'll find something, mate. It'll all come out in the wash.' And he walked away, heading for the doors to the terrace, nodding to himself like a plastic dog on the parcel shelf of a minicab.

James watched as Stephen slid out of the room, unnoticed by anyone else. And then he followed him.

'You should leave, you know. This weekend.' Stephen stood in the gloom, leaning against a pillar by the walled vegetable garden. Light and music spilled out of the house, and the sound of fists thumping on tables as the drinking games continued, enthusiastically, sloppily. But out here it was quiet. James held the glass conservatory door behind him, propping it open with one of the cushions from the wicker chairs so that it did not slam shut. He felt like someone in a detective story. What was he doing, creeping around in the dark, eavesdropping? But instinctively he felt there was something that he must find out.

He held his breath in the dark.

'It's the perfect time. It is!'

Stephen laughed. He had taken his jacket off after dinner, they all had, and his bow tie, and now he stood in his rolled-up shirtsleeves, grinning into his phone. He was giggly, coy; he might have been a teenage girl, twirling the phone cord around her little finger. James had never seen him like this. Whoever he was talking to, it was someone who softened his edges, who made him laugh. It was someone he was in love with.

Stephen lit a cigarette, the flame flaring in the black night, and the paper crackling as he inhaled. 'It's beautiful here. I just wish I was here with you, instead of a group of fucking drunk blokes. I know, I know, they're good guys. No . . . no, you can do it. Don't think about that. You wouldn't be, though. No one can ruin anyone else's life. We all make our own choices, darling, we all have to follow our own paths. And yours is heading right to my front door. It'll be just you and me, and no one will be able to touch us. You can be happy again. You do deserve to be happy, you know.'

The woman was unconvinced, it was clear. Stephen's silver tongue was doing its best to convince her, but she was wavering, unsure. He wasn't giving up, though. Gently push, push, pushing away at her, relentless as the tide.

'Come on. He's away. No unpleasant rows while you pack, no undignified begging from him to deal with. You and the kids can be gone before we're all back. I'll tell Lilian to get the rooms in the attic ready for them. I've had them all painted and done up, you know. Pearl's is beautiful. Oyster pink. They're ready and waiting.'

Pearl's is beautiful. Oyster pink . . . James felt sick. He wanted to sit down, but he was too far from the chairs, and they would creak anyhow, alerting Stephen to his presence. And he didn't want that. Not now. Not yet. He needed to hear this out. He clenched his fist, digging his nails into his palm. Stephen sighed, a note of frustration creeping into his voice.

'You can bring her as well. For now, at least. You can't exactly leave her there by herself. When we get back, we'll sort it out. Pack her back off to him. I know . . . I know she's not. Come on. "Come live with me and be my love, And we will all the pleasures prove . . ." See what you've done to me? Quoting poetry like a lovesick swain. Anyhow. At the end of the day, she's not your problem. And it'll do Cass good to have some time alone with her dad. God knows, he's hardly spent any with her up until now.'

James screwed his eyes shut so tightly that fireworks went off behind them. He didn't know whether to run towards Stephen or away from him. His instincts were entirely split. To charge, full of fury, at the man who was trying to annihilate his family

338

behind his back, the man who he had trusted, respected, revered even, and who was dripping honey-tinged poison into his wife's ear; to batter him into silence and destroy the sounds coming out of his mouth, to crush them into nothingness. Or to turn and run, as fast and as far as he could, heart pounding in his chest, blood pounding in his ears, until he was out of reach and could escape the sound of his voice, could expel the memory of it from his brain. *It'll do Cass good to have some time alone with her dad. God knows, he's hardly spent any with her up until now.*

It hurt, the words hurt James physically; they burned in his chest and flowed like hot tar into his veins. They hurt, because they were true. He was a useless husband, and a worse father.

In the end, he did neither. Instead, he managed to stand still and quiet until he could breathe again. Then he turned, and, shutting the door silently behind him, went back into the house. He would wait. He must make himself wait. Stephen Garside would keep until tomorrow. Will, on the other hand, he must talk to now.

'Did you know?' he asked Will, once he was back in the house. He had come back in from the garden to find that most of the rest of their party had either passed out or gone to bed. Will and Johnny were sitting at the dining table still, a bottle of port and a game of liar dice between then, but when James came back in, Johnny took his chance to go.

'I can leave the stag in safe hands,' he said, winking. 'I've got to get some kip or I'm going to be shooting myself tomorrow, let alone any clay pigeons.'

'Thought you rock-and-rollers were used to late nights?' Will teased, blearily.

'Yeah, well, this rock-and-roller's got a child with him full time these days, and has been up since five singing "The Wheels on the Bus". I'll see you guys in the morning.'

James reached for the thick hoodie that was draped over the back of one of the leather club chairs nearby. Suddenly he felt cold and in need of comfort. He poured himself another drink, that he didn't need, and sank into the chair. Will nodded at him, his eyes unfocused and his cheeks red. 'Great weekend, James. Well done. You're a real friend.'

James nodded. 'Got to give you a good send-off, mate.'

Will grunted and a shadow passed over his face. 'Yeah. Send me off into the great unknown. Like an ashtronaut.'

James smiled. There was a moment's silence. Then, 'Did you know?'

Will looked up at him, and raised his glass to his mouth. 'Know?' He looked around the room, as though searching for an intruder, then put his fingers to his lips. 'Shhhh. Know what?' he whispered. He was very drunk. Would he even know what James was talking about? Maybe not. But he had to ask. He had to know how many people knew about his humiliation.

'About Stephen Garside. What he's been doing.' He couldn't bring himself to say it.

Will's head jerked back, and James could see that he knew exactly what he was talking about.

'Shit.'

'Ah.'

'Mate. I'm so sorry.' Will's voice was sharper when he spoke this time, had lost some of its drunken fuzziness. The shock of James's words had sobered him up a bit.

James had been expecting Will to have known; something inside him had told him that he did. That what Piggy had intimated related to him. And overhearing Stephen Garside outside had made him more sure of it. But when Will confirmed it, it still came as a shock,

340

'Right.' He couldn't say anything else, not yet. His mouth wouldn't make the words come out. He took a swig of port and winced. It tasted sickly, cloying. It stuck to the roof of his mouth. He nodded, trying to make sense of it all, trying to think of something to say. He couldn't go to pieces. Not now. That was not how he – how they – had been brought up. Stiff upper lip, and all that. 'Right,' he said again. And then he began to cry.

Will's voice was guilty; he sounded almost panicked by James's distress. 'Shit, James, don't cry, man. It's not worth it.' James looked up at him in horror.

'It's not worth it? How can you say it's not fucking worth it?'

Will stood, wavering a little as he did so, and put both hands on the edge of the table to steady himself as he began to make his way around to the side where James was sitting. 'I've been trying to put it right, James, I promise. Trying to get people to listen to how great a guy you are. But he's got a lot of sway. And – well, at the moment, I don't.'

James looked up at his friend, shook his head. 'What are you talking about? How can you possibly put it right? What sway? He's certainly got sway with Izzy, that's for sure.'

'Izzy? What the fuck's Izzy got to do with anything?'

Will and James stared at one another. And through the fug of too much red wine and cigar smoke, James realised that they were having two separate conversations. He ran his hands through his hair.

'Stephen Garside's outside trying to persuade her to leave me for him.' Will gaped as James continued. 'What else has he done? What is it that you've been trying to put right, Will?'

Will took a deep breath. Then he sat back down, in the chair next to James, and began to talk.

Chapter Sixteen

Saturday

They walked up the hill, in their navy hoodies with their nicknames in yellow on the back, specially purchased and printed for the weekend. Will 'Skinny', James 'Boner', Bart 'Boman'. In his left pocket, Will carried the engraved hip flask that he had been given as a christening present. It was battered and scratched now, but full of whisky, and its heavy presence gave him comfort, made him feel secure.

Not that he should need the bolstering effect of a shot of single malt. It was his stag weekend. He should be buoyant, exhilarated. He should be enjoying jokes about it being his last weekend of freedom, laughing with his friends at them, not-so-secretly desperate to trade in the freedom of bachelorhood for the safe comfort of married life. But he wasn't. Every joke rang too true to be funny. Under their hoodies, they all wore the rugby shirts James had had printed up for the weekend.

He tried to shake the feeling off. He was here with his friends, the wedding was still a fortnight away. Stop counting the days down as though it's an execution, he told himself. Colette's beautiful. She's bright and kind and young and she'll make the perfect wife. And it was all true. He just wasn't sure that she was the perfect wife for him.

The groundsman who was leading their group for the day took a step back as Will readied himself to shoot, standing behind him, near James, who would shoot second. He raised his arm so that his assistant, positioned a hundred yards or so to his right, in charge of the trap, could see that they were ready. For a moment, as the clouds turned dark, they were outlined, almost, against the grey sky. Stephen, James, Bart, Will, Johnny. The groundsman lowered his arm. And Will raised his gun.

'Pull.'

The shot rang out. Above them, a single circle of putty-coloured clay shattered into pieces.

Behind Will, as he continued to shoot, the other men watched and waited their turn. James would be up next, then Bart, then Stephen. They had drawn names out of a hat to choose the order. Apart from Will. He would go first, of course. As he waited, James fumed. He'd never felt anger like this. It was pure and unadulterated. He had no idea how he had managed to keep it from bubbling over until now. All night he had lain awake, hot under the cool cotton sheets of his bed, listening to the bones of the old house creak and settle, his jaw clenched as he ran over what he had heard, from Stephen and from Will, again and again.

You and the kids can be gone before we're all back. I'll tell Lilian to get the rooms in the attic ready for them. I've had them all painted and done up, you know. They're ready and waiting . . .

I've been trying to put it right, James. I promise. But he's got a lot of sway.

Had he been naive? Too trusting? Should he have suspected something earlier? James didn't think he was a stupid man. But maybe this was the evidence that proved otherwise. Maybe everyone had known, all along, what Stephen Garside had been up to. His friends, his family, his colleagues. Ex-colleagues. Maybe they had all been treading around him, uncertain how much he knew, unsure of how much they could say. Or laughing at him. Daft old James, can't see what's going on under his very nose. Which would be worse? Whose betrayal cut the deepest?

Around and around he went, so that by the morning he was aching with tiredness, physical and mental. His eyes scratched and his head felt hot and thick. He was in no shape to go shooting. Still. He would be fine. A cold shower and a hot coffee, and a bit of fresh air, and he would get out there and show Stephen fucking Garside what he was made of.

Will came to the end of his round. 'Six out of ten. Could be worse, I suppose.' He handed the gun to James. 'Bit hung-over still, I guess. Go on. Show me up.' There was an apology in his smile as he handed James the gun. As James took it, he lightly touched his fist to Will's shoulder. Will was not the one he blamed.

'Yes, go on, James. Show the rest of us how it's done.'

James froze. Had it been anyone else who had spoken, he would have thought nothing of it. On the face of it, after all, it was not an inflammatory remark. But because it was Stephen who had said it, and because it was James he had said it to – it was different.

'What are you trying to say, Stephen?' James turned towards him, gun in his hand. The rest of the men were silent.

Stephen shrugged. His gaze was amused. 'Nothing at all. Just that I've heard you're a pretty good shot. Always find your mark.'

Was he deliberately taunting him? The meaning behind his words was clear to James. *I've heard you always find your mark, but you'd better show me you can do it, because I haven't seen any evidence of it yet. I'm the winner, you're the loser. In this shoot, as in life, I will beat you*. Those were the words he heard. But was he the only one who heard them?

'Oh fuck off, Stephen. Just fuck the fuck off.' James's hand shook on the stock of the gun.

A small smile played on Stephen's lips, and he raised his eyebrows. He nodded slightly. Maybe he realised that James had overheard his conversation the night before.

'What is it, James? What's the matter?' He wasn't going to give an inch. If James wanted to do it this way, he was going to have to play the part of accuser as well.

That was fine with James. He was too angry, now, to stop himself.

'I know,' he said, and the relief of it made him weak. 'I know what you did. What you're trying to do. Why?'

Stephen's eyes had become hard. The veneer of friendly bonhomie between them was gone.

He shrugged. 'Why not?'

James shook his head. 'Why not? No. There's got to be more to it than that. Do you love her? Tell me you love her.'

Now it was Stephen's turn to shake his head. 'She's a very attractive woman, your wife. I want her.'

'That's different.'

'Yes. I suppose it is.'

'But it's not just her. Why have you been blocking me? I thought it was weird. I knew times were tough, but I thought it was wrong that I couldn't even get an interview at half the places I approached. Not even a meeting. And then I found out why.'

'Guys.' Johnny's voice was quiet next to them.

'Not now, Johnny.' James was determined to settle this, once and for all. For ever.

'Why would you do that? It's like you wanted to destroy me. Destroy everything I'd worked for, everything I cared about.'

Stephen shook his head. 'You shouldn't be so emotional, James. You're reading far too much into this. I just wanted Izzy. That's all. I wanted her, and I knew she'd be more likely to leave someone who couldn't get his feet back on the ladder. That's all. It really wasn't anything personal.'

Suddenly James was very aware that he was holding a gun. And that Stephen wasn't. He took a deep breath. He could feel a bead of sweat running from his brow, down his temple.

And then Johnny spoke again, more insistent this time. And James heard the fear in his voice.

'Guys. Stop. Look.'

James and Stephen turned at the same time, almost as one. And stared. Less than a hundred yards away, Bart and Will stood facing one another, just as they themselves had done a few moments ago. But something about this scenario was different. Bart also had a gun in his hand. But he was pointing it at Will.

'Shit.' James's voice was a whisper. He glanced across at the groundsman. His face was white, and his hands were outstretched in a gesture of helplessness.

'There was a spare gun in the back of the Land Rover,' he said, quietly. 'I always carry a spare. Just in case, like.' He shook his head. 'I always carry a spare,' he said again. James held his hand out to quieten him.

'It's all right,' he said. 'No one's blaming you.' The man stared at Bart and Will, his head moving slowly from side to side.

'She's leaving me,' Bart was saying to Will. 'She's leaving me. It's your fault, isn't it? What did you tell her? What did that bitch of a girlfriend of yours tell her?'

346

Bart's hand trembled, and the men, almost as one, instinctively took a step back. Will shook his head. 'Bart. I don't know what you're talking about. I don't know anything about it. But I'm sure we can sort it out. Come on. We can sort this. Come on. Put the gun—'

Bart jabbed the gun in the air in front of him, and roared, 'Shut up. Shut up!' He spun around to James. 'Put your gun down. Put it down now.'

James nodded, and held the gun out in one hand, before slowly lowering it to the floor, his eyes on Bart all the time.

'OK, mate. It's OK.'

'I'm not your mate. I'm not any of your mates.' The gun was back on Will now. He held his hands up in the air at shoulder height, his face crumpled and frightened. But he was trying to stay calm. James could tell. There was a shadow of the same look on his face that he had always had at school when he had been caught doing something he wasn't meant to – panic underneath, covered with a layer of tranquillity. You would only see the panic if you knew him well.

Now, though, the panic was winning out. Sweat was breaking out on his forehead, and his eyes were flickering from Bart's face to the gun. Back and forth, back and forth.

'Get in the car.' Bart jerked the gun towards the Land Rover. Will looked over at it. 'Where are we going?'

'Just get in. In the driver's seat.' He glanced at the groundsman. 'Where are the keys?'

'The keys are in the ignition. I always leave the keys in the ignition. So they don't get lost. So we can move on to the next trap quickly. I always leave a spare gun in the back of the car.'

Bart gestured to Will, who walked slowly to the car and got behind the wheel. As he did so – and as Bart walked around to the passenger side, the gun trained on Will the whole time – he looked back at James. The two men's eyes met. And James wondered whether it would be for the last time.

The day before

I would suggest you obtain a credit report. For you both. The tone of the woman's voice bothered Caroline. It was as though there was something she knew that Caroline didn't. Superior.

She didn't say anything to Bart before he went off to Will's stag weekend. Didn't want him to know that there was a problem, to worry. The household admin was her domain. And she was the one who wanted to buy the house, after all. But on Friday morning, as soon as she had waved him off, in his special hoodie that made her heart twinge, because she was so glad he had been accepted as one of the gang by her friends, she opened the laptop and logged on to a website offering free and instant credit ratings. There might be some mistake in the system, she supposed, some old unpaid bill, even, lurking on his records that she could sort out without him ever having to know about it.

Individual not found.

Caroline stared at the screen in confusion. Individual not found? Why? She must have done something wrong. She clicked back to the beginning of the questions and started again.

Five minutes later, she found herself staring at the same screen. *Individual not found.* She couldn't understand it. She had entered all of his details correctly, name and date of birth, that was all straightforward enough, and their address. The only possible error could be in one of his previous addresses. She had taken them from his old mobile phone bills, two addresses. One where he had been for a few months, a rented flat somewhere in west London. The other where he had lived with his previous girlfriend, a house in south London. Not far away, in fact, by the postcode. She didn't recognise the address, though. Maybe one of them was wrong?

She typed the first address into Google. It came up, straight away. A smart block of serviced apartments, exactly where he had said it was. Of course it was where he said it was, she admonished herself, why on earth wouldn't it be? But something wasn't right. She double-checked the postcode on the screen. All as she had typed in. So it wasn't that. Almost without thinking, she picked up the phone, and dialled the number for the apartment manager given on the website.

'I'm trying to reach Bart Beauman. That's right. Oh, has he moved out? Oh dear.' She listened as the woman told her that Mr Beauman had not lived there for some years. She didn't sound surprised that Caroline was trying to track him down.

'Well, thank you for your help. I'm sorry to have bothered you.'

The woman laughed. 'You and all the rest of them, darling.'

Caroline paused. 'I'm sorry. What do you mean?'

'Mm? Oh, it's not like you're the first person to call looking for Mr Beauman since he moved out. If that was even his name, which I wouldn't put money on.'

'I don't understand, of course it's his name. Why wouldn't it be his name?'

'People do strange things, don't they? Change their names, cover things up. Especially when they're running away from something or other. And Mr Beauman had an awful lot to run away from. Fifteen grand's worth of unpaid rent on his flat here, and that's just the tip of the iceberg. You ask me, whatever it is you're trying to get out of Bart Beauman, let it go, darling. You won't see your money again, not from that one.'

As soon as she had put the phone down, Caroline ran to the loo, where she was sick, retching until her throat was raw and her eyes watered. Fifteen grand's worth of unpaid rent? How could it be true? How could it possibly be true? And yet, as she wiped her face with a cold flannel and gulped water from the tap to try and stop her head pounding, she knew that it was.

When she had calmed down enough, she sat back down in front of the computer. The world felt as though it was vibrating around her. Her face was hot with tears that kept on coming, in rushes. Just as she thought they had stopped, they would start up again. All she wanted to do was crawl into bed and pull the covers over her head, and go to sleep and hope that when she woke up Bart would be next to her, and none of this would have happened. But she knew that she had to find out the truth. She had pulled the end of the thread, and the whole blanket was unravelling. And with it, her dreams of a baby were disappearing.

She picked up the mobile bill with the other address on, the one where he had lived before he and his girlfriend had split up and he had moved into the flat. What happened, Bart? What went so very wrong, that you ended up running from so much debt? Was he trying to pay it off now? Was it something to do with the previous relationship?

That was it. That had to be it. The woman he had been with before – Elizabeth, that was it – the one who had cheated on him. It must be something to do with her. Caroline searched her memory for clues. What had he said about her? Not much. He had avoided talking about her most of the time. He had said something once about her shopping a lot, she thought. Maybe that was the answer – she had run up huge credit card bills that he had been forced to pay off? It didn't explain why he had left his rent unpaid. But it must be something to do with it. She didn't know how. But she was determined to find out.

Caroline pulled up outside the address that she had typed into her sat nav. It wasn't what she was expecting at all. Bart had always talked about the house he had shared with his ex as being 'a little cottage, two up, two down. Nothing grand, but we were happy there. At first, at least.' Well, this might have been two up, two down, but only an incurable optimist would have described the house in front of her as a cottage. It was a grey concrete block, built sometime in the sixties, probably, with small square windows, two to each floor. It sat in a row of half a dozen similar houses, at the front of an estate. Behind them were two high-rise blocks made out of the same dust-coloured slabs. Caroline checked the address. This was definitely the right place.

She took a deep breath, and walked up to the front door.

The woman who opened the door to her stared at her suspiciously. She was around Caroline's age, wearing a hoodie and jeans that were frayed at the bottoms, with bare feet. Her hair was pulled back into a messy ponytail. 'Whatever you're selling, I don't want it. Can't you see the sign?'

She pointed to a small notice to the left of the doorbell. *No junk mail, no door-to-door salesman, no free papers.* She turned her head back to the room behind her. 'Clara, stop it, stop teasing your brother. If you don't stop right now, you'll be on the naughty step. I can still hear you, you know.'

Caroline gazed in surprise. The woman's voice was clear and almost clipped. It was not the voice of someone who had been brought up in a place like this; it was the voice of someone who had found themselves here unexpectedly.

'I'm sorry. No – wait . . .' Caroline pleaded with the woman, who was about to shut the door in her face.

'What is it? I'm busy.'

'Yes. I can see. Sorry.' She struggled to get her words out. 'It's just – look, you're obviously not the person I was looking for, but I wonder if you can tell me who lived here before you.

A few years ago, I think. I'm trying to find her. Elizabeth, her name is.'

The woman gave a small nod. 'That's me.'

Caroline shook her head. 'No – I mean, sorry, I'm not saying that's not your name – was she called Elizabeth as well? I suppose it's not an unusual name, especially if you're our age. Jubilee babies.' She smiled.

The woman sighed. 'No, I don't know who lived here before me. But I've lived here for years. I'm Elizabeth. Elizabeth Beauman.'

She had fainted when she heard that. Come round lying over the threshold, the woman, Elizabeth Beauman, standing over her, looking worried. 'Bloody hell. You've livened my day up. Are you all right?'

She had sat Caroline up, leading her into the kitchen and giving her a glass of water, making her eat a piece of toast at the table. Hadn't asked her anything until she had sat down next to her with two mugs of strong tea. 'Get that down you. You'll be OK. I used to faint all the time when I was pregnant with these two. Came round in a tube carriage one time, I'd shut the whole Victoria line down at rush hour.'

'I'm not . . .' Caroline couldn't bring herself to say it. Not here. Not in this room, with this woman sitting in front of her, concern in her eyes. She swallowed. 'You must think I'm insane.'

'No. Not insane. I would like to know who you are, though. Who you are, and why you're looking for me.'

She told her the whole story. The fact that she was talking to Bart's ex-wife should have made it difficult – impossible, even. If she'd had to predict how she would react in this situation, she would not have imagined that she would be sitting at the woman's kitchen table, drinking tea and telling her everything. How they had been so happy to start with, how in love they had been. 'Sorry,' she said, again. 'It's not really appropriate, this. Is it?'

But Elizabeth looked at her with sad eyes. 'It's all right,' she said. 'I understand. Everything you felt with him, I felt too. That's what he does.'

She told her how things had begun to get difficult, how they had started to row. About her mother, about how ill she was, and how Bart seemed to hate it when Caroline visited her. 'He hates the attention being taken away from him,' Elizabeth told her. 'He was the same when the children were born.'

'But . . . I can't understand it. I'm sure he loves . . .' Caroline paused. The existence of Bart's children, undeniably his, the sound of them playing upstairs where Elizabeth had sent them, like a vision of what might have been for her, for them, was almost too much to bear. But she made herself go on. 'I'm sure he loves his children very much.'

'Ha. That's a joke. He hasn't seen them for over a year. Didn't even send cards on their birthdays.'

'Over a year.' Caroline gasped, despite herself. He had visited them, visited her, since they had been married, then. Had come here . . . when? What lie had he told her. She shook her head, as though to shake the truth away.

'Well. Maybe it's all too difficult for him.' Her voice quavered as she tried to defend the indefensible.

Elizabeth raised an eyebrow, and sipped her tea.

Caroline continued. 'I mean, it must be hard, seeing them. Well, seeing you, really. Remembering.'

'Remembering what, exactly?' Elizabeth didn't sound guilty, or angry. Just curious.

Caroline didn't like to say. It felt like treading on someone else's memories. On their story. But she was angry, now. Elizabeth must know what she was referring to. How could she sit there and play the innocent, after that?

'Remembering how you cheated on him. With his best friend! How could you? I know Bart can be difficult, I know things must have been hard for you both.' She looked around the poky kitchen. She couldn't imagine Bart living here, not in a million years. He must have been like a caged bear. 'But there are some things you just don't do. Some lines you don't cross. And the money. What happened to all of his money?'

Caroline stopped. And stared. Elizabeth was not angry. Had not jumped up to tell her to get out. She was laughing.

'Oh God,' she said, 'I'm sorry. It's not funny. It really isn't. But – Jesus.' She wiped her eyes. 'The gall of the man. The sheer bloody gall of him.'

She raised her head, and looked Caroline in the eye. 'Look, I don't mind you coming here. I really don't. I, of all people, know what living with Bart Beauman can drive you to. But if you're going to sit in my kitchen and drink my tea and accuse me of all this, then you need to know the truth.'

Caroline nodded.

'The money. Why do you think I'm living here, Caroline? Do I look like someone who wants to bring her children up on a shitty estate like this? Do you think I want to be here?'

Caroline shook her head. It was a grim, miserable place. 'I'm here because I've got no choice. Because my ex-husband, your husband, spent every penny of what I had, and more. Used everything I had as collateral against loans, and then disappeared, leaving me paying for them. Holding the baby? Holding two babies and a piles of bills. I had the bailiffs round here every day for six months after he left. My children went to sleep to the sound of them hammering on the door. It was a really lovely lullaby for them.'

Elizabeth's voice was bitter now, and full of bile.

'The saddest thing? I didn't even kick him out. He left. Even after Sarah, I didn't kick him out.'

'Sarah?' Caroline asked the question, but she was sure that she already knew the answer.

'Yes, Sarah. My best friend. The bridesmaid at our wedding. The godmother to my daughter. Who lived a glamorous life in New York, jetting in every so often, blessing us with her presence.'

'New York?' Caroline whispered. Oh God. She knew what was coming.

'Mm, she's a hotshot lawyer out there. A beautiful, well-off lawyer, and the woman who slept with my husband. Christ, I'd spent two years either pregnant or breastfeeding; sex was hardly top of my to-do list. Caroline, it wasn't me who slept with Bart's best friend. It was Bart who slept with mine.'

Bart paced. He had to decide what to do. And he knew he had to decide soon. Time was running out. They weren't going to wait around for ever. Sooner or later, if he did nothing, the decision would be taken from his hands.

He was confused. It was the tiredness and the hunger, he was sure. He shook his head. Caroline was here, outside. So maybe she wasn't leaving after all? Maybe she had changed her mind? He looked at Will. He no longer looked like a threat. Grimy, covered in sweat, his wrists bound behind his back, he just looked like Bart felt – desperate, and exhausted. Bart almost pitied him.

And suddenly, Bart was overcome by a deluge of loneliness. He had messed things up so badly. And all he wanted was someone to tell him that it was OK. Someone to talk to. If he was going to die in here, if the police were going to come charging in and shoot him, then he wanted one last conversation with someone who might understand before he went.

He moved away from the window, and turned towards where Will sat in the corner.

'I'm going to take the gag off,' he said, and his mouth felt dry and thick. God knows how Will's must feel. He experienced a second of guilt, but then crushed it back down. No. It was not his fault. None of this was his fault. He had been driven to it. He was a good man, an honourable man.

Will nodded, relief in his eyes.

Bart hesitated. What to do with the gun? He didn't want to put it down. It was his comfort, now. His only defence. But to take it over to Will was . . . Was what? The man was tied up. He couldn't do anything. *Hold on to the gun. It's your friend. Your only friend. Keep it close.*

Bart stepped into the shadows, and leant down so their heads were level.

Harriet yelled. The pain swept through her like lava running down the sides of a volcano. It felt like her pelvis was at its epicentre, and her body was being riven with great judders of power and pain and fear. The contractions had started shortly after the phone call came, and Izzy had put the handset down on the side in the kitchen, where she and Harriet had been drinking tea, discussing whether curry and sex really were likely to bring on labour, or whether it was all just old wives' tales. She had been wide-eyed and pale when she hung up, and Harriet had assumed it was bad news about Ginny.

'Oh no, is it . . . has she . . .'

But Izzy had shaken her head. 'It's not Gin. Harriet. You need to sit down.'

'No. What? Tell me – Izzy, what's happened?'

'It's Will. And Bart. It's – I can't really believe it. Harriet – Bart's got a gun. He's taken Will hostage.'

And shortly afterwards, Harriet had known that she wouldn't be needing curry or sex to bring on her labour after all.

'Come on, Hats. Good girl. Good girl. You're doing so well. Come on, hold on. Hold on to me. You can do it.'

Harriet summoned all her strength, and did as she was told. She held on to Izzy as though for dear life, while all around her swarmed lights and midwives and noises. She couldn't focus on any of them. They didn't matter. All that mattered, all that she could concentrate on, was Izzy's voice. It was the only thing that she had to hold on to.

Harriet threw her head back and bellowed.

Will waited until Bart was as close as he was going to get. He could feel his breath on his cheek as he reached around the back of his head and fumbled with the rag that was tied around his mouth. Desperation for it to come off, to be able to breathe freely again, almost overtook him, and he forced himself to fight the urge to struggle. He must stay still, compliant. For these last few seconds, he must be patient.

Bart breathed heavily as his fingers worked to release the tight knot that he had tied, while keeping the gun tucked in under his right arm. He smelled of sweat and dirt and panic. Will watched his face from the corner of his eye. Should he have known? Should he have been able to see, back when Bart first appeared on the scene, that there was something wrong with him, something that would lead to this? But there was nothing, not really. He had been suspicious of him a little, yes. He'd been a bit too flash with his cash, a bit quick to slot into Caroline's life in every way, take her over. But Will had put that down to unreasonable jealousy. He'd liked the fact that Caroline still held a bit of a torch for him, that she would always come and talk to him first at parties, want to sit next to him at dinners. It was flattering, and he loved her, had grown up with her. He didn't want to be with her, she was too much a little sister to him. But when her head had finally been turned so dramatically by Bart, to the point where Will almost became invisible, it had smarted a little. So he'd put his feelings down to that. Was there something else that he should have seen, that could have prevented this?

But however hard he looked, there was nothing. Nothing about Bart had betrayed the turmoil that lay beneath.

Will felt the knot finally come loose, and with a little grunt, Bart pulled the fabric away. He took a single, deep breath of air unfiltered by dirty sacking. It was bliss. And then, with a determination that came from somewhere deep inside, giving him a strength that he had not known, he launched himself up and forwards with a great yell, ploughing his head into Bart's and knocking him backwards, the gun in Bart's hands still as he flew across the room.

They all heard the gunshot. They were only a hundred yards or so away, after all, though it felt like miles. Everyone's head turned at once, when it came. The police officers, the ones who weren't armed and positioned. The rest of them, from where they stood behind a hastily erected barrier: Stephen Garside, Johnny, the groundsman, the owner of the house. James. And Caroline.

Her hand flew to her mouth and her knees buckled. James held her firm around the waist. 'No!' she cried out. 'Oh please, no.' And even as the words left her mouth, she wondered who she was crying for. Will, or Bart?

The officer in charge spoke quickly and firmly into a walkie-talkie. He said something they couldn't hear, and then all of a sudden there was a surge of men moving towards the building, their bodies hunched and low to the ground, like a swarm of insects, and then two bangs, loud, so loud they made her teeth chatter, and bright flashes of light, and she screamed out, sure that one or both of the men she loved were dead, and she was powerless to help them, powerless to do anything at all other than stand and watch as the field was overrun with things happening that she did not understand.

Chapter Seventeen

March, 2010

It was the middle of March and a glorious, sun-drenched day when it finally happened. The sort of day Ginny had always loved so much. Later, Caroline looked back and remembered how they had walked through the grass, chatting about nothing much, she and James either side of Julian, trying to jolly him along and make him feel less alone, and wondered whether they should have known. That today would be the day. People said they did, didn't they? When people died after a long illness. 'There was something different in the air – a feeling of change.' Or, 'It felt as though something was lifting – and then they told me he had gone.'

There had been nothing, though, as far as she could tell. No premonition or sense that this day, this visit, was anything other than just another in the string of near-identical days and visits that they had undertaken in the last few weeks. No feeling of finality, of the closing of a chapter or the imminent departure of her mother's soul. A daughter ought to feel something before it happened, surely? Ought to at least sense that unbreakable umbilical cord relinquishing its hold as it loosened and let go. But then Caroline had proved to herself and to everyone else recently that she was a bad daughter.

It happened quickly, in the end. The nurse told them when they got there, expecting it to be just another visit, that Ginny had had a bad night, and that she was very weak. They had all nodded. She had been weak for days, weeks. This was nothing different. This was par for the course, these days – the pattern of their lives. But the nurse's face had told a different story. 'You might want to spend some time alone with her, all of you,' she had said, and Caroline had grabbed her father's hand, instinctively, for ballast, feeling it curl around her own as they stood, trembling, in a row, before this nurse, Nurse Waldegrave, who had been so kind to them all and who Caroline now suddenly felt like punching. She could not be saying what it sounded like she was saying. Ginny was not going to die. Not now. It was too soon. It was always too soon.

She hadn't opened her eyes. When was the last time she had done so? Caroline couldn't remember. A day ago? Two? Two days ago, she thought. She had been awake then, or mostly; drifting in a half-world of sleep and confusion. But there had been lapses like this before, whole weeks where she had slid down into what looked like the final stretch, and then she had rallied and come back to them, sitting up in her bed, gazing at the flowers on the table next to her with pleasure. This would be the same.

But it wasn't. Caroline had faltered at the door, not wanting to go into the room where her mother lay, dying. That was what she was doing. She might not have had a premonition, but now she was here, she could not miss it. It was the sound Ginny made. A deep, visceral noise that Caroline wanted to recoil from. It sounded so painful, as though the breath were being pulled out of her from somewhere deep within. James and Julian had already been in to say their own private goodbyes. And now it was her turn.

'It's an awful sound, I know, but she's not aware of anything,' the nurse said gently, from behind her. 'She's quite comfortable.

It's much more distressing for you than for her.' And she squeezed Caroline's shoulder, and then waited until she had taken a step into the room, then softly shut the door behind her. Caroline quelled the feeling of panic that rose up in her. She had to stop herself from turning and running after the nurse. It was the same feeling of desperate urgency to flee that she remembered from being a child, and getting up to go to the loo in the middle of the night. She'd creep across the hallway, and sit, legs dangling with nerves as she peed, the fear rising up inside her. The window was behind the loo, and she would imagine getting up and turning to flush and seeing a face in the window in front of her, shadowy, with deep, staring eyes. Eventually she would not be able to bear it any longer, and would leap off the seat and race back to bed, her thighs still damp and her heart racing as she flung herself on to the bed and pulled the covers up over her head. Her mother would always come to her when she heard the familiar pattern of footsteps, the slow, sleepy pace followed by a pause, and then the desperate fleeing. She had known, had always known, when Caroline or James had been in need of comfort, and she had always given it.

If only she could do the same for her mother now, Caroline thought, as she forced herself to stay in the room, to walk slowly over to the bed where Ginny lay, and take her hand. It felt dry and papery, as fragile as those little Japanese flowers she used to play with that you put into bowls of water and watched as they unfurled. But Ginny was past comfort, even if Caroline had been capable of giving it. She had travelled too far down the road for that.

She wanted to apologise. To tell her mother how sorry she was for everything. For taking her for granted for so many years. For assuming that she would always just be there, for not appreciating her enough. For having been so distracted recently, for the badness that she had brought into their family when she married Bart, for the attention she had given him that she should have given to Ginny, if only she had known. If only she had known how little time there was.

'Mama?' she said, finally. 'Mama, I need to tell you some things. Quite a lot's happened recently. Harriet's had her baby. It's a little girl. She's beautiful. She's called Florence.'

Caroline bit her lip.

'You were right about everything, Mummy. So why didn't you say something about Bart? You saw, didn't you? You must have seen.'

She wiped the tears from her eyes.

'Well if you didn't see it, then you weren't the only one. Bart – he did some really awful things, Mummy. But I don't want you to worry about that now. The important thing is, everyone's going to be all right. We're all going to be fine.'

And finally it all came out, and she sat there at her mother's bedside, and took the last opportunity that she would ever have to tell her everything that had happened. How brave Will had been, how Bart had been hurt by the stun grenades when the police went in, but not badly. How he had looked at her when they took him away on a stretcher, surrounded by police, his eyes sad, pleading almost, and how it had taken all of her strength not to go to him and hold his hand and tell him it was all right she loved him, she was here. How instead she had turned away. About Elizabeth, Bart's first wife. About the fact that he had been married before, had lied to her, had lied to them all. About his children, the children that he had hidden away, their face a painful shadow in Caroline's mind now because of their resemblance to Bart. They were like echoes, echoes of the children she and Bart might have had. About Bart's gambling debts, and bad business debts, strings of them in this country and in others too, probably. The lie that she had uncovered just as she was leaving Elizabeth's house that day.

She had turned to the other woman, and squeezed her hand. 'Thank you,' she said. 'Thank you for being so honest with me.'

Elizabeth shrugged. 'I'm sorry for you. Sorry he's still doing the same old thing. Don't think he'll change, Caroline. I hope what I've told you today has convinced you of that. He won't change.'

Caroline nodded.

'If I were you, I'd shut down my bank accounts, get a divorce, and get as far away from Bart Beauman as you can. Don't hang on till you're in my position. Don't leave it too late.'

Caroline smiled bleakly. 'You know the sad thing? From where I'm standing, your position doesn't look all that bad. Sorry, I know that sounds awful. It's just . . . we've been trying for a baby since we got married. I know, I know it's probably a good thing that I didn't get pregnant. Clean break, and all that.' She took a deep breath. 'But I can't help it. I still can't help feeling that if only I'd been able to have a baby, everything might have been all right. And at least I'd have that. You know? At least I'd have that.'

Elizabeth frowned, and shook her head. 'Oh Caroline,' she whispered. 'You were never going to get a baby. Not from Bart, at least. I'm so sorry. I'm so sorry that he did this to you.'

Caroline shrugged. 'It's not your fault,' she said. 'Us women spend too much time saying sorry, don't you think?'

Elizabeth nodded. 'Yes. But in this case, it is my fault. Or a bit my fault, anyhow. Because after I had Archie, I knew I didn't want any more children. And neither did Bart. So he had a vasectomy.'

Caroline sighed. It was still the lie that hurt the most. How he had let her carry on trying, wishing, hoping. Day after day, month after month. How many tears she had shed for a baby that, she knew now, was never going to come.

Still. She was young enough, the dream didn't have to die for ever. Just for a while. And until then, she had her nieces and nephews, she had her friends' children. She had her new god-daughter, little Florence, who she was on her way to see now.

Before she left, she bent down and kissed her mother's forehead.

'Bye, Mama,' she whispered. 'I love you.' And Ginny opened her eyes, just for a moment, and looked straight at her daughter. Caroline held her hand. Neither of them spoke. Then Ginny closed her eyes once more, and her hand softened in Caroline's, and she was gone.

Harriet gazed at her baby daughter. She was tinier and more perfect than she had expected. She had felt so enormous in the final weeks of her pregnancy that she had been convinced she was carrying a hefty lump of baby, a massive boy with a huge head and thick, sturdy limbs. So it was a surprise when what emerged, after a long labour, was this little six-pound girl with skinny, scrappy arms and long, slightly wizened fingers.

'I did it,' she had gasped up at Izzy, who was holding on to her shoulders and weeping, as Florence was passed to her. 'I did it.'

'You bloody did,' Izzy said, wiping her eyes, 'you clever, clever girl.'

She had taken a photograph of Harriet then, wide-eyed and flushed with hormones and achievement, her baby cradled on her chest.

Neither of them had mentioned the obvious, the fact that Harriet had done it pretty much entirely by herself. They didn't need to, for what was there to say? He was not here, and that was that.

Only it hadn't been that, because shortly afterwards Izzy's phone had rung, and she had sat next to Harriet's bed listening to what the person on the other end was telling her, and automatically reached for Harriet's hand.

'What?' Harriet had asked, aware through her exhaustion that something was wrong, something had happened.

Izzy had glanced at her, her brow furrowed. 'OK. Don't worry, I'm here with her,' she'd said. 'It'll be fine. Just get him here as soon as you can. He's got a beautiful baby daughter to meet.'

'Iz, what's happened? It's Will, isn't it? What, what is it?' Harriet had started to push herself up in the bed, panicking. Florence was fast asleep in a crib next to her.

'He's not hurt,' Izzy had said quickly. 'Well, not badly.'

'Oh God.' Harriet put her head back on the pillow and closed her eyes. 'Oh God, no, no, I can't bear it, I can't cope.'

Izzy had leant forward. 'Hats, listen to me. He's OK. He really is. He's coming soon. But there has been . . .' She had paused, at a loss how to describe the events that James had just relayed to her.

'A development. The seige – it's over.'

Now Harriet looked at the photo Izzy had taken that day, remembering. Izzy had told her what had happened, quickly and bluntly, like pulling off a plaster. How Bart had gone mad, it seemed, and taken Will hostage, holing up in a shed on the estate with a gun that Will had eventually managed to get away from him. She had almost lost Will. If things had played out slightly differently. But they hadn't. Florence was here, and Will was still here, and Bart had been taken away, leaving Caroline weeping on her brother's shoulder in a cold field.

Will had turned up at the hospital just a few hours later, his cuts and bruises patched up, still wearing the stag weekend hoodie, looking somewhat the worse for wear. The nurses assumed that he had simply been at a particularly raucous stag, and gave him disapproving looks as he made his way towards the room where Harriet and Florence lay sleeping.

She had opened her eyes to see him standing there, dishevelled, his eyes red as he gazed in at Florence, his large hand touching her tiny one, very gently.

'Are you OK?' she had whispered, and he had turned to her, his face a mixture of apologies and thanks. There was a lot he wanted to say. She could see it in his eyes. But at first he simply said, 'Yes. I am, now.' And she had known that he wasn't just talking about what had happened with Bart.

Harriet picked Florence up out of her Moses basket and kissed the top of her head. She was dressed in a pink all-in-one covered with roses. Harriet had indulged her shopping habit fully in preparation for her daughter's birth, and in addition she had been sent so many little outfits that the girl's wardrobe was almost bigger than her own. 'Hello, my little sweet pea,' she whispered. 'Daddy's coming to see you soon. Yes he is. Daddy's coming.'

He had asked her that evening whether she would consider taking him back. As she lay in the hospital bed, tired, sore, overwhelmed by love and relief and adrenalin and struggling to absorb everything that had happened.

'I'm sorry, Hats,' he had said quietly, as he held Florence. 'I'm so sorry. I should never have let things end between us, not the way they did. I handled it all horribly badly. I can see it now, so clearly. It's like I was living in some sort of bad dream. And now everything makes sense.' He looked at Florence. 'This is where I'm meant to be. With Florence. And with you. I just want to be with you.'

She had turned her face towards him. She couldn't believe what she was hearing.

'I never loved her, you know. Not really. It was never like what we had. I phoned her, earlier. After they took Bart away.

It made me realise . . . I couldn't marry her. I called it all off.'

'How is she?' Why am I asking that? Harriet thought. I shouldn't care. But somehow it felt like the right question to ask.

'Furious.' Will smiled, awkwardly. 'But . . . I think she'll be OK. She seems more worried about cancelling all the flowers and what she's going to do with seven bridesmaids' dresses than anything else. I don't think it ever would have worked. In the long run.'

Harriet shook her head. 'So why . . . why did you propose to her, then?' she asked.

He sighed. 'I don't know. I really don't know. I guess . . . I suppose you forcing things got me thinking. And it made me realise that maybe I did want to get married, after all.'

'Just not to me.'

'No, I don't mean like that. I mean . . . Look, I felt backed into a corner when you told me how you felt. Trapped. The only way I could react was to push you away. But then, it's like it sparked something off inside me. So when Colette came along . . .' He shrugged. 'I don't know. I was readier than I realised, I suppose. You set the ball rolling and then disappeared.'

Harriet bit her lip. 'I didn't disappear anywhere, Will. You dumped me, and I moved out. You knew where I was. You could have . . . JESUS.' She could not carry on. She didn't have the energy, couldn't risk losing her temper in front of her baby who was not even a day old. This was not the time or the place.

'Get out, Will.'

He looked confused. 'But Hats. Didn't you hear? I want to be with you. I want you to come home. Both of you.' He gestured to Florence. 'I want you back.'

'I said get out. Put my daughter back in her crib, and leave, or I'm calling the nurses to make you go.'

She smiled at the memory of it. He had looked so utterly surprised by her reaction. Had clearly been expecting her to open her arms and welcome him back, bountiful and grateful. Well fuck that.

Still, he had showed his mettle since then. Had visited every day, without fail. Had driven her and Florence home from hospital, unpacking all of their things and lining it up all neatly in the hallway of her flat before leaving. When she had opened the fridge she had found it stocked full of her favourite M&S treats, and the freezer too, things that she could chuck, one-handed, into the oven. There had been fresh flowers on the table and her post had been sorted into piles. He had come round every day after work, and sometimes at lunchtime, bringing her box sets of *Thirtysomething* and *Roseanne* to watch while she was breastfeeding, taking the rubbish out and putting washes on. He was trying to show her that he had changed. And maybe he had. The old Will wouldn't even have thought of any of those things, would have considered a box of chocolates and a bottle of wine suitable recompense for most misdemeanours. Still, she had not been able to bring herself to get over the hurt. Did not feel that he had quite grasped what it was that she really cared about – not the break-up, but the fact that he had been prepared to go ahead with the wedding, to give Colette what he had withheld from her for so long.

The doorbell rang, and she carried Florence over to the buzzer. 'Here he is,' she whispered in her ear, 'your daddy, who loves you so much. Here he is.' That much was undeniable. There was no mistaking how much Will adored his daughter, had done from the moment he had set eyes on her. That was a mark in his favour.

She opened the door. Will was standing in front of her, as she had been expecting. What she had not been expecting was what was standing alongside him. It was a grandfather clock, as tall as he was, with a night and day face. Its pendulum swung slowly from side to side.

'Morning,' she said slowly, staring at it.

'Nine fifteen in the morning, actually,' Will replied, gesturing to the face of the clock.

'Will . . . what . . .'

'Just wait,' he said, stepping forward and lifting Florence from her arms so that she could look properly at the clock. 'I know you've always wanted one. I got Harry to help me find it.'

She stepped closer and examined the wood. It was a beautiful piece. The wood was fine-grained and polished to a shine, the face was ornate and in good condition. She smiled as she imagined Harry searching for it. He knew exactly what she liked.

'Most people get an eternity ring when they have a baby, don't they?'

'You're not most people. We're not . . .' He trailed off. 'Look, Hats, there is a reason for this. It's not just because I know you wanted one, and I always said they were stuffy and pointless. That too, but that's not the main reason. The thing is . . .' He looked at Florence, who was waving her hands at his face, took hold of them and kissed them, then returned his attention to her mother.

'I wish I could turn the clock back. It's all I keep thinking. If only I'd realised what we had, and how much getting married meant to you. If only I'd not been such a fucking idiot, and proposed to you before you felt you had to push me – and I'm not blaming you for that. It was my fault. It was all my fault. You had to do it to make me see, to open my eyes. And it worked. It's just that when I did open them, finally, someone else was standing in front of me. I wish I hadn't done any of it, Hats. I wish I'd never got involved with Colette, it was all wrong. I wish I'd had the balls to back out of it sooner. I wish . . .' He paused. 'Well, basically, there's only one thing I don't regret about the last year, and that's this one,' he nodded at Florence, 'and the night we spent together at Julian's party.'

'Hardly a night.' She smiled, despite herself. 'A couple of hours.'

'OK,' he conceded. 'I'm trying to make the whole thing sound more romantic, all right, give me a break. Our daughter's listening, I don't want her to think her parents are complete reprobates. Look, maybe it was a stupid idea. But I thought this would show you. How sorry I am. And that when you looked at it, it might remind you that every day, I'm wishing I could change what happened, but I can't. I'm sorry, Hats. I can't. And I wish more than anything that I could. I just want you to know that. I need you to know that.'

Harriet looked at him, at Will, holding their child. It was Will she loved so much. Always had done, always would. How could she turn him away? If it had been anyone else, she might have been able to. But not Will. Not now.

She reached for his hand, and pulled him towards her. 'OK,' she said. 'OK.'

Will's face crumpled with relief, and he kissed her, Florence nestled in the space between their chests until Harriet panicked that they were going to suffocate her and pulled away, her face wet with tears. She looked over Will's shoulder, smiling. 'There's just one problem,' she said, and his eyebrows met in a question mark. 'How the bloody hell are we going to fit that thing into your cottage?'

Izzy stood in the empty café, her keys in her hand, unwilling, just yet, to shut the door behind her and let it go. She had taken the sign down, and it was leaning up against the wall, ready to be loaded into the car and come home with her. A keepsake. A reminder that, for a time, Pearl's Place had existed, had been

hers, and she had made it work. For a time. She had sold the
lease on to a local couple who were going to turn it into a
sandwich shop, and she hoped that they would make it work.
They were nice people. 'You're welcome to come back and do a
shift behind the counter any time,' they had said, jovially, 'if
you miss it too much,' and she had smiled and said she might
well take them up on that, knowing that once she left today she
would not set foot in the place again. It was all too tied up with
everything, with Stephen Garside and her and James fighting
and being so miserable, and the whole sorry mess of the last two
years. No, Pearl's Place would not be a part of her life any more,
beyond the sign that she would hang in the kitchen, and that
would become part of the furniture. It was time for new
beginnings, for all of them.

For her and James, in particular. They needed a new start
most of all. Had already begun the process of rebuilding their
marriage, slowly, painstakingly. After the stag weekend she
had not been sure whether it was salvageable, whether she had
broken the trust between them for ever. But she had known, as
soon as she had taken that phone call in Harriet's hospital room,
that if she did nothing else, she had to try to get it back.

'I realised when you rang from that field how much worse it
could have been. How I would have felt if it had been you in
that shed,' she had said when James had finally arrived back
home, tired, shell-shocked, worn out with the strain of seeing
Will emerge from the stone lodge, blinking and pale, dealing
with the police, supporting Caroline and watching his brother-
in-law go off in the back of a police van.

'I couldn't have borne it,' she had continued. 'It would have
broken my heart.'

James had looked up at her. 'But Will's fine,' he said. 'Bit
battered, but fine.'

Izzy had shaken her head. 'No. I mean if it had been you

doing what Bart did. It suddenly made me see – it could have been you.'

'Iz. I would never—'

'But who would have thought he would, either?' she interrupted him. She had to get it out. 'We all thought he was fine, he was perfectly normal. And we sat here, in this kitchen, and had dinner with him, and laughed at his jokes, and waved him and Caroline off at the end of the night, God knows how many times, and then suddenly, one day, he snaps. And you've been under so much pressure, with money, and work, and Cass, and us, and who's to say you might not have suddenly woken up one day and just not been able to bear it any longer? And if I knew that I had contributed to that, if I had driven you down that road . . .' Izzy was sobbing now, and James stepped forward and gently encompassed her in his arms. Her fists were tight up against her chest and she couldn't breathe properly; she felt as though her body was a ball of elastic bands stretched to their limit.

'Darling. Sweetheart. It would never have happened. Listen to me.' He took her face in his hands. 'Bart – this isn't the first bad thing Bart has done.' Izzy listened. 'He's hit Caroline. More than once.'

James's face had pain and rage writ large across it as he told her what Caroline had told him on that field. The knowledge of his failure to protect his little sister from the pain that he had not seen, had not realised existed, burned inside him. 'I can't believe it. But it's true. He's a fucking nasty piece of work, and he's never coming near her again. He hit her, he covered it up, he made her believe it was her fault. Classic stuff, I suppose. And I'll never forgive myself for not seeing it.'

'Oh James. Oh darling. The poor girl.' She held his hands.

'I know. But that's the thing. It would never have been me, Izzy. Bart's – well, there's more to the story, and Caroline can tell you herself. I know she'll want to talk to you. But he isn't like us. He isn't like me.'

Izzy nodded. 'I just – it just made me see. How awful I've been to you. With everything. I've been a terrible wife.'

'I haven't exactly been a shining example of husbandhood either, have I?'

Izzy buried her face in James's chest. 'How did we fuck it up this badly? We were doing OK, weren't we? I don't even know what happened.'

'We stopped paying attention, I guess.' He rested his chin on her head. 'We got complacent, maybe? Stopped seeing what was important.'

'And we lied to each other.'

'Yes. We did.' James pulled back from her and looked her in the eye.

'Izzy. I need to know. What I heard Stephen Garside saying on the phone . . .'

She blinked. She had to be honest with him now. Had to tell him the truth, however much it might hurt both of them. He was going to ask her if she had slept with him, and she would have to tell him. She steeled herself.

'Were you going to leave me? I don't want to know anything else. It doesn't matter. I thought he was my friend.' James gave a little shake of his head. He had been so stupid. Of course Stephen Garside hadn't been his friend. Men like Stephen Garside didn't have friends. 'I just need to know – were you planning on going to him?'

And she had let out a gasp of air, and shaken her head. It had not been the question she had been expecting. But she had to keep the promise she had made herself. 'Honestly? I don't know. I don't think so. I don't think I could have gone through with it. I don't think I could have taken Pearl and Alfie away from you, and taken them to his house, and played happy families. I think the answer is no. But if you're asking did I think about it?' She took a deep breath. 'Then I'm sorry, but the answer's yes.'

She turned now, hearing the bell on the door jangle as James pushed it open. They smiled at one another, and he picked up the shop sign and tucked it under his arm.

'Ready?' he asked, holding out his hand to her.

She nodded. 'Ready,' she said. And without looking back, she pulled the door behind her, locked it, and posted the keys through the letter box.

Stella sat in front of Benjy's desk, a new black fountain pen in her hand. In front of her was the contract for the novel that she had started writing on the sofa in her living room all those months before, and which, she thought now, might well be the reason she was sitting here at all today.

Her hand hovered over the dotted line. She read the title one more time. *Freefalling.* She had seen the word a thousand times at the top of her manuscript as she was writing it. Printed on the contract, though, it looked different.

'Get on with it,' Benjy grinned. 'Won't be long before you're staring at the book cover. Now that really will be a good day.'

She nodded, and signed her name. Stella Albright. It was real. She had a book deal, she was going to be an author, published by one of the best fiction publishers in the country.

'Did you ever believe you were going to get here?' Benjy asked, and his voice had lost its joking tone now.

She shook her head. 'No. I really didn't. I didn't . . .' She felt a lump rising in her chest, and pulled herself together. *Come on. This is a happy day. This is a good day.* But it felt important to acknowledge how dark most of her days had been until recently. 'I didn't think I was going to get anywhere, for a while. I thought – I thought I was going to die. And the worst of it was that I didn't really even care.'

'You cared enough to finish this, though. And I, for one, am bloody glad you did.' Benjy rubbed his fingers together and grinned.

'Yeah. I did. It was the thing . . . the only thing that I had to hold on to, you know?' She cleared her throat. 'Everything else had gone. Johnny, Viking . . . It was really fucking bleak back there, Benjy.'

'I know it was, kid. I know.'

'Anyhow . . .' She shook herself. 'It's all good now. I'm excited, you know? I feel like – I feel like it's all beginning.'

'That's because it is.' Benjy picked up a bottle of sparkling water from his desk and poured two glasses, holding one out to Stella.

'Glass of fizz, modom?' He handed it to her with a mock flourish, and she raised it in a toast.

'To *Freefalling*,' Benjy said, touching the rim of his glass to hers.

'And to landing on soft ground,' she said in reply.

She left the office half an hour later, flipping her sunglasses down against the glare of the midday sunshine. And then she changed her mind, and pushed them back up again. She wanted to feel the light in her eyes, the sun on her face. She had been hiding behind the shades for too long.

The book deal was a good one, and meant that she had enough money to pay her rehab bills and buy out Johnny's share in their house. She had cleared out the third bedroom, the little box room that he had always used to keep his guitars and music equipment in, and turned it into a little office for herself. Viking's room was no longer half empty – he was back living with her full time, and Johnny had him one night a week. Last night had been his night, and now she was going to meet them and collect Viking and take him home. There they were – she could see them as she walked over Waterloo Bridge; they were on the South Bank, by the carousel. Johnny was holding Viking up so he could see the horses going round and round, and Viking was squealing. For a moment, as Stella watched them, she felt sad. Seeing them together like that made her wonder whether she had done the right thing in letting their relationship fade. Johnny would have happily come back to her when she came out of rehab and he could see that she was well again, that she was not going to slip back into that darkness. Should she have tried to make it work? Accepted that Johnny would never change, that she would always be sharing him, that Delilah might have gone but there would always be another Delilah waiting in the wings?

No. She walked down the steps towards Johnny and Viking. The lightness she felt in her heart now told her that she had made the right choice. She was not spending every night sitting at home wondering where he was and who he was with. It was none of her business any more, and the relief of it was immense.

They looked up as she neared, and Viking grinned and waved.

'All signed and sealed?' Johnny asked.

'Yup. It's a done deal. You're looking at Stella Albright, author.' She gave a little curtsey. Johnny held up his hand for a high-five and she faced her palm to his. Before she could remove it, he wrapped his fingers around hers.

'I'm proud of you, you know,' he said. 'Really proud.'

She didn't speak. She hoped that he wasn't going to make some big speech, or try and convince her that they should get back together. But he just looked at her.

'I should have seen, earlier,' he simply said, in the end. 'And I shouldn't have just left you to cope by yourself when I knew that you weren't coping. I'm sorry.'

Stella nodded. 'Thank you,' she said. She took Viking's hand and smiled as he gripped her fingers with his own.

'We made a great boy. You wrote a great book. And I made an album.'

'A great album.'

Johnny shrugged. 'An album. It's not bad going, you know. Despite everything.'

Stella squeezed his hand. 'No. It's not bad going. Come on. I'll buy you an ice cream. To celebrate.'

It was two weeks after Ginny's death before Julian could bear to start going through her belongings. He slept in his dressing room, the small single room that faced their master bedroom, on a foldout sofa bed that they had used to put occasional guests up in. Somehow it was easier to sleep in here, where the bed felt different anyway, than to face the half-empty space of their big double bed alone. Her reading glasses and little water jug on her bedside table, the book she had abandoned some months previously as her concentration and eyesight had finally failed her, its page folded down where she had left it. It was a book she had read before – a comfort read, she had called it – and Julian had picked it up and opened it where it fell, hoping that it might give him, too, some shred of comfort. It did not, and he put it down again.

He'd have to take her books to the charity shop at some point, he supposed. There were piles of them, all the novels that had given her such pleasure throughout her life, that she had laughed and wept over, that meant something to her and nothing to him. They would all have to be boxed up and lugged to Oxfam or Cancer Research. No. Not Cancer Research. What good had they done Ginny? The thought of them profiting from her death, in however small a way, made him feel gruff and resentful. Some children's charity, that would be better. He would have to look into it. Yet another item to add to the list of jobs that appeared as if from nowhere after someone died. 'It's good to keep busy,' the hospice staff had advised him, after she had gone. 'Keep yourself occupied. Time will pass. It just does.' Kind smiles, cups of tea and custard creams. They were right, he supposed. But he didn't want to keep busy. Didn't want to have to. All he wanted was his wife back.

Much of the time, Julian noted, almost dispassionately, as he opened Ginny's wardrobe and gazed at her twinsets and silk blouses and neatly lined-up pairs of shoes, he felt sulky, like a child. His was not the brave, honourable grief of a noble tragedian, it seemed, but the tantrumming, self-pitying emotion of a five-year-old boy whose plans had been spoilt and whose bottom lip trembled with the injustice of his life. How levelling bereavement was. He had not realised. Had not known how it would strip him bare and reveal the very essence of himself to the world. He opened a mahogany drawer, and stared at the dozens of pairs of stockings, neatly rolled up, each in its own little cubby hole created by the plastic divider that sat snugly inside the drawer. Tan ones the colour of Rich Tea biscuits, navy ones, black ones. A single pair of bottle-green ones. He reached in and took those out of their slot, feeling the mesh beneath his fingers. There was a little snag in the fabric, and his thumbnail caught on it, pulling the thread and making a run. Julian held them to his face. Oh dear. They wouldn't be wearable now, he thought, not with that run in them; it was a long one, Ginny would never go out with . . . He stopped. Ginny would never *have* gone out with that in her tights. *Have*. It was a word he was going to have to get used to saying. It was a word he already resented.

What would he do with all of this? Tights, Ginny's underwear, her carefully polished shoes. The long winter boots he had bought her so that she could walk Mr Butterworth without getting cold when he paused for long sniffs at lamp posts. Clothes were one thing, could be given away; jewellery would be distributed among Caroline and Izzy and Pearl, he supposed; Ginny would have left instructions for that in her will. But these things, so intimately her, could not be parcelled out like packed lunches to strangers. And yet the thought of throwing it all away, taking it to the tip or parcelling it up in black bin liners to be crunched into landfill was horribly upsetting to think of. The things she had taken such care of thrown out with the trash like old newspapers and tea bags. He could not do it. But what else could he do? Suddenly Julian understood why people ended up leaving the rooms of the dead as they were, like shrines, as though they had just walked into another room. Doing anything else just involved too many decisions. He shut the wardrobe door.

He abandoned the bedroom, and decided to make himself something to eat instead. People had been bringing him lasagnes and pies – cottage, and steak and kidney, and chicken and leek – and other easily freezable dishes in china bowls ever since Ginny died. The freezer was full of them, despite the fact that he had now eaten pie for supper four days in a row. He felt like – he didn't know what. Something lighter. He opened the fridge and surveyed its contents, and then shut it again. He wasn't sure where to begin.

Caroline had been shopping for him the day before, delivering four hessian bags packed full of supplies. He had just put the milk and eggs and salad in the fridge, along with a chicken and a few other bits that looked as though they should be kept cold, and the bread in the bread bin. Everything else he had left out on the side. He looked at it now. It was a fairly random collection of items, arranged like that. Some cans of tuna, the posh sort, in olive oil, fillets not chunks. A bag of easy-cook Basmati rice, some spaghetti, a box of oatcakes. Raspberry Bonne Maman jam and a pack of croissants and some tinned peas, a couple of avocados that were still too hard, a new bottle of olive oil, a bunch of bananas, a pack of 'essential' blueberries and a pot of multivitamins for the over fifties. Julian peered at the label. It claimed to provide 'specially balanced nutrient combinations to support your changing health needs'! He put it down again. What were his 'changing health needs'? He had no idea. He stared again at the assortment of food in front of him, wondering how on earth he could turn it into something resembling a meal. It had been a long time since he had done any cooking, other than boiling an egg or two occasionally.

The display looked like one of those cookery shows Ginny had liked, where they gave the contestants a mystery bag of ingredients and challenged them to create a meal out of them. She loved – she had loved – sitting in front of the TV, tutting as they came up with some dreadful-sounding concoction. 'It's quite clear,' she'd say, turning her head a little towards him but keeping her eyes on the screen, 'they should take the lamb chops, marinate them in the yoghurt and half the mint, put the rest of the mint into a lovely tabbouleh with the bulgar wheat and cucumber, and make a nice little toasted chickpea relish to go on top with the sundried tomatoes and a bit of ground coriander. Never just use the puff pastry to make a tart. Anyone can do that. How is a puff-pastry tart impressive?' Julian would nod, and gaze at the telly, trying to see how she could look beyond the random ingredients that the contestants had been presented with to envisage this fully fledged meal, but he never could. It was like those Magic Eye pictures in shopping centres, he had never been able to see those either. James had had a book of them when he was younger, and Julian had spent three hours once trying to see the hidden picture that James insisted was there, before giving up and throwing the book across the room in frustration. 'It's a whale, Dad, can't you see?' But he couldn't.

'Come along, you silly old fool,' he muttered to himself.

'You're going to have to get a grip on things.' He took out a chopping board and an onion, peeled it and began to slice, without really knowing why. It just seemed to him that lots of recipes began this way, and it was as good a place to start as any. At least he felt as though he were doing something. Kedgeree. The thought came to him suddenly. That was what he would make. There was smoked haddock in the fridge, he remembered unpacking it yesterday and noting that it was the posh, undyed stuff. There were eggs, and he could boil those. What else? He rummaged around in his memory. Something spicy. Curry powder? He looked along the spice rack, his fingers working their way through ground ginger, cinnamon, turmeric . . . garam masala? No, he didn't think it was that. Allspice? That sounded right. He wasn't sure. He took the top off and inhaled, getting the powder on his fingers as he did so. It smelt right. Sort of. Well. He would give it a go, make it up as he went along. How difficult could it be?

Pretty difficult, as it turned out. An hour later he had used every saucepan in the kitchen, as well as three chopping boards, and was no closer to having an edible plate of food than he had been at the beginning. The smoked haddock was cooked – or what was left of it after he had hacked it into irregularly sized chunks with a serrated knife that was too small for the job. It didn't smell very good. He'd poached it in milk and peppercorns, but it had overcooked and become stringy. The rice was cooked, but again did not look how he remembered Ginny making it; somehow he had managed to both over- and undercook it, so that what he had ended up with were grains that were slimy on the outside and hard in the middle. He had picked some herbs from the pots on the terrace, and wasn't sure what they were, but had stirred them into the onions as they cooked. It had made them smell a bit Italian, and faintly of cat pee.

'Damn and blast,' he muttered. 'Damn and bloody blast it!'

He slammed the frying pan that he was holding down on the wooden worktop, and the herby onions flew in the air, scattering the side. In the corner of the room, Mr Butterworth woke, and whimpered. 'Sorry,' Julian sighed. 'I'm sorry. Looks like it's going to be pie again for us, Mr B.' He stared at the carnage before him. He should clear it up, really. But he couldn't summon the energy to face throwing it all away. To face his complete ineptitude. He would have a drink first. He went to the cupboard where the spirits were kept, knelt down, feeling his knees creaking as he did so, and poured himself a large measure. Not too large, though. He didn't want to sink into the widower's trap of booze before breakfast.

As he put the bottle back in the cupboard, his eyes lighted on something that had not been there before. Something new. Strange. It was a folder, one of the pale green paper folders Ginny had always used to organise her paperwork, recipes and receipts and suchlike, but this one had his name on it. *Julian* was written in Ginny's neat hand on a small white sticky label in the top left-hand corner of the folder. He picked it up and took it out, holding it in his left hand without opening it. It was quite new, the cardboard had not yet faded, and the label was still shiny and clean. It had been put in here quite recently. Thoughtfully, Julian poured soda water into his glass as he stared at the folder, feeling suspicious of what it might contain.

Sitting at the table, he ignored the mess around him and put the folder down in front of him. *Julian*. What could it be? It was not her will. That was with their solicitor. It was not a letter, for why would it be in a folder, in the drinks cupboard? Why had she not put it on his desk, in the drawer or on his blotter, if it was something important? Why not give it to him herself? Why was he sitting here wondering when he could just open the damn thing and find out?

He took another mouthful of his drink, and then did just

that, quickly and businesslike, pretending to himself that he was doing something as inconsequential as turning over a page of the newspaper.

Darling Julian, he read, and the sight of the elegant, sloping handwriting brought tears to his eyes.

I expect you've been making a mess of my kitchen, haven't you? There are some wipes underneath the sink, the Flash ones. I always used to think they were an awful waste of money, but I've come round to them recently. They do make life a lot easier.

Anyhow. I'm not writing this to talk to you about Flash wipes – actually, I suppose I am, in a way. I thought you could do with some help. You've never had to do much for yourself until now, have you? I always ran around after you. I'm not complaining – I was glad to do it. It was my job, and I hope I did it well.

Julian could almost hear the faint note of uncertainty in her voice. He blinked. You did do it well, my darling. You did it so well I haven't got a fucking clue what I'm doing without you.

Too well, maybe. I don't suppose you've got the faintest idea what to do with yourself now, do you?

He smiled. Once again, even in death, they were in sync.

If you had gone first, I would have been the one sitting at your desk right now, staring at a pile of bank statements and passwords, without the faintest idea of where to begin. But that wasn't the way things have worked out. Instead, you're the one lost at sea, trying to work out what slot the washing powder goes in and where the cling film lives (above the fridge, with the foil).

Of course, you might move from here, in time. Or you might remarry, and your new wife will want to do things differently if that happens. But until then, you'll need to carry on, and you'll need help. Oh, friends and neighbours will bring you food and ask you if there's anything they can do, but you can't exactly ask them how often the plants need watering, can you? And it won't be long before they'll fade away, anyhow, and just assume that you're managing, because you wouldn't dream of letting them think otherwise. I know you. I'm so sorry I won't be here to look after you, my darling. I can't bear the thought of you floundering along. So I thought I should leave you some instructions.

It's been strange writing all of this down. The running of our home. It's felt like my legacy. In a way, I suppose it is. It's what I've spent the last forty-odd years doing, after all. Not a very impressive legacy to leave, some might say, no different to that of thousands of women up and down the country. But it's mine, mine and ours, and I'm proud of it. In my own small way, I feel like I've made a difference, even if it is only to my own family.

Everything you need is here.
With best love, always.
Ginny
Xx

Everything you need is here. Julian turned the pages of the file that she had carefully slid into the paper folder. Each sheet of paper was inside a plastic cover, their carefully typed-out instructions protected from the inevitable cack-handed spillages that would otherwise mark them. They were separated into categories. Laundry. Cleaning. Mr Butterworth. Friends and neighbours. Recipes. The file was stuffed full of information. Where she took his shirts to be laundered and how much to pay the cleaner, the name of the vet that Mr Butterworth liked and the one not to book him in to see because he bit him, the dates of all the family birthdays so that he could send cards, and the things that their grandchildren would not eat for when they came to visit. There was even her kedgeree recipe in the back of the folder. Garam masala. It was garam masala that he should have used, not allspice. Of course. He touched the page with his finger, reverently. She was right, and yet she was wrong. Everything he needed really was here. Apart from her. Apart from her.

A week later

Ginny had always known the right thing to do. And her folder had given Julian the idea. It was as though she had been sending him a message. Bringing them all together. He had phoned Caroline up, and asked her to help.

'Can you ring round, darling? I think we should have a bit of a get-together.'

He had sounded positive for the first time since her mother

had died, Caroline had thought as she put the phone down. Not all right, still sad and wobbly. But a note of hope had crept into his voice, like the first spikes of snowdrops poking up through frosty ground.

They all sat, the whole gang, around the Rathbones' kitchen table. Julian at the head. Izzy to his right, James next to her, Pearl and Alfie rampaging around among everyone's feet as usual. They would be all right, the two of them. The money Stephen Garside had given Izzy had been returned. James had told Caroline what had happened, his face serious. 'There was no . . . actual affair,' he had said. 'Apart from a kiss.' His face had been pained. 'I can forgive her that. I know I haven't been easy to live with recently.'

Caroline had taken his hand. 'We'll be OK,' she had said. 'We all will.'

James had wrapped her up in a bear hug. 'I hate that I didn't see it. Didn't stop him,' he said into her ear, his voice muffled by her jumper and his emotion. 'I'm your big brother. I'm supposed to look after you.'

Izzy and James were both going to work with Will, on a new venture that he had come up with, based on her idea of providing middle-class families with posh versions of takeaways. Izzy was developing the recipes, Will and James were in charge of marketing and finance. Julian seemed to think that they had a real chance of making it work. And it would be good for James and Izzy to work together. Build them back up, as a team.

Cass sat on James's other side. Caroline's newly acquired niece. She was a funny girl. Awkward, and quiet, but she had a kindness and gentleness to her that reminded Caroline of Ginny. And something about her smile. She was living with James and Izzy now, for a while, while her mother was on a spiritual retreat in Mysore. She might not have much to say to the adults still, but she was sweet with Pearl and Alfie, playing with them all the time. Alfie was climbing up her legs now, his podgy arms reaching up to be picked up. And anyone who was approved of by those two was all right by Caroline.

She looked down, and started to serve out the dauphinoise, cutting it into neat squares, making sure everyone had enough.

'You've made this rather well, Dad,' she said. 'Mum would be proud.' Julian gave her a little bow of his head.

Stella and Johnny were there, together yet apart. Stella looked happier than she had for a long time. Recently she had looked faded at the edges, jumpy. Now she was glowing, glossy, full of confidence and energy. It was Johnny who seemed to have faded into the background a little, but that was no bad thing as far as Caroline was concerned. She sniffed as she handed him his plate of food, and he seemed to sense her disapproval, because he gave her a diffident smile as he took it. It would do him good to let Stella take the spotlight for once. Realise what he had had, and what he had let go. She was better off without him.

And then Harriet and Will. Back together, little Florence in her carrycot next to them, conceived on Julian's birthday weekend, apparently. Her mother and father smitten in that brand-new-parent way. Overwhelmed with love and exhaustion and wonder at this little scrap of a thing that they had made, just the two of them, and who had exploded into their hearts and lives with such voracious force. It made Caroline's heart burn. But somehow, not as much as it had when she was with Bart. Why was that? She still wanted a family, it just didn't seem so urgent. Had the dream of a baby with Bart been a way of trying to bind him close to her, to hold on to something that she knew might slip away? She shuddered. Thank God. Thank God it hadn't happened. Or the ties would have become unbreakable.

After lunch was finished, and the boys were clearing up, Caroline went over to where Harriet and Izzy were talking about reflux, Harriet bouncing Florence on her lap as she dribbled and gurgled happily.

'Come outside, will you?' she said, gesturing to the terrace where Stella stood, wrapped in a cardigan, smoking. 'I just want to . . . Well, come.'

She followed them out, carrying four of her mother's little champagne coupes on a tray.

'What are we toasting now?' Stella asked, cigarette between her fingers.

'Don't worry, yours is elderflower. Home-made by Mama.' Caroline handed the glasses around. 'We're toasting us. The four of us.'

'Good idea,' Izzy said. 'We deserve it. It's been quite a year.'

'Exactly. Just think. Everything that's happened since I got married. It was only a couple of years ago. I've got unmarried, for a start.'

Stella wrapped her arm around Caroline's shoulders and squeezed her.

'Me too. But I also picked up a coke habit.'

'And dropped it,' Harriet reminded her, holding her glass in the air and touching Stella's with her own.'

'You had a baby. A lovely baby,' said Izzy.

Harriet smiled. 'Yes. And screwed up my relationship.'

'Not for good, though. I almost managed that one as well.' Izzy's expression was rueful. 'And somehow I seem to have picked up a stepdaughter.'

'Mama's gone,' said Caroline, and she had to take a long breath to steady herself. 'But after everything, after divorces and rehab and babies and fights and affairs and sieges . . .' She laughed, despite herself. 'Bloody hell. It's quite a list. When I got married, I thought I knew everything there was to know about love. But I didn't know anything. I thought it was all good, all positive and supportive and something that made you happy. I didn't know how dark it could get. I didn't know how much you could love someone who was hurting you so much. But after all that, we're still here. The four of us. Together. It's quite something, you know.'

And Harriet, Stella and Izzy all nodded. They were standing in a circle, and one by one they raised their glasses one more time.

'I guess we've all learnt something about the darker side of love,' Stella said quietly. 'To us.'

And the others joined her. 'To us.'

JESSICA RUSTON

To Touch the Stars

The darkest night brings out the brightest stars . . .

Renowned for style, glamour and sophistication, Cavalley's creates the most luxurious millinery in the world. For fashionistas and film stars, a hat designed by Violet Cavalley is the ultimate indulgence.

Talented and beautiful, Violet Cavalley has poured her heart and soul into building her multi-million-pound business and raising her three children. It seems that everything she touches turns to gold.

But Violet is not the woman she appears to be. And her adored children conceal secrets of their own. Behind the Cavelley family's gilded facade lies a streak of darkness. Darkness that now threatens to destroy them all . . .

Praise for Jessica Ruston's *Luxury*:

'Exotic . . . glitzy . . . Deliciously indulgent' *Marie Claire*

'With exciting twists, this sleek story is utterly thrilling' *Closer*

'Glamour, wealth and scandal – a fantastic debut' *Company*

'It's what long-haul flights were made for' *Elle*

978 0 7553 7032 0

headline
review

Now you can buy any of these other bestselling
titles from your bookshop or
direct from the publisher.

FREE P&P AND UK DELIVERY
(Overseas and Ireland £3.50 per book)

Luxury	Jessica Ruston	£6.99
To Touch the Stars	Jessica Ruston	£6.99
To The Moon and Back	Jill Mansell	£7.99
The Return	Victoria Hislop	£7.99
Heaven Scent	Sasha Wagstaff	£6.99
It Happened One Summer	Polly Williams	£6.99
The Best of Times	Penny Vincenzi	£7.99
The First Wife	Emily Barr	£6.99
The Birthday	Julie Highmore	£7.99

TO ORDER SIMPLY CALL THIS NUMBER

01235 400 414

or visit our website: www.headline.co.uk

Prices and availability subject to change without notice